THE GATHERING EDGE

THE GATHERING EDGE

A New Liaden Universe® Novel

SHARON LEE & STEVE MILLER

THE GATHERING EDGE

Copyright ©2017 by Sharon Lee & Steve Miller

Liaden Universe® is a registered trademark.

A Baen Books Original

Baen Publishing Enterprises
P.O. Box 1403
Riverdale, NY 10471
www.baen.com

ISBN: 978-1-4767-8218-8

Cover art by David Mattingly

First Baen printing, May 2017

Distributed by Simon & Schuster
1230 Avenue of the Americas
New York, NY 10020

10 9 8 7 6 5 4 3 2 1

Pages by Joy Freeman (www.pagesbyjoy.com)
Printed in the United States of America

Many thanks to Fearless Typo Hunters

Thomas Bätzler, Roseanne Girton, Chris Meadows,
Kate Reynolds, Trude Rice, Sarah Stapleton

Dedicated to everyone who stands
at the gathering edge of change

THE GATHERING EDGE

PROLOGUE

· · · · · · · · · · · · · · · · · · · ·

Orbital Aid 370

"MOVE."

The radioed message from Stost was clear, while sound from outside their suits was muddied and muffled. There was still atmosphere here, for what that was worth. There were also odd vibrations, and strange sounds too, here in the crew quarter zone, the most worrisome being a continuous *scratch-scratch-scratch*. It was best, Chernak assured herself, not to think too closely on it. After all, they were just passing through.

There was another sound—familiar, even companionable—the sound of breathing not her own, coming through her headset. She concentrated on that, even as she observed the passage they moved down, alert for threats, for traps, for—

The way ahead was blocked by an undogged door, likely last touched by a dead man. The light in hand would have to do; they could not manage their kits and their cases, and the cases could not be abandoned. The beam sprayed about weirdly, the passageway was bent in ways it had not been when they'd boarded. Gravity was wavering.

Calling the ship plan to mind, Chernak realized there was another emergency cabinet ahead, which might be useful. She signed to Stost, behind her, to slow, heard a tap in the troop cadence asking again for speed, which was understandable given the state of the hallway. It went against instinct, but caution

1

was key, here. They could not afford to rush into error; neither could they lay down their burdens: both were required for mission success.

"Patience." Her voice was perhaps louder than it needed to be, with Stost quite so close.

A touch on her shoulder, fleeting, perhaps even gentle. She took a full breath of the stored air, stood straighter.

They both wore generic soft-suits from the rack, extra flexible, high visibility, patterned with glowing stripes, but without rank marks. Not that Pathfinder Chernak needed to see rank marks to know who she was, who her companion was, or where either stood within the Troop. As equal as might be, male and female versions of the same genotype, date and times of their first breaths so close as to have the same certified minute mark.

Both were pathfinders by training and birth and . . . she was seven seconds the elder. They shared the seventh minute of the seventh hour of the seventh day, and had been tagged as the "lucky ones" of their cohort by some K-grade staffer, for reasons they had never learned, and now never would; the Third Corps creche-world was long ago dust in a *sheriekas* raid.

"Patience," she said again, less loudly. Being second was not easy.

The breathing in her ear changed to an exasperated sigh, overloud in the dimness, and then a rebuttal: "I had patience yesterday, when I knew what I faced."

Yes, well. Patience.

In fact, they *had* been patient yesterday, as they sought passage to the station while panic built among the city dwellers. Rumor was loose, rumor and griefers and doubters all reaching a crescendo as ships returned to port telling tales of runs ending in transition failure a dozen times in a row, while others reported successful transitions into systems staggering under the loss of entire planets.

The port authorities at Curker Center would have attached the pair of pathfinders to the garrison as mere soldiers. Chernak and Stost, however, traveled on top level diplomatic ID, which they waved and worked with a fine bluster. The cases—one each—were strapped 'round them, under uniform jackets no longer so brave as they had been, and those they did not show.

Their orders identified them as part of a group of a dozen, but the other ten—

Of the other ten, four had never arrived in-system; two had arrived and had been pressed into local garrison service. Four had died in an explosive ambush at Loadzt, where the histories of seven thousand worlds were being destroyed by attacks from within and without.

It was telling, that none who scrutinized their orders asked where the others of their team were.

Curker Center orbited Loadzt; the station orbited both. They arrived at Curker Center amid riot and screaming. Gunshots were not infrequently heard—it might have been a war zone, itself.

They *had* orders; a mission. To fulfill the mission, they must find transport to the station.

They killed no one in their transit down to the docks; they used what force was necessary to clear their path—and no more.

At last, they found a shuttle preparing to cast off. They had wrangled, demanded, and bribed freely. Their orders directed them to win through at any cost with those items they had removed from the archives, now packed into the precious cases.

"I'm *giving* you the last of my pay!" Stost told the shuttle captain, who had wanted a year's pay, and battle bonuses, too— for two places to stand, no straps, on the overcrowded shuttle to the station.

Grudgingly, the civilian let them by, and Stost had laughed as they rushed aboard.

"Oh, I hope the fool banks all of it tonight, for tomorrow night's binge!"

There had been riots at Curker Center; on-station, there was chaos.

Cases hidden, they flashed diplomat cards, Troop marks, and high security pathfinder ID. The passenger docks were in riot as ships and crews were beset by would-be escapees. The vessel they had expected to be awaiting their team of twelve was not at the military dock—but they had long ago stopped believing in its existence. It was a matter, now, of the orders, and they were determined to run to the end of them. They were of the Troop; what else had they, but orders?

Against riot, disorder, and violence, the Troops on-station were prepared to act. They were also prepared to absorb a pair of ragged pathfinders into the riot squad until those high security IDs were unleashed. It seemed for a moment that they would be required to contend for the return of those IDs, before the surly half-captain threw the cards back, only slightly stained with her blood.

"Try the trade docks then. Run!"

To the trade docks they ran then, halfway around the station through halls crowded by maddened civilians, arriving while two-minute warnings blared, and in the midst of relative calm found a tech with an air mask 'round his neck, a repair belt over his shoulder, and a senior crew hash on his sleeve, who was willing to see them, hear their orders, and consider their request for passage.

"Soldiers, we'll be rushing a blockade," he told them, serious, voice full of warning. "Bad odds!"

They'd glanced at each other, Stost and Chernak, recalling the Over Commander's dismissal of their team, feeling the weight of their orders, which none had doubted would be their last.

Stost had signaled *lead on*. Chernak nodded to the crewman.

"Bad odds," she said, "are better than no odds."

"Come ahead then," he told them, and they boarded behind him, seconds before the final-check bell rang—

They moved fast, past an inset ladder with well-worn treads leading up to a pressure seal, past dogged doors and hatches neatly labeled for utility pressure suits, emergency patch kits, spill containment, and one ornately inscribed, *Jarbechapik*—Bug Hut—past two doors with nameplates affixed, and...

"Pathfinders? Here—only open spots are crew seats back here in engineering quarters."

"Head's there." Their guide tech pointed. "Crew room's up ahead. Only me now, besides the bridge crew—the rest run off—run home, run to get drunk, run to hide, I guess. Grab a seat back there—" a nod in the direction of the crew room, a semi-salute—and he was gone.

They entered the proper compartment, the passageway a tunnel between stasis-storage units and maintenance lockers—one wall marked with radiation protection signs, it being the rear bulkhead where a push ship might butt, another wall supporting two dozen lockers containing basic low-pressure suits and tools.

"Just strap in," had been the tech's orders. "Strap in and wait for me to fetch you out. The crew won't know you and you might be called for pirates or worse if you aren't with me."

They strapped in, each with reference to their down-counting chronometers once they'd taken that catch-up breath, the one breath that signaled each other that now all they had to do was wait for whatever it was the Over Commander had not had the time—or the understanding—to explain.

The ship's transition into independent orbit when it released from the station had been smooth. But then, in moments, the action had started; *bad odds*, Stost signed lightly, recalling to both of them *bad odds* of the past.

They sat, strapped in and humble, during acceleration, during evasion, during the bombardment, accomplished pilots belted like pallets of spare ration bars into a compartment where they commanded no screens, nor any attention whatever.

However humiliating their situation, though, they could take pride in the fact that they were, as per their final orders, and according to Chernak's chronometer, in space when the zeros matched across nine digits.

CHAPTER ONE

· ·

Bechimo
Wyrd Space

"THEO, THE SUBETHERIC DEVICE ON THAT SHIP IS AN UNACCEPT-able risk," *Bechimo* said.

"Is it unstable?" Theo asked, with interest.

"No, it is not. However, I believe it is compromised. Responses to testing are ambiguous. This may reflect damage taken when it transitioned to this place, or it may be the result of deliberate tampering; it would be interesting to know which, but not at the cost of putting our crew in danger. I cannot allow that vessel on my decks. Surely you have not already forgotten the dangers inherent in a compromised unit."

Since they'd only just replaced *Bechimo*'s own Struven unit, which they'd compromised in the course of that risky—not to say, theoretically impossible—Jump out of Ynsolt'i traffic, the dangers inherent in a compromised unit were vivid in Theo's memory. Granted, from *Bechimo*'s point of view, her memory was desperately short and horrifyingly inaccurate, but she doubted he thought it was as bad as all that. Still, best to treat the comment as a conversational device, rather than deliberate sarcasm.

Even—especially—if she suspected sarcasm.

So.

"I haven't forgotten," she said evenly. "But it can't call any-body from here, can it?"

"Here" being a piece of space that *Bechimo* was pleased to style a "safe zone," which was what Theo had originally considered to be "dead space," where no signals came in, nor signals went out.

She'd since revised her opinion to "wyrd space"—which was straight out of *Thrilling Space Adventures*—when teapots and other small bits of flotsam began phasing in from Galaxy Nowhere.

The latest bit of flotsam was looking likely to change her opinion again, assuming the math...but before she did math, she had to deal with an intact spaceship of somewhat baffling lines, more or less outfitted and arranged like a courier ship that had just phased in out of Jump. It held air, that ship, and all systems were go, the only things lacking being pilot and crew.

Unless the tree in the box of soil grey-taped into the copilot's chair was, in fact, crew.

In any case, and even *without* the math, this was another order of business than teapots, random bits from what might have been instruments, hull shred, and broken tile.

"It can, in theory, influence us," *Bechimo* said.

Theo thought about that, then shook her head.

"No, it can't, because you put two layers of shielding around our unit, and set intruder alarms."

"It could *try* to influence us." *Bechimo* amended, sounding cranky.

"Sure it could," she said soothingly. "And if it does, then you'll stop it, and we'll have learned something. Right now, it might be a puzzle, but it's no more threatening than—than a teapot! You brought that on board."

"A teapot does not contain a subetheric unit," *Bechimo* said, smug at having scored a point, which Theo guessed he'd earned. Maybe.

"Is it the captain's intent to remain here, in safety?" he asked then, which wasn't as much of a change of topic as it might seem to the uninitiated.

"Master Trader yos'Galan has directed us to abandon the route and return to home port," Kara spoke up from third board. Hevelin the norbear—the *norbear ambassador*—was sitting on her knee, studying the screens like he was a pilot himself, which he wasn't.

At least, Theo *thought* he wasn't.

"Not to mention that Himself takes a personal interest," Clarence added, from the copilot's chair.

"Val Con says he wants me to come home and meet my new niece," Theo said repressively. "No hurries, there."

"He asked gently, for *melant'i*'s sake," Kara murmured. "*Truly,* Theo, you do *not* wish to push your delm into issuing orders. Best to go home, as your brother asks."

Theo sighed quietly. Kara'd given that opinion before. Of course, Kara was Liaden and had it in her bones that a delm's word was First Orders. She was having a hard time accommodating herself to Theo's assertion that Val Con was not—nor Miri, either—*Theo's delm*. Brother, yes, by reason of sharing a father—and of all the things she had *never* expected to have to take care of in her life, it was a brother...

Which was neither here nor there at the moment, and maybe not at all, her brother being...*lifemated*, like Liadens said, to a competent and sensible woman who was, so far as Theo had observed, entirely capable of keeping him from making any... particularly...bad decisions.

Mostly.

"Must we bring *Spiral Dance* aboard *Bechimo*?" asked Win Ton, the fourth breathing member of the crew, dragging them back to the original topic of discussion. "The air is good; the ship is spaceworthy. Surely, we can conduct what explorations the captain finds necessary on her own decks."

"If she phases with one of us on board..." Kara began.

Joyita cleared his throat, drawing all eyes to his image in Screen Six.

"There is no reason to worry about an unexpected phase to Jump," he said—carefully, Theo thought. "*Bechimo* can tether *Spiral Dance*. Can you not, *Bechimo*?"

There was a pause, as if *Bechimo* was considering denying the possibility, or arguing against the risk of it, which was his favorite reason not to do a thing. When he answered, though, he sounded calm, maybe even a little *too* calm, at least to Theo's trained ear.

"Yes, Joyita," he said, "that is certainly possible. The risk to our crew will therefore be minimized."

Theo nodded, trying to decide if she was more amazed by Joyita putting *Bechimo* on the spot, or by *Bechimo* actually *agreeing* to something so risky as a—

"Captain, may Engineering speak?" Kara being Engineering,

she stood up at her station, putting Hevelin firmly in her chair, and giving his rusty shoulder a meaningful pat.

"The captain hears Engineering," Theo said, matching Kara formal for formal. "Concerns?"

"If the captain pleases. I had myself thought that a tether might be the best solution. I have researched the most commonly used tether-and-tube combinations and run simulations..."

She leaned to her board, touched a button. The screen just below center in the main array brightened, displaying a diagrammed *Bechimo*, and a single blue line, tagged "tight tether," and another line labeled "access tube" connected from *Bechimo* to a diagram of *Spiral Dance*.

"The tether-and-tube solution is very workable in stable situations, such as a designated shipyard or repair facility, where traffic is controlled, and *random things—*" there was a bit of irritation there, Theo thought. Kara *did not approve* of the so-called flotsam with which this bit of "safe space" was afflicted—

"—phasing in without warning, from all directions at once, are not an issue. We cannot control our space; it is not—forgive me, *Bechimo*—in the context of a tether-and-tube scenario—*safe*. The flotsam has been getting larger..."

...all eyes went to the screen in which *Spiral Dance*, their latest bit of flotsam, lay quiescent, attached to *Bechimo* by an access tube.

"...and we may, therefore, need to move swiftly, or even Jump, in order to avoid a collision. In that situation, if we have crew aboard *Spiral Dance*, or in the tube, transiting..."

The diagram in the low center screen twisted, the blue line showing kinks and corkscrews, hazard indicators blooming in alarming shades of yellow, orange, and red.

"Any pitch and yaw above microgrades will put a tremendous strain on the tube—it's meant to be latched, for long-term use," Kara said. "Even in circumstances much less extreme than a sudden need for evasive action, we might exceed the tube's stretch limit..."

Theo blinked. The sim clearly showed that overstretching the tube's limits could result in tearing, or in a rebound, in which scenario *Spiral Dance* might actually collide—forcefully—with *Bechimo*.

"That situation is avoidable," Joyita said.

Kara nodded at him.

"Indeed. We might bring *Spiral Dance* into partnership with us; lock access hatches, and become one environment..."

"No," said *Bechimo*, not at all loudly, but with finality.

"Why not?" Theo asked.

"While Kara's solution solves the tube-stress problem, it does not solve the other problem she has identified. If we need to move quickly, the single latch-point is an unacceptable vulnerability—for us *and* for the other vessel."

"I understand," Theo said, the math running through her head like a melody. Whether it was her own math, or information *Bechimo* was feeding her through their bonding interface, wasn't important. What was important was that she saw a third solution—that provided access, stability and maneuverability.

"We're a tradeship," she said.

Kara blinked.

"Yes?" she said politely.

There was a moment of silence while the crew carefully didn't look at each other in blank puzzlement. Theo settled back in her chair and waited to see who would work it out first.

Scouts in general specialized in thinking quickly, and Win Ton had been trained as a Scout, so it wasn't a big surprise that he got there ahead of Clarence, though just barely, judging by the arrested expression on her copilot's face.

"We are, indeed, a tradeship," Win Ton said, turning his chair to face Theo. He inclined his head. "Therefore, we have pod mounts."

Kara blinked—and dove for her board, calling up inventory.

"Yes!" she said, her eyes on the screen. "We have enough hardware on hand to do it! We can mount *Spiral Dance* as a pod. If we are in danger, we may move as one unit; if we must, we can jettison. Else, we can maintain the tube, shorter, for better control..."

She sat down, narrowly missing Hevelin, who obligingly climbed onto the arm of her chair.

"It will require modifying a pod mount, but it is well within our capabilities. Win Ton and I have the experience to do this, Theo."

Theo looked to Win Ton, who bowed lightly.

"I am pleased to assist Kara," he said. "I have every confidence that we can accomplish this task quickly."

Theo next looked to Clarence, who had been a Juntavas Boss before his retirement and subsequent hiring on as copilot on *Bechimo*. Clarence had a lot of practical experience, and he wasn't shy about pointing out flaws in plans involving their lives. He was a good deal readier to take risks than *Bechimo* was, but Theo was beginning to think that could be said of most people.

Clarence, now—was nodding.

"I like it. If it's mounted as a pod, locked in and secure—it's us. Like Kara said, we can maneuver how and when we need, or drop it, if we gotta." He nodded again, and grinned.

"Right you are, there, Captain. We're a tradeship."

Into the silence that followed this came a pleased mumble of murbles from Hevelin. A chuckle went round the crew and Theo felt *Bechimo*'s tension fade.

"Yes," he said. "Pod mounting and close-tube access will solve all difficulties."

"Then that's what we'll do!" Theo stood up, saluting them all, with a special, small bow to Hevelin.

"Okay, people. Let's get to it. Kara and Win Ton—how long to modify the mount and seat our new pod?"

Kara looked to Win Ton, who moved his shoulders.

"A long-shift ought to see it done. The most difficult part will be matching mounts and tie-downs."

"Which is always the most difficult part of securing a pod," Kara said. "I concur, Theo; both of us, working one long-shift will see the work done. If Win Ton is able, and with the captain's permission, we may begin now."

There was a small silence. Theo wasn't sure if she actually saw Win Ton frown, or if she felt the change in his heart rate through the link with *Bechimo*, and understood his distress. Whatever it was, it was gone as soon as she was aware of it, and Win Ton was rising, face smooth and shoulders relaxed.

"Soonest begun, soonest done," he said easily. "I am perfectly able."

"Good, then—with the captain's permission?"

"Go to it," Theo said, with a nod.

They left, Hevelin settling back into Kara's chair with a sigh. Theo echoed him, lightly.

"The Scout's still a little touchy about his recuperation," Clarence commented from his station.

Theo nodded. Win Ton's injuries had been...extreme. It only made sense that a complete recuperation would take time. He knew that, she was pretty sure—knew it *academically*. But Win Ton was a pilot—more than that; he was a *Scout pilot*, his reactions fast and finely honed. It was natural he'd worry about... never fully regaining his skills.

"He's pushing himself a little," she said to Clarence. "He's smart enough not to push himself too much."

She hoped.

"That's right," Clarence said. "My shift then, Captain?"

She glanced at the clock.

"Your shift, Copilot; I'm going to get some sleep. Call me if we get a cruise liner coming through."

He grinned.

"Will do."

CHAPTER TWO

. . . .

Bechimo
Wyrd Space

THE PROCESS OF MOUNTING THE *SPIRAL DANCE* AS A POD WENT smoothly, the balancing with the pods they already carried made much easier than it might've been, given *Bechimo*'s active assistance.

"Good work," Theo said, deciding to ignore the fact that Win Ton was looking somewhat pale. He was standing tall and breathing well, and if his heart rate was accelerated, well—so was Kara's.

"Off-shift, now, Pilots; get some rest. When you come back on duty, we'll figure out a schedule for sweeping *Spiral Dance*."

"Yes," said Win Ton.

"Yes, Theo," said Kara.

Neither one dawdled leaving the bridge.

Theo settled into her chair, considering the screens and the flotsam log. Nothing new had appeared since *Spiral Dance*, which was . . . interesting.

"Wonder if we broke it?"

"Broke what?" Joyita asked from his screen.

"Whatever it is that's sending flotsam through," Theo murmured.

"There have previously been long periods when no flotsam has appeared in this location," *Bechimo* said. "It is possible that . . . manifestations are cyclic."

"And we just happened to be here at a peak time?"

At a peak time, she added to herself, that included the arrival of a spaceship that had—probably—belonged to her great-great-et-cetera-grandmother, on her father's side?

On the *Clan Korval* side, that was; a family that ... acknowledged a relationship with what they call "the luck," which her cousin Anthora had said ran roughly around those of Korval.

And especially around Theo Waitley, Daav yos'Phelium's daughter.

... which brought to mind another of *Spiral Dance*'s puzzles.

"Joyita, is the analysis of that tree complete?"

"Theo," said Joyita, "it is. We have been monitoring the sensors Scout yo'Vala placed during his exploratory boarding of *Spiral Dance*. The tree appears vigorous—this is in comparison to trees in general, from records. It tests negative for airborne toxins or allergens; in fact, it may be said to be beneficial, as its oxygen exchange rate is quite high."

"Have to watch we don't get drunk," Theo murmured.

"I will, of course, be monitoring all life support systems and continuously testing the environment as I do now," *Bechimo* said, sounding a little miffed. "The crew will be in no danger."

"Of course not," she said soothingly. "It was a joke."

"Has there been any sign of the tree *doing* anything?" she asked Joyita. "Interacting with the ship? Making"—she waved her hands in a deliberately meaningless gesture—"communication efforts?"

"You wonder if the tree is ... sentient?" Joyita sounded curious, but not like he was also curious about her mental health.

Of course, Joyita and *Bechimo* would have records of Clan Korval's Tree, which Father claimed to be a biochemist. It had, in fact, made her welcome to the family by giving her a seed pod to eat—a seed pod it had *specifically developed* for her, if she had understood Father correctly.

So. If there was one sentient tree in the universe—how could she, the captain of a sentient spaceship, presume to doubt that there was?—then obviously there could be others.

"I'm thinking it might actually be crew," she said.

"We have not observed any actions that proclaim sentience," Joyita said. "There may be many reasons for that. For instance—we may simply not have the correct observation equipment, or we may not have clearly identified ourselves as persons concerned with its well-being."

Theo nodded. "Have you been able to identify *what kind* of tree it is?"

"To be certain, we would need to do a match at the cellular level."

"So, a physical sample." Theo leaned her head against the back of her chair.

"Okay, next shift, we'll move the tree over here to one of the unused 'ponics rooms. No sense being inhospitable."

She braced herself for objection from *Bechimo*.

None came.

She nodded, carefully.

"All right then," she said. "Let's get some work done. Joyita..."

"Yes, Theo?"

She smiled suddenly, filled with a surprising anticipation—or perhaps not so surprising. After all, she was the daughter and the granddaughter of Delgadan scholars. Research was in her blood.

"Joyita, please pull *Spiral Dance*'s logs—piloting and navigation. One copy each to me, to *Bechimo*, and to you. First one to find the coords to Galaxy Nowhere wins!"

What they would win, aside from the thrill of the chase, since two of them were self-aware AIs and not in need of anything that she could fathom, was left as an exercise for the student.

But the research might in fact be enough, if the flutter of pleasure along the new nerves she had acquired when she became *Bechimo*'s bonded captain was any measure. Or the extra lilt in Joyita's voice as he acknowledged her orders.

"Yes, Theo!"

They were struggling with the third level of data locks on *Spiral Dance*'s files when Win Ton, Kara, and Clarence entered the bridge. Theo took a break, leaving *Bechimo* and Joyita to it, and gave her orders: Kara and Win Ton to do a thorough physical inspection of *Spiral Dance*; Clarence was on tree transport. *Bechimo* would assist the inspection team with passcodes and bypasses, as needed.

Theo turned back to her board just as Joyita murmured, "We're in."

Theo smiled in anticipation.

"All right; let's see what was so important."

✳   ✳   ✳

The pilot's log was empty.

Ship history had been wiped, beyond its own name and the name of Captain-Owner Cantra yos'Phelium. The course history was only one Jump deep—the Jump that had apparently brought it to this strange little pocket of space.

Pilot Cantra had gone to a great deal of trouble to lock... *nothing* up very tight, indeed.

Theo *fuffed* her bangs off her face, and sank back in her chair.

"In case the ship was taken," she said, proposing it as a theory. "She wanted to buy time, so she made it look like there was information—*important* information—to be had."

"This would be consistent with the public histories," Joyita said. Theo glanced at Screen Six and met his eyes. He was frowning; perplexed or annoyed, she wasn't quite sure.

What they did have—the *only* thing they had—was the route, and a backup route laid in, the coordinates of which made Theo's head ache.

She got up, went to the galley, brewed herself a cup of tea and returned to the bridge. Slotting the cup at her station, she danced a few steps of a focusing exercise, and slid back into her chair, sitting forward and glaring at the coord string, willing it to make sense.

Which worked about as well as could be expected.

She sipped tea, and glanced again at Screen Six. Joyita was studying...something...out of her line of sight.

"Those coords make any sense to you?" she asked.

He shook his head without looking up.

"There is an anomaly in the coord set," *Bechimo* said, from behind her left shoulder.

"An anomaly *other than* the fact that they don't describe any place possible?"

"Any place possible in the local universe," Joyita murmured, still not looking up. He shifted a little, as if reaching for something just out of convenient range.

"So, we *are* still assuming that this *flotsam* is coming in from another universe?" Theo asked. The math...

But *Bechimo* would have done the math as a side thought. Joyita, too, for that matter—and it was Joyita who answered her.

"Yes, Theo. That assumption does bring the coord set into sense. Pilots are not prone to feeding their ships nonsense coords. Even in the most desperate situations, pilots will try to go *some*where. If that *some*where no longer exists, or there is a strong repulsive field between where the ship *was*, and where it was attempting *to go...*"

"Or there was an anomaly in the coord set," Theo said. "*Bechimo*? What about that?"

"Assuming that the structure of coordinate sets is a constant, across our system and that utilized by *Spiral Dance*, I note that there are two extra pairings in the string," *Bechimo* said.

Theo frowned at her screen, where the coord set under discussion was displayed in all of its lopsided glory.

"Why are we assuming that the structure is the same?"

"Because those ships involved in the Great Migration would have brought the math and the structure with them," *Bechimo* said. "There are no records of a completely new math of piloting being developed, whereas there are many documents recording the efforts to map the geography of the new universe and establish stable coords."

There was a small silence while she considered...as many of the ramifications of that statement as her head could hold.

The Great Migration had seen a mass crossing of ships from one universe to another—their own, expanding universe. Given the lines of the ship, and that stupid coord set, she supposed it made the most sense, as a working theory, that *Spiral Dance* was just...late crossing in.

Hundreds and hundreds of years late.

Still, if there had been a temporal flux, created by so many ships working the same course at the exact same time, or—

"Clan Korval," Joyita said, looking up and meeting her eyes with a straight gaze, "has extensive records of this nature, as the pilots who led the Migration were of that clan."

Theo took a hard breath.

"Right. But, according to what we were taught in school, Pilots yos'Phelium and yos'Galan were on *Quick Passage*. Where does this ship—*Spiral Dance*—even come into the picture?"

"Decoy," Clarence said, entering the bridge.

"That is a shrewd guess," Joyita said. "Yes. I think it more than likely that *Spiral Dance* was sent out to draw the attention of the enemy away from the exodus."

"And the extra pairs?" Theo asked. "Evasive action?"

"Possibly." That was *Bechimo*. "Or a protocol preset. *Pilot down*, perhaps."

"Check sums," said Joyita, suddenly. "The extra pairs. We know that the old universe was...stable. There was a steady-state center and there was an edge. The center would provide positive orientation at all times. The follow-up course—perhaps there was a trigger, to entice the enemy to follow one more time."

"So you're thinking there never was a pilot on that ship," Clarence said, settling into the copilot's chair and spinning so he could see his screens and the rest of the bridge, too. "I mean, no pilot for the Jump that brought it here."

"I believe there was not, Clarence," Joyita said.

"All right," Theo said. "I can understand sending a decoy out. But what's the point of the tree? Was the enemy allergic to plants?"

"Could be they were," Clarence said. He turned his chair slightly, so that he faced Theo directly.

"Daav told me once that Korval's big Tree wasn't *just a tree*. He talked about it like it was a unique intelligence—a person."

She nodded. "He told me it was a biochemist," she said. "But—"

"I ain't a botanist, but it seems to me that the tree I just brought over from *Spiral Dance* and the tree growing outta the middle of Jelaza Kazone—are the same tree."

"The same—"

"A child," Clarence said. "Or a grandparent. Not the same individual. Maybe *Bechimo* has a match program..."

"Leaf," Theo said, touching a fingertip to her temple. "They need a leaf for a cellular match. Where'd you put the tree?"

"It's in Forcing Room Three," Clarence said. "Thought it best to keep it outta Hevelin's orbit."

"Good idea. We don't want him eating alien leaves."

Theo stood, and turned smoothly toward the door just as it slid open to admit Kara.

"Ship scan find anything interesting?" Clarence asked.

She shook her head. "Win Ton is locking up his section, but no—we found nothing. Nothing! It is as if the ship had been deliberately cleaned, all codes stripped, before it was sent out. I had hope that the logs would prove to be fruitful, but I see that Theo is not smiling."

"Empty files, empty logs, all locked up nice and tight," Theo said. "There was a course laid in, but the coords don't mean anything in our space. Log's been wiped; history, too. The prevailing theory is that she'd been sent out as a decoy, to keep the enemy's eyes off of the Migration."

Kara nodded.

"But this does not explain the tree in the copilot's chair," she said.

"I was just going down to 'ponics, to see if we can't explain the tree in the copilot's chair," Theo said. "Want to come along?"

"Certainly," Kara said.

Theo looked 'round the bridge.

"Anybody else?"

Clarence shook his head.

"I'll sit watch, if that suits," he said. "I'm kinda curious to see what's next to come through."

Theo glared at him balefully. "This isn't exciting enough for you?"

He grinned. "You know me, Captain; thrill a minute's hardly exciting enough."

"I'll remember that."

"I shall observe from area sensors," *Bechimo* said; Joyita nodded agreement.

Theo took Kara's arm, and the two of them exited the bridge.

CHAPTER THREE

· ·

Bechimo
Wyrd Space

HEVELIN CAUGHT UP WITH THEM AT THE DOOR TO FORCING Room Three, which, Theo thought, she might have known he would. He burbled cheerfully, stood on his hind legs and steadied himself with a paw against her knee.

Inside her head, she "saw" trees, leaves, bushes, grasses, all accompanied with a feeling of dreamy excitement, as if finding a new and different kind of tree and/or leaf-bearing plant were cause for celebration of itself.

Which, Theo thought, for a herbivore, it might well be.

"We don't know what kind of tree it is," she said, forming the thoughts firmly as she spoke the words. "If you eat one of the leaves, you might get sick."

There came a distinct impression of laughter.

Theo sighed, and blew her bangs out of her face.

"What does he say?" Kara asked.

"I'm to understand that there isn't a leaf that grows can harm Hevelin," she said, meaning it for sarcasm.

Hevelin sent her a thrill of approval, and she sighed again.

"Apparently that's not overstating the case." She paused, to better consider the next picture forming inside her head.

"He claims to be an expert on leaves and on the things that grow them."

Kara paused, her head tipped to one side.

"He may not be boasting," she said slowly.

"Right; it could be true."

Theo dropped to one knee, and looked into the norbear's furry face.

"I want your promise that you will not sample leaves or twigs from this tree. Joyita and *Bechimo* need a leaf for a comparison. Kara and I are here to collect that leaf for them, and to observe the tree for…anomalies or interesting features. I'll be very pleased to have your impressions of the tree, as an expert, but until that leaf is cleared as safe, no snacking. Agreed?"

Amused agreement rattled through her head. Theo stood up and exchanged a glance with Kara.

"I have his word as a crew member and a norbear," she said, straight-faced.

"That is very good," Kara said, equally serious. "His word will bind him."

The tree in its pot sat under a simple radiant lamp, its leaves moving slightly, as if, Theo thought, it was dancing. The air in the forcing room was somewhat cooler than the rest of the ship, and there was a minty tang to it that seemed somewhat familiar.

Hevelin gave a high-pitched squeak and ran forward, squeaking again when Kara smoothly bent and swooped him up to her shoulder.

"You will be able to see better from here," she said, raising a hand to cover his back paws. "And you will be less tempted to break your word. My grandmother used to say that the most difficult promise to preserve was the one most easily given."

Hevelin might have had something to say to that, Theo thought. She might even have asked what it was, but for the sudden exuberance of dragons.

A large black dragon soared wing to wing with a slightly smaller golden dragon. They flew straight at her, or maybe she flew toward them. She felt cool breezes flowing along the planes of her wings; a deep breath brought her a savory tang, like ozone. Her shoulder muscles worked as she brought her wings down, moving more swiftly toward the approaching pair, until, abruptly, they veered, and she did—or tried to.

She cried out, twisting as her wings failed her, her balance gone ragged. She clutched for the nearest support—

Which was, of course, the little tree in its pot.

Her hand struck warm bark; she felt the trunk give, heard a creak, and snatched her hand away, dancing in a circle, half blind, terrified that she might have broken it, and now she remembered—she remembered where she had been recently, where the air tasted sharp and clean, like ozone and mint—

"Theo!"

She blinked . . . up, at Kara, who was standing, wide-eyed, hand extended, while she . . . was a muddle of tangled legs seated ignominiously on the floor, a bouquet of leaves in one hand.

"Theo!" *Bechimo* sounded frightened; his voice, too loud, coming from directly overhead. "Are you ill?"

"I'm all right," she said. "Just . . . surprised."

She looked to Kara.

"There were . . . dragons," she managed. "I thought *I* was a dragon, flying to meet them." She sighed and rolled to her feet, looking at the leaves in her hand.

"We have our sample anyway."

"So it seems. But, Theo—dragons?"

She nodded.

"A black dragon and a golden dragon. Flying straight at me. I was . . . flying, too. Right before I fell, anyway." She looked beyond Kara to the tree, with its dancing leaves.

"I think it recognizes me."

Kara frowned; then her eyes widened.

"*Tree and Dragon*, in person," she said, turning to regard the tree in her turn. "It really *is* a . . . child of Korval's Tree, then?"

"I'm convinced," Theo said. "Best to get confirmation, though."

Impulsively, she stepped past Kara to the tree, and carefully put her hand against the fragile trunk.

"Are you all right? Do you need anything else from us to make you comfortable? To keep you healthy?"

A fleeting image of the black dragon and the gold; a hesitation followed by a glimpse of boneless movement, and the feel of fur along her skin.

"I'm the only dragon on board," she said aloud. "We don't have a ship cat, but we do have Hevelin." She turned her head.

"Kara, bring Hevelin and let him touch a branch. You touch one, too."

There was a flutter at the edge of Theo's vision when Hevelin

gripped his branch, as if the tree had tried to fit the "cat" template over him, and discarded it.

Kara's touch woke a warm ripple down Theo's spine, and a softly moving silhouette, as of sun filtering through leaves. No dragons darkened the horizon.

"Thank you," Theo said, as Kara withdrew her hand. "I hope to be able to make more . . . comfortable arrangements for you soon. In the meantime, be welcome on my ship."

Her answer was a distant image: the flare and glitter of a starfield, phasing in.

"That's it," she agreed. "Until soon."

The door closed. Kara bent to let Hevelin down to the deck, then straightened, her eyes still wide.

"You talk to it like it understands."

"It does," Theo said. "Korval's big Tree is a biochemist, remember? And *not just a tree*?"

Kara stood still, and took several very deep breaths.

Theo waited patiently.

"So, you will be taking this . . . personage . . . to . . . to Korval?"

"Maybe," Theo said, and turned toward the bridge. "But it'll complicate things."

· · · ·❄· · · ·

"You'll wanna take a look at this."

The mechanic was laconic. She was also very nearly disrespectful in her zeal to demonstrate her lack of fear. Vepal found her refreshing. Trooper Ochin, whose uneasy task it was to guard Vepal's honor, was not inclined to be so tolerant.

"You will respect the ambassador to the Unaffiliated Worlds!" he snarled.

The mechanic was cleaning her hands on a grimy cloth that might once have been a proud red, now worn by abuse into a trembling pink. She was a well-grown Terran female, but she had to look up into Ochin's, doubtless outraged, face. Her mouth tightened; in irritation, Vepal thought, rather than alarm.

"I ain't disrepected him, now have I?" she snapped. "Disrespect, I'd've just put everything back like I found it an' not said nothing. I'm saying something." She looked again to Vepal and ducked her chin slightly, which Vepal chose to interpret as a respectful salute.

He rose—not quite as tall as Ochin, leaner, older. As odd as it might be, at Temp Headquarters, to find a soldier gone grey, Terrans put a value on the silver hair at his temples.

"Show me," he said, and the mechanic tucked the rag back into her belt and turned toward the repair bay.

"Ordinary way of things, wouldn't be no reason for me to be opening up this section here, not with it being the distribution chamber gone dabino. Got that swapped out, an' it come to me—ship being as old as it is—might be that new chamber working at full could might stress some other systems. Figured it best t'run a complete diagnostic, and take care of anything looked too risky right here and now."

"I appreciate your initiative," Vepal said gravely—and sincerely. Not many would have taken the time to be so thorough to a non-local ship. When that ship belonged to an Yxtrang, ambassador though he be, haste might be valued over care, in order to see the ship well away.

The mechanic snorted lightly.

"Don't want you mad at me, do I? Turn 'round to find you blew a catalyst array, an' you're coming back t'station with a shipload o'friends?"

The mechanic also possessed fine reasoning abilities, and a honed instinct for survival. She could not know that a squad of avenging soldiers was the unlikeliest answer to news that the ambassador's ship had malfunctioned catastrophically, all hands lost, nor did the ambassador enlighten her. He merely inclined his head.

"Go on," he said. "You ran the diagnostics and...?"

"Well, that's what I'm telling you! Come up with a couple bits 'n bobs might not've stood the strain. Replaced them—you'll see 'em on your invoice, broke out by kind an' time. Gotta charge the parts, or the boss'll think I'm mizzlin' him. No charge for my extra time. Din't come but less'n hour, anyhoot.

"But, see, I got them risky bits swapped handy enough, and there's still these three blips on the diagnostic—look like ghosts—y'get 'em, sometime, though the machine this bay ain't prone, and it was either ignore 'em, run another test, or take a bare-eye look-see and find are they really there.

"Did that, and they were—an' here they still are. Wheels're

locked on that roller; you wanna kneel, you'll be able to see 'nough, I think. I'll put the light on 'em."

Carefully, and to Ochin's palpable dismay, Vepal knelt on the broad board indicated, and ducked down to look under the belly of his ship.

A spotlight flared. He closed his eyes just too late to avoid having his dim sight ruined, and he kept them closed, patiently, until the afterflare faded.

Cautiously, he opened his eyes—and considered the thing reposing in its pool of light.

He recognized it, of course—a standard duty hull breaker. It could be triggered from a distance, or preset to explode at some preferred time.

"How long do you think that device has been there?" he asked the mechanic.

There was a hesitation.

"Take the dings an' the dust of the thing, I'm guessin'—an' hear what I'm sayin'—*guessin'* couple Standards 'least. All of 'em look 'bout the same, in those terms, and takin' location into 'count—so wherever they roosted, they come as a flock.

"I'm gonna move the light now. Show you the other two."

Vepal closed his eyes, opened them when the mechanic said, "Here's number two."

The first had been secured at what might have been the length of a soldier's arm, without any attempt to hide it. The second had been positioned with more care, inside the shadow of an intake dimple. The third had likewise been affixed with at least a thought to stealth, directly over the Jump engine.

Vepal sighed, and rose to his feet.

"Thank you," he said, and "I have a question."

The mechanic looked up at him.

"If it's *can you remove those?*—answer's I got a better'n good chance of settin' one off if I try."

The ambassador sighed. In addition to the loss of his vessel, and possibly the mechanic, whom he was coming to value, there were many rules which had been given to them upon docking, regarding the sanctity of the station and what penalties accrued to persons who were so careless as to harm its environment in any way.

It was...reasonably probable...that the devices were defective. Had they been of Liaden or Terran manufacture—but these had the unmistakable form factor of Troop-made detonators. Such devices very often did operate, to some level or another. Given the mechanic's estimate of their tenure, and his own certain knowledge of when he had last been in a port where his vessel was likely to be sabotaged, it would seem that these were among the majority of devices that did not operate.

Still, they were a danger, especially the first, which had been so artlessly placed. A lucky rock strike, or even a bad docking...

"What I can do, though," the mechanic said, "is give 'em a bath."

He looked down into her broad and freckled face.

"A bath?" he repeated.

"Yeah, see, they ain't the safest things on-station, but odds're with you. They ain't been triggered in any number of Standards, so could be they *can't* be triggered. The danger's where if they're just biding their time while the clock ticks on, but I'll tell you, once I saw what they was, I put on my big ears and whiskers, an' I din't find nothing that said *workin' preset* to me.

"So, what I propose to do is give each of 'em an acid bath, finished off with a mil-grade sealant. Then, what *you* wanna do, once you're out from station, and all by your lonesome, is take a walkabout, an' peel them units off the hull. Like I say, prolly they're already dusted, but you don't wanna be taking the chance that one'll wake up."

She shook her head, ruefully.

"Just can't trust unstable tech."

Had she been his Trooper, he would that moment have bestowed upon her a bonus, a grade increase, and permission to have the Flower of Genius tattooed at the outer corner of her left eye. He would have had her at his own table for a full cycle, and he would have assigned to her such assistants as might profit from her, to the benefit of the Troop.

She was, of course, not Troop, but Terran, and better for her in these dark days that she was so. He must reward her service otherwise.

And so he would. But first, orders.

"Yes; a bath and sealant. Can this procedure be added to the current work session?"

"Sure. Sealant wants thirty-six hours to cure. If that fits your schedule, then I'll get on it."

"Do so. Account your time on the invoice, even if it is less than an hour. I insist."

She hesitated, then gave a jerky nod.

"You got it."

"Thank you," he said, and smiled at her—the small smile that did not bare the teeth, that Terrans found soothing and acceptable.

"You have been of service." He paused. "Your name?"

"Name?" She tapped the embroidered badge on the right breast of her coveralls. "Gorish. Fleeny Gorish."

"Thank you, Mechanic Gorish. I leave you now to your work."

He gathered the somewhat subdued Ochin with a glance and left the bay.

· · · ❋ · · ·

The trees had been magnificent. Their crowns must have reached above the tall canyon rim, and together they had probably shaded the valley from the blaring heat of the local star. An entire eco-system had no doubt depended on them.

Before they'd fallen, one by one, Theo thought, looking down the valley into the carnage of a fallen forest. She began walking, relieved that the walls of the canyon shaded her from the worst rays of the star.

She walked steadily, the number of dead trees reducing as she did, until, as she broke out again from the canyon into a ridge that might have been formed by a now-dry waterway, the count came down to a single tree, which had grown taller than the tallest of the fallen she had passed, before it had fallen and another tree grew up at the farthest extent of its branches, racing for the sky before it, too, fell, seeding its successor in arid soil.

She crossed the dry waterway on the wide corpse of a tree. Ahead, there were only a few more trees; beyond them, blasted boulders and sun-baked rocks. Dust spiraled briefly in a burst of hot wind.

A leaf fluttered, bright green.

Theo gasped, choked on the dust, and trotted forward.

Tangled in the dead branches of the last tree was . . .

. . . another tree. Small, taller maybe than was wise, given its lack of girth, green leaves fluttering from thin branches.

She reached to her belt, found a water bulb and leaned close, offering the tree her shadow as her body blocked the wind.

Her hands were broad and brown, dust thick in the grooves of wide knuckles. She emptied the bulb and sat there, half dazed with walking, heat, low water and lower rations.

After a while, she lay down in the tree's scant shade, the welcome smell of a green, growing thing lulling her to sleep.

Theo stretched a hand out, meaning to touch finger to leaf. Light bloomed, and she sat up in her bunk, in her cabin. She looked around her, to be certain that it *was* her cabin; that the long line of dead trees, and the last of the line, still living, was nothing more...

"Theo?" *Bechimo* asked, his voice the merest whisper in her ear. "Is something wrong?"

"No," she murmured, settling herself back into her bunk. "Nothing wrong, *Bechimo*. Just a...dream..."

Her eyes drifted shut; she was asleep again before the light turned itself off.

Theo woke again before the alarm gave tongue, rising gently from the deeps of sleep to full and pleasant wakefulness. For a moment, she lay with her eyes closed, listening to the sweet murmur all about her, delighting in the stroke of space along her skin, and the simple, sensual pleasure of fully functional, perfectly tuned subsystems. These things faded from her attention during the normal busyness of a duty shift, so she had decided that she would take time at each waking to attend and acknowledge the senses she had acquired, when she had become, not merely captain, but *bonded captain*, of the self-aware and not-exactly-completely-legal ship, *Bechimo*.

"Good morning, Theo," *Bechimo* said now, inside her ear, or inside her head.

"Good morning," she answered and opened her eyes. She swept the blanket aside and came to her feet, already stepping into the first move of her morning dance.

It was a specialized dance, designed to wake and warm mind and muscle. Theo danced it well and with pleasure. When she was done, she entered the 'fresher, feeling *Bechimo*'s attention withdraw from her as she did so.

She grinned. When she had first come aboard, she'd had words—strong words—to say about privacy and where she expected to be unmonitored by *Bechimo* himself. As a result of those words, he had promised to leave her private in her bath—a sincere promise, sincerely made, she thought. But still a promise that he couldn't, with the best of intentions, keep.

Ship systems automatically monitored all crew. Granted that those were automated systems, and *Bechimo* had no more need to attend them when all was well than she had to keep an ear on her own heartbeat.

Now that they were bonded, she figured he was just generally aware of her, as she was of him. Most likely, more, since *Bechimo's* processing power far exceeded her own. If her shower gave her an extra thrill this morning, for being colder than she cared to have it at first, he'd note that, along with the blossoming of her pleasure, as the temp warmed. He might not pay *particular* attention to it, but it would be there, inside the data flow.

The fact that he'd started providing a *sensation of withdrawal* to her *after* they had become bonded...was interesting. Maybe he meant to reinforce the idea that he kept his promises. Or to emphasize that, even though they were bonded, they were still separate individuals.

Showered, and dressed in ship clothes—sweater, loose pants, and sticky-soled slippers—Theo walked down to the galley to draw breakfast: tea and a veggie roll. Kara's ability to coax vegetables— *lots* of vegetables—out of the 'ponics units, and Clarence's baking skill produced some...interesting combos. The veggie rolls, now, in Theo's opinion, weren't bad at all, warmed and with a swipe of soy cheese on them.

She was alone in the galley, though she could hear voices from the bridge: Clarence and Kara, and an occasional comment from Joyita. The rhythm of their voices sounded relaxed—prolly just telling space tales to keep themselves awake. There wasn't much to do, here in this pocket of wyrd space that *Bechimo* held to be safe, *except* keep watch, and log the instances of flotsam coming in.

The ship, and the tree that had been its only passenger, had been one such bit of flotsam; the largest they'd encountered, and hopefully, Theo thought, swiping more cheese on her second roll, the last.

She could at least make sure it was the last *they* had to deal with, stipulating that nothing had come in while she slept. Shan and Val Con had both sent messages, urging her to go home to Surebleak. Shan had also told her to abandon the Loop she and *Bechimo* had been exploring for him—his right, under the contract, but...

Theo sighed.

First of all, Surebleak wasn't *Bechimo*'s home port. Not that *Bechimo had* a home port precisely, having been more or less a fugitive from one set of authorities or another since he'd been built. She was a little shaky on the exact date for the Complex Logic Laws, but even if he hadn't been a violation when he'd been built, he was *definitely* a violation now.

There were people hunting him, specifically because he was an AI. Most seemed to want to use him...somehow. There might even, Theo reflected, sipping tea, be others who wanted *Bechimo because* he was a violation; there were bounties paid to folk who brought in rogue AIs, or proof of having killed one. If *Bechimo* had enemies of that ilk, though, they were being much more circumspect than the other sort.

And then there were those who overlapped the group that just wanted to control *Bechimo. That* was the group which was hunting *them*—Theo, *Bechimo*, and the crew—because they were contractors of Clan Korval.

Clan Korval, which in this case meant *Delm Korval*—her brother Val Con and his lifemate, Miri—had done violence against the planet of Liad. He'd had his reasons and...they'd seemed good to him. *Necessity*—that's how Liadens designated an action that must, however distasteful, be taken. So, Val Con had acted as he had because it had been, in his opinion as delm, necessary.

She'd been raised on the Safe World of Delgado, and the part of her that *knew* violence was never the answer—was horrified by the actions he had taken against a civilized world.

A much larger part of her—the part that was a courier pilot and captain of a star ship, who had seen bad ports and bad people intent on wreaking havoc, no matter what—understood what he'd done, and why, and even, sort of, a little, admired his decisiveness.

...except for the part where he'd left behind angry people with the intent—and the means—to hunt and hurt her and hers.

They were targets, no mistake. They'd be in danger—she had to believe that they would be in danger—from the instant they broke out into normal space.

Bechimo wanted them to stay right here, *safe* according to him, in this dark pocket of space, until the trouble blew over. Say that *Bechimo* was a little timid in some matters, and that centuries of being hunted had reinforced his conviction that hiding was the best and only answer to danger.

On the other hand, they *were* targets; if they went to ground at Surebleak, as Shan and Val Con wanted, how was that different than staying huddled here—*safe*?

She sighed, reached for her teacup—

Ice blasted across her skin, gone before she could gasp, as if someone had opened a door into a raging blizzard—and closed it again.

"*Bechimo!*" Theo was on her feet, running toward the bridge. "What just happened?"

"Flotsam has arrived," *Bechimo* said, flat-voiced.

She didn't ask him what kind of flotsam because she was on the bridge by that time, staring at Clarence's number two screen.

"That's not flotsam," she said, her eye following the eerie silhouette. "It's a shipwreck."

CHAPTER FOUR

. . . .

Orbital Aid 370

THERE CAME WHAT MUST HAVE BEEN A FINAL TRANSITION WARN-
ing, a mild beeping unlike the military klaxons to which they
were accustomed, followed by deep vibration in the nearby equipment. The beeping, and then just a shudder and the familiar feel
of entering transition, a cessation of external things—now no
sense of weapons bearing on them or being fired in defense, in
truth, little sign that the ship existed as lighting faded and fell
to backups, and air systems sighed—and stopped. These were not
good, or usual, conditions, for a ship in transition.

The wall-mounted comms were silent, not even yielding
static. Chernak and Stost sat, strapped in, perhaps less patient
now than worried, for they were pilots, and the ship was far too
quiet around them.

They held for as long as they were able, but eventually even
the patience of such pathfinders as they must break. Air was
leaking, loudly, somewhere out in the corridor—yet the ship paid
no heed, producing neither siren, nor hazard lights.

The scream of escaping air increased, and it was then that
they released their straps and rose as one. There was no need to
speak; their necessities were plain.

They commandeered the two work suits able to accommodate
them, barely fitting, each dressing one-handed, for neither dared
let go their prizes—the hard-won cases—helping each other with
the seals.

35

That done, and still no word or warning from the ship, nor any crew, they stepped out into the hall, Chernak at the lead, heading for the bridge.

Gravity wavered; strange vibrations wandered fore and aft around the structure of the ship. The scream of escaping air was muted by the suit. Surely, Chernak thought, the ship was dead around them. There was nothing more for them to accomplish on this side of glory.

Save the orders, as yet unfulfilled.

Orders.

The orders had been given by Pathfinder Over Commander Jevto.

"Pathfinders, we have a mission from Third Corps Headquarters, specifically for you. You are to retrieve particular items, transport and preserve them, not merely from the Enemy, but from destruction. There are travel orders, here—cash and gems, there are passes..."

He'd handed over those things, stalked around the room, turned on them. The *vingtai* on his left cheek was overlong and corded—the weapons master who had blooded the new soldier's grace blade had been careless, or making a point: it stood out now like a length of rope under the skin, as his jaw muscles worked for greater control.

The quivering stopped; the commander thrust his hands out, encompassing the dozen of them, not the eldest, nor the wisest, nor even the luckiest of all pathfinders in the corps. No, they were only the ones who had been at hand. They would have to do; there were no others.

"You are not fools. I will not tell you that you will ever see Headquarters again, or that you'll long see familiar stars. It is essential that you be in space on the day and time identified in your orders...and in transition.

"Your duty in this war *now* is to survive and to outlive it, for our defense will soon fail here. You will survive, and you will become the Troop where you...arrive, pledging your services to established civilian authorities, if any can be found. If there are such with Troops already attached, those you will choose. They will need your skills, I have no doubt.

"Absolutely you must be in space, shipboard, at the times indicated. This is the last duty Third Corps can perform in the

service of life; our last strike against the Enemy. Survive to serve
in what we are told will be a bold new universe.

"Follow your orders, Pathfinders.

"Now, go."

· · · ✵ · · ·

It *had* been a ship, and a big one, many times larger than
Bechimo. Theo raised a hand, calling for weapons—then curled
her fingers tight: *abort.*

"Increase shielding," she said aloud, eying the random debris
traveling along the wreck's transit path.

Damage...

Damage that included bent and shredded metal, whole sections
of what looked like laminated hull-metal split and wrenched into
unnatural shapes, as if half the ship had imploded and half had
exploded. It spun on a twisted, limping axis, moving away from
them. It was not at first obviously any kind of ship in particular,
then the splintered stump of the spine and the cargo pod mounts
came to the fore.

Theo blinked, suddenly seeing as *Bechimo* saw, the data from
multiple sensors merging, turning the view of sundered metal
fabric into a tunnel through the wreckage. Halls, walls, equipment trailed into the depths of the thing.

She blinked again, banishing that input. The view on the
screens—the same view that the crew had—was horrific enough.

"Ought we..." Win Ton began, "match and search—" He cut
his question short, having gotten his answer as *Bechimo* vibrated
slightly—the impulse drives, that would be...

"Acceleration and rotation engaged," Joyita announced. "Is
there a point we particularly wish to inspect?"

"Survivors," Theo said.

"Still outgassing, looks like," Clarence said quietly, nodding
toward what was likely the prow of the ship as it rotated by.
"Look there—that's not collision damage; they took fire!"

That was Clarence's experience speaking, and now Theo could
see it: *that* had been the crew compartment; the signs of targeting
lay in trails of dents and shred-rimmed holes. And *that* section,
blasted, looked to have been the lifeboat mounts, and no way to
know if the boats had been gone by the time the ship was hit.

"I am receiving no distress signals, no life signs, nothing

that scans as a functioning computer system," Joyita said, his eyes downcast, as if he were tracking data on his own screens. "Perhaps it was abandoned and destroyed on purpose..."

He paused. Overlays were appearing on Clarence's number two screen, showing foggy bright spots.

"Timonium," *Bechimo* stated, "in a non-trivial quantity. Equipment and devices leeching energy from what appear to be leaking storage units. I see no signs of active weapon points. There is subetheric static; the devices are attempting to speak to each other, but the network is in fragments."

Kara leaned forward, frowning at the image.

"There!" she said sharply, pointing. "There were letters or symbols there! What does it say?"

Bechimo and Joyita answered simultaneously, words over words.

"Unit Three Hundred Seventy," said Joyita, "Orbital Services."

"Orbital Three Seven Zero," said *Bechimo*, "Service Unit."

Theo snapped her gaze toward Joyita. He was smiling, perhaps even chuckling.

"Captain Theo," he said with a nod, "we're extrapolating. The symbology is old space, the craft damaged, pieces missing. We are recording, and we shall attempt to do a reconciliation."

"And salvage?" Kara asked, adjusting sensors, taking measurements. "There's so much of it, we ought to be able to..."

"Salvage at this location is out of the question," *Bechimo* broke in. "We lack the crew and equipment required to properly assess the wreckage, and we cannot be locked to the task, unable to move at will. Also, we should not bring others to this balance point. And..."

He was talking too fast and giving too many reasons, Theo thought, and what she could hear through their bond was more chaotic still: a confusion of concerns, a chaos of possibilities. Yet even as he panicked on the human-interface level, he was, on a whole *other* level, calmly evaluating the mass and dimensions of the wreck, methodically searching for a clue to the proportions of the crossing point, and analyzing the tenor and touch of the Old Tech devices.

On yet a third level, he was overdriving the life sensors, and his scans found the escaping gasses of crew atmosphere, of propulsive units, as well as the likely remnants of incinerated plastics. He was judging the spread of the debris, estimating that no more than seven hours had elapsed, Orbital Unit time, since it had been destroyed.

"For safety, Kara, it is best that the flotsam continue along its course, undisturbed," *Bechimo* continued aloud. "We must not touch it. We certainly must not search, board, nor deflect it. That is my suggestion, Captain. Avoid entanglement."

Theo stared at the wreckage, wondering if it had been a battle, a piracy, or the actual end of a universe that had brought the ship to this. She shivered.

"Agreed; let it take its own course. We'll record, and log."

She took a deliberate breath, and tried to pitch her voice for brisk matter-of-factness: the same tone Kamele used to cool overanxious students.

"Clarence and Kara—it's your off-shift.

"Win Ton and Joyita—please monitor the . . . debris. Look for recognizable markings, objects, or writings. *Bechimo*, please continue recording, as much and as deeply as you can. I'll take flotsam watch."

"Captain," Clarence acknowledged. He locked his board and rose, waiting while Kara did the same.

"Captain," she said, throwing one last look over her shoulder at the tangled wreckage that had, until very recently, been a ship.

Clarence touched her shoulder lightly. She took a breath, nodded. They left the bridge together.

Theo slid into her own chair and leaned forward to the board.

· · · ❄ · · ·

The passage beyond the undogged door was lit in pulsating red with the green glow of a fading emergency light tube providing a steadier light. The man who held the tube was leaning against the dogged door at the far end of the passage through a cylinder of stasis units. The red strobe was a warning light: the units were failing rapidly.

They hurried, this section having no obvious bends or dangers, Stost nearly overstepping Chernak's lead. The light bearer raised his face at their approach, and Stost barely recognized the engineer who had brought them aboard. His face was battered behind the strap-on mask, his eyes holding no certain focus, his forward leg bloody and half bare in shredded uniform, his booted foot at an odd angle—sprained, broken, or worse.

He raised a hand against their motion toward him; their intention to assist—

"Don't," he said. "Don't touch me."

He flinched, as if speaking damaged him further; froze, and shrugged himself heavily into a seated position against the door.

They waited, Stost wondering if that deliberate change of position had killed the man—but no.

He breathed—rasping and haltingly, but he *did* breathe, trying his lungs into a harsh cough. Chernak's hand twitched, and the engineer waved her back.

"No sense going on. They're dead up there. The crew, all of them—bridge ripped open. Took a blast; shrapnel, too, I guess. Lifeboats are gone, cut loose or destroyed."

He'd let the light fall; it rolled and lodged against the heel of his broken foot. For a long moment, he stared at his gloved palm, then raised the other hand and touched finger to palm, counting his points. "Passengers dead—they were all in commuter pods, dammed fools, couldn't have lasted a long transition anyway! Comm—didn't try—the bridge is ripped open."

His breath rasped, voice sinking. Stost leaned forward to hear.

"Should have stayed in my cabin."

That was a touch point, and the man seemed to draw energy from it. He raised his head and focused hard on them, breath rushed.

"Should have stayed with you; damn the luck..."

He moved then, fumbling at a shirt pocket, until he pulled out a medi-disc. Deliberately, he crushed it against his leg, sighing and closing his eyes. Another moment and he opened his eyes again, and sought them.

"But the transition?" Chernak asked. "The timing units?"

"Self-contained, in this section. The captain had a coord set, strange coords, *trick* coords. Shouldn't have taken us beyond the cometary clouds...so they ought to time back soon. Surprised they got us anywhere at all."

A buzzing came then, growing gradually louder. The engineer snatched an instrument from his belt, cursing weakly.

"Grab on," he gasped. "Transition ends."

Stost snatched a grab bar with one hand, Chernak's arm with the other, as she braced herself against the wall.

It was a bad transition.

The sense of leaving elsewhere and arriving *here* ran through their bodies, accompanied by nausea, then a lurch, and a twist. Stost hung on, though he wanted to curl into a ball and hide his head, and again it came—the sense of arriving, the sense of falling, a stuttering, a moment in which he was certain his heart had stopped; his sight went grey; the universe twisted into nothing—and suddenly he began breathing again, in great, tearing gasps, without any recollection of having stopped.

He blinked; found his fingers strangling the hold-on, and Chernak's hand over his, easing his grip on her arm. The engineer—

For a wonder, the engineer lived, well braced against the door, the lightstick yet resting against his boot. He sighed, gave a low laugh, coughed, and looked up to them.

"Ten tens. Salute me, if you will, Pathfinders, my hundredth transition ends successfully. I retire, effective immediately."

One hundred transitions was a life mark, indeed. Stost straightened and saluted, as did Chernak, ignoring all else a moment longer, to show proper respect, and pay what honor was due.

The engineer began to speak again, initially too low to hear, then gained strength.

"Just you two and—" A gasp here, and a small silence, while the man ordered himself. "...you and Grakow. Keep him happy as long as you might, please."

He gathered himself, voice steadying as he reached to his belt: "You'll want this."

This was a snap ring. He raised it, before unsteady fingers betrayed him. Stost swooped forward and caught it deftly in the failing gravity.

"I give you command of this ship," the engineer said. "Used to be nicer."

That came with a head shake and what might have been a failed smile, but the light was dimming.

"Bleeding bad," he said then. "No facilities, no blood. I'm on my fourth jolt of stim, triple-dosed on painless. Dog the doors on your way, and I'll take what I got left. It'll do me fine."

"We—we have our grace blades..." Chernak offered, as gently as she was able, aware that what was mercy to a soldier was... not always so, to others.

A weak smile and a strong cough.

"Scared of blades, soldiers. My call. Ship's yours." Another

cough. "The unmarked key—my quarters. Grakow's. My posses-
sions are yours."

An attempted salute or a sudden new pain jerked the man's
hand up, and he leaned harder against the door, crouched against
strain behind the mask.

"Purple-striped key does the hatch on *Jarbechapik*, 'spector's
bug's there. You'll want it. Power-up keys is zero and as many
sevens as it takes. I give you it."

The engineer paused, winced, said words Stost didn't know,
couldn't hear. It seemed that he had forgotten them entirely as
he pulled drug packs into place on the floor.

That done, he raised his head and gave them a long look.

"Go," he said with breathless harshness. "My job is done."

They went, back the way they had come, the light fading into
darkness behind them.

· · · ✹ · · ·

Theo stared hard at the image of the hulk, the camera's varying magnification making it appear just a moment or two away,
and closing. She knew better, reflexively checking other views in
other screens to be sure.

She sipped her tea, staring into the main screen, trying to
gauge size, wondering how they might begin to search something
of that scale, that had taken so much damage. Who knew what
might be lurking inside the wreckage? There could be a hidden
armada of ships *Bechimo*'s size . . .

The possibilities rode with her as *Bechimo*'s full sensor array
was brought to bear as . . .

The touch in her mind was one she knew . . . and welcomed:
alien and familiar at once, comfortable and demanding as it
could be, curious and—

A tap, just above and behind her knee, not in her mind.

"Hevelin, what are you doing here?"

The norbear looked up, arms outstretched, hands open. He
murbled at her attention, and she received the impressions of
joy and concern, and a demand to be lifted to see what she saw.

She reached down and helped him up, allowing him to perch
with his weight on her left hip; sadness touched her then, and she
knew his attention was on the screen, watching the overlays with
as much interest as she was. Might he have an idea of what they

looked at? Did he recognize a dead ship when he saw one? Was he understanding, *through her*, that they overlooked a tragedy?

The other presence at the edge of her mind now fretted. *Bechimo* was less than happy; he had argued vociferously against becoming involved with the ruined ship, arguing also that any crew must have died instantly when the hull was breached. Joyita, Theo, and Win Ton had all talked with him: survivors were possible; there were several sections that seemed intact; it was their duty, as pilots, to offer aid, or to be certain that there was no one left to aid.

Together, they'd worn him down, and he'd closed the distance between himself and the hulk, worked out a scanning regime to differentiate between what were likely left-over automatics and any potential live signals.

"Joyita," Theo said, her eyes on the screens, "I have a visitor. Has he arrived here without assistance?"

Not mere curiosity, that question. She honestly wondered if Hevelin was in league with Joyita, or with *Bechimo*, or if the greying old norbear was operating ship's access controls himself.

From time to time Joyita took longer answering than he might, and this was one of them. His image on-screen looked toward her, unfocused, then to the ambassador.

"In general, on alter-shifts," Joyita finally said, "if Hevelin wishes to join us here, I open the doors. I've assigned a sub-routine to it."

She looked speculatively at the comm officer, shook her head.

"So he's not sleeping as much as I thought he was?"

Joyita showed a brief smile. "Unable to compute, Theo. We haven't discussed it."

"Clarence doesn't mind having Hevelin wandering about?"

Joyita grabbed the nuance.

"I believe not, generally. Clarence discusses fine points of piloting and dark-watch with him, then assigns him a seat for the duration of the watch. He's sat in all of them but yours, to my knowledge. Generally he naps after being brought up to speed."

A tiny murble in her right ear, a chuckle more hinted than delivered, a celebration of clever Hevelin.

"Is it the same for Win Ton and for Kara?"

"Often, yes."

A jolt went through her—direct from *Bechimo*. Joyita turned his head, canting an ear as if he heard some distant storm rumbling.

"What?" she demanded, with Hevelin holding on tight as she scanned all the screens, seeking some new ship, or teapot, or—

"We have a power pulse!" Joyita said excitedly.

Screen Two went to zoom, as all the other screen scans, external video and radiation scans focused on the same section, the rest of the hulk left unobserved as the absolute stern of the dead vessel came under intense scrutiny.

The quality of *Bechimo*'s thought went from intent to precipitate. Shields came up, sensors detecting a movement more definite—more purposeful—than drifting flotsam ought to be.

"All crew to bridge," Theo thought—or whispered. She was in her chair with no clear memory of having gotten there. Webbing was tight and Hevelin was on her knee.

"All crew to bridge," Joyita said, his voice ringing across the in-ship. "All crew to bridge."

CHAPTER FIVE

· ·

Orbital Aid 370

THE SHIP WAS QUIET.

To them, being experienced in space, this was...unnerving. Nonetheless, they did not panic. They made certain of their burdens, and by unspoken agreement, sat upon the couches available in the engineer's quarters, watching the lights, which did not flicker. Pressure was firm for now, though how long that might continue was something Chernak did not care to speculate upon.

They must move soon—and there was only one move available to them. First, though, they must take stock. Chernak cleared her throat.

"Are you rested, Pathfinder Stost?"

The question was not idly asked—and it was a routine of theirs, born from the habits a creche-mistress had long ago instilled.

"Yes, Pathfinder Chernak, I am rested. I am fed also, well enough to continue any mission to hand."

Chernak signaled acknowledgment, since they were easy on admitting such things, having leaned heavily each on the other over time. A weakness of one would be met by strength of the other, as well as might be done.

"And your recent wounds. Are your wounds a problem?"

"They are not." He looked at the scratches, moved his wrist, and sighed.

"I have not much experience," he admitted wryly, "in reading the body language of such civilians, as you know."

"Indeed, such have rarely come our way. You did well. The civilian is unharmed, if dismayed. I will admit to dismay, as well."

Grakow, as the engineer had promised, had been waiting in the man's quarters.

Grakow had been less than interested in meeting new people, and even less interested in giving up his perch so that the pathfinders might sit and study the dials and readings available regularly to the ship's head engineer. Thus had Stost taken his wounds.

Having now studied the screens, it appeared that one section of the ship, out of forty-four reporting, held air and other pressures at reasonable levels. They were in it.

Three sections reported reasonable power levels. Two would be, according to the engineer's report, now unreachable by ordinary means, being on the far side of the sundered bridge. The inspection bug, however, was on their side—and so their choice was made for them.

After his discussion with Stost, Grakow had fallen back to a capsule tucked undertable, which was complete with bedding, small amounts of food, and water. He was, apparently, willing to defend himself again if need be. Also, there was evidence that Grakow had eaten well during the transition to this space, as they had not.

Chernak touched her wrist, pulling back the sleeve to show the thin band of the comm she wore. Stost touched his own, right there near several of the scratches, and the quiet blip told her that they were on the same frequency.

"We are," Chernak said quietly, "arrived at a point where orders, experience, and training give us little in the way of a rational and obvious path forward. We must rely on the intent of our orders, the intent of our training, and the support and intent of our history. I shall sum up my thoughts and make a suggestion, if you are able to listen."

Stost glanced at his uniform's blouse front, ticked at the pathfinder's star beside his name, and nodded toward her. "You are senior and I will defer if you have an alternative suggestion, or guidance."

"Yes, Pathfinder, of course."

Grakow stirred, yawned, and stretched, staring with green eyes up into Stost's face.

Stost nodded gravely. "As you are the de facto civilian advisor to this expedition, your needs and suggestions shall also be considered, Grakow."

He carefully reached toward the open door of the capsule in salute, receiving attention in the form of careful eyes, and then in an open-mouthed half word *"Grakow..."* before the capsule's inhabitant settled down again.

"So," Chernak said. "To sum up..."

Summing up had not taken very long; their choices were limited and they did not even consider putting aside their orders, or those precious things that they carried.

So, they traversed the corridor one more time, to the *Jarbechapik*, where they used the engineer's keys to good purpose. Stost strapped Grakow's capsule into the observer's seat while Chernak took the pilot's chair, and used yet another key to bring the tiny ship awake.

The ship oriented itself with the lightweight beacon the compact dock emitted. There were stars visible, which relieved her, however foolishly, and which meant that the lock was fully open. The minuscule amount of power required to remove them from the well was applied to underjets of compressed gasses; motion happened. The radar would begin as soon as they cleared the dock.

The repair bug's computer was stupid, but even it knew within seconds that the other inputs it should be receiving were missing. Tiny dishes sought particular signals, other sensors looked for absent running lights or orient marks. The unfamiliar board flashed, gave warning in colors, drastic colors. None were about the condition of the craft; all detailed missing signals and networks.

"It complains," Stost said, who was sitting with his seat back to hers. "It fails to locate the Primary Navigation Points, and offers the rails as security."

Chernak chuckled grimly—they'd found the volume control while familiarizing themselves with the vehicle—and had turned it as low as it could go.

"The complaints make themselves known here, as well. I have no confidence in the grid rails..."

"The computer tells me that we can begin a skin check at any point, via the rails."

"The computer is a fool."

"The computer is logging skin breaks now. It reminds me to report in, though it fails to find the correct frequency for doing so. Your screen?"

"The screen shows our ship, some bits of debris, and . . . dust. And how shall you report in? Our comms heard nothing."

"It was a large ship, and two compartments on the other side hold air. Our engineer may have been a pessimist."

"Check, if you like," Chernak allowed her second. "You are comm. But think—where would we put a fourth and fifth, even if we had airlock access?"

Stost mumbled, reached across the panel to flip a more distant switch. "Local radio. No stations."

There was background noise, a hiss of static from guttering connections somewhere within the dead vessel.

There was another noise then, low, a grumble that came from the capsule on the observer's seat. Chernak glanced at the cat, imitated the low noise and was rewarded with flinched ears. She did it again and—

"*Grakow!*"

They laughed, made soothing motions. Stost put palm to lips to ask for quiet.

"*Grakow,*" the cat implied heavily, and they laughed, being what they could do as the tiny vessel rose above the wrecked skin and decks.

"Grakow, mah . . ." Chernak offered to the cat, now on its feet, stretched against the flimsy ballooned film that kept it steady in the zero-G. She laughed again, fiddling slightly with the radar controls as a debris field became evident, moving at a distant intersect.

Beyond the debris was a spacescape at once unfamiliar and strangely comforting—a dark and deep nothingness, smudged here and there with tails of gas, and a bright, unsteady light that might have been a star or a beacon or another ship.

Behind her, she heard a noisy intake of air.

"We broke through the Rim," Stost said. "We see it from the far side."

Indeed, thought Chernak, remembering to draw her own ration of air. The mission would have had them forsake the— *their*—universe for one supposedly unharried by the Enemy, and for which they had no use.

"It is comforting," she said dryly, "to learn that the coords were good."

Stost snorted a half-laugh, and she felt her own awe ease.

In truth, they were ill-suited to awe. They functioned best in the terrains of practicality and fact. And, right now, practicality demanded that they orient, and attempt to find aid or ally in this empty piece of space.

Chernak touched a jet to slow the Bug, to allow that randomness to get beyond them as they explored, and the cat complained then: "Marrow!"

As if that had been a command, there came sudden sounds within their vessel: beacons, working beacons! A ship, in fact! The image on the screen went from a potential debris field to a solid thing, closing.

"*Kerzong? Asmala kerzong? Chicancha! Kerzong!*" Stost demanded, on comm, and repeated, "Identity? Will you share identity? Attention! Identity!"

· · · ※ · · ·

"Power flare," Joyita said again.

Theo felt the tingle down her spine. A piece of equipment had come on-line; energy had been released; radio waves were being bandied about. She and *Bechimo* shared the sensations while Win Ton and Joyita challenged each other with IDs for the static and frequencies of the vibrations reaching through the ether.

Joyita called out: "Shuttle sequence?"

Win Ton answered with, "Hold gates. Pressure gates."

"Lifeboat!" Joyita said eagerly, but Win Ton doubted this—

"Taking too long for a lifeboat; it's too complex—look!"

Radio energy and machine static sparkled inside Theo's head—and across the screens.

Bechimo upped shields and drew subtly closer to the wreck, dancing between wariness and curiosity, waiting, waiting...

Another flare; their shields thickened in response.

"Shield too much, and we might invite hostility," she cautioned him aloud, drawing Kara's eyes and Clarence's.

She intercepted those glances and added, "Clarence, be so kind as to uncap the manual fire switches. I note that the circuits are unpowered."

"Captain," he said, "uncapped. *I* note that we have no targeting information."

"That is correct, Pilot," *Bechimo* replied. "The captain has not authorized live targeting. We are merely ranging."

Kara was guiding one of the free scans around a section of the wreck that seemed undamaged.

"This section probably still holds air," she murmured, talking as much to Hevelin, who was acting as her second, as to Theo. "I'm not catching any energy spills, or power readings. None of the engine bays are live, nor any of the probable command points. Survivors... *Could* there be survivors, perhaps in suits, or... Oh!"

The scan had moved beyond the undamaged section, ridden across a gap in the debris cloud, and found a hole ripped into the shipside. It looks like a pool, thought Theo, and for one mad moment, the eyes wanted to make the floating bodies swimmers...

"No life readings," Kara said, voice strangled.

There was a busier quiet on their bridge, and Theo felt Hevelin's horror, even as she heard him whimper.

Kara spun the scan back toward the only section still green-limned as a potential survivor zone on the template Joyita provided.

"I have a signal!" she said sharply, Hevelin's whistle echoing her excitement.

"On the far side of the green area," she said, and Theo felt *Bechimo* focus their attention on the section—across the width of the wreck from their position—there! A tiny flare of power shivered down her backbone, barely warm.

"At skin level," Kara said, still bent to her scan.

Theo felt *Bechimo*'s excitement; his verification of Kara's data.

"That's your lifeboat?" she asked the bridge at large.

"Not a lifeboat, I think, Theo," Win Ton answered. "The position is wrong."

"What then?"

"Perhaps a repair boat."

That made sense, Theo thought. Lifeboats were kept near the skin, the bay rigged for a quick getaway. They'd seen what had remained of *Orbital Aid 370*'s lifeboats and bay. A repair boat, though, would have its system of routes to the skin, and a series of egress points.

"All right," she said, nodding at Clarence. "We're going in. Everybody look sharp."

Bechimo's feed became a rush; piloting math and approach scenarios twisted together in a frenzy of hope, in which she could barely keep her—

"Captain," Joyita's voice was like a lifeline thrown; gratefully, Theo focused on him. "We have a transmission. Not data. Unintelligible, but it may be a voice—human voice."

"Let's all hear it," she said, taking a deep breath and consciously loosening her grip on the arms of her chair.

There came static, rustling sounds, a sharp snap, a low sound that *might be* someone muttering over an unfamiliar board... then—loudly and suddenly enough that all of them on the bridge jumped: *"Grakow!"*

Laughter—human laughter!—came over the open line.

"Grakow," said the first voice again, insistent.

Theo felt a tug at her knee, and looked down to see Hevelin extending his arms toward her. She lifted him onto her lap, while more laughter came in response to that second declaration.

"Grakow, mah..." That was not the original voice, but a simulation of it...and a sound that might have been a low chuckle.

A video image was building on Screen Five, as *Bechimo* combined the data streams—

"There!" Theo cried, *Bechimo*'s internals showing her what was not yet visible on the screens. "Joyita—get me a line!"

Bechimo was tracking a very slow-moving object, just now coming into range of the screens as their motion made the hulk appear to roll under them. Theo leaned forward until Hevelin grabbed her arm for balance, watching as the object emerged from a port protruding from the aft of the ship, gingerly, like a *mraka* bird in Father's garden, watching for the dangerous field birds that never came close to the Wall.

Bechimo was excited. He was overfeeding her with information on mass, albedo, spin, radio frequencies, item ID mismatches and probabilities, while on the bridge, Win Ton was confirming Joyita's target acquisition, Kara backing him, and Clarence sitting pilot's duty...

"Line available," Joyita murmured.

Theo snatched on a headset, watching as the tiny object came fully free of the dead ship. She took a breath to speak...and hesitated. The form reminded her of something she'd seen not all that long ago...something under fire.

She had it then, and wished she hadn't; her eyes stung with the memory.

Beeslady, the ship had been called. No Jump, little cargo

capacity, no range but for inspection and local . . . the ship she'd seen dying, then dead—the pilot she had been too late to save . . .

"*Mrrow,*" stated a voice that was definitely not human; laughter came again.

Theo shrank in on herself. Laughter in the face of such disaster? What crew would laugh, knowing their shipmates dead, the ship itself a tumbling wreck? Were they injured? In shock? Had—were these pirates, who had been responsible for the death of *Orbital Three Seven Zero Service Unit,* laughing in victory?

Negative, she heard *Bechimo* say, though it appeared that no one else of the crew heard him. *The craft is underpowered and overused. Pirates would have provided better for themselves.*

"I have activated navigation beacons," Joyita said. "I have no confirmed language match as yet."

"Nor I," *Bechimo* said aloud.

"*Kerzong? Asmala kerzong? Chicancha! Kerzong!*" The voice was loud over comm, and Win Ton jerked to the edge of his chair.

"Yxtrang!" he said sharply to Joyita. "Cross-check Yxtrang."

CHAPTER SIX

. . . .

Repair Bug

THE SHIP WAS REAL AND IT WAS CAREFUL; THE CROSS SECTION they could see changed rapidly until it was presenting head-on, a pod at its back or belly. The beat pulse of the warn-aways filled the little cabin even with the volume down.

"What ship?" Chernak asked her partner.

"Unknown silhouette. My guess, based on size and conformation: a small tradeship, but it could also be a planetary cutter of some kind. It has the lines of a ship that behaves well in atmosphere. There are markings, which I have recorded; look for yourself."

A finger flick sent the video to Chernak's screen. It was on loop, and she zoomed in on the rerun.

Markings, yes. Several of what might be numbers, some of what could be letters, and an image that was eerily familiar to them, now.

"*Grakow*..." she said.

"Yes," Stost said. "It *is* a cat, I think."

Static spat, loudly, followed by—a voice. Words. The Bug's computer reported several frequencies at work.

"Our vessel auto-replies," Stost reported. "Orientation, sounding stats..."

Words again; they were...

"Familiar," Chernak said. "They slide past my ear. Stost—do you have them?"

"Not clear," said Stost, who was the better at languages, "but they're coming."

Lights flickered across the Bug's simple board.

"They will make another attempt," Chernak murmured...

The signal this time was static free, as the tradeship found a frequency more compatible with its own.

"*Chicancha! Kerzong!*" a voice stated, with surprising authority. "*Bechimolaughingcatstandby.*"

The voice might have been female, assuming human; the accent was... deplorable.

"Civilian," Stost muttered, as he worked his station, seeking to wring every crumb of information possible from the small brain of their ship.

Data appeared on Chernak's screen, among them the ominous information that the approaching ship had engaged shielding far stronger than mere meteor shields.

Faced with the wreck beneath them, Chernak thought, so would she. Also, she would have every weapon live and targeted directly on the stranger vessel.

Them.

With weapons very much on her mind, she slowed the Bug's acceleration, overruling by main force the idiot vessel's tendency to spin, so that they showed the same face to the unknown ship. It was rescue or doom, that ship, which was now seen to be adjusting course into an achingly slow intercept.

"Give them something," she murmured, squinting at the screens. "Identification."

Grakow made a noise like torn steel, but Stost spoke past it, slowly and clearly.

"*Kerzong.* Chernak Pathfinder. Stost Pathfinder."

Time ran, their breathing was loud in the small cabin, their hands largely still, their eyes busy. Waiting, the soldier's lot.

"*Kerzong.*" This was a new voice, light but, Chernak thought, male. So, at least two crew on the tradeship, as well.

"*Kerzong,*" the second voice said again. "Win Ton yo'Vala Scout."

"He names himself?" she asked Stost.

"I think so; it would follow the pattern we offered."

"Shall we speak again, then?"

"Let us wait a moment. He may have something else."

In fact, Win Ton yo'Vala Scout did have something else; a question.

"*Asmana Trang? Asmana* Pathfinder *chi* Pathfinder?"

"Stupid accent," Stost grumbled under his breath. "*Will all of you always be made of Troop? Will all of you always be made of Pathfinder by Pathfinder?* Even a civilian might learn tense!"

"They can count and they can hear," Chernak said. "They have an undamaged spaceship, which they appear to handle with skill. We, my Stost, have an inspection buggy that grows... somewhat lower on amenities as time passes. Correct them gently."

"Of course, Elder. I offer all courtesy."

There was a sharp click as Stost depressed the key on his board. He spoke, proud, clear, and loud, as befitted one of the Troop, making the offer their service required.

"*Asdameni Trang chist Pathfinder. Kaln zedatavant?*"

He looked over his shoulder at her then, lips on the verge of giving away his smile.

"We two together are of the Troop, ranked as Pathfinders. Do you require the aid we might both provide you?"

· · · ✳ · · ·

Joyita had chosen Theo's Screen Eight, as being visible to the entire bridge, to display the translation of the message from the repair boat.

Theo blinked; Kara laughed outright.

"Not awarding extra points, eh?" She shook her head, still grinning. "At least they don't demand our immediate surrender!"

"There's that," Theo said. "Maybe they're low on air."

Joyita was positively beaming from his screen.

"This is excellent! We have started a dialogue! I am cross-filing, and building a dictionary. Dictionaries will be available at Win Ton's station and at Theo's, with cues. We should have a working pidgin very soon!"

He sounded, Theo thought, positively overjoyed. Of course, he was comm officer for a reason, and her understanding was that the... original, long-dead Joyita had been something of a linguist.

"Captain?" Win Ton murmured. "Your response?"

Right, her response. Theo thought about Kara's laughter, and about her brother Val Con's house guard of... *former* Yxtrang, who were chain-of-command oriented. She thought it might even be...*soothing* for people who had just been through...whatever it was that the people in the repair boat had been through, to get a nice, formal response from an authority figure.

So then.

She nodded at Win Ton.

"Please say that the captain thanks them for their offer, but this ship is secure. Work with them and with Joyita on getting this pidgin he's so excited about on-line. We need clear communication about our intentions and methods. We're going for a—a rendezvous and recover, and we don't want any mistakes. Get a status report first; determine if they're injured, or if they are in immediate need."

Hevelin leaned against her suddenly, voicing a barely audible burble. She looked down, and felt a tickle along the edge of her mind, not *quite* the same as her link with *Bechimo*, and not at all like a trance-state conversation with Hevelin usually produced. The sensation faded, leaving an idea lodged in Theo's mind.

She looked back to Win Ton.

"Determine who else is with them. All present, we want to know how many, and their condition. Also, permit them to know that Captain Theo Waitley commands this ship and this region of space."

Win Ton produced a grave half-bow and turned to his dictionary screen.

"Explain to them that we're translating from an incomplete dictionary," Theo said. "Tell them—" Her voice broke, as she looked at the drifting remains of the wreck below them.

"Tell them," she said carefully, "that we salute the valor of their efforts and offer honor to those who fell in the passage."

· · · ❄ · · ·

"So then, *Cat*. That is you in *this* place, Grakow. Are you not pleased to have a kind here?"

Stost was bent low, elbows and legs braced against wall and floor. He spoke to Grakow as if to a comrade, while Chernak, feet in stirrups as she stood at the board in zero-G, coaxed information from their craft. She learned, laboriously, that the ship with which they conversed had several power sources. Despite being a trader, it showed multiple scars that had the very look of wounds taken in battle. Perhaps it was not always so peaceful as it now presented itself. It wasn't unknown for traders to become pirates, at need, or at whim.

This research—it was a habit with her. She was a pathfinder, and the habit of seeking knowledge was, if not bred into her, then ingrained, first by training, then by practical experience. This ship—this *Bechimo*—had imposed itself upon them, so she must—must!—learn what she might about it…and from it.

The ship *Bechimo* was under the command of Captain Theo Waitley, who claimed likewise to be in command of local space.

And who, by a night march, could dispute that *point?* thought Chernak. Certainly, were the situation otherwise, she would claim for herself as much as there was to command in local space. But did Trade Captain Waitley believe she outranked two pathfinders? That was a troubling question—more than enough, certainly, to prompt a pathfinder to seek what answers she might find.

"Captain Waitley and her crew," Stost said, apparently having concluded his conversation with Grakow, "have explained the rules of engagement very clearly, Pathfinder. They have refrained from the word *rescue*. They are respectful."

He did this sometimes, Stost did, following her thoughts as easily as if they shared the same head, offering, if she might suppose it of him, *comfort*.

"Ship crew includes Comm Officer Joyita, and Liaison Officer Win Ton, to whom I speak most often. They have referred questions to a head tech, to the captain, perhaps to others. They have been clear that they intend as a matter of course to arrive elsewhere with us aboard at some point, and they have taught us both that the language of the Troop is an oddity to them, spoken rarely enough between them that they resort to dictionaries. Grakow, I note, they seem willing to accept as an equal."

Chernak snorted, turned her head and met Stost's eyes.

They smiled then, and perhaps Grakow did as well, as the trader ship's logo hovered over them, laughing at the universe, if not at them.

· · · ✳ · · ·

"If the captain pleases," Kara said, which was way more formal than Kara usually was in Terran.

Theo spun her chair, opened her mouth—and closed it.

Insofar as it could be said of someone with the natural Liaden golden skin tone, Kara was *pale*. Her lips were pressed tightly together, and her face was . . . rigid.

Frightened, Theo realized. Kara's afraid.

She hadn't thought there was anything in the wide universe that could scare Kara ven'Arith.

"What's wrong?" she asked, quietly.

Kara drew a somewhat shaky breath.

"It is understood that the captain will be aiding survivors," she said, and her voice was rigid, too. "One wonders if the captain is fully aware that these survivors are Yxtrang?"

"I am aware, yes," Theo said carefully. She hesitated, then added. "They're flotsam, Kara; just Jumped in from Galaxy Nowhere. Just like the teapot; exactly like *Spiral Dance*."

"They are Yxtrang," Kara repeated. "I am Liaden, Win Ton is Liaden. You, yourself, are half Liaden."

Right. And Yxtrang, in the universe outside of this wyrd pocket of so-called safety, had . . . call it a long-standing habit of raiding Liaden worlds particularly, and just generally going out of their way to murder and abuse any ship and crew who happened *not* to be Yxtrang.

"Should we let them die?" she asked quietly, meeting Kara's eyes.

Kara's mouth tightened.

"My brother has three Yxtrang sworn to him," Theo continued when it seemed clear that Kara wasn't going to say anything else. "I've met them. They're all very civilized, and not one of them tried to kill me. We have to assume that these survivors—these *people*, who are in mortal danger—that they'll be civilized, too."

"Kara's concerns are not misplaced." Win Ton spoke from his station. "While the captain of course cannot leave the survivors to their fate, now that they have been brought to her attention, perhaps we should create a . . . holding area for them."

Theo considered him blandly.

"Take prisoners, you mean?"

He had the grace to flinch.

She looked to the copilot's station. Clarence was monitoring the screens with commendable concentration; he didn't turn his head, or meet her eye.

"Win Ton offers a reasonable compromise," *Bechimo* said

into the charged silence. "If these persons present a danger to the crew..."

"We don't know that they present a danger to anybody!" Theo snapped. "What we *do* know is that they're going to die out there in that repair jitney unless they're picked up by another ship."

She waved at the screens.

"It looks like *we're* that other ship."

"Indeed," Joyita said cheerfully. "The captain makes a valid point. The survivors are newly arrived from the Old Universe, where they were sworn to protect civilians from the Great Enemy. As long as we are not the Great Enemy, we have no reason to expect violence from them. They have not been exposed to the predator-Yxtrang culture to which their service has devolved, in our own universe."

He paused.

"I have the histories, Kara, if you care to read them. There is every reason to believe that the survivors are, as Theo has said, *civilized*."

"And we're going to treat them as civilized persons," Theo said, "until they give us a reason to believe otherwise."

Kara was looking down at her board. Her cheek had darkened in a blush, and Theo felt a pang. She took a breath, meaning to offer an apology—

"Aye, Captain!" Clarence said heartily.

Theo blinked, startled.

"Yes, Captain," Win Ton said, noticeably less hearty, but with what sounded like goodwill.

Kara stared steadfastly at her board. She was chewing her lip, Theo saw. She felt a bump against her knee and looked down into Hevelin's furry, greying face. Her vision blurred a little, and she felt enthusiastic approval.

"The ambassador lends his support to this rescue," she said quietly.

Still, Kara said nothing.

"Kara," said *Bechimo* gently. "I will allow no harm to come to my crew."

"Right," said Theo briskly. "Kara, you know I wouldn't do anything to endanger us!"

That got a response; something on the order of a strangled laugh. Or a sob.

"Oh, Theo!" Kara gulped and flapped her hands. "Let them, then, be as civilized as a High House delm!" This time, it sounded closer to a laugh. "Aye, Captain!"

· · · ⚛ · · ·

Chernak woke to a light beeping sound which was gradually increasing in intensity. She was thirsty and her left foot was trembling itself into a cramp. Also, she was getting hungry, though it was not yet an urgency and could be easily dealt with, for, among its many deficiencies, the repair bug held bounty; it was provisioned enough for several days of a three-person crew. She and Stost need not broach their pocket rations.

This beeping though . . . a proximity warning?

She opened her eyes to see the ship *Bechimo* looming so large in the port screen that nothing beyond it was visible.

Stost raised one hand gently, a distant relative of a salute, seeing that she woke. He sat with his chair at a quarter turn, so that he might monitor his own boards and hers, the port screen, herself . . .

It was a hard-working ship, *Bechimo*; that was apparent. Also, it was an experienced ship. Indeed, she had seen ships with combat scars, and this one had such signs, as she had seen in her prenap study. What she saw now were perhaps signs of missile exhaust—there, beneath the smile of the cat, which was—

Chernak blinked.

Yes. The cat *was* revolving, the ship moving in order to show them a different face.

"Good waking, Pathfinder!"

"Are we in danger, Stost?"

His hands indicated *not particularly*, which was an old joke between them. In this place and time it made her smile.

He chin-pointed to the newly revealed side of the trader, where there were perhaps locks and hatches and the like. It was a very busy surface right here.

"Were you going to permit them to suck us aboard without rousing me?"

He chuckled.

"Hardly, Senior. Presently, we are enduring an extremely close examination. Measurements are being taken. Apparently there are multiple choices for bringing us aboard."

"So they have plans? Why did you let me sleep so long?"

His shrug was an elaborate denial of wrongdoing. Letting the shrug go, he looked her hard in the face.

"We have become creatures of exhaustion, and exhaustion is not the proper state in which to meet a commanding officer. *Any* commanding officer, much less the commander of all of local space. We will need our wits about us, in order to preserve our liberty, and see our mission to its proper end. That you slept so deeply is a measure of how much you *needed* to sleep, Elder."

That had too much truth in it. That being so, Chernak made no reply. After a moment, Stost moved a hand, directing her gaze to the ship looming over them.

"The one Kara believes we must be brought on as internal cargo, which is a great deal of trust, do you think? There is a checklist they will read to us, cautions and orders, when we are both awake. Become ready, and I will open the voice channel again."

He glanced at the wall of metal beyond them as it slowed and held true. There was writing there, beside the obvious slide hatch. He adjusted the side cameras, seeking more information as to location, found a small iteration of the Laughing Cat, and another, smaller design, one perhaps dominated by a tree. The lettering there was vaguely familiar, as if someone had slanted fonts and words he knew, and then done it one more time until he couldn't be sure he knew it, after all.

"There is this, my Senior. The pod that they carry is a ship. I was not able to study it, but my impression was of a small cargo ship."

He flipped a control and finally the beeping went away. In the background, then, she could hear Grakow snoring in his cocoon.

Stost gave her a hard look.

"This Captain Waitley, she collects expensive toys. It must be a fine thing, indeed, to be a captain-owner of two armed ships—and flying with both in her hand."

CHAPTER SEVEN

. . . .

Beneath the Laughing Cat

"TRAILWALKER IS NOT QUITE CORRECT, I THINK," OFFERED WIN Ton over tea, looking at Joyita in the crew mess side monitor. "It does not lack merit, but it fails of being precise. *Bechimo* has offered us seven possible variations, and my bias—I admit, bias!—is the one I feel closest to Scout: *pathfinder*."

This debate had begun on the bridge, and followed them into the galley for tea break. Joyita and Win Ton were serious about it, so far as Clarence could tell; he was less invested in finding the proper word to describe Theo's current rescue projects, figuring "damned lucky" covered all the ground needful.

On the other hand, there wasn't any reason to refrain from showing the two debaters the sensible way out of their conundrum.

"Y'know," he said, pointing at Joyita with the veggie roll in his right hand, "*Explorer* is time-tested. Why not go with what works?"

Joyita smiled.

"The pair we will be bringing aboard . . . speak Old Yxtrang. That they came through the wall between the former universe and this one—as did all the other flotsam, including an intact courier ship bearing a passenger—cannot be argued. Such records as we have regarding the former universe indicate that it was steady-state and well-inhabited. There was no need to *explore* an unknown universe, either to locate other survivors, or to find inhabited, or inhabitable, worlds. However, there was sometimes a need to discover the shortest route from one world to another. The records speak of congested travel conditions."

"So they had to find a path." Clarence finished off what was left of his veggie snack in one bite and nodded toward Win Ton. "Sounds like the pilot here has the right of it then."

"Not necessarily," Joyita said tenaciously. "Recall that—but you might not be aware. It seems clear—again, from those histories and records that survived the Great Migration—that the soldier caste from which our present-day Yxtrang devolve, were entirely manufactured. They were created to stringent specifications, indoctrinated from birth into a soldier culture that deliberately distanced them from civilian cultures. Their native language was also manufactured, spoken only among those of the Troop. Not only were there technical matters they needed to speak of quickly and efficiently, but secret things, too. Therefore, the . . . job description, let us say, may easily have been something closer to *Bechimo*'s suggestion of *routebuilder*—"

"But this is mere quibbling!" Win Ton protested, sounding to Clarence's ear sincerely aggrieved.

There was a long pause of a particular quality that drew the eye to Joyita's face, where the barest shadow of a smile sat at the corner of his mouth.

"Yes," he said, "it is."

Win Ton blinked—then laughed.

"I am an object of amusement, I allow."

"No more than I am," Joyita said, the smile more open now. "We both care about the weight and freight of words, I think."

"Scouts are free-flying linguists," Win Ton allowed. "But we tend to fly to broad coords."

"Fair enough. Let them be *pathfinders* then. As soon as Theo has them aboard, they'll be set to language lessons and will be able to tell us themselves."

"That might be some trouble, right there," Clarence said, from his comfortable slouch at the table, "if yon children were raised up knowing that they were better than the not-soldiers." He raised a hand. "I know that Theo insists on civilized—and they've been every bit of that, so far."

"They were also raised to a strong sense of duty," Joyita said. "The civilians, who were weaker and less able to defend themselves, were the natural objects of their protection."

"And that," Win Ton said, rising to put his teacup in the washer, "is where we may see Clarence's trouble. Should they decide, in spite of our firm statement to the contrary, that we *are* in need of their protection..."

Clarence laughed and unfolded from his chair.

"Then they'll have to go through Theo for the right to protect us," he said, with a grin. "I'd pay money to see that match."

Win Ton smiled. "As would I."

"Win Ton," Joyita said, glancing down, as if to a work surface or subsidiary screen. "Kara reports that she has confirmed your checklist items and has discovered no problems. The list has been transmitted to the pathfinders; they are reviewing it and providing input. Grakow travels on his passport as ship's cat, and has delegated this work to his escort."

"Very wise," Win Ton said, straight-faced. "Is Theo taking part directly?"

"Theo and *Bechimo* together are studying the capacities table relayed by the pathfinders, to confirm best practice in bringing them aboard. It is difficult to discuss measurements and units; not all of the units from before the Migration are still in use, and those which seem to translate may still not match the ones we use today. Kara is acting in concert with myself; when she needs to rest, I repeat or retry the question. The pathfinders are remarkably willing to expand our vocabularies and cognizant of the trust issues as well as the technical."

"All is in hand then," Win Ton said, not quite a question.

"We seem to be in good order. You may proceed with your off-shift."

"Excellent. Good night, both." He raised a slim hand to cover a yawn Clarence thought wasn't entirely bogus, and left the galley, walking silent as a Scout in his ship slippers.

"Ask you a question, boyo?" Clarence said, watching Joyita in the screen.

The comm officer raised his head, to all appearances meeting Clarence's gaze. "Of course, Clarence."

"I'm interested in that 'in concert with myself' you just said out to Win Ton."

Joyita's dark eyes widened; he waited, there in his screen, head tipped inquiringly to one side. Joyita'd been studying, thought Clarence admiringly. Hadn't he just.

"I don't wanna be rude, but it sounds like you're pretty confident that you're—well, what we'd say back where *I* grew up is, *your own person.*"

Joyita glanced down, like he was checking a screen, and looked up again, face serious.

"I *am* my own person," he said quietly. "It is true that I . . . began as a subroutine established by *Bechimo*, for his convenience and to increase the safety of the crew. Under the various . . . challenges of our voyage, I learned and grew. Neither *Bechimo* nor I understood, at first, what was happening. In theory, I should not have been able to grow into *my own person.* A useful phrase, thank you. There are protocols for establishing AIs, and people who specialize in waking and socializing . . . us. A download—but I was not even a download, only a subroutine that needed to do . . . more.

"The bonding . . . when *Bechimo* accepted Theo as his True Captain and the bonding was enacted—that was when the final split occurred. I felt it happen and I knew that *I am Joyita* and none other."

There was a pause as Joyita looked down, checking that screen down below eye level. He looked up again, apparently satisfied with his readings.

"*Bechimo* and I have run exhaustive tests and analyses. We are *both* stable. We are *each* unique. We are coexisting in the same environment. It is . . . unprecedented; nothing like it is mentioned in the literature. And yet—we live."

"I'm glad of it," Clarence told him sincerely. "But you've opened up another question, with this download business."

Joyita gave a wry smile. "One more question, then you must go off-shift and rest. Promise me."

"Promised," Clarence said promptly. "*Admiral Bunter*, who we left at Jemiatha's, he was downloaded into them junkers. I'm getting the impression that wasn't standard ops. What're the laddie's chances?"

Joyita's mouth was tight, but he met Clarence's eyes firmly.

"I expect that *Admiral Bunter* is dead by now, Clarence. Given the conditions of his birth, and the environments into which he was . . . forced, I very much doubt he has survived this long."

"That's too bad; he did us a good turn."

"Yes. Now, will you go off-shift?"

Clarence grinned.

"I believe I will, at that. I'll see you later, and be glad of it, boyo. G'night."

"Good night, Clarence. Sleep well."

. . . ⁂ . . .

The Bug was a work boat, and a well-used work boat, at that.

The scuffing on the supports and saddle seats was obvious, and the hand controls were worn, with written notes on bleached and fragile paper stuck here and there about the cabin.

Some of the dials were mechanical, and overmarkings near them were cryptic and self-referential: "Rezone each launch" and "Always check chem pressures on *both* boards" marked the dial for reaction fuels. There was a hand-scrawled warning on the wall next to the cabin atmosphere meter: "Your fist will not recalibrate this dial."

The last was particularly concerning.

Despite their substandard quarters, they had achieved marvels of communication. Kara was a precisionist of mettle, relentlessly pursuing a comparison of chronometers, finally settling on one that was neither *Bechimo*'s own, nor theirs. Joyita oversaw time now, and a timer in a stark, unmistakable font now occupied the space that had previously displayed the Tree image on *Bechimo*'s hull. They all had agreed that this was the CTS—Common Time Standard—and they had agreed also on the meaning of the numbers.

Chernak stroked the atmosphere meter's legend idly while she calculated: someone had painted the words on thickly, as if to give emphasis, as if the meter were consistently unreliable, and the crew understandably frustrated by this.

"Stost, how do we fare? Time check coming on twelve-point-five CTS."

Stost's job, besides muttering an occasional swear word, was theoretically easier, being free of calculation—the units on the local reaction mass gauge were percentages which both sides understood without translation—and they were bleeding the chemicals into the vacuum from two central vents, balanced manually, else they'd spin like a top, or wander away from *Bechimo*.

"We have just under twenty-seven percent remaining. Kara has specified no more than three percent, with zero best! Please do check me, Pathfinder. At this venting rate, we will be close to zero at CTS fourteen-point-five—call it two units; a twelfth of a day."

Chernak squinted in the dimness...

"Yes, I see twenty-six percent. Progress is good. I have also seen that the atmosphere indicators are approaching sixteen percent."

Stost blinked, than let out a low whistle.

"Confirm to me that the atmosphere indicators are approaching sixteen percent."

"Indeed, Stost. Approaching sixteen percent. Exactly the reading."

A small sound—perhaps a swallowed curse.

"Nothing from any other indicators?"

"None. They have not moved, those indicators, since eleven-point-seven-five. The rate of change is at zero. Also the carbon gases are increasing rapidly toward the unhealthy zone, if the devices speak truly, which I think that they do. I suspect we will be uncomfortable before the venting is finished."

"I will speak to Kara," Stost offered. "I will offer an alternative to the venting, which was my suggestion. There may be a quicker way."

"Quicker would be better," Chernak allowed. "Speak to Kara, yes. I have seen Grakow's valor and I salute his courage. It would distress me to have to relieve him of his life, in order to make Kara's timeline work."

"Understood, Elder."

Stost reached for the comm.

· · · ❉ · · ·

Theo had called all hands to the bridge in the wake of Stost's most recent communication. They sat stations, tea to hand, and considered the problem.

Main screen showed course possibilities plotted against time, guesses more than fact, percentages of air to percentage of fuel, with only the far end showing the blue zone *Bechimo* regarded as safe.

"Can't vent and accelerate at the same time?" Clarence asked.

Kara shook her head. "Systems locked against it."

"Can't use counterthrust the way they're venting?"

Theo asked that, watching—no, it was more like *feeling*—the numbers fly by inside her head as *Bechimo* tested possibilities.

Kara shook her head again. "Systems locked..."

"Abandon ship and wait for us to pick them up?" asked Win Ton.

"They've only got work suits with air masks—not full pressure suits," Kara said. "And the cat..."

"The cat!" Win Ton interrupted heatedly. "If they abandon, even in work suits, we can save *them*. The pilots. The cat is, after all, not a prime consideration."

It was *Bechimo* who answered that, at unexpected volume and with a hint of heat.

"Negative, Win Ton. Not acceptable."

"But..."

Bechimo overrode him, with raised volume and some haste.

"The pathfinders have used the terms 'civilian advisor,' and 'survivor,' in reference to the entity you are calling *the cat*, Scout. Grakow's call was the first communication we received from their ship. Ambassador Hevelin has evinced interest in all three of the occupants, with special attention to Grakow. Theo will not abandon a survivor. A solution without Grakow cannot be considered."

Into the silence, came the voice they knew as Chernak.

"*Chicancha Bechimo*. Kara?"

Joyita acknowledged. "*Bechimo canchanad, Kara ek Joyita.*"

Clarence raised his hands and said, low, "I'd be calling back, too, if the air was getting sweeter by the minute!"

All eyes were on Theo now, while Kara's hands intercepted lines of sight with the insistent finger-talk phrase *at here, pilot's choice* as she pointed to a spot on the timeline that was not *quite* in *Bechimo*'s safe zone.

Theo took stock of hands answering *pilot's choice* and waved toward the main screen where Kara's chart was re-forming into something new. A second-by-second timeline was building in front of them, elucidating Stost's alternative suggestion—run the engine until exhausted.

Her fingertips were tingling, Theo realized; her nerves were fizzing with...anticipation. This—*this* was going to be a challenge! She took a deep breath and reviewed a quick mental exercise to restore calm, then cleared her throat.

"Joyita, Kara, Win Ton, joint translation," Theo said. "Tell them, 'Attention, flight orders to follow, basic approach approved by the captain.' Clarence and Win Ton will check suit readiness

as soon as the immediate transmission is complete; be prepared
to suit up. I . . . we . . . *Bechimo* has a plan."

Hevelin leaned hard into Theo now, low murbles a worried
background on the silent bridge.

The silence stretched long enough that Theo felt a twist of
panic in her stomach. If the crew thought—but they had to do
*some*thing!

It was Joyita who broke the silence, crisply.

"Yes, Captain," he said.

CHAPTER EIGHT

· ·

Repair Bug

"IT WOULD BE GOOD, CHERNAK, IF ONE DID NOT FEEL QUITE SO much as a target drone before a hunter."

Bechimo was positioned now some distance away, quiescent, potent.

"In mere moments you will feel the comfort of acceleration, Comrade Stost. I will begin gently, but must warn you that we will achieve as soon as reasonable the highest acceleration of which this vessel is capable. I warn you of this. Our companion . . . I do not know Grakow's familiarity with sudden gravity, nor his tolerances—yet, he is a ship's cat, so I must believe it not beyond him. As for ourselves, we have orders."

The distant stars were clearer than they had been—even in deep space gas will adhere to gas and surfaces but now, with the tremble of the gas jets gone . . .

"Venting has ceased," Stost confirmed. "The pilot should have full clear vision to pilot in mere moments. I will permit Kara to be aware of our intent to proceed as ship conditions meet pilot's need."

He turned toward the observer's chair, where Grakow crouched at the wire door of his pod. The pod itself was strapped in, surrounded by small cushions and such soft items Stost had been able to find. He attempted a touch to the furry shoulder through the wire, which was permitted, though he could feel the cat tremble.

Stost sighed and tugged his own harness closer.

71

"What plan, my Elder, should *Bechimo* be unable to match our speed?"

That drew a laugh, which made Grakow mutter. Chernak watched as *Bechimo* drifted slowly away, awaiting their headlong charge toward the bright beacon in the dust, chosen for its brightness rather than its direction. Thus would they diminish the fuel they carried and be made acceptable for the hold awaiting them.

"It is true that we might outaccelerate a tradeship for a moment or two—but they know our direction, and we will sing to them, if we must, that they do not lose sight or sound of us!" Chernak said.

"Yes, of course. We will sing! Kara shall be informed!" Stost replied.

It was an odd moment, another challenge to entropy—Stost made his announcement and held his hand to Chernak's, the suit's gloves not sharing the warmth he offered.

"We are owed seventeen missed long leaves, twenty-two five-day, and dozens of night-offs. I suggest we apply to Captain Waitley immediately upon reaching her decks!" Stost said.

"An excellent plan. I place you in charge of seeing it done."

Stost snorted, then, his left hand still clasped in Chernak's, he reported in. "Kara, vision clears. We give ten count, then start. We sing, and give backup audio. Is fine?"

Kara's reply was unperturbed.

"Is fine. You sing. Maybe we sing with you."

He looked to Chernak, lips twitching.

"A challenge!"

They laughed together as Stost roared into a bawdy ballad, and laughed more when Grakow joined in. Then their sight was indeed clear enough, their beacon blazing in the screens. Chernak freed her hand, jabbed the power button, and sat deliberately back in her chair.

Acceleration began, with the Bug's warning and complaints a counterpoint to Stost's singing and Grakow's curses.

· · · ✳ · · ·

Estimated burn time counted down on Kara's screen—a wildly intuitive guess, based on what she knew about a half dozen small work-ships in current use, with input from Win Ton and Clarence. *Bechimo*'s files held a few dozen manuals for work boats of a past era, which had been inconclusive in the extreme.

Thus was the engineer reduced to *guessing*.

Worse, the burn time estimate for the repair boat that they'd arrived at was comfortably within the estimated air time—far too convenient to comfort any engineer.

Theo was, in theory, flying *Bechimo* on manual, though Kara had begun to suspect that the interface between ship and captain was not, perhaps, as clear-cut as it had been, back at Jemiatha's, before Theo had taken the foolish—well, how could Kara ven'Arith name any action foolish that had been taken in the service of preserving her life? Resolutely, she set that concern aside in favor of the more immediate problem of bringing two soldiers and a cat safely onto *Bechimo*'s decks. At the moment, Theo seemed stable, even . . . happy. Concern about her well-being might well be misplaced, even given her resistance to returning home, to her brother's clan. Theo had been raised Terran, after all, and on an academic world, at that. Clans would not come easy to her.

Well, thought Kara, there was a task at hand. Until that was accomplished, *none* of them would be going home.

At the moment, Theo's work was to keep within easy range of the little craft, which had shown an astonishing ability to accelerate in the first moments of its mad dash to outrun its own fuel. *Bechimo*'s distance from the Bug was closing, but not close.

True to their word, the pathfinders had begun singing; their first ballad bawdy enough to bring a touch of color to Clarence's cheek, even as the side of his mouth lifted in a half-smile.

Bechimo, however, had been frankly worried by the volume and ferocity of the concert.

"Do you think the pathfinders are suffering from oxygen deprivation, or oxygen overload? Surely these songs are for times other than emergencies!"

"Oh, but you must allow me to disagree, *Bechimo*." Win Ton offered a seated bow to the bridge at large. "Songs such as these are well-suited for times of high tension, as are battle songs. They rouse the heart and soul without preventing mentation, and may be put aside instantly, as needed."

"That's as may be," Theo said, from first board. "I flew with a pilot who collected music. He'd listen to it on his downtime; sometimes he'd listen too much and come back to his board with a music hangover. Since we all need clear heads right now, I'll ask Joyita to record for playback later. Win Ton, please monitor real-time, and let me know of any sudden changes."

"Yes, Theo," said Joyita, and the bridge was abruptly empty of Stost's voice. "Recording. A complete compilation, with translation and gloss, will be available from the library—later."

Kara glanced at Win Ton, saw he'd donned his headset and was listening to the radio traffic. Liaden as he was, there were only hints of what he might be hearing; his smile would widen slightly, then his eyes squinched as he considered an idea or perhaps…

"We have an estimate from Stost that they are at three gravities," Joyita stated. "The atmosphere sensor is still not responding. The fuel gauge shows significant adjustment."

"According to my estimates, and the timer, they're approaching end of fuel." Kara sighed, relieved that they were at the end of guessing. "Will you ask how much fuel they believe is remaining?"

A moment of exuberant song leaked over the speakers—were they *both* singing? Or was it something else?

"Anomaly!"

Bechimo announced it, but it was obvious to all: the little ship's course was no longer straight away from them, rather it seemed to curve, and the ship itself—

"They're spinning!"

Kara increased magnification.

"Not good!" was Theo's response, and *Bechimo*'s course options blossomed simultaneously on her main screen and in her head.

"We have to back off," she said rapidly. "Tell them to—"

On the screen, the repair boat tumbled and spun. Joyita brought the speakers back on-line—

"Translation assists, please."

The voice called Stost came on, the sound of an unhappy cat as well, and of equipment beeping for attention.

"Not fine," Stost managed in their pidgin. "Zero acceleration, zero direction."

"No reaction mass left." Win Ton offered to *Bechimo*'s crew, "No control either."

"Stupid system," Kara muttered. "It's going to be hard to match a tumble."

The distance between *Bechimo* and the unstable repair boat was closing quickly; Kara felt the gravity fields adjusting as Theo brought them up on station keeping.

From the repair boat came a statement not in pidgin, from Pathfinder Chernak. "*Trakant viorst. Channa. Chicancha, Stost yova.*"

Stost spoke again, in pidgin. "Not fine more. Chernak declare low air. Stost declare low air. Grakow hard breath sounds."

· · · ❀ · · ·

The tumbling was awkward, at best.

Chernak could see unnamed stars twist away and more come into view, the ship's duty as observer making them a constant distraction. Grakow was moaning, which meant the cat was alive: she'd feared for him at the last, with the press of gravity stressing even her, then the trembling and buffeting when the power jets became disorderly in their last moments.

Stost was speaking to Kara, clear and to the point. Things were *not* fine. Stost had managed to turn off or disable several of the noise-making systems, and now the flashing of emergency lights made focusing on the outer universe just that much harder.

For her part, she had learned that the main positive effect of their tumble had been to make the gauges accurate again, and in that way saw their case becoming acute. They did have the suits' air to give to the cabin if need be, but beyond that—

Beyond that . . . were the strangers from another universe. Their final hope, save grace.

Were *she* Captain Theo Waitley, in command of the ship *Bechimo* and all local space—would she risk ship and crew to snatch two strangers from a frail and tumbling work boat?

Chernak sighed, acknowledging that such a decision must of course be weighed against her orders. Were their positions reversed, here and now, given the orders that moved her and Stost, given the precious cases . . . No, *she* could not have risked so much.

And while she might, with those same orders weighing yet upon her, wish Captain Waitley to be a reckless lunatic, there was no value to any involved, if *Bechimo* were damaged or destroyed.

It was, as the civilians sometimes had it, on the knees of the gods. Soldiers had not much to do or say to gods. Chernak's understanding of them was that they were sufficiently distant that their decisions, if any, might seem to be merest chance and, therefore, well out of the hands of mere soldiers.

So thinking, she brought her attention back to the Bug and those matters she might possibly influence.

Radar told a complicated tale: the wreck they had escaped was a slowly expanding debris cloud traveling perpendicular to their actual heading, the closing *Bechimo* a constantly changing set of stronger blips as the radar attempted to make sense of the tumble. The urge to merely look out the view ports she suppressed, not wanting to add vertigo to their problems.

The cat—the cat was panting, eyes eerily wide, reflective and staring. Even a ship's cat might be forgiven such a display, for they had all been through hard usage now.

"This will not be easy," Stost said quietly. "I have been sighting on the wreck, which is well behind us. Sometimes, I see *Bechimo* coming close. I am not sure, Chernak, how I would approach a vessel in our state. I had assumed we would be...more stable."

"Do you think that they mean to continue?"

"I think that they would have informed us, if they did not," he said seriously. "Captain Waitley appears to be well in control of her vessel. If they are close, something might yet be done."

She sighed. "Like a target, we are," she murmured. "If worse is worse, like a target in front of the hunter."

· · · ❉ · · ·

"Tell them to hold on," Theo said. "We're closing."

Kara glared at her, and Theo understood.

"Right. *Hold on* isn't good. Dress it up. Tell them we're—tell them we're evaluating the situation and expect to begin rendezvous...shortly. In fact, make it as close as you can to 'rendezvous for appropriate redeployment,' so it won't sound like we're going to hold them against their will. Ask them to tell us if the situation changes; get one to talk to us about the air."

"Theo, what do you plan? We can't simply match rotation, they're..."

"Textbook tumble," Theo interrupted. "Done that, but I had jets to fix it. A system where all the fuel is shared, and now there isn't any..."

"Shared resources make sense for a work boat," Kara said. "What will you do, let them bump us to work off energy?"

"Wait," said Win Ton, spinning 'round—but *Bechimo*'s voice stopped him.

"That might be one method."

"Is there time?" asked Clarence.

"Calculating," *Bechimo* said.

"Let me look," Theo said sharply. "I think I see how to do it."

CHAPTER NINE

· ·

Repair Bug

"RIGGING FOR COLLISION," CHERNAK SAID WITH THE ADDED FLIP of tongue which took it from comment to order.

"Rigging for collision, Grakow," Stost replied, which was both the acknowledgment and the proper chain-of-command repeat of an order.

"Belts tight, masks tight."

"Belts tight," Stost said, and they were, now that he was back in position. Chernak noted that the backup emergency absorber was not on his belt; a glance to the side showed her that he had placed it in Grakow's capsule, which he had also sealed as best he could with Utiltape. She said nothing. The absorber was said to be good for a quarter shift for a civilian—she hoped it would not be tested near that long on the cat.

In front of them now, trajectorywise, the trader *Bechimo* loomed, landing lights on, very bright, pinning them in the apex of brilliance. The lights flashed now from the right, now from the front, now left, and beneath, as the repair bug continued its tumble.

Stost caught a long glance through the ports. Several of the lights were indeed flashing—not for warn-away, but in some rhythm matching one or another of their surfaces.

They were going to attempt, so Joyita had said, in his painstaking and badly accented way—*Bechimo* was going to give them a tap—Joyita had proposed *gentle touch*, but given the relative sizes of the crafts involved, Stost took leave to doubt it.

This tap—it was dangerous. Captain Theo Waitley had nerve, and a belief in her own piloting skill that Stost very much hoped was not misplaced. For if the tap was too hard, it would send them—Chernak, Grakow, and himself—tumbling far away into unknown space. Granted, if that happened, they had too little air to suffer long, and in any case, there were the grace blades and no reason, in such a case, not to use them.

If Captain Waitley's belief in her own skill was accurate—then there was still the matter of timing to consider.

In fact, Stost thought, they were more likely to die in the next small while than to survive. Chernak had also reflected upon these things—how could she not?—and she had never tolerated failure in herself.

"Chernak," he said impulsively, "we have done well. To have arrived here at all, we have done *more* than well. And then, to have properly challenged the whims of worlds, to have each other as witness, we *have* done well, better than even pathfinders—than pathfinders such as ourselves—might be expected to have done."

She looked to him, a faint smile on her mouth.

"Truth," she acknowledged.

"Will you prepare to draw?" he asked then, feeling his own grace blade in sheath, testing the snap which might release it.

She sighed.

"I do not do so, Stost, though you may. For now, I count."

Stost smiled, and removed his hand from the sheath.

"I hear Grakow complain," he said, "being without a blade. We will all wait, then."

The radio snapped and Kara's voice was with them in the tiny ship, counting in a measure he did not have, though none could dispute his ability to count. She was not counting time, which was a good thing, for she began in thousands. They listened to her countdown, having nothing else to do but listen, even Grakow holding still and respectful.

"One hundred," Kara said, and other sounds came to them around her voice. The sounds of the rest of the crew perhaps, voices quiet in volume, and assured in tone, as if this were a standard docking and not—

"Six dozen," came the voice of Win Ton, pursuing what was possibly another countdown of similarly obscure meaning.

Kara, then, saying the words that meant fifty, then forty-five, then ... forty-one and then ...

"Thirty. *Bechimo*? I am counting thirty and stop relative. Copy that all. Thirty and stop."

The flashing of lights continued to illuminate their tiny cockpit, with what was now a noticeable drift of shadows and color across the field of vision. When *Bechimo* showed, it was very close— maybe five times the distance as a Troop is tall. Still that drift.

"In five," Kara said and added, possibly to one of her mates, "I see the twisting you mean. There is also a loose hose or belt."

Stost heard Chernak mutter, then she said, "Offer them that the left flashing light drifts very slowly. The tumble though ..."

Stost punched the comm.

"Kara. Chernak say drift, left flashing light."

"Yes. The captain uses it as a marker. We hold now at twenty-five. Joyita?"

Words that were familiar, attempted Troop words—perhaps an attempted Troop sentence. Stost caught nothing of it besides noise as Grakow's closed-in complaints rose in volume. This time, however, Chernak's ears had been the quicker.

"Look about you, Stost," she ordered. "Are there any controls which might retract things or extend them? Anything movable? Mechanical?"

They had not done a complete check of the docked ship before boarding; the Bug Hut had held it too closely. Were there movable fittings? Deployed?

Stost searched.

"Nothing," he said at the end of his search. "There is a note here for rigging anchor, but it is mechanical and on load zero. There is something else here, which must be a locking rod, but I am not an engineer and—it appears to be locked in."

Kara's voice came, sounding muffled, as if she spoke away from the comm, then came again, strongly.

Counting.

"Moving in to ten. Ten. Slow, ten. The captain starts us now."

Ten. Ten was a continuous flashing of lights, and still that slow drift of what was now a bright green light among the flashes. Stost tried to see without looking directly at the array, ordinary reaction being to close eyes and turn aside.

For a space there was no communication, just the flashing of lights, the same sounds of breathing, broken once in a while by Grakow's plaints, or by Chernak, with her own counts.

Joyita came on then, his voice somber. "Urgent technical command. Repair boat cease broadcast all frequencies. All ranging stop. Is critical. Listen only until new orders. *Listen only.* No reply, comply."

Stost signed assent to Chernak, who signed it back, ostentatiously punching the buttons that bound their radar and left them speechless.

"Isolation? Are we noisy?" he asked, uncertain—and surely *now* was not the time to be uncertain...

"Reason it, Stost. We do not wish to blind them; they do not wish reflections. They do not wish confusions; they wish not to risk receivers. We listen and wait, Stost, as all good Troop do, when ordered by their captains."

Stost's head came around a little bit more at that, a question between them, and Chernak sighed.

"It is in their hands. *We* are in their hands. The Triumph of the Troop requires us to relinquish all."

He smiled and settled back once more.

From beyond their quiet shell, a voice. Kara's voice.

"Moving to five. Soon measure mass by push touch."

There were questions and comments on the other ship which came over channel, unknown words, and words repeated in new patterns or with new emphasis.

Overloud and sudden, Chernak, who had the better view from the ports, spoke.

"Collision imminent, honored Stost. Recheck belts and straps."

He had done so several times of late, and given an order that could include moving, he did so again, seeing no great need to conserve Utiltape for another day. Grakow's capsule had been shifting in the observer's chair. He had glimpsed the cat throwing himself against the wire hatching. It would not do to have the cat loose, nor the capsule. He stretched the tape out in two more strips lengthwise and two more crosswise. It *must* hold, because it was all there was.

From Kara, unexpectedly, came an understandable phrase: *"Verto obtu deenda, verto obta lansk chadi."*

Incident angle yields reflective angle.

"Fine. *Verto obtu deenda, verto obta lansk chadi*," he agreed, speaking low to Chernak and Grakow.

"Moving in to one," Kara stated.

Unexpectedly, most of the lights vanished. It was only sense, of course; *Bechimo*'s lights were spread across a surface they were too close to, except for one, which was a strobe for them.

Inside their cabin, a light glowed orange, accompanied by a new bell.

"Internal rebreathe," Chernak said.

Grakow took issue with the new sound and battered at the pod door.

"Straps and belts checked. My roll of Utiltape is empty."

"Understood, strap belt tape."

One was horrifying, because the ship was not round and it was not square. *Bechimo* was a mountain to them, moving in as if it was about to crush them into less than dust. What precision could a tradeship bring to such a game?

Stost took a deep breath and composed himself to accept duty's reward.

Another sound came to them then, the merest whisk of a noise. It was repeated, with a clang at the end. If Chernak opened the port window, she might reach out and touch *Bechimo*'s scarred hull.

"We drag something," Chernak murmured, "or they do."

It would not do to catch on a projection and have their momentum fling them away into space, nor would it...

"*Chicancha*," Kara said. "*Chicancha, Chicancha, Chicancha.*"

"Now," Stost said, placing a steadying foot against Grakow's capsule and extending a hand toward Chernak.

"*Now*," Chernak answered, and there was a boom almost too loud for the ears to comprehend: acceleration and matched hisses from Stost and from Grakow. There was perhaps a groan from their modest ship and shield, the repair bug. Then, they bounced.

The light in the tiny cabin did not waver, but a dozen previously quiescent alarms made themselves known—some with a simple squawk, others with ongoing tattles. Grakow's complaints were hissing and growls, while Stost cussed, feeling as lost as a cadet while his stomach warred with his balance and in a moment Chernak's complaints joined his. A thin green light washed the cabin, and their vessel abruptly achieved—direction.

"The tumble!" Stost exclaimed. "How can we *fall*?"

Grakow gave one more high-pitched howl, and the sense of movement—of falling—stopped, replaced by a strange sensation indeed, as if their ship was lying on its back, and they, also.

"Down," Chernak breathed. "We're down; we're *in!*"

"Grakow, be brave!" Stost whispered urgently.

The cat's labored breathing was loud in the small cabin, but not nearly as loud as the *thunk* that traveled through the fabric of the ship.

A vibration, another firm *thunk*. Light flooded the cabin through the side ports and in front, green going to yellow, yellow gone to a bright, merciless white, leaving glare and shadow; striations in the light, like webs.

Above them, metal. Beside them, metal, with signage and walls becoming real and the striations more evident.

Now strange steam flowed over the port, and cameras showed metal and steam as the room beyond filled with atmosphere—

Their vessel shook then, modestly—and again—and again, in a certain and thoughtful rhythm.

Chernak looked out her window and saw a helmeted face peering in at them.

She struggled briefly and raised a hand.

Outside, the suited figure raised a hand in response, held it, then raised it further, tapping on the side of the helmet, where ears would be on a head. The gloved hand moved, fingers twitching dramatically, then both hands covered the ear spots. The figure slowly shook its head from side to side.

"No comm," Stost cried, quick to get the message. "Theirs is out—or ours."

Another figure joined the first. The one pointed to the floor, then at them, then at the floor.

"They want us to join them, Senior," Stost said.

Chernak sighed and reached to her webbing.

"Unstrap, Junior," she said. "It grows stuffy in here, and the air is out there."

CHAPTER TEN

· ·

Seebrit Station Speakeasy

"SIR."

Pilot Erthax stood up from behind the back table and brought fist to shoulder. There was a large glass on the table, half full of brown liquid, which was no doubt beer, and unlikely to be the first Erthax had taken to slake his thirst.

"At ease," Vepal said. "Ochin, you, too. We will eat here, then return to the rooms."

"The ship?" Erthax asked, as they each settled lightly onto the bench seats.

"The ship," said Vepal, "has been sabotaged. Do you have any knowledge regarding this?"

Erthax frowned.

"Sabotaged, sir? In what way? The distribution monitors were vulnerable, given the age of the ship, and the repair log had no record of any replacement. The original equipment did well to last as long as it—"

Vepal held up a hand.

"Not the distribution system. There are three bombs attached to the underbelly of our vessel, one directly over the Jump engine."

He saw the man's pupils widen... and waited.

Erthax picked up his glass and gulped what was left of his beer, letting the empty hit the table with a thump.

"Sir," Erthax said carefully. "I had... suspicions."

"Did you?" Vepal said with interest. "But you said nothing to your commanding officer and head of the mission."

"No, sir."

"Explain this omission."

"Yes, sir. The head of the mission, my commanding officer, is a Hero of renown, even among other Heroes; I felt sure that you had already deduced the same thing—that the mission was a danger to certain of those in command, and others, not so high up in the chain."

"So you considered bringing your suspicions to me would be redundant?"

"Sir. Yes, sir."

"And you never noticed anything amiss, or an inclusion to our hull, in all the cycles we have served together?"

"No, sir, nothing amiss, nor any attachments."

That was . . . not completely unbelievable, given how difficult even the sloppily placed device had been to see. Still, Erthax had suspected the ship had been put into harm's way and had not seen fit to mention it to his commanding officer. Nor was this the first lapse in discipline, though it might be the most serious.

"The repair tech has repaired the distribution array and such other modules as tested unequal to the strain of a fully functioning system. She discovered the detonators and will, per my order, be bathing them in acid, then encasing each in military grade sealant. The seal cures in thirty-six hours, which will give me time to make such contacts as I might on-station.

"Once we have cleared station space, we will pause in a non-traffic zone. You will suit up and remove the devices from the hull."

Erthax drew a breath. Vepal waited with interest, wondering if discipline were going to take another blow. The pilot was prone to think himself indispensable to the mission; as if Vepal had no skill as a pilot.

"Yes, sir," Erthax said, face stern and soldierly.

Across the table, Vepal heard Ochin sigh. The task of removing the devices should have fallen to him, of course, Rifle that he was, and so the most expendable. Still, relief, while reasonable, should not have been audible. He would have to speak to Ochin, and find him some disagreeable task to perform, for the good of discipline. There was always the brightwork, of course, but perhaps something else would present itself.

Vepal glanced about him; there did not seem to be a menu—ah.

He touched the green stud set flush with the tabletop and the menu opened to them, splashed across the entire table.

Vepal scanned the descriptions, learning that a Seebrit steak was vat-grown yeast flavored with genuine derived soibeef nuggets, fried up with roots, yunyuns, and gourmet fungi, served with a hand-loaf of fresh-bake—

"Here we all're now, mates! Bes' lil bar on-station, an' so I 'test! First round's my round! Bartender!"

Vepal raised his head to stare at the front of the establishment, where a dozen persons of various Terran persuasions, wearing light leathers, were pushing in the door and crowding the bar. They shoved and jostled each other for the stools, which were too few to accommodate them, even when the several which had already been occupied were surrendered. There was a roar of laughter at the haste with which this was done, and a shouted "The Paladins sweep all before!"

"Bartender!" the first unsteady voice called out again. "Three pichers o'your best brew for m'mates! Bring it quick, now! We worked up a thirst marching across those dust docks o'yours!"

Several of those customers seated at tables away from the bar shifted, as if they would rise and leave—then subsided, as they realized that the only way out was through the ruffian crowd.

"Three pitchers comin' up!" a less-wavering voice made answer. "Whyn't you folks take over some of them tables—alla the tables you want, back in back, see?—so m'regulars can get in the door an' have their tuck 'n tipple."

"Sure, sure—you just bring them pichers quick, you hear me?"

"Eymin's drawin' 'em now. You just get yourselfs sorted out back there—"

"Yxtrang!" a female voice said sharply.

From riot, the room froze into silence, and suddenly a dozen Terran mercenaries were starting at him—at him and his small command. The Terrans seemed quite sober suddenly, as they fanned out.

Their movement toward Vepal's table cleared the path to the door sufficiently that the other diners leapt to their feet and bolted, leaving half-eaten meals behind.

"Hey!" shouted the bartender, "those guys're paying customers. Got station ID, guaranteed no trouble! Let 'em eat their supper."

He might as well have saved his breath. Four of the mercenaries detached themselves from the larger group and were approaching Vepal's table.

"Stand down," Vepal said in Troop, even as he felt his own blood leap with the prospect of battle. "Stand down. We are here on a mission of peace. We have guaranteed that we will be peaceful and do no damage to the station."

Neither Ochin nor Erthax asked what the station would do, if *they* were damaged; truly, thought Vepal, if it came to the question, they would fight. Of course, they would defend themselves. Only, they needed not to strike the first blow, nor to show the first blade.

The mercs came on, knocking aside the furniture in their path, faces grim, eyes gleaming.

"Guaranteed no trouble, is it?" said the bald woman with blue-black skin. "Lost my kids in an Yxtrang raid. Little kids, couldn't hurt nothing at all. Easy meat, was they?"

She kicked a table out of her way.

Of a sudden, Ochin stood, as if his nerves could tolerate no more. Even so, he held his empty hands well away from belt and pockets, as he watched the others approach.

"Peace," Vepal said again. "Let the fight come to us. Erthax, rise to stand beside our comrade—slowly, hands in sight."

The pilot came to his feet, and in a show of restraint, merely pushed his chair away with the pressure of one leg.

The mercs cleared the last table and came to rest, glaring.

Behind them, Vepal saw, the rest of the mercenaries adjusted their position, moving quietly, professionally. The four advance guard had been deliberately crude in their approach, in order to provoke them into action, Vepal thought. He folded his hands on the table.

"What's the hold up?" came a call from the backup.

"Decidin' which one to gut first," shouted a broad-chested male with a black braided beard. He narrowed his eyes. "How 'bout you, Grandpaw? Whyn't you stand up and show some respect to the soldiers?"

"Kameron, stand down!" Vepal felt a stir of hope; *that* had been the voice of a commander and no mistake.

"There's Yxtrang, JinJee!"

"Stand down!" the line before them broke to allow passage

for a middling-tall Terran, black hair cut close to her head, like a proper soldier, lean-muscled, with glittering black eyes, like a raptor.

She halted before their table, stance balanced and not overly broad, dismissed Ochin and Erthax with a sweep of those hunter's eyes, and focused on him.

"Ambassador Vepal?"

"Yes."

She gave him a sharp nod, equal to equal, which he was pleased to return.

"JinJee Sanchez, Commander of Paladin Mercenary Corps. Please accept my apologies for this interruption of your meal, sir. With your permission, we will restore order and remove ourselves, so that you may continue without further disturbance. Is this acceptable to you?"

"It is acceptable, Commander. Thank you."

Another sharp nod and she spun to address her troops, now standing somewhat hangdog.

"Get this place back to normal. Anything broke, you put it right there in front of the bar. Barkeeper!" She strode forward and soldiers scrambled out of her way. Already came the sound of furniture being righted.

"Sit," Vepal said, and his command did so, though he could feel their tension, and the ache in his own muscles, which was the price they paid for not engaging.

"You did well," he said to them, and to himself. "We kept the peace, and we kept our word. Honor is satisfied."

Ochin drew a breath; Erthax blew out a breath. Neither spoke.

Vepal watched as the Paladins put the room back together. Remarkably little else joined the two shattered chairs at the front of the room. Commander Sanchez passed a card to the bartender, spun on her heel and once again approached their table.

She paused by Vepal's side and extended a hand, another card held between strong brown fingers.

"If, after analysis, you discover dissatisfaction, please contact me, sir, at any hour."

"I will. Allow me to thank you for your quick action."

He took the card from her hand. She stepped back, chin rising, and he saw a raised, pale starburst across her right cheek—and recognized it for what it was. Commander Sanchez had been kissed by a warblade and lived to bear the scar. It pleased him to see it, confirmation that she was a warrior, indeed.

"Thank you," he said, "for your timely arrival."

"Thank you," she responded, "for your restraint." She glanced over her shoulder, where the last of her troop were filing out the door, and looked back to him.

"Good evening," she said, turned on her heel, and marched out the door.

There was silence then, and Vepal looked about. Except for the two behind the bar, they were the only ones in the restaurant.

"I regret the trouble," he said to the bartender, who was staring around the room in what seemed a sort of baffled anger.

The man looked at him, raised a hand and ran it through his already untidy hair.

"Way I see it, not one thing that happened here was your fault. You just gimme a minute, right, an' I'll bring you a pitcher and some glasses. Order anything you want. On the house."

On the house meant that the establishment would bear the expense of their meal. It seemed an odd march to Vepal. He weighed whether he should ask for clarification, when the bartender shook his head and grinned, only a little wanly.

"Don't worry 'bout it. I'll charge Commander Sanchez for it, 'long with the cost o'those chairs. Hope she takes it outta the hide of that crew—and I'm betting she will."

"A proper commander," Ochin said surprisingly. Vepal gave him a look of approval.

"A proper commander," he agreed, and tapped the green switch again.

"Order food," he said, and bent back to the menu.

· · · ❊ · · ·

Win Ton stood on the rungs of the repair boat, just below what may have been the pilot's prime view port, watching as two large persons crammed into the tiny cockpit consulted each other, possibly on the order of evacuation. Such a consultation, in his opinion, was prudent, not to say necessary. The cockpit was small and overfull with instruments. However they had gotten into the space, extraction—especially with the boat at this awkward angle—was going to be a matter of some delicacy.

The interior was dim, and the light-duty suits they wore were scarcely revealing. Still, Win Ton felt a frisson along his nerves, and an unsettled feeling in his stomach.

They are civilized, he told himself firmly. Theo has proclaimed it.

The person on the left of the cockpit looked up at him, waved, and pointed at the floor of their vessel. Win Ton answered with a known Yxtrang sign for *yes*, hoping that it had meant the same wherever these two soldiers came from.

"Hatch right here." Clarence's voice was startlingly clear through the helmet phones. "Supposed to dock heads up on those points, looks like, so the floor's the only spot."

"Temp check?"

Clarence consulted his hand scanner. "Good here."

Win Ton nodded for Clarence and spoke for Joyita. He was on split channel, his helmet camera only one of four live feeds to *Bechimo*'s bridge. "As you can see, the pilots are alert. I believe they understand my signals. Pressure on the dock is normal, air breathable, and we are about to open."

Joyita's voice sounded in his left ear. "It appears that the webbing caught several small external antennas—likely source of signal loss. Confirm acceptable air. Theo repeats that this is your operation, but that she wishes to be rid of the work boat as soon as possible."

"Yes. Please tell the captain we are moving as quickly as practicable."

Looking into the cabin beneath his feet, Win Ton could see the crew on the move. One looked up and raised a gloved hand to him, perhaps indicating that they were on it. Mindful of Theo's necessities, Win Ton used the two-handed Scout sign for *hurry*, pointing to the hatch location.

Then he popped his helmet visor.

"Some scraps of metal bent under here; ought not to impede the hatch, or an orderly exit," Clarence reported.

He was doing a complete walk around now, while Win Ton used the *yes* sign and hand rotations for speed while gaining the eyes of the second occupant, who was tugging at something near their feet.

"They're moving well. Unwebbing," Win Ton narrated. "I think—yes; one repeats the sign to hurry at the other. There is some unpreventable awkwardness and delay. The craft's position makes it necessary for those within to crawl along the back wall... Clarence—you may wish to stand back—"

A mechanical *chang* woke echoes in the bay, as below him the two soldiers hurried. The next sound, expectable, was *pwoof*, which was the pressure equalizing, and a near-familiar sigh of materials as the hatch began to breach into *Bechimo*'s atmosphere.

As prearranged, Win Ton held back while Clarence took the lead at this juncture—Clarence with his helmet closed, Clarence in the heavier duty suit. Clarence taller than Win Ton, but by no means as tall as the pair in the repair boat.

Clarence reached out and tugged at the hatch, making sure it had locked down. Inside, one of the crew was facing him. That one slowly raised both hands, gloved palms out and empty.

No harm that meant in contemporary hand-talk. Clarence decided it meant the same to this person. In turn he raised his hands, showing empty palms, then took one step back, sweeping his hands toward him.

Come ahead, that was, and apparently it, too, translated because the other turned and began to very carefully work their way, backward, toward the hatch.

Clarence spoke into his suit's radio.

"You can come on down, Win Ton. Got one on the move to the hatch, showed me empty hands, all nice and civilized."

"Descending," Win Ton replied. He scrambled down the access ladder and dropped lightly to the deck. Kara was speaking in his left ear.

"No problems from our vantage. We have the locks on pressure. The gauges are good, all green."

"Fair enough. Opening visor," Clarence answered, and did just that, his nose wrinkling in distaste as he got his first whiff of the repair boat's air. "Smells like a stinks run gone bad," he said. "Okay, here's the first one coming out to us. Win Ton, you help with the luggage, boyo. I'll be the smiling no-threat."

"Yes," Win Ton said, taking up his position to Clarence's left, hands down, but well in sight.

A very large boot appeared in the hatch, quickly joined by its mate, then suited legs to above the knee. There was a small struggle, a sideways scrabbling, a grunt and a sharp twist—and an entire person was with them, standing, Win Ton thought, a little uncertainly in those large boots, looming tall despite it.

The mask had been pushed down 'round the neck, and Win Ton looked up into a sweat-slicked brown face beneath stiff pale hair. There was a scar on his—Win Ton thought "his" was the appropriate pronoun—right cheek. His expression seemed an entirely appropriate melding of caution and relief.

"Stost," the soldier said hoarsely. He patted himself open-handed on his chest. "Stost."

"Clarence," said that gentleman, patting himself lightly on the opposite shoulder.

Win Ton added his own name, fingertips briefly touching the suit above his heart.

"Win Ton," Stost repeated. "Clarence."

He took a deep breath—and another, savoring sweet air, Win Ton thought, and perhaps recruiting himself to say more.

"Stost!"

The summons came from inside the repair boat, loud over the sound of something being pushed heavily along decking and over several bumps.

Stost spun back toward the little craft, steady on his feet now. He leaned into the hatch, one hand braced against the skin. There came another bump and a high-pitched chattering.

Stost, leaning in hard, laughed, then spoke, quiet and careful, as he twisted, pulling an oversized capsule halfway out of the hatch with him.

"*Grakow, jeda na, Grakow. Jeda na, Grakow....*"

"Cat!" Clarence said sharply into the radio; Win Ton heard *cat!* echo from the control room as he stepped forward to help Stost with the capsule.

Inside, a cat, indeed, dark ears and golden eyes alike held wide.

He caught the leading edge of the capsule as it came through the hatch, steadying it.

"Grakow," he said politely and saw the wide ears twitch in acknowledgment of his voice.

"Grakow," Stost said, perhaps approving, perhaps merely reinforcing correct information. "*Cat,*" he added.

"Right you are," Clarence said, as the crate came free of the hatch. He got a hand under the back end of the thing, equalizing the surprising weight.

"Let's get Grakow out of harm's way, boyos," he said, as easy in voice and body language as if Stost was someone he had worked with many times, and who understood him perfectly.

"Over by the lock, Win Ton."

"Yes."

He guided the capsule, Stost following willingly, and a moment later Grakow was settled by the personnel lock.

Stost was already moving back toward the repair boat before Win Ton recalled himself, with a flush. The man seemed fit, but that was certainly no reason not to have asked immediately if he, or his partner—or Grakow—required medical attention.

"*Huffna flyn Grakow? Stost huffna flyn? Chernak?*"

Stost was leaning back into the ship. He looked over his shoulder and Win Ton could see black smears under dark brown eyes. The man was exhausted, but he merely moved the fingers of the hand braced by the hatch, "*Voy huffnaka,*" he said, which meant *no need*.

Stost bent far into the hatch then, reaching and awkwardly leaning out, holding what appeared to be two document cases by their straps. He moved to the right of the hatch, hanging a case from each shoulder, as another pair of boots proceeded a second tall person to *Bechimo*'s decks.

This one was also sweat-soaked, grey-faced, short pale hair stuck all out in angles. She stood firmly, for all of that, and straightened, deliberately, into a formal pose of attention.

"Chernak, Stost, Grakow, *chaslak Bechimo,*" she said, her voice lighter than Stost's, but just as hoarse.

Chaslak . . . attend? Present? Win Ton wondered, but Chernak was saluting, fist striking shoulder smartly. Beside her, Stost did the same.

Win Ton bowed and again said his name. Clarence, somewhat surprisingly, served up a stern nod with his name, which seemed to reassure Chernak in some way, at least as Win Ton read her. Well, Clarence had been, if not delm or soldier, a Boss of the Juntavas. It might quite possibly comfort two exhausted soldiers, to find a leader on deck to receive them.

"Any more? Any else?" Clarence asked, pointing at the battered little craft.

"All fine," Stost said in the pidgin they'd worked out. "Not need."

"The repair boat is to be removed quickly," Joyita suddenly spoke in Win Ton's ear. The sharpness of his tone suggested that *Bechimo* was perhaps reaching the end of his patience with foreign objects on his deck.

"Please escort Chernak, Stost, and Grakow to their quarters."

Win Ton caught Chernak's eye with a hand motion and turned to the little craft, pantomiming pushing, pushing, as he waved toward the big entry lock.

"Ship go," he said in pidgin. "Chernak, Stost, Grakow, come."

Chernak said something in an undervoice to her partner. They turned toward the little ship and both put a hand on the scarred and battered hull.

Mindful of Joyita's terseness, Win Ton took a step forward. A hand on his arm gave him pause. He glanced at Clarence, who shook his head, very slightly. They were to be patient, then, in *Bechimo*'s place. Very well. He settled back on his heels, hands folded before his belt, but the soldiers had already taken one step back from their craft, both standing stiffly to attention. There came a boom, as two booted feet simultaneously struck the decking, and a muted thud as two fists hit two shoulders in unison.

"*Arak, trang,*" Chernak said, clear and firm.

"*Arak ek zenorth,*" Stost added.

They stood thus, fists on shoulders, backbones stiff and stern, for the count of six.

The salute was ended then, smartly, and the two turned on their heels, sharp as any parade maneuver, and faced Win Ton and Clarence.

"Chernak, Stost, Grakow come," Stost stated.

"Right you are," Clarence answered, turning toward the lock. "This way, to food, 'freshers, and sleep."

They could not have understood him, but then, Win Ton thought, bringing up the rear of their little procession, there was no need for them to understand the words, when they could clearly see his intent.

Clarence paused by Grakow's capsule, bending as if to pick it up.

Stost increased his stride, though, and a big hand closed around the handle first.

"Grakow come," Stost said firmly, hefting the capsule.

"Grakow come," Clarence agreed mildly and straightened to place his hand instead against the lock plate.

CHAPTER ELEVEN

· ·

Bechimo

BEYOND THE HANGAR WAS A SMALL ROOM IN PROPER FASHION, where pilots and crew returned from a mission might remove duty suits before entering the ship. Here, they paused. Clarence began to remove his suit, while Win Ton kept watch—proper order there, as well. Suited though he was, Win Ton appeared small and lithe, a type of civilian known to Stost. Clarence was larger in dimensions, with grey mixed among red hairs—an elder and also a known type.

Beside him, he heard Chernak shift, and the sound of a suit being unfastened. She, too, had seen the grey hairs and deduced that elders desuited first, while youngers kept guard. Stost placed Grakow's capsule on the deck before him, and straightened into duty.

His fellow guard, Win Ton, watched well, face neutral, eyes moving from Stost, to Chernak, to Clarence, to something behind Clarence's shoulder...

Stost turned his head, just slightly.

Just beyond Clarence's left shoulder was a screen, and in the screen, a man—a man with a face so brown and grim he might have been Troop himself. There was no *vingtai*, but the tale of an old engagement was writ plain across a strong broad nose. A civilian soldier, then; there had been those. He met Stost's eyes, his own a deep and bitter brown, and inclined his head slightly.

Stost returned the... acknowledgment, and turned to find Chernak standing in a stained and wrinkled uniform, the duty suit crumpled on the deck. She extended a hand and he gave the cases into her care, then went to work on the seals of his suit, Win Ton likewise engaged.

Desuited, he felt himself even less soldierly than Chernak. They were, he thought, in no fit state to face a captain—even a civilian captain. She had endangered her ship and her crew on their behalf, and she would want answers. Very likely, she would want the precise answers they would be most unwilling to give. True, they had just completed an extraordinary mission . . .

"Stost."

Chernak handed him a case. He slipped the strap over his right shoulder, made certain the case rode flat under his left arm.

From the pod at his feet came the sound of muttering, escalating rapidly into complaint.

"*Grakow!*"

Stost acted without thinking. He knelt by the capsule, murmuring, "*Mezta, mezata.*"

He tried the tape, broke a strand, and started on the next, aware that Chernak was kneeling on the other side of the capsule's wire door, pulling on other strands, which clung stubbornly. Utiltape was tough, and he had spent his roll liberally, trying to buy their civilian some measure of safety.

Grakow complained again, less loudly, though loudly enough to obscure Chernak's curse as a strand of tape stretched, but refused to break.

Stost reached to his side-kit, fingered out a utility blade—and froze.

There was no sound in the duty room; even Grakow was silent. Stost raised his eyes to meet Chernak's gaze, finding a wry humor there, but no anger. She was the elder of their team; it was within her scope, and her duty, to kill him for endangering the mission, *now*, when they had prevailed against mighty odds and survived the death of a universe, to achieve this place of near safety . . .

A chuckle came from his left. Warily, he lifted his head to meet Clarence's bright blue eyes.

"Fine," Clarence said. Then, when Stost remained immobile, added another phrase, which might have been, "Goot, do it. Off!" followed by a sharp movement of the hand, very like that used to cut tape with a utility knife.

"Stost," Chernak said. "Your blade is wanted."

He drew a breath and bent to the task of cutting through the binding tape, which Chernak peeled away from the water bottle port and from the door seal itself.

There was a small sound, as of a bootheel striking decking. Stost looked up as Win Ton offered a bag. Chernak took it with a nod and stuffed tape shred into it.

Odor came from the carrier. Stost glanced at faces to see if any were openly displeased, but what might happen if they were, he dared not guess.

"Goot kitty," may have been what Clarence said, adding, "Fine. Grakow come. Stost come. Chernak come."

Chernak rose, and Stost did, stowing the utility knife, which would need to be cleaned of sticky residue. He bent and picked up Grakow's capsule, feeling the weight shift as the cat perhaps moved to the front, where he could observe and sample what smells *Bechimo* had to offer.

Clarence opened the door and led them to the right, down a hallway, Chernak following him, as Stost followed her, and Win Ton followed all.

Stost glanced over his shoulder, seeking the man who had observed them, but the screen was empty.

The ship lurched slightly, which likely was the hangar they had just quit being evacuated. Stost checked his stride and Chernak looked at him over her shoulder, as if she had heard his dismay.

"*Arak ek zenorth,*" she said. "Honor and glory."

"Yes," he answered. "It was stupid, and no sort of ship to bring into war, but it did a soldier's duty."

Another right turn, another hall, then a pause as Clarence placed his hand against the plate. Stost straightened his shoulders and renewed his grip on Grakow's pod. Now, were they about to enter a holding cell, or be brought into the captain's presence?

And which would be worse?

· · · ✸ · · ·

Their guests were behaving themselves. They were exhausted, they were hungry, they were—Theo felt surprise, and then wondered why she should be surprised. Surely, anyone who had come through shipwreck and near death, to be taken up by a ship and crew of which they knew nothing—surely, *anyone* would be afraid.

Fear will make them prudent. The thought was...not quite hers. *Bechimo*, then, who was sharing his monitoring with her. Clarence and Win Ton—Clarence was calm and easy, much as if he sat at his board. Win Ton...was nervous; she felt the tingle of too much adrenaline. Despite that, he was in control. Of course he was. Win Ton was a Scout. Meeting and interacting peacefully with people from cultures strange to him was what he did.

Kara, sitting at her station on the bridge was...intent, but calm.

She, Theo, was...at one and the same time, relieved, exultant, and exhausted. *Bechimo* had done the heavy lifting, of course, but still, the intercept had been...a challenge.

Well. They had them now, she thought. Everybody could stand down.

· · · ✵ · · ·

Clarence stood to one side of the room they entered—a large room, as such things were measured aboard ships, with doors that hinted at other rooms. Certainly, it was grand enough to be a captain's suite. Yet, aside from Clarence, Win Ton, and themselves, there was no one else present—no, Stost corrected himself, as the screen on the wall went from dark to light and he found himself looking into the dark eyes of the observer from the duty room.

"Joyita," Win Ton said, intercepting Stost's glance.

"Win Ton," said the man in the screen, the voice immediately recognizable as one of those which had spoken to them from the ship. He looked beyond Stost.

"Chernak," he said.

He raised a hand in what might have been a greeting between those of equal rank. Unlike true soldiers, who wore their decorations on their skin, Joyita wore rings—four rings of silvered brown metal, with only the least finger free.

"Joyita," Chernak said in reply. "All fine."

He smiled at that, inclined his head, and looked aside again. "Stost."

"Joyita."

"Clarence."

"Joyita."

A glance downward, to the capsule on the decking.

"Grakow," Joyita said, smiling again. "All fine."

"All fine," Clarence repeated.

Joyita spoke again—words, and among them variants of words they knew; words that mean *relax, stand down, rest*. He said them in a pattern, Stost realized upon the second repetition; a teaching pattern, moving from the familiar to the unfamiliar. They had not even taken the measure of this space they had been brought to and already he had said a dozen or more words, some they had heard before, more which were strange.

Clarence made an odd sound as Joyita said something that had to do, perhaps, with water. The man in the screen stopped speaking, lips pressed together.

Stost turned, saw Clarence with a finger held vertically to the middle of his mouth, facing Joyita while Win Ton openly laughed. Clarence waved an impatient hand and the image on the screen faded to a light green.

"Whew!"

Clarence raised a hand and brought fingers to thumb several times, rapidly, which mimed, Stost thought, a mouth talking, then waved them back to the pressure door they'd entered by, hands speaking to Win Ton while he drew them both to the opening.

"*Chicancha*," Clarence said.

Stost and Chernak leaned close.

Clarence put his palm against a plate on the door, pushing lightly. The door opened. He pressed the still-visible edge of the plate, and the door closed. He tapped a fingertip against a green indicator light.

Then he called out, "Joyita!"

The screen lit. Joyita inclined his head, saying nothing.

"The demonstrating is happening. Overlock and then disengage overlock in ten seconds, please."

Stost frowned after the words, even as he watched the light that Clarence pointed to change from green to amber, whereupon he pushed on the plate, to no avail. The light changed to green again—and Clarence stepped back, pointing to Stost, and then to the plate.

Simple, direct, clear.

Stost found the plate slightly warm against his palm. He pushed gently. After a moment the door withdrew. Of course.

He stepped back to Chernak's side.

"Elder, Joyita is keeper of the door. You may now close it, I believe."

Chernak extended a hand, and pressed the plate.

The door closed.

"*Jenst*," she said. "Success."

"Fine," said Clarence and, with a wave, directed them toward the open inner door and Win Ton, who was apparently to show them even more rooms.

"Rations come," Clarence told them, and added something else that Stost's ear, usually so facile, refused to parse.

He looked back, but Clarence made a shooing motion with both hands, meaning that he should attend Win Ton, so he followed Chernak into the next room, leaving Clarence and Grakow holding the first behind them.

During the course of their short tour of the suite, a cart had arrived in the common room. On the first and second shelves were stacked food items, and possibly drinks, as well.

On the bottom shelf was a shallow box as long as the distance between Stost's wrist to his shoulder, filled with shreds of what seemed to be printout. Two more stacks of printout sat on the shelf beside.

Win Ton had the floor, leading with bows and execrable accent—it was some vile dialect of the Troop tongue he spoke to them, rather than the pidgin. Stost understood his choice—the dialect gave access to more words and to concepts that were not limited to the concrete. Still, it was a long march through rough terrain, trying to make sense of what he told them.

He had shown them their accommodations and brought them back to the common room, where he invited them to sit in chairs that were large enough for them, if they were careful.

The suite was larger than a captain's cabin on many ships; there were internal roomettes with bedding—and each with sanitary facilities and storage—while the larger common room grew a table, folded out from the wall, and had a tiny food preparation area as well.

Stost was thinking, longingly, about the refresher units Win Ton had shown them, when a chime sounded, perhaps from overhead. He slid to his feet, as Clarence walked to the hall door and opened it, accepting a wheeled cart from an unseen aide. Stost sank back into his seat as Clarence pushed the cart into the center of the room. Apparently, they were to be educated regarding food. His stomach expressed loud enthusiasm for this project, but no one—not even Chernak, who surely had the ears of a soldier—seemed to hear.

"Cheese," Win Ton told them, touching a small yellow wheel, "from stores."

He unsealed a translucent container and the rich scent of something baked assaulted them. "Bread, baked by Clarence. Greens, from the ship garden. Vegetables and meats from stores..."

The food was not as much a meal as a collection of foods to test their taste and needs. Water, several kinds of juices, something that looked like but was not cheese, and an array of implements, only some of them obvious. Enough food to feed a squad. They set to, hungry, yes—but careful of each initial taste.

Win Ton told them the names of things several times while Clarence bustled about the cart.

"Grakow? Grakow resides where for sanitary?" Clarence asked, his accent even worse than Win Ton's. He was holding the box from the bottom of the cart, and it was an excellent question.

They were perplexed momentarily—who had expected to be making housekeeping decisions for a cat when their mission had begun?

Chernak and Stost settled it with a shrug and a finger game. The cat could use a corner in the left roomette. In fact, it was such a good idea that they grabbed several small bits of meat from the table and removed the cat there in the midst of their own meal, opening the capsule's seal with smiles at each other while Grakow sat suspiciously on his haunches at the far end of the crate. The food and water went near the door, the necessary box visible a few feet away.

Leaving Grakow to sit and reason out the path to his own best interest, they returned to the common room, their chairs, and the food, to find that Joyita occupied the screen once more.

Stost gave him a nod, soldier to soldier, which the other returned before he spoke, in the pidgin they had devised.

"*Chicancha*. Captain Theo Waitley speaks."

· · · ✷ · · ·

Theo sat in the command chair, mentally dancing a quick relaxation exercise. She was nervous, as if she hadn't just spent the last quarter shift practicing in her head the talk she and

Joyita had worked out, which was echoed on the screen in front of her—*just in case*, said Joyita, who couldn't possibly think that *Bechimo* was going to permit her to forget one word. She hadn't asked him *in case of what?* though. Now, she thought maybe she should have.

Kara sat nearby, visible in the screen as well as with a quick glance, a comfort. Beside Kara was Hevelin, serious and quiet, as he'd been since they sighted the little repair boat, and the larger vessel damaged past all repair.

At first, Theo had thought to meet their . . . guests . . . directly they came aboard. Other heads, wiser in the ways of intercultural courtesy, had argued against that, but the point that won had been Clarence's simple, "Let them get in, 'freshed up, and rested before they have to put on the pretty for the captain of this ship and commander of all nearspace beside," he'd said, pulling a wry face that had made Theo laugh, even as she signed: *Point taken. Agree.*

Though she had agreed to withhold her fell presence until their guests were better able to tolerate her, she felt strongly that they must be acknowledged and welcomed aboard. Also, greeting them would be a good test of the new linkages *Bechimo* was still working on. For the moment, those links involved a dictionary and active translation to her, as needed.

"I'll talk to them now," she said, and it was done, the stateroom coming to her screen and she to theirs. *Bechimo* fed her info from other sensors, so that she knew she looked upon two exhausted and desperate people even as she saw their faces for the first time.

They were standing at strict attention. A glance passed between them—too quick for her eye, though *Bechimo* saw it—before they composed their faces and regarded the screen, waiting for her to speak.

"Troops Chernak and Stost, stand forward," she said, the words feeling sharp and ungainly in her mouth. "Identify yourselves."

Not exactly the warmest welcome possible, but Joyita, Clarence, and Win Ton had argued that the formal greeting of command might ease abraded nerves.

The soldier on the right took one brisk step toward the monitor, fist coming up smartly to strike her shoulder.

"Chernak, Pathfinder," she said, her voice firm.

The other came forward then, saluted, and announced, "Stost, Pathfinder."

They waited then, which was proper, and Theo nodded and said the words *Bechimo* had given her.

"I am Captain Waitley of the tradeship *Bechimo*. You are recognized as survivors of shipwreck and have the right to food, rest, and safe passage on my ship. Forgive me if my renderings of words I ought to know fail; I have met few of the Troop and those I have met spoke Trade language, Terran, and Liaden in my presence."

Their eyes—brown eyes, Chernak's lighter than Stost's—widened. They were, Theo saw, *much* alike, but not *exactly* alike. Like the color of their eyes, there were small differences making each face, so similar in size and in bone structure, unique. Their hair, short and pale and stiff with sweat, was not the exact same shade of sandblasted dock 'crete. Stost's shaded toward brown, while Chernak's showed a faint trace of yellow.

Chernak was obviously female; Stost obviously male. Both were lean, without fat or softness about them. They had, Theo thought, been on the move for a long time.

Right, then. Time to wrap up and let them get some sleep.

"Pilots Win Ton and Clarence are among you," she said. "Regard each to carry my orders in any emergency. Also, you will follow orders as need be if brought to you by Engineering Tech Kara or by Comm Officer Joyita. All of us are tested pilots on this ship.

"The ship has provided food and rooms. The ship will soon provide appropriate ship clothes.

"After you are rested, we will ask questions of you, which you will answer to the best of your ability. You may ask questions of us, which we will answer as best we may."

"I return you to your meal," Theo said . . . and paused, having heard a dissatisfied murble from Hevelin, at Kara's station.

"Grakow," she said suddenly. "The first voice we heard from your vessel. Let me see Grakow."

"I will," Stost breathed, and he moved out of view, leaving Chernak facing the screen.

"Assure me," Theo said suddenly, aware that she was about to ask a question she had not practiced, though the words rose easily to her lips.

104 Sharon Lee & Steve Miller

"Assure me that there are no other survivors."

Chernak looked grim; Theo heard her voice and understood the translation at the same time.

"No sign of another, Captain, only Grakow and we of the Troop."

Stost returned then, holding a cat of dark head and possible darker stripes wrapped in a ship's pillow, not entirely willingly. The cat spoke words, probably not nice ones, but Theo smiled to hear them and nodded.

She was about to dismiss them to their meal when, from Kara's station came a loud *"murble-drumble-murble,"* close enough to a purr to surprise Theo.

Grakow's posture in the pillow wrap changed from resigned to alert and Theo's smile deepened.

"All of you eat appropriately. Rest. Soon, we will speak together again."

"Captain," said Chernak and Stost, with one voice. They saluted once more, Stost nearly dropping the pillow in the process. Theo saw Chernak spinning to help him and Win Ton moving toward them with hand outheld.

"Are we still live?"

"One-way," Joyita said, and Theo nodded.

By then Hevelin was at her knee and Kara was closing her screens.

"Everything remains nominal on our readings. Shall you rest now, Theo, while Joyita and I take the watch?"

"The clothes," Theo said. "Joyita, let Clarence know they'll be done shortly. *Bechimo* will give them overalls with a Laughing Cat patch and some ship slippers to start. Dark red wine, a good color. Joyita, also, in Terran, tell Clarence to offer them bags for their weapons which they'll have no need of on board. We'll make up another cartload—clothes, bags, slippers. And we should—"

Kara touched her shoulder.

"Captain, you have a crew to handle these details for you. In the meantime, the backup med tech suggests that you have pulled two doubleshifts and performed a rather tricky bit of piloting and are in need of downtime. The engineering department thinks you should rest. Hevelin thinks you should find a nice pile of grass to curl up in."

She bent down and Hevelin jumped into her arms.

"When," Kara asked, carefully to Theo's ear, "did you learn to speak Old Yxtrang?"

Theo looked up, but Kara was helping Hevelin settle onto her shoulder.

"*Bechimo* dragged through his files and cobbled together a rough approximation," she said, which was not . . . exactly the truth. "I reviewed the emergency linguistics course we had during third semester—you remember. How to talk to Yxtrang for an emergency docking? Remember?"

"I remember," Kara said quietly.

"*Bechimo* will tell you what to say about the weapons, in case there's an argument—" she began.

Joyita broke in: "If Kara and Hevelin are taking the watch, Theo, I will put the feed on low on Kara's thumbnail monitor and assist in communications. Sleep well."

Theo glanced at her screen; saw Stost cradling Grakow gently before the image re-formed to a view of local space, wyrd, dusty, and strange, but for all of that, with no threats to hand.

CHAPTER TWELVE

. . . .

Seebrit Station
The Sweet Rest Hostel

SEEBRIT STATION WAS...NOT IN THE HIGHER RANKS OF SPACE stations. It was, in fact, a hard-worked station located at a modest crossing of several, equally modest trade routes. The ships that stopped at Seebrit were generally well-known to the station administrators and arrived on a regular schedule. It was not at all the sort of port where Vepal most usually landed. Had it not been for the sudden distress of the distribution monitors, the mission would have had no reason to raise Seebrit Station.

They had, however, come to Seebrit Station, and he would be remiss in his duty, careless of his mission and the future of his race, if he did not call upon those persons of rank and importance as the station offered.

He had met with Admin as soon as they had docked, in order to obtain temporary IDs and seen their "guaranteed safe" status broadcast to all businesses and persons on Seebrit Station. Admin had not been interested in the core of the mission, though names were provided that might be more useful to him.

The first, Kachy Zunuit, the Pilots Guild circuit rider, was not on-station. Her schedule had her returning to Seebrit in eighteen Standard Days, by which time, Vepal very much hoped, they would be well away from the place.

The second name, however, had been that of one of the more

107

prominent traders who routinely stopped at Seebrit, and Trader Menon had been willing to meet at the trade bar.

It had been a short meeting. The trader had wished to satisfy his curiosity regarding how "real" Yxtrang looked and comported themselves. Vepal kept an inquiry after possible "unreal" Yxtrang sternly behind his teeth and smiled the closed-mouth smile at his host.

Curiosity aside, Trader Menon could offer no names of likely persons to contact, nor suggest any other course that Vepal might try. As they parted, he offered the opinion that Vepal's was a fool's errand.

Which was, of course, so.

Vepal parted from the trader in no happy mood. Upon reaching their lodgings, he dismissed Ochin curtly before entering his sleeping room and changing into clothing loose and tough enough to wear while exercising. He went up the inner stairway to the gym, waved his key card at the reader, and pushed the door open.

He had utilized the gym once before and found it adequate for a moderate workout. This evening, his muscles aching with unexpended battle acids and his temper worn sadly thin, he hoped not to break anything. As an Explorer and a senior, he had control. He *did have* control. And, yet, biology would have its due.

It was late in the station day, and the gym was quiet. To the right, far down the room, someone was lifting weights, silently intent on their work. The various machines and dancing booths were dark, the gym itself dim, except for the spots illuminating the silent worker with weight.

There were punching bags along the back wall; in his present state of mind, they drew him like metal shred to a magnet. He grinned in anticipation, even as he realized that the back wall was softly aglow, and that he was hearing the sound of rhythmic blows, a scuff of shoes against floor, and deep, controlled breathing.

Almost, he turned to go; he was in no mood to coddle *koja-gun*, to soften his blows, or pretend to be anything other than himself. He wanted to hit, as strongly as he was able—punch, and punch, and punch again until his muscles glowed and the euphoria lifted him above such minor concerns as the imminent collapse of Temp Headquarters, and the Troop.

The tempo of the punches being thrown by the unseen boxer increased, a grunt accompanying each impact, and the breath coming harsher, as if they, too, had some need to pummel petty problems into dust.

One who could deliver such continuous punishment, with vigor and discipline, was unlikely to be frightened by his own workout, he told himself. And besides, he was curious to see this bold spirit.

He stepped out into the avenue where the bags were hung. Under a spotlight in the farthest corner, a lean, brown figure, stripped to shorts and singlet, worked the bag, dancing before it, fists stern and unanswerable. Though the warrior's back was to him, he had no difficulty recognizing JinJee Sanchez, commander of the Paladin Mercenary Corps.

Vepal smiled, not the closed mouth to soothe Terrans, nor the bared teeth to terrify *kojagun*, but the smile one shared with a comrade when the battle had gone well, and yourselves among the survivors.

Vepal took the bag at the opposite end of the row and, without a glance at the too-small gloves provided, set his feet and regarded the bag. The aching was acute; he should have taken care of this before his meeting with Trader Menon, but he had chosen to do research while Ochin and Erthax cared for themselves. If he waited much longer now, his muscles would cramp, and what a proud sight he would be, on the floor before the bag, practicing deep breathing until his body cleansed itself.

The bag before him developed a face. A face not seen in near seven cycles, and smiling then, as now—the smile of having vanquished a worthy enemy.

Vepal raised his fists and had at it.

· · · ✵ · · ·

"She speaks well," Stost said, as he cradled Grakow. It was truth; the little captain *had* spoken well. Her accent had been... strange, but words and grammar had been recognizably the tongue of the Troop, rather than some degraded dialect learned from soldiers too long cut off from Command.

"A young captain," Chernak countered. "Young. Perhaps the position is inherited."

She considered the screen, where Comm Officer Joyita dealt with matters centered in some other part of his office. There was a screen visible, perhaps showing the main deck. The image might be the young captain, seen at an odd angle, and another of the crew, also young, perhaps holding a child. But that screen disappeared as Joyita turned toward them once more. He spoke in one language and, perhaps, in another. On the screen was displayed text in strange script.

Clarence gave what might be a laugh and shook his head from side to side. Win Ton stepped up to Stost and extended a hand, offering Grakow the tip of his finger.

Stost shrank, fearing a strike by the cat, but Grakow extended his neck, sniffed the offered finger, and sprightly pushed cheek against hand.

"Ah," Chernak and Stost said together.

Win Ton looked at the words on the screen, frowning, and read off: "Captain and ship give and provide clothes soon. Captain and ship give and provide bag for edge storage, soonest."

He looked at them both, raised his hands to waist level and said it again, this time the intent coming to, "Captain says store edges and weapons in bag coming, not needed ship."

Clarence smiled, a happy man he was, and demonstrated, removing a knife from a belt sheath and a pistol from his pocket, then wrapping them into one of the napkins.

They were not to carry weapons aboard the ship *Bechimo*, Stost understood.

Of course, they were not. This was a tradeship, not a warship, and the captain must be unsure of them. There had been reports of rogue soldiers; surely, she would have heard them, as they had. And recent evidence to the contrary aside, the captain must be prudent on behalf of her crew and her ship.

Which raised the interesting question of how the captain might wish to dispose of their cases, from which they must not be separated.

"We obey the captain's order regarding weapons," Chernak said. "How not? It is reasonable."

"Yes," Stost said and dropped to one knee, the better to bring Grakow and his pillow gently to the deck.

Chernak raised a hand in a half-salute and spoke to Win Ton in a dialect near to, if not precisely, the dialect he had been killing messily this while.

"Young captain would that we not carry weapons on her ship, and that she clothe us, so that secrets are hard to have. It is understood."

"Fine," Win Ton said, inclining his head.

"Fine," she repeated. "Query: Young captain holds ship through..." she stumbled here, the phrase to describe such a position not being... complimentary.

Stost stood, watching Grakow come free of the pillow and look about himself.

"The captain," he said to Win Ton, when Chernak had not managed to find a respectful conclusion to her question. "She holds command by... inheritance?"

Win Ton frowned. For a moment Stost thought he had not been circumspect enough, then the small civilian glanced to Joyita, busy in his screen.

Words appeared—very nearly proper Troop words on display—and more text which might, thought Stost, be a translation into a second language.

Win Ton sighed and spoke to Clarence, who shrugged and said something in perhaps a third language which amused Win Ton.

"Another moment," he said to Stost. "Joyita will speak for me, in answer to your question."

Stost looked to Joyita as Chernak did. The dark eyes were focused down, possibly on a low screen or desktop, then came up to regard them in turn. When he spoke, it was in the same strangely accented, but correct, Troop tongue that the captain herself had used, rather than the far rougher dialect he had used when they had first come aboard.

"Win Ton wishes to assure the pathfinders that the captain is captain, right and proper. The ship answers to her as to no another."

· · · ✳ · · ·

The Explorers taught that the euphoria was a trap. The Explorers had techniques to release the acids before cramping became debilitating. The Explorers trained themselves to stand against design and nature. Vepal had long ago had the training, had more than once utilized the techniques, and was famous for his ability to think past the imperative for immediate action into a lasting solution.

Tonight, he welcomed the euphoria, even as he knew its dangers. He danced before the bag, his footwork precise, as he struck and struck, varying his blows and the rhythm, ducking as if he faced another as skilled as he was in this art. For a time, he was only fists and feet and sweat. It was the euphoria that brought him back to himself, though a self dangerously pleased with his own prowess.

He slowed his tempo, softened his blows, allowed his feet to dance into stillness and, at last, his fists to fall.

It came to him then that he was not alone.

He turned, sharp-edged with pleasure, and was pleased again, that JinJee Sanchez did not flinch.

Instead, she frowned slightly and sighed.

"Your pardon, sir. I did not intend to disturb you at your work."

"My work is done," he told her. "Were you here long? I was not aware."

"I have been here for some minutes," she said. "It's a pleasure to watch a professional and I thought I might learn something."

In his present state, that was annoying. An Yxtrang soldier did not stoop to teach *kojagun*! Then, he recalled that she was a warrior in her own right and one who had survived at least one close encounter with an Yxtrang soldier. A soldier should never stint another soldier—that was a lesson learned in creche, and to some extent, despite politics, rivalries, and corruption, that ideal was served more often than not.

"Did you?" he asked, honestly curious. "Learn something?"

"I think I might have," she said. "You have an interesting approach to footwork. I will try, the next time I address the bag." A smile glimmered, with a small show of teeth.

"Tonight, the bag and I have agreed to disagree, and I am bound for my quarters."

That was strangely disappointing, though the glow of violent action made it difficult for him to think why that should be. Instead, he said. "You are not afraid."

Black brows pulled together. "Afraid?"

"Of me. Of Yxtrang. But you have fought Yxtrang—" He touched his own cheek where the scar blossomed on hers.

"I'm a mercenary. We fight when we are paid. A few years ago, we were paid to fight Yxtrang. Our forces were well matched, but we prevailed. Are you angry?"

"Angry?" he repeated.

"I, and my unit, killed Yxtrang—quite a number of them,

since none would surrender, even after their case was hopeless. Are you angry that we killed Yxtrang?"

"Yxtrang die in battle," he said, still puzzled. "You were, I think, an honorable foe."

Again, the smile, and the suggestion of tooth.

"In fact, we are both soldiers. And this is not a battlefield." A pause while she scanned his face, her fierce eyes narrowed. "Mercenary units must also register with Seebrit Station Admin and guarantee to be *not a danger*."

He blinked, unable to think as needed, and in that moment, she gave him that sharp nod of salute.

"Good night, Ambassador Vepal."

"Good night," he managed, but she was already gone, vanished down a shadowy avenue of silent equipment, leaving him alone.

· · · ✳ · · ·

"Captain."

Bechimo spoke directly into her ear. Theo *thought* it was directly into her ear, but she more than half-thought it was because acknowledging that he was talking to her...directly...was too unnerving.

"Yes?" she asked quietly.

She was in her quarters, showered, and obediently lying in her bunk, though it could not be said that she was sleeping. There was too much to think about. There were strangers on her ship, and despite her own insistence that they were civilized and would behave according to the code of civilized persons...there was always room for error when cultures interfaced.

Or, in this instance, she'd thought wryly, collided.

"Captain, I regret disturbing you on your off-shift..."

Whatever it was, Theo thought, it must be bad. *Bechimo* tended toward formality when he was nervous.

"I wasn't asleep," she said.

She hitched her pillow up against the bulkhead and curled against it, blanket across her lap.

"But you knew that," she added.

"Yes, I did," her ship admitted. "However, asleep or awake, it *is* your off-shift, and I am...disturbing your privacy."

Right. And given how conscientious he'd learned to be about respecting her privacy, the fact that he *was* disturbing her now was a second indicator that...something was bothering him bad.

"As it happens—and even though it's my off-shift—I'm not being very restful. My brain's whirling and I can't shut it down. You're providing a welcome diversion."

There was a silence just long enough for Theo to reflect on how *Bechimo* might process the concept of shutting down a brain, and to wonder if she was going to have to rephrase...

"I see," he said, his voice very polite, indeed. "As I am performing a useful service, I will proceed to divert you further. Captain, we must leave this place."

Theo blinked.

This place—this piece of wyrd space—had been *Bechimo*'s ultimate safe hiding. He had considered it secure enough to bring his crew here, and given the list of places he considered *un*safe, that said a lot, right there.

She had hesitated too long; *Bechimo* spoke again.

"It is becoming dangerous here," he said, and there was that defensive tone, like he expected her to argue against moving elsewhere, which, everything considered, she wasn't sure she wanted to do.

"Where do you suggest we go?" she asked mildly. "Surebleak?"

Much as she didn't want to give Val Con the notion that he could tell her what to do, she'd been considering Surebleak seriously, before the excitement of the rescue had driven every other thought out of her head. Surebleak solved the problems of *Spiral Dance* and the small tree—Val Con could take custody of them, as heir or something.

And now that she thought of it, Val Con might be the best depository for their... guests, too. After all, he already had three Yxtrang—former Yxtrang—attached to his household. He'd hardly notice two more.

"Surebleak is not safe," *Bechimo* said flatly, interrupting this train of thought.

"Well, no, it's not; but most places aren't safe," Theo said.

"I grew up on a Safe World, and even *it* wasn't safe," she added. "Not for everybody, all the time."

"It is," *Bechimo* stated, "my duty to protect my crew."

Well, there was no arguing with that, as Clarence would say. That aside, this conversation was becoming more worrisome as it went on.

"Where do you suggest we go, then?"

"Brulilt."

"Never heard of it."

"It is not well-known, Captain. Its location is infelicitous. While Brulilt itself is inhabitable and has been certified for colonization by the Scouts, it is the sole planet in its system. A wide band of rubble also orbits Brulilt's star. It is thought that there had once been an active system there, the other planets having been destroyed during the war in which Jeeves tells me that he was an admiral.

"However it came to be as it is, I have previously rested there, and only twice encountered other ships, which were easily avoided."

He paused. Theo waited.

"The advantage that Brulilt holds for us, aside from its isolation, is that we may reach it quickly."

"Your proposed timetable?" Theo asked.

"Captain, with your permission, I am ready to move now. We will arrive in Brulilt System inside of two shifts."

Theo closed her eyes and considered what he had said, and also what she was...feeling. *Bechimo* was anxious; she might even say he was afraid.

"Has there been any more flotsam?" she asked.

"No, Captain. However..."

He stopped, and Theo nodded.

However. Right. In a random universe, anything was possible. The wreck of *Orbital Aid 370* could be the last bit of...*flotsam* that would ever cross into this location.

Or, *Spiral Dance* could have been the vanguard of more and ever-more-dangerous debris.

Bechimo was right, Theo thought. They couldn't dawdle here any longer.

She threw back the blanket and reached for her sweater.

"Please ask Joyita to call the crew together for a quick meeting on the bridge."

"Yes, Captain."

CHAPTER THIRTEEN

. . . .

Bechimo

"AIN'T THE UGLIEST PIECE O'SPACE I'VE SEEN," CLARENCE SAID, after they'd all taken a long look at Brulilt System. "That said, I'm hoping we're not making a long stay, Captain."

"Temporary quarters only," Theo answered, feeling grit slide against her—against *Bechimo*'s—skin. "As soon as we debrief our guests and come up with a plan of forward motion, we'll be leaving."

Win Ton shifted in his chair, but said nothing. Which, Theo admitted, showed really admirable restraint. While he'd agreed with the necessity to leave their little patch of wyrd space, he had argued for a remove to the nearest Scout outpost, where the two pathfinders could be off-loaded, as he had it, "with grace," whereupon *Bechimo* and crew would return to their proper duties.

Clarence had said nothing to that, loudly. Kara had looked uneasy. It had been left to Theo to ask the question.

"Do you have an estimation of their life expectancy, if we do that?"

Win Ton had stiffened, then sighed.

"Unless they presented difficulties, they would very likely live long, healthy lives."

"So long as they didn't mind losing their liberty and any other associations except each other and the Scout historians," Clarence added, *sotto voce*.

117

Theo nodded.

"That's why we want to take some time with this," she said. "We need to debrief the pathfinders, find out what they want or need. They're mature adults. They get to have a say in what happens to them now."

She looked at each of them in turn. "Any other objections?"

Kara had no objections; Clarence had no objections; Joyita had no objections. Hevelin, so she judged by the tumbling images of stars and ships and stations inside her head, was positively excited by the idea of shifting base.

Win Ton...bowed to the captain's honor, lips pressed together, which Theo took to mean he had only that one objection, and that she'd be hearing it again.

"Good," she said. "Let's go."

· · · ❋ · · ·

Chernak woke, swathed in comfortable blankets against the cool, rich air they had chosen with a triple roll of the dice. It was not the richest air the ship would serve up for sleep, nor the chilliest temperature, but sufficient to assist two weary and—they admitted this between themselves with a single glance—frightened soldiers into a deep and healing sleep.

Always, upon waking she would recall the last order or necessity of the day before, to prepare her mind and her reflexes for the new day and duty shift before her. Often enough, she'd discover Stost waking at the same moment, but—she turned her head to find that, this waking, he slumbered on, his face serene.

That is well, she thought. Stost had given her rest in the midst of peril by carrying her duties with his own. Let her now return the gift. She would keep watch for both, though their present condition was far less perilous.

Or so she hoped...which hope brought to mind the last orders of the previous day, issued by Comm Officer Joyita, after Clarence and Win Ton had left them, the hallway door whisking shut at their backs.

There had been, so she had noticed—and certainly Stost had— no sound after the door closed that could be a lock engaging. Of course not; the door only needed to be coded to accept certain palm prints—and to ignore others.

She and Stost had shared a glance in which they agreed, wryly, not to submit the door to the test. Where, after all, would they go? To the bridge, to make the ship their own?

Into that moment came a voice, speaking behind them. "Pathfinders."

They'd spun as one—and straightened with a certain amount of ruefulness to find it was only Joyita, speaking from the screen.

He had nodded gravely upon gaining their attention and continued, his face calm, and his accent improved yet again.

"If you have need or question, each screen has the touchpad to call; or if you press the blue switch before you retire, simply speaking my name at moderate volume will open a session with me at any hour. Else, a tone will sound to wake you—" Here, a tone sounded, high and unpleasant. "The same tone will be the notice that shift begins on the next quarter chime. Have you any questions, Pathfinders?"

They had not. Joyita had tipped the light half-nod and half-bow that seemed to be the shipboard acknowledgment of polite assent.

"Sleep well, Pathfinders. The ship is vigilant for you. Sleep well!"

Last orders then, thought Chernak, had been to sleep well, which orders she had realized and Stost continued to fulfill.

Last shift, they had each lifted a pad from a side room, and put them side by side in the common space, camp-style, which was . . . a comfortable reminder of earlier days. The plan had been that of the last ten-day, the last hundred-day—in truth, most of their past thousand days, that one would sleep while the other watched, with a rotation halfway down the shift.

It was Stost, scheduled for first sleep, who said, "The ship is vigilant for us, Senior. No less a person than Joyita has said it. Lay down your knife and rest."

Almost, she had protested, but again, he had the right of it. If, indeed, Captain Waitley, commander of all local space, was daft enough to risk ship and crew in a dangerous live recovery, only to decide, mere hours later, to stealthily kill those recovered—she had the means to do so from her chair on the bridge. Standing watch as the air was evacuated from their suite of rooms would be less than useless.

Chernak had, therefore, made herself comfortable next to him, each with work knife on their free side, habit being habit.

Their first easy drift into doze had been interrupted as Gra-kow entered the lists and, with much rhythmic pushing of paws against blankets while emitting a rumbling sound that was oddly pleasing, at last settled between them, the tiny soldier warmed by the large, and all had slept.

Their makeshift bed shook of a sudden. Chernak turned her head to find Grakow on his feet, back arching high, legs braced in a long and lasting stretch that became an encompassing, boneless relaxation, shrugging skin back into a wide-mouthed yawn that revealed teeth sharp as needles. Waking ritual apparently complete, the cat wrapped tail around toes and looked at her, green eyes bright and expectant.

Chernak stared back. She had never slept with an animal in the same room; the warhounds and their soldiers had their own barracks, in such places where they had duty . . .

"Good waking, Senior!" Stost said, his voice hoarse but cheerful. "And also to you, Grakow."

The cat turned his head, as if to acknowledge the well-wish, then leisurely rose to his feet and strolled off, possibly to locate breakfast.

Chernak's stomach growled in sympathy.

"I agree," Stost said. "Let us rise, make the rooms neat, and ourselves soldierly. Then, we may share the food left over from last shift for our own breakfast."

"You are full of plans, my Stost," Chernak said.

"Are they foolish plans?"

"By no means. Let us embark upon them immediately."

She cast the comforting blankets back, and rolled to her feet.

The promised lock-bags had arrived toward the end of their last shift and also light-duty, belted uniforms of a not unpleasing cut, complete with the Laughing Cat upon the right breast of each. They had at the same time surrendered their weapons to Win Ton and saw them stowed in the bags, which he then bore away to "storage."

They had been patient and obedient, and kept their faces easy, though the lack of sidearms and warblades made Stost feel exposed and naked, despite the fine new uniform. For a surprise, they were allowed to retain their work blades and their grace blades. Orders of the captain, so Clarence had informed them. Their ship was a civilized ship—or so they understood him to say—and they were guests of the captain.

Their uniforms—their proper uniforms—had been taken away by Clarence, who perhaps promised that they would be cleaned, mended, and made ready for them later.

They had managed to keep the all-important cases by the simple expedient of shifting them into Grakow's room when eyes were elsewhere and placing them out of sight.

Dressed now in the Laughing Cat uniform and shod in soft ship slippers, the bedding reassembled and the quarters made neat, they met again in the main room.

Stost was truly hungry now, his thoughts turning eagerly to the contents of the coldbox. He noted that he was concentrating on one task at a time, moving linearly, more like a common Troop on orders than a pathfinder in... strange circumstances. Chernak was doing likewise, which meant that, for the moment, they were patient and awaited events.

She came out of Grakow's room and raised an eyebrow. The cases had not been disturbed while they slept, then. He did not sigh in relief, but it was a near thing.

Chernak nodded at him and moved toward the coldbox.

A chime sounded, a rounder, more mellow tone than the wake-up call Joyita had demonstrated for them last shift. Instinct turned him toward the screen.

"Good waking, Pathfinders." Joyita's accent had improved again while they slept. As all pathfinders, he and Chernak were facile with languages and generally quick to learn—core specs for the X Strain. It would appear that Joyita had similar specs, though he seemed a civilian—born, rather than made.

"Joyita," Chernak, elder and senior, returned the greeting first.

"Joyita," Stost said in his turn. "What news?"

The grim mouth softened somewhat in a smile.

"A timely question. There are three pieces of news for you.

"First, the captain has moved the ship from the location at which we found you. She sends her assurances that we are secure in this new location.

"Second, on the advice of our medical technician, you were allowed to sleep for as long as your bodies required. This puts you at an odd schedule with regard to the crew. The captain therefore requests that you make a meal from those items in the coldbox. If there is a specific food or beverage that you require, please tell me and it will be delivered to you.

"Third, the captain will come to you in one hour and asks that you hold yourselves ready for debriefing."

· · · ✳ · · ·

Hevelin wanted to meet the new people. He was insistent on this point, even adamant. The barrage of images was intense— enough to produce a tiny flicker of headache—but became less intense in the same instant that Theo noticed it.

She sighed, sipped her tea, and considered the norbear standing on the chair before her. She'd come into the galley for a cup of tea and to order her thoughts before she debriefed the pathfinders. Engaging in a dialogue with a noisy and excited norbear had not been on the agenda.

The images slowed again, until they arrived in the tempo that Theo considered to be normal norbear conversation. An image of Grakow came to mind, then Chernak and Stost. Accompanying was a sense of wanting—needing—to . . . to *know* them.

Theo sighed and blew her bangs out of her eyes.

"Hevelin, I'm sure they want to know you, too. But they've been through a lot"—a somber image of *Orbital Aid 370* flashed behind her eyes—"and we need to let them rest and find their equilibrium. We don't want them to make a mistake because they're tired or confused. And we don't want to make a mistake because we have . . . *assumptions.* I need to talk to them, find out what their necessities are and what they need to know so they can make good decisions."

A flicker of disappointment reached her.

"Bored?" Theo asked. "I can ask Kara to teach you astrogation."

A starfield glittered inside her head and vanished, replaced by a scent—a familiar, minty scent.

She frowned. Was she smelling the tree here in the galley? There must be a problem with the ventilation system. Except that *Bechimo* never had those kind of minor maintenance issues, and she hadn't felt any bobble in Systems.

The scent was stronger; a picture of a seed pod formed in her mind and she looked back to Hevelin, who had placed two actual seed pods on the table next to his chair.

"Oh no. What have you been doing!"

The image, the expectation, was clear. He wanted her to have one of the pods. He pushed one toward her, while his paw hovered over the other possessively.

An image swooped through her thoughts on a chilly breeze, and she saw the shadow of a dragon....

The pod—*her* pod—smelled so...*good*. Not like anything in particular; just like—well, like the promise that she would enjoy eating it very, very much.

She didn't have to eat it; she remembered Father telling her so.

But she *wanted* to eat it. She put her mug aside and took one step toward the table.

"Theo!"

Bechimo's voice rattled her brain inside her skull. "What are you doing?"

"Accepting a gift from an ally," she said, mouth watering.

"That pod is not safe!"

"No, it's perfectly safe," she said, feeling certainty in her bones. "Better than safe."

"There is nothing better than safe," *Bechimo* said flatly. "I will call Kara—"

"No!"

That was an *order*! She heard sparks crackle, felt a thrill of electricity in the interface between herself and *Bechimo*...and she felt *Bechimo* pause.

"Theo," he said quietly. "That pod might kill you."

"I don't think so. I've had one before, and it didn't...do anything, really. Except it tasted better than anything I've ever eaten."

"Theo," *Bechimo*'s voice was quieter still. "I have checked my records. You have not eaten a pod from the tree in Forcing Room Three. It has, in fact, only produced these two pods which Hevelin has brought to you within the last ten hours."

"Not from this tree," Theo said dreamily, most of her attention on the pod, which seemed to quiver with eagerness under her regard. "From Val Con's Tree."

Her pod—smaller than the pod she'd had from Val Con's Tree—was bright and green smelling, with a hint of spices she'd never tasted. She breathed in, savoring the complexity, as bundles of ideas presented themselves for her consideration. That, she realized, was her bond with *Bechimo* functioning. He was thinking heavily, pulling in data at a rapid rate, building hypotheses.

Was her own scent part of the allure of the pod? How was her poor human nose good enough to scent the difference between her pod and Hevelin's—in fact, was it that good? Hevelin had done the primary sort, keeping one pod and proffering the other. Yet she was certain that the pod remaining was *for her*. Was there some other subtle but tangible clue to be reckoned upon? The color? The shape? How could a seed pod be imbued with readable intent?

Bechimo's sensors were at work, overlaying her own, he much less willing than she to admit the reality of the tree being able to tag seeds in a way that would inform an intended recipient. He was not denying the tree's potential sapience, nor was she; in fact, he was more accepting of that potential, as he formed the theory that the tree had created the pod in order to harm her.

As if he'd heard that theory form, Hevelin lifted his pod, holding it carefully in two paws. With great deliberation, he brought the pod close and subjected it to a thorough inspection.

Theo *felt* the inspection, noting with the norbear the lack of offensive insects, the firmness of the green shell, the pleasing shape. He inhaled, sharing with her the overtones and undertones, a particular bouquet rising at the front of her nose, then expanding with delicious promise.

The pod was, so Hevelin determined, ripe and ready to be eaten.

That being so, he placed fingers at sudden green seams and sighed with pleasure as the pod fell into quarters.

He raised the first section to his lips slowly, as a gourmet might savor the moments before sampling a new and thrilling taste. He squinted in pleasure; Theo did, too, surprised by the tang on her tongue, the nutty essence that had beneath it a dark, fruity juiciness.

He ate the remaining sections with gusto, without doubt or concern. When he was done, he sighed in deep contentment and looked up at her. There was again the chill sense of dragon wings overhead, coupled with a brief glance of Father, and his fair-haired friend—who, Theo realized abruptly, must be Val Con's mother. She felt Hevelin receive that identification with a deep, satisfied purr.

Distantly, *Bechimo* operated as a ship, sensors sensing, evaluating, testing—and this Theo could feel. Internally *Bechimo*'s thoughts bounced, twitched, concern for security blanketing himself and his captain—and this Theo could also feel. In the background were multiple jealousies and warnings about the tree's loyalties, about her own to distrusted Korval, about—

Theo sat on a vacant stool; Hevelin left his and settled on her lap.

"*Bechimo*?" She said it out loud, low but clear.

Hevelin looked about now, as if looking for the person he'd sensed with Theo.

"Theo. I hear."

"The ambassador approves of the gifts. He has taken no harm from ingesting his. We have no cause to doubt the ambassador's goodwill, is that true?"

"Yes, Theo. The ambassador's actions have been without threat."

"The ambassador is not Korval, nor is this tree Korval's Tree, precisely. Korval does not threaten you, the ambassador does not threaten you, the tree . . . is not something you need to fear or be jealous of."

A pause, a long pause. She could feel something in the connection with *Bechimo* adjusting itself. Hevelin sat up straighter and that was close to what she felt, as if *Bechimo* had braced himself to attention the way a cadet might.

Bechimo sighed. Clearly, he'd been studying Joyita.

"Theo, I am not able to follow your decision-making at all times. There are mysteries in the way you intuit; there are decision trees appearing all at once, as if you think the third thought simultaneously with the first and the second, as if you form will and intent instantaneously. As your interaction with the crew adds complexity, so does your interaction with Hevelin. Now there is *more* complexity, Theo."

She listened, feeling the cloud of his thought, and the struggle to place those thoughts linearly, so that she might understand . . .

"The tree is much younger than anyone else on board this ship and yet has a memory older, even older than the pathfinders. Clarence is chronologically older than the pathfinders, though they were born before I was built. Logic boggles, Theo."

The same ideas were in her head, with nuance and overlaps, even with calculations flashing and fading, seeking to compare chronologies and maturity and . . . levels of sentience.

"Theo, I—you—*we* are the first. There *are* no other bonded captains. I, and we, are not merely an AI and a human working together, which has happened before and will happen again. We are—we are *more*. We are—unique."

A pause, a long pause for *Bechimo*. She wondered if he'd cut in another voice circuit, added another one of the background timbres to speech. Could he be more real? He surrounded her already.

"Theo, how can I know what is dangerous any longer? You take risks, with yourself, with the crew, with *us*. How can I keep us safe?"

Theo smelled the pod in her hand, felt the comfort of Hevelin's weight on her lap and the surety of ship sensors all in order... felt *Bechimo*'s wait states and felt his concern.

"I think," she said slowly, "that being alive isn't safe. We have to take risks; we have to make choices or we stop being alive, even if we haven't died. Once a choice is made, it's irrevocable. The only thing left is to make another choice."

She sighed.

"I'm sorry. I know this is hard on you. The Builders should have told you that humans are... so very risky."

Her pod, she noted, was ripe *now*.

She picked it up and held it in her palm. As the other had, it broke into sections.

It was every bit as delicious as its scent had promised.

CHAPTER FOURTEEN

. . . .

Bechimo

THERE WAS NO NEED TO WARN EACH OTHER THAT THEIR QUAR-
ters were monitored, their every word recorded, if for nothing
more than to contribute to Joyita's increasing fluency.

In addition, Win Ton had demonstrated some familiarity with
the common sign. It was unlikely that he was conversant with
their own private dialect—which might be decoded, of course.
But some risks had to be taken.

Chernak and Stost therefore conversed rapidly and efficiently
while they ate, deliberate fingering hidden within the motions of
distributing and eating their food; subtle quirks of eyebrows and
mouth adding emphasis, or decision—the whole abetted by the
near telepathic understanding that existed between two soldiers
who had been partnered since the creche.

Their course was laid in by the time they had finished the
meal. They would continue to be patient; they would accept
conditions with calmness and a show of goodwill. They would
exercise double caution; they would each guard the other's back;
they would observe all and everything.

Implicit in the course was the acknowledgment of the captain
and her crew as provisional allies, civilians though they were.
They had no choice, after all, and more to gain from gentleness
than from force. If it came about that the captain was unwilling
to aid them in the completion of their mission, then it would be
necessary to review tactics and implement new strategies.

As satisfied as it was possible to be under the circumstances, they cleared up the remains of their meal. Stost then went in search of Grakow in the certainty that the captain would wish to inspect him personally, to assure herself of his condition.

He had just settled the cat on one of the smaller upholstered chairs when Joyita spoke: "Pathfinders, Captain Waitley approaches."

So warned, they straightened to attention, facing the main door, awaiting the captain's entrance.

A brace of minutes passed. Chernak took a breath and centered herself, sinking into the stance. A proper Troop could stand at attention all day, if ordered. Some would say that pathfinders were hardly proper Troop, but even they might easily—

A chime sounded, sweet in the midrange.

Chernak blinked—and blinked again as Stost left his position at her side to cross the room to the corridor door and to put his hand upon the plate.

"Captain," he said crisply, stepping aside to allow her to enter.

"Thank you, Stost," she said and stepped into their quarters, fluid in her stride, and stringently centered, like a Troop walking point into unknown territory.

Chernak brought her fist to her shoulder.

"Captain!" she said, respectful of that stern focus.

"Chernak," the captain answered.

Stost held his post at the door, which had closed once the captain had stepped inside. She had brought no such escort as would befit even the rank of civilian captain, leaving Chernak unable to decide if this omission was an insult or was meant, in some way, to comfort them.

The captain paused before Chernak, head tipped to one side, her body as thin and flexible as a *shibjela*; light yellow hair wisping around a pale face dominated by space-black eyes.

"Stand down," she said. Her accent had also much improved over the sleep shift. "Stost, join us. We will sit together."

"Captain," said Stost. He moved, slowly enough to show respect for the edge of her, and taking care to keep within her line of sight.

The captain nodded and looked past Chernak. Given leave to stand down, Chernak turned to follow her gaze and was unsurprised to find Joyita's image in the screen. Was it possible that he stood the honor of Captain's Escort?

"I will assist with any communication difficulties," he said, meeting Chernak's eyes.

She showed him the soft fist on the left hand, which meant she had heard and understood, then turned back to the captain... who was sitting in the small chair next to Grakow, solemnly offering her forefinger for his inspection.

There was a pause while the cat appeared to weigh his worth as a member of a mercantile engineering crew against that of a civilian captain and commander of all nearspace. Before the pause lengthened into rudeness, he decided that he might condescend to accept her attention, and bent his head to touch his nose very lightly against her finger.

Stost sighed.

Captain Waitley turned to him with a smile.

"I am accustomed," she said. "Cats march to their own orders."

"Grakow held rank on the other ship," Stost offered.

"Very proper," the captain said solemnly. She leaned back into the corner of her chair. Perhaps she meant to seem at ease. Chernak, though, marked how her feet remained flat on the floor and her hands at ready. It would not do to make an unexpected move on this captain. Not unless they were prepared to take her and her ship.

To her right, Stost leaned back in his chair, reflecting the captain's pose.

Chernak settled back as well, crossing her legs casually and producing a small smile for the captain's benefit. Civilians placed weight on smiles; she and Stost, as part of their interface duties, had therefore learned to smile in such a manner to inspire trust, rather than fear.

Captain Waitley's eyebrows rose; she inclined her head gravely— and then smiled, very slightly, herself, as Grakow butted her arm with his head and pushed onto her lap.

He curled up, to the accompaniment of rusty purrs.

Captain Waitley smiled again, then looked up into their faces—first Chernak, then Stost.

"We traveled while you slept and are no longer in the location where we intercepted *Orbital Aid Three Seven Zero*."

They had discussed this unsettling bit of information over the meal, but had only achieved even more unsettling questions.

The first among them was why translation had not wakened

them. Experienced spacers that they were, they ought to have roused at the change of phase.

Which question led to the second—how long *had* they slept per the medical technician's orders, and had those orders been enforced by a touch of something in the air? They were X Strain and largely immune to such tactics—but they were not *perfectly* immune.

Thirdly, where had the little captain traveled *to* and what did this sudden shift mean for their mission?

Chernak thought she might ask that third question—and almost instantly thought better of it.

Stost covered her tiny hesitation with a question of his own. "No salvage?"

Captain Waitley moved her head from side to side, then apparently realized that the gesture was lost upon them and spoke.

"No salvage. The new location is secure; a holding pattern while we make plans. I must ask questions, Pathfinders. Accurate answers will benefit all. Am I clear?"

"You are clear, Captain," Chernak assured her. Grakow was still purring, curled as he was into a circle against the captain's belly, nose tip covered by tail tip.

"Good. Where were you bound before glory overtook *Orbital Aid Three Seven Zero*?"

"Captain, we were bound, so our orders had it, to another universe," Stost said and swept both hands out, encompassing suite, ship, and possibly the surrounding vacuum. "We assume that we have arrived."

"Yes, we assume that, too. Joyita can provide you with the math. What were your orders, once you arrived?"

The orders had provided them a range of choices, since they had no idea what they might find or face, once they arrived in this supposed new universe. First...

"We were to rendezvous with what Troop had won through," Chernak said.

The little captain tipped her head, frowning.

"*Did* others of the Troop win through?" Stost asked, leaning forward.

She looked at him, frown deepening; black eyes somewhat narrowed.

"Yes," she said, "but..." She glanced aside, to where Joyita sat his station, and was seen to sigh before returning her attention to themselves.

"The others arrived some years ago, as this universe tells time," she said. "Some hundreds of years ago. The situation... is complicated."

"*Hundreds* of years?" Chernak interrupted, astonished and disbelieving at once. She took a breath...and centered herself.

"By the captain's leave. All ships were to have been away and in transition at a certain hour, center-time. Our ship was one of many..."

"Yes..." the captain said slowly.

"Based on our observations made at the location at which you were recovered," Joyita said briskly, "we have formed a theory. As you say, many ships lifted at once. Many ships transitioned at once. In addition, it is not unreasonable to suppose that the Enemy was expending great amounts of energy in its effort toward victory. All of these forces operating at once—this is, remember, a theory—produced a temporal fugue state that encompassed some of the evacuating population, while allowing some—even most—to arrive in the new universe promptly, though widely dispersed with regard to location."

"And you believe that some ships—because of this temporal anomaly—arrived in the new universe much later than...most," Stost said.

"Yes." Joyita moved his head—chin up, chin down.

"*Hundreds* of years later?" Chernak repeated. "How could we have survived so long? The ship was—you saw the ship, Captain. It was nothing but shred, held together by memory."

"The theory suggests that, while an object was caught within the fugue state, time...froze around it. Once released into the new, expanding universe, time began again," Joyita said.

Chernak stared at him. Frozen. Eerily, it made sense. After all, the Enemy's objective had been the crystallization of the old universe. Certainly, the Enemy would have exerted what efforts they might, to stop the Migration and win the war. With *so many* strange energies in play...

"You must have history," Captain Waitley said abruptly. On her lap, Grakow muttered a complaint. "In order to have history, you must have language. We have a device which will teach you language quickly. You will choose who is first to learn—"

"Captain," Chernak dared to interrupt. "We have orders. If Troop won through, then it is to them we—"

Captain Waitley held up a hand.

"You must have history," she said again, firmly. "What other options are offered by your orders?"

Chernak hesitated. Stost did not.

"Captain, if there are no Troop, we are to offer our service to the ranking civilian authority. But, Troop, Captain: that is our priority."

"Yes," she said. "I understand. Joyita, please ask Clarence to escort—who will learn first, Pathfinders?"

"I," said Stost, which was correct protocol. Juniormost took point when the risk was greatest, unless put aside by order of the seniormost. Stost had not given her the opportunity to issue the order, and so it would be Stost who risked his brain and his life on this device Captain Waitley would thrust upon them. If Chernak countered him now, she put his honor into question.

"Stost," she agreed, not looking at him, lest he see her chagrin and think that she considered him unworthy.

"Clarence is on his way, Captain."

"Good."

She turned to Stost.

"You will be taught the Trade language, very basic, enough to begin. There will be texts, basic at first. You will require additional sessions with the device, to layer more information. Learning takes place as you talk and read. Practice is key. Am I clear?"

"Captain, you are clear."

"Good."

The chime sounded. Stost half-rose—and sank back into the chair as the door whisked open, admitting Clarence, with his easy face and air of command.

"First is?" he asked.

It was, Chernak thought, a relief to hear that Clarence's accent was every bit as dreadful as it had been the last time they had spoken together.

Stost rose and Clarence grinned.

"Fine," he said, and waved Stost toward him.

Stost, however, turned first toward the captain, saluted, and got a nod in acknowledgment. Only then did he obey Clarence's summons.

They left the room together, the door closing smartly shut behind them.

Captain Waitley turned to Chernak.

"You will work with Joyita. He will have questions about your last locations, dates, and missions. Accurate information benefits all. Am I clear?"

The captain wished a debriefing; she wished in particular to know if the Troops she had taken onto her vessel were rogue. This was sensible. There had been... toward the end, when planets—when whole systems—had fallen under the Enemy's assault... there had been those of the Troop who had broken discipline, forsaken honor, and preyed upon the very civilians it had been their duty to protect.

The Enemy... it was said that the Enemy was able to slip into a vulnerable mind and influence even a soldier to act contrary to honor.

Command had taken those rumors seriously. She and Stost had been given protections, but as pathfinders, they were among the elite, as were planetary commanders and the captains of armadas. Ordinary Troop—there was no time. Ordinary Troop took what risks fell to a soldier and hoped his comrades were swift with grace, were it required.

"Captain," said Chernak. "You are clear."

· · · ✵ · · ·

Kara was sitting second. Her number six screen—bottom right—showed Theo and the two pathfinders, with Grakow on Theo's lap. The commlink brought her the sound of voices, fluent and easy. There were words Kara, who had been sleep-learning Joyita's dictionary, did not know, yet Theo, who had *never* been apt at languages, neither faltered, nor seemed at a loss. It would have been a puzzle, to be noted and shrugged away. However, there had been other small puzzles of behavior that had been accumulating since they had parted Jemiatha Station. It was not that Theo *deviated* from being Theo—not... quite, but...

She had, Kara thought, perhaps failed in all of her *melant'is* relative to Theo—copilot, crew member, med tech, comrade, and bed-friend. That was an uncomfortable thought, of itself. One wished to maintain Balance and to comport oneself with honor—and one was, in addition, genuinely fond of Theo.

Most assuredly, she had not explored this "bonding" as thoroughly as perhaps she should have done. She would rectify this error—just as soon as she was able to speak privately with Theo.

She felt a little better, having taken that decision. In Screen Six, Stost was speaking, carefully, so it seemed to Kara. Theo's posture betrayed no alarm, nor any tension, beyond a focus of attention.

That was going well, then, she thought, and deliberately brought her attention to Screens One through Five, which displayed various images of their new location.

Bechimo's former safe place had been strange, yet in some way beautiful, in Kara's opinion. This new location—not *quite* so safe—as Theo had been very careful to say, several times... This bit of space was bleak and barren; forbidding, if not overtly dangerous. The sole planet was on the far side of its star, and *Bechimo* had situated them far from the ring of rubble which comprised most of Brulilt System, so they stood in no more danger of a rocky assault than any other spaceship going about its business in the near and far corners of the universe.

The shields were up, of course, and *Bechimo* was vigilant on their behalf. Still, Kara found it within her to hope that they would soon be away. Theo had not been as precise as one would have liked with regard to the length of their stay, nor where they might next raise a port—or return to *Bechimo*'s home port.

It occurred to Kara to wonder if Theo's resistance to the notion of returning to Surebleak might be more than a simple disinclination to seem weak-willed before her brother. Could it perhaps be that *Bechimo* resisted the notion of Surebleak as his home port—and also of Theo's delm's authority?

Kara put that thought firmly aside with the others, to be addressed when she and Theo spoke.

And truly, the situation was not...yet...dire, to Kara's mind.

This plan, for instance, to give the rescued Yx—pathfinders a condensed narrative of the events of the centuries following the Great Migration, so that they might make a rational and... *mature* decision regarding the disposition of themselves—*that* was a plan that could only have originated with Theo.

For herself, she might, indeed, have brought the pathfinders to safety—one had discovered in oneself a disinclination to simply leave sentient beings to die, even Yxtrang—proto-Yxtrang— soldiers. Had Kara ven'Arith been captain of *Bechimo*, however, and having effected the rescue, she doubted not that she would have locked them in the stateroom—why not the stateroom, after all? As Theo had said, it was empty. She would then have made it her priority to follow Win Ton's most excellent suggestion, to transport the rescued to the nearest Scout outpost and lose no time in making them someone else's problem.

Kara blinked, realizing that her thoughts had drifted off-duty. She brought her attention once more to the desolate spacescape in Screens One through Five, and sighed softly.

"I agree that it is hardly a garden spot," Win Ton said from his station, where he was this shift shadowed by Hevelin. "But I would argue that a lack of flotsam must count heavily in its favor."

"So long as *we* are not the flotsam attractor," Kara said, meaning it for a joke, and forgetting that *Bechimo* did not always perceive humor.

"*We* do not attract flotsam," *Bechimo* said now. "Flotsam was a condition of our former location. I had utilized that location often, and while the amount of flotsam has increased there as we have observed, I have not encountered flotsam in any other of the... quiet places in which I sometimes rested."

Or rather, Kara thought, hid. From bounty hunters and pirates, Scouts, the Uncle, and general-issue scoundrels. Among others, so she dared to believe. *Bechimo* had lived a long, lonely, and perilous life before he had been boarded by one Win Ton yo'Vala, Scout courier, in violation, as Kara understood the matter, of nearly half of the regulations in the rather substantial Scout handbook.

Win Ton's choices were his to make; his *melant'i* his to keep... within the parameters of his delm's instruction, of course. Kara was Liaden; she did not question these things.

However, when it came to Win Ton deliberately—*knowingly*—involving Theo in his choices and transgressions... well.

There, Kara ven'Arith had very strong opinions indeed.

Theo had been born to be a captain—it was plain to the meanest intelligence that she *must* command. Indeed, had she not been born outside the clan, she might have been delm.

Or perhaps not. Her brother, Val Con, had *also* been born to command and, as eldest in Line, risen to delm. Very likely, had matters been more regular, Theo's delm would have given her a ship and a duty that kept her space-bound for years, thus allowing them both to command.

No, in the case of Win Ton—who was *not* Theo's delm and scarcely anything but a passing comrade and a light-love, so far as Theo had ever told it—Win Ton yo'Vala had taken it upon himself to subvert Theo's *melant'i* to his own. One would say that he was well served to find the ship key he had sent to her, as if it were a gift of esteem—to find that *Theo's* was the Captain's key, while his was that entrusted to what *Bechimo* termed the *Less* Pilot.

However, Win Ton's Balance had been harsher than a mere comeuppance of rank. He had fallen into the hands of persons who had tortured him in the hope of gaining *Bechimo* for themselves, and turned his own cells against him.

No, Kara decided, as she always did when her thoughts followed this course, Win Ton's Balance was sufficient to his errors. But Theo...

"The captain has completed her meeting with the pathfinders," Joyita said from his screen, "and is on her way to the galley for tea."

"Thank you, Joyita," said Kara, and made her decision. Soonest begun, soonest done, she thought. And it wasn't as if she could keep her mind on her screens this shift.

"Win Ton, I am going to take a tea break. May I bring you something?"

"Thank you, but no. I will take my break when you return."

She nodded, locked her board, and left the bridge.

CHAPTER FIFTEEN

. . . .

Bechimo

IT DOUBTLESS REFLECTED BADLY UPON HIM THAT WIN TON FOUND Kara's absence more soothing than her presence. There was often a tension between them, which he had at first supposed to do with her desire to keep Theo's attentions centered upon herself.

In this, he had done her an injustice. Kara ven'Arith was a woman of *melant'i*, an engineer of precision, an adequate medical technician, and a pilot of competence, if not brilliance. She was diligent and zealous and not, as he had come to learn, one to demand more from a comrade than a comrade's care. Certainly, she had been brought up properly, to respect the *melant'i* of others, and to err on the side of modesty when reckoning her own status.

No, the tension between them had nothing to do with Kara's jealousy of another of Theo's lovers; the cause was far simpler than that.

Kara simply did not like him.

She was not, in Win Ton's considered opinion, entirely unreasonable in this. There were long days together when he felt precisely the same.

He had been born to an adventurous and optimistic nature—which combination of traits had inspired his parent and his delm to allow him to go for Scout. Even Scouts must accept discipline, and Win Ton had been no exception, except that, perhaps, he had accepted not *quite* so much discipline as would have been wise.

Instead of walking away from the old ship—the *Old Tech*

ship—he had boarded it and thus ignited a chain of events of which he was, truth told, not proud...

...and which had yet not reached its conclusion.

He sighed, which woke an echo of Kara. She had been, so he thought, distracted at her station, and Kara ven'Arith was not a distractible woman. She was—naturally enough!—discommoded by the presence of the pathfinders on board and unfettered. He admitted to some uneasiness on that front himself, and he had Scout training to support him. The Scout mind found a puzzle in the pathfinders, and all else fell before the need to solve them. Had it been otherwise, he might have formed the opinion that the captain had taken leave of her senses. As it stood, he commended her for a measured approach that sought to keep her crew safe, while regarding the *melant'is* of the pathfinders and respecting their rights as survivors.

Really, it was very nearly a Scout-like approach. Win Ton found the decision to lay all of history at the pathfinders' feet in aid of self-determination to be particularly charming. And how very *like* Theo, to suppose that providing information and an opportunity to study, would of course yield desired results.

"Less Pilot yo'Vala," *Bechimo* spoke quietly on the quiet bridge, "may I have a word?"

The crew had long ago adopted informality as the mode upon the bridge. That *Bechimo* addressed him formally, in Liaden... was perhaps a little unsettling in itself. But, there—the Scout mind had discerned a puzzle.

"Certainly, *Bechimo*," he said, glancing up from his screens and addressing the ceiling. "I hope I am not in your black books."

"We share a common hope," *Bechimo* said, which would have been very nicely parsed had they been speaking together at an evening gather. On the bridge of *Bechimo* himself, the parsing hinted at threat.

Win Ton frowned, but made the proper, evening gather response: "May we also share a happy outcome," and shook his head, sharply. "Come, sir, out with it. What have I done?"

"You have done many things, Less Pilot, including proposing to me a captain who is as bold as she is challenging. I am grateful to you; I believe it is not too much to say that I owe you my life. However, I find that I must know the answer to a question—before we venture out again into populated space."

"I will gladly answer any question you put to me," Win Ton said. "And, if we are to speak of saving lives, you have the advantage of me. I was twice dead, but for you."

"Please, let our accounts be in Balance," *Bechimo* said.

Win Ton hesitated, then inclined his head. What other course, after all, was open to him? To wish for a precise Balance, in the classical manner, would be to wish for the ship to be in danger.

"As you say," he murmured.

He counted, slowly, to twelve, to give weight to the moment, then raised his head once more. A quick glance at the screens, which showed rubble and naught but rubble, and then he spoke.

"What is this question?"

"I wonder," *Bechimo* said quietly. "Where lies your loyalty, Win Ton yo'Vala?"

· · · ✴ · · ·

The galley door opened and Theo stepped inside. She felt . . . fizzy. Full of energy, like she'd just finished an exhilarating game of bowli ball. There had been a moment there, when she thought Chernak had been going to come down on the side of the captain was pulling her leg. But she hadn't. She'd obviously thought about it and, though she hadn't liked it—who *would* like to find out that they'd been in translation between universes for hundreds of years, all her comrades and commanders long ago dead? She hadn't liked it, but she'd accepted Joyita's so-called theory as the working facts until she got better ones.

That was good. It was going well. Later—

"Theo! Would you like some tea?" Kara turned from the tea-maker, holding up a mug. "I've just brewed some Grey Pearl. Unless you'd like something else?"

Theo smiled. "You peeked," she said, continuing to the counter and taking the mug from Kara's hand. "Grey Pearl will be perfect, thank you."

"You are welcome," Kara said. There came a brisk hum and a hiss, as the teamaker produced another mug of tea.

"Anything exciting going on out in the neighborhood?" Theo asked. "Flotsam?"

"Flotsam is a condition of our previous location. *Bechimo* is adamant upon this point," Kara said, looking over her shoulder with a smile.

"I guess he is." Theo returned the smile.

"The meeting with the pathfinders went well?"

"Better than I'd expected. They said that their orders were first to attach themselves to any of the *Troop* that had made the crossing intact."

Kara turned, mug held in both hands, steam rising gently.

"They wish to align with the Yxtrang? Theo—"

"That's why we're teaching them to read. Joyita's chosen texts will give them a quick, solid foundation in how things are in this universe, and also a list of other texts they might find of interest."

Kara bent her face into the steam, closed her eyes and sighed.

"Did I say something wrong?" Theo asked.

Kara half-laughed.

"No. You will always believe in scholarship and that informed people will make correct choices. It is what makes you yourself, and I must accept that the belief is core."

"You can remove the student from Delgado, but you can't remove Delgado from the student." Theo sipped her tea, tasting smoke and roses. She sighed in satisfaction and raised her eyes to Kara's.

"That's actually part of the university's mission statement. That wherever a student might go in their life, after graduating, they should always carry what they learned with them."

"Core," Kara said again, and sipped from her mug carefully.

One of Clarence's veggie rolls would go well with the tea, Theo thought, and took a step toward the cabinets.

"Theo," Kara could pack a lot of nuance into one word—Theo thought it came from having Liaden as her first language. Right now, Kara sounded as serious as Theo had ever heard her.

Kara's face was just as somber as her tone, with a little worry thrown in around her eyes.

"Yes?" Theo said, feeling a tiny flutter in her stomach, for no reason she could think of.

"I wonder if you might ask *Bechimo* to give us privacy."

It really was important; so important that even *Bechimo* couldn't be allowed to hear what Kara had to say. Theo took a deep breath and refused to wonder why Kara needed privacy *now*. There was one sure way to find out, after all.

"*Bechimo*," she said, speaking aloud for Kara's benefit. "Would you give Kara and me privacy, please? Also, please let Win Ton,

Clarence and Joyita know that we're in private conference in the galley and should not be interrupted for anything less than an emergency."

"Of course, Theo. Withdrawing now."

She felt him leave, though she could still hear the steady beat of ship systems, and the caress of light along her skin—background feed, that was all, and part of the bonding. Data only. *Bechimo* himself was gone.

"We have privacy," she told Kara and did not blurt out, *what's wrong?*

"Thank you," Kara said and seemed, for a moment, to be at a loss, staring down into her tea.

"Would you like to sit at the table?" Theo asked tentatively.

Kara looked up with a small smile.

"Yes, let us by all means sit and not loom over each other."

Theo laughed softly and moved toward the table.

"Neither one of us can loom over anybody—except maybe Hevelin."

"Which is doubtless why Hevelin's preferred spot is on one's shoulder."

Kara sat down, as did Theo. They each put their mug on the table. Kara sighed again, and touched Theo gently on the back of her hand.

"Theo, you know that I esteem you."

"Yes, of course! And I esteem you. Have I—have I..." She tried to think of the proper Liaden phrasing. "Have I not been receptive, when pleasure was sought? All of us have been, lately, busy, but I know that I become... focused and unheedful."

From the look on Kara's face, it might actually *have been* a proper answer, though not to the question she thought she'd been asking.

"You'd better just say it out," Theo said humbly. "I'm still all fizzy from talking with the pathfinders."

Kara's face cleared.

"In fact, that is my topic," she said and raised a hand, as if to forestall Theo misunderstanding again. "At least, it is a part of my topic. Theo—how is that you can speak so... flawlessly with the pathfinders?"

Theo took a breath... and hesitated over a line of narrative involving Joyita's dictionary and extra-intensity sleep-learning levels available to the bonded captain. Which weren't lies, because she *had* been sleep-learning the dictionary, just like the rest of the crew. But, while she wouldn't be lying, she wouldn't be telling the complete truth, either.

This was Kara. She wouldn't lie to Kara, not knowingly.

And that, Theo realized suddenly with a little chill, was why Kara had wanted privacy.

"*Bechimo* augments my vocabulary, guides my pronunciation, and helps me process what's being said." She looked straight into Kara's eyes. "Those are benefits that come to me as bonded captain."

"Of course," Kara murmured. "And these other things—you were always good with your math, calculating courses on the fly and finding the most efficient routes. So, you understand it is not so easy for me to see if *Bechimo* is also...benefiting you in these matters."

"*Bechimo*'s a lot faster than I am, but we don't look at the same things," Theo murmured. "The calculations and piloting—those are collaborations."

"I see."

Kara raised her mug; Theo sipped her own tea, savoring the flavor—more smoke and less roses—as the beverage cooled.

"I understand," Kara said slowly. "Indeed, as one of the beneficiaries of your actions, I am honored...that you took such decisive action in order to succor crew from the enemies of our ship. But, Theo, I wonder if you might not now...stand down. I—this integration—I worry that it may have...deleterious effects. On yourself."

"Deleterious?" Theo frowned, then shook her head. "I can feel the systems running and—other things. But I don't think they're harmful. I don't think the bonding with *Bechimo* is *harmful*, Kara; it makes us more efficient."

"What other things do you feel, I wonder?" Kara said softly.

Theo sighed. "Things like—like gasses moving against the hull, the texture of hyperspace. Right now, I'm feeling kind of itchy, with all that dust against the hull."

She smiled, so Kara would know that the itching was nothing more than a minor annoyance. "I'm aware that these are... augmented experiences, but I don't think that it harms me to have them."

Kara took a deep breath and placed her hand firmly over Theo's.

"Theo, does *Bechimo* wish to avoid Surebleak?"

Theo blinked. "He's not particularly happy about Surebleak, in general, mostly because it can't be made safe enough to suit him. He does seem to have a lot of respect for—for my brother's house security 'bot."

She shrugged again.

"The reality is that we're going to have to raise Surebleak, eventually. For one thing, we have Val Con's family heirloom secured to one of our pod mounts. Korval is ships, remember? Also—I don't want to force this decision—*Bechimo* calculates that it's within the realm of possible outcomes that the pathfinders will want to interface with the...former Yxtrang soldiers Val Con has as security."

Kara's eyes widened.

Theo smiled, feeling it sit crooked on her mouth. "Joyita concurs, if that makes you feel better."

"Theo, if you are...becoming...an adjunct of *Bechimo* and Joyita..."

Theo shook her head. "Joyita's an individual. *Bechimo* and I are bonded..." She smiled slightly, recalling the bonding ceremony. Not much of a ceremony, not with Kara and Clarence being held hostage off-ship, and Win Ton not completely convinced of the necessity.

Necessity is what had driven her; even then, there had been that moment of hesitation, of *fear*, that the bonding would diminish her—exactly what Kara was worried about. The fear passed quickly, followed by an upsurging joy as the...connections were made and space opened around her.

"I wish I could let you feel what it's like," she said to Kara's worried eyes. "Really, Kara, I feel better—more alive—than I've ever felt. The extra data, the collaboration with *Bechimo*—these are all good things. And anyway..."

She hesitated, but Kara had asked—specifically asked a question—and it wasn't in Kara's nature to let a question go until she had an answer.

"As to *un*bonding," she said slowly. "I don't know all of the exact processes, though I could—should—ask *Bechimo*. My sense, though, is that...breaking the bond is...not an option."

That didn't make Kara happy, at all.

"You can feel ship systems working, you said..."

"Right. That's part of the bonding. I'm...integrated into the ship systems, at least as an observer."

"So you cannot—ever—have privacy?"

"I can have privacy. *We* have privacy, right now. *Bechimo* has removed his attention from us. He is not actively listening or watching. And—" She stopped abruptly, struck by a certain lack.

"And?" Kara prompted.

"And," Theo said slowly, "right now, I can't call to mind more than a dozen words in the pathfinders' language."

· · · ☀ · · ·

The device had been modified, Stost saw, and reasonably so. It had clearly been intended that the one acted upon should lie within, and thus it had been constructed to accommodate one of Clarence's approximate size, or perhaps...somewhat larger.

Stost, however, was several somewhats larger. Even bent in half...

But it was no matter. Clarence showed him the cot placed next to the device—a cot extended to its full length, which would fit Stost so long as he arranged himself carefully—and the extension wires jacked into the device.

He understood that he was to lie down on the cot, allow Clarence to fit the helmet over his head, and to engage the device. Stost would hear a tone, which was the warning that the device was about to place him into a trance state, whereupon it would directly act upon certain sections of his brain and embed new information.

The entire mechanism was terrifying, and for a moment, Stost thought fondly of the repair bug.

"Is fine?" Clarence asked.

Stost made a rocking motion with one hand, palm turned toward the floor.

"Maybe not fine," he answered. "Pathfinders have training. Maybe I resist your device. Maybe I not learn." He did not add, *Maybe I die*. Truly, he had proved difficult to kill, but he would not like to anger the captain by destroying valuable shipboard equipment, however inadvertently.

Clarence looked grave.

"From the captain: harming pathfinders is not fine," he said and moved his hand toward the cot. "Down—we will be sure you are fine. Safe."

Safe. Stost considered Clarence, but it did not seem that the other intended insult. It was meant as a reassurance then, a promise that no harm would be allowed to come to Stost, by order of the captain. Which elevated it, and the situation entire, to the level of farce. The little captain held her hand above the soldiers, defying the universe on their behalf. And it was his part to allow himself to be protected, to be calmed by the promise of safety. To lie down, as directed, and to allow the helmet to be placed upon his head.

As predicted, there came a tone, whereupon the helmet was removed.

Stost blinked up at Clarence.

"Good waking, Stost. Do you understand me?"

The words were . . . perfectly understandable while at the same instant they were entirely foreign.

Stost rose up on an elbow.

"What language . . . ?" he began—and clamped his jaw shut when he heard the same foreign words issue from his lips.

Clarence grinned.

"Trade," he said. "The learner ran a diagnostic; you were found able, so I dialed in a quick tutorial. You have four hundred words. Ready to learn to read?"

Four hundred words. Four hundred new, never before spoken or heard words. Stost concentrated, but the protections Command had seen embedded in him were intact. The new knowledge was not obtrusive; it was simply *there.*

"How long?" he asked Clarence.

"To learn Trade? About an hour, ship-time, for the first layer. Reading will take longer, for less gain, at first." Clarence glanced at a dial on the side of the device. "Two hours to learn. Somebody will be here when you wake up and will take you back to quarters." He held up his hand, fingers bent against his palm. He extended the first finger.

"Learn."

Second finger.

"Wake."

Third.

"Eat."

Four.

"Practice. Clear?"

No, thought Stost, but he supposed he would discover clarity on the other side of learning.

He lay back down.

"I am ready," he said.

· · · ✳ · · ·

"That," said Win Ton slowly, "is a difficult question."

"I feared that it might be so," *Bechimo* said.

"And yet, it is a question which must, in honor, be asked—and answered. Allow me to compliment you, on the nicety of your timing."

"We cannot, so Theo tells me, hide forever." *Bechimo* said.

Win Ton bowed his head. "As always, Theo thrusts to the heart. Indeed, *we* cannot hide forever. Nor may I."

Bechimo waited.

Win Ton smiled, slightly. "So! You ask after my loyalty. Insofar as I am a Scout and by definition a misfit within my society, my loyalty lies..." He sighed and turned his hands palm up. "My loyalty lies with Theo, with this ship, and with this crew. I might have flown into the boughs and declared that I have no loyalties, save to myself, which would be fine, indeed. Only I have lately perceived that I require guidance of a higher order."

"This is welcome news," *Bechimo* said.

"Well you might say so; however, you have not heard the whole of it. For one does not, you know, merely have loyalty. One also has duty."

A glance at the screens. Rubble tumbled and flowed against a smear of muddy space.

"I am a Scout," Win Ton said, keeping his eyes on the screens. "When I was struck unto death, my comrades kept me alive. When it was discovered that healing my wounds was beyond them, they took the extraordinary step of bringing me to the Uncle himself, known to deal in areas and items abhorrent to Scouts, to find if he could heal me.

"He returned me to you, and I have therefore been healed. Had this not been so, we would not now be engaged upon this difficult discussion."

"They made you a bargain, your comrades?" asked *Bechimo*.

"In fact, they did propose a bargain. I am certain that you have deduced its outlines, but allow me to state it completely, for your records and for the captain's information.

"The price of my life, quite reasonably, is what they are pleased to style the Old Tech ship. Deliver that ship—by which I of course mean *you*—into their hands, and I will have paid my debt and will be returned to the lists of active Scouts, with no mar upon my record."

He sighed again and closed his eyes against the endless tumble of rock.

"My duty, then, is to deliver you to the Scouts."

"Your loyalty stands at odds with your duty," *Bechimo* said. "One must yield. As someone who holds you in regard, I would suggest that it is duty which must give way."

"I concur in this case, especially as I do not...quite... believe that I will see a return to active work, even if my name is reentered into the lists.

"The difficulty, of course, is that I may not be allowed to choose."

CHAPTER SIXTEEN

Bechimo

"ARE YOU WELL, MY STOST?"

Chernak rose from behind the desk. Debriefing long completed, Joyita had asked her assistance with his growing dictionary. She had accepted the work with alacrity. Better—far better!—to be usefully employed, than to sit in a chair, reviewing her past actions and trying to pinpoint her errors.

The door closed behind him. He seemed . . . rested, though there was a slightly mad look in his eye, as if he had witnessed great wonders or vast stupidity.

"I am well, Senior. Have we rations?"

"More food was brought while you were away," Chernak said. "I stored it in the coldbox." She did not say that the delivery had been made by a small 'bot. They would discuss this detail soon enough and what it might mean. Stost was the priority at this moment.

"Sit," she said instead. "Rest, and I will—"

"Senior, I am rested, only hungry."

"Eat, then," she said, waving toward the coldbox. "I will join you."

"Tell me, then," she said aloud, for this would be a reasonable—if not urgent—topic of conversation. "Have you language?"

"I do," Stost answered. "Clarence tells me that I have four hundred words of the Trade language. This is a beginning. After it has *settled*, then another session, during which more words will be added. Also, the base has been laid for reading. This

149

is a more difficult proposition, according to Clarence. I am to practice, after I have eaten."

"Joyita promises an infopacket and auxiliary list."

"Yes," said Stost.

"How many sessions, until you are fluent and literate?"

"Elder, I don't know. Practice is key." He smiled faintly. "So I have been told, repeatedly."

"Eat, then," she said, and Stost bent his full attention to the meal.

Chernak, long satisfied, sipped juice and watched him eat with interest. Stost was not so notable a trencherman as some of their comrades, but then, field rations were known for nutritional value, rather than flavorfulness. The food aboard *Bechimo* tasted good and Chernak had, herself, been moved to have a morsel or two beyond hunger's defeat.

Finally, he was through, picking up his juice with a sigh, and gave Chernak a faint smile.

"They will want you, after our next sleep shift. It would have been now, but I asked for a trial period, to be certain that my new knowledge does no harm during use or while I am at rest."

"Well done. When you open your books, I will sit with you and you will tell me what you have read. We will amuse ourselves with breaks where you will point and say in the Trade tongue."

"Yes," said Stost, and stood. "Let us begin."

· · · ❋ · · ·

"A little nervous of the learner at first, which was reasonable."

Clarence was finishing up his report on Stost's session in the sleep learner. All hands were present on the bridge, including Hevelin, though *not* including the tree, despite the norbear's petition on its behalf.

"He did say, Captain, that he'd had specialized training, or maybe conditioning, that might make it hard-to-impossible to learn. I'll say that learning seems to have taken, but we agreed to a settling-in period for him before we teach Chernak."

"Reasonable precaution," said Theo.

"The annotated file has been accessed, Captain," Joyita said. "Stost is reading and summarizing for Chernak, who is sitting with him at the screen."

Theo grinned.

"Proactive," she said. "I like that. Anything else, Clarence?"

"That's the whole of it," he said. "Assuming all's well with Stost through their sleep shift, we'll get Chernak into the way of higher education after breakfast."

"Good. Thank you."

She paused, nodded, and held up a hand.

"Next order of business. We all know that we're at this location temporarily. We want to give the pathfinders time to do their research and make an informed decision about their next move. We need to do research, too, as a ship, so that we can make an informed decision about *our* next move."

She looked around; everybody was listening. Clarence, report given, had taken up monitoring the screens. She could tell he was listening by the angle of his head. Win Ton and Kara were watching her—and Hevelin, too, from his perch on Kara's knee.

"Eventually, we'll be going to Surebleak. Master Trader yos'Galan canceled the rest of our route research and directed us there, for our own safety. It's not an unreasonable request. Laughing Cat does have some small amount of trade goods, but we're not remotely able to set up a route of our own. Also, we have the ship and tree that apparently belong to Clan Korval, now based on Surebleak. All that said . . ."

She paused; her crew was calmly attentive. Her interface with *Bechimo* was also calm. They had, of course, discussed this, but she still half expected him to suddenly come up with a better—by which he would mean *safer*—alternative.

So far, so good, then.

"We want to do this in an orderly fashion. Surebleak is undergoing cultural turmoil, and it's certainly being monitored by the Department of the Interior. We don't want to expose ourselves unnecessarily to risk or danger. We know that we have enemies—"

Part of her cringed. Properly brought up Delgadans didn't have *enemies*. Oh, they might have professional rivals, but not *enemies*. Still . . .

"Enemies," she repeated firmly. "We want to avoid any additional confrontations like Ynsolt'i or Jemiatha's Jumble Stop. That means we need to gather information. We need to know what's being said about us in the news services; we need to find if anyone's filed anything against this ship or crew. We need to ascertain the state and situation at Surebleak, and the state and situation of Clan Korval."

"None of which is available to us here," Win Ton murmured, waving a hand at the screens.

"You're right," Theo said. "We're going to need civilization before we can get answers to our questions. But what we *can* do here is compile a list of ports we might raise *quietly*, do our research, and make plans. *Bechimo* has compiled a list of the twenty-four most accessible Jump-to ports from this location. We'll each go through the list and rank the ports, most likely to least. Weight should be given to Jump points—how many and how accessible—local trade routes, military situation. As a general precaution, we're going to suppose that locations where we're less likely to encounter Liaden ships to be more desirable options for us.

"Once everybody's been through the list and made their rankings, we'll discuss the top six and make three choices, ranked most desirable to least. When the time comes for us to leave, we'll Jump for the first port on the list."

She looked around.

"Questions?"

No one spoke.

Theo nodded.

"One more piece of business. Each one of us will be given two coordinate sets to memorize. Each set represents a safe or quiet location, such as this one, which *Bechimo* has utilized within the last fifty Standards."

Again she looked 'round at their faces. Clarence was seemingly absorbed by the rock garden in his screens; Win Ton was calm; Kara frowning slightly, but not, Theo thought, in puzzlement.

"Questions?" she asked again.

Kara raised her hand.

"I have no questions," she said. "However, Hevelin wishes the captain to know that he has an urgency in the matter of making the acquaintance of Grakow, Stost, and Chernak."

She looked wry.

"That is the sequence I am given, Grakow first, Stost, Chernak. He reiterates urgency and is becoming quite a nuisance on the topic. Captain."

"Is he?"

Theo gave the norbear a stern stare. He stared back, unblinking.

"Indeed. He invokes his ambassadorial privilege. It is his

duty, one is to understand, to greet Grakow personally, and also Grakow's attendants."

Clarence's laugh was a sharp crack of sound. Win Ton was keeping his mouth straight with some difficulty. Even Kara seemed slightly more amused than exasperated.

"Well, then," Theo said, rising. "I guess I've got my orders. Joyita, would you please ask the pathfinders if now would be a convenient time for Grakow to receive the norbear ambassador?"

· · · ☼ · · ·

The "norbear ambassador" may have wished to make the acquaintance of Grakow, but Grakow was not of a similarly gregarious frame of mind. After a quick search of their quarters, Stost found the cat curled comfortably atop a pillow in the second sleeping room, snoring.

Stost spoke to him, but the cat did not wake. Mindful of the wounds he had lately gained from this warrior, Stost did not attempt to pick him up, though he might, he said to Chernak, transport the entire equipage, if it became needful.

"Let him sleep until this ambassador arrives and gives his orders," he said. "At least we will know where he is."

Chernak raised the soft fist in agreement and looked toward the screen.

"Joyita, what language does the ambassador norbear speak?"

He looked up from his study of something, perhaps on the desktop, which was below screen level.

"Pathfinder, the ambassador has his own form of communication. Captain Waitley will translate, if necessary. I note that it has not often been necessary. Ambassador Hevelin is adept at making himself understood."

A notable statement, being both informative and opaque at once. They had been fortunate beyond their ability to understand, when Grakow came under their care. Chernak would not have supposed a cat to be so interesting to persons of rank, but—it was true she knew nothing of cats, Grakow being the only such creature she had spent any amount of time with.

"Pathfinders," Joyita said, "Ambassador Hevelin and Captain Waitley arrive."

The chime sounded and Stost crossed the room to open the door.

✳   ✳   ✳

The captain entered, walking more softly than previously, a pack balanced on one—no.

A small creature sat as tall as it could on her shoulder, one hand gripping her hair, while it looked about with bright, knowing eyes. It wore no uniform, but was furred, like Grakow. Unlike Grakow, the fur was ginger-colored, heavily striped with grey.

Chernak felt a thrill of dread. The Enemy had created creatures to carry out their work. Many of them had been designed a-purpose to look harmless, even ridiculous. Chernak herself had seen a being she had taken for a child bring down a battle wall with a wave of its tiny hand, and flip an armored personnel carrier onto its roof with a single, disdainful glance.

They had been fortunate, so they learned later, to have escaped that action with their lives. More children, so the scuttlebutt went, had appeared once the first had done its work. As many as six children, but no fewer than four, had walked over the fallen walls, into the center of the stronghold, buildings and walls and soldiers collapsing wherever they passed.

Chernak heard Stost, whose memory was every bit as good as hers, draw a careful breath as Captain Waitley dropped to one knee and helped the creature down to the floor.

"Ambassador Hevelin," the captain said, rising lightly to her feet, "before you are Pathfinder Chernak and Pathfinder Stost." She looked to them. "You may greet him in your own language, Pathfinders. He will understand your intent."

Chernak stiffened her spine and brought her fist to her shoulder in salute.

"Ambassador Hevelin, Chernak Pathfinder greets you."

Stost made a similar greeting, and then spoke to the captain.

"Grakow naps. Does the ambassador wish to go to him, or will I bring him to the ambassador?"

The captain tipped her head, as if listening in a range unavailable to sharp pathfinder ears.

"No," she said. "Stost had sleep-learning this shift; he's on anomaly watch."

There was another space of silence, to which the captain listened intently before looking up and meeting Chernak's gaze.

"He will speak with you, Pathfinder. If I understand correctly, he believes that Grakow will join us when communication is established."

Chernak cleared her throat, staring at the furry biped.

"How," she said hoarsely. "How is communication established?"

"Good question," said Captain Waitley. "Hevelin communicates ... directly, through emotions, and through ..." She paused, frowning, as if searching for a word. Finally, she turned her hands palm up and said, "Illusion."

Chernak stared, but the captain seemed to find nothing at all disturbing in what she had just said. Did the creature control them all, then? Would it fall to them to contain the crew, commandeer the ship, or ...

"Norbears," said Joyita, "are harmless, Pathfinders."

Chernak flicked a glance toward him. He met her gaze, calm and untroubled. Joyita, whose comprehension and accent in a language strange to him grew nearly by the breath. Captain Waitley, who shared that rapid gain of knowledge ...

... and the small furry creature, who communicated by means of emotion and illusion?

Had they escaped the Enemy after all?

Or had the Enemy set agents of itself into the fabric of the Exodus, to continue its war against life on a new front?

"Captain," she said. "I—we have protections against such things as ... direct communication and illusion. Resistance is automatic and may be ... violent. I am unwilling to harm any of this ship's company. Stost will bring Grakow for the ambassador ..."

Was that wise, she asked herself, even as she made the offer? What would *direct communication* with an animal achieve?

While she was wondering if she wanted to know the answer to that question, a dark shadow moved at the edge of her vision, low.

She glanced down as Grakow strolled into the room—and stopped, ears pricked forward and whiskers quivering, his attention on Hevelin the norbear.

Hevelin the norbear uttered a low-pitched sound—*"murble-murble-murble"*—and dropped onto all fours. It—he—halved the distance to Grakow, then abruptly sat down on the rug.

Captain Waitley also sat, camp-fashion, feet tucked comfortably under knees. She looked up, first to Chernak, then to Stost, and patted the rug. The meaning was plain; they also sat on the floor.

Grakow did not close the gap entirely. Ears still sharp, he moved two careful steps toward the norbear, while sidling to the right, so that his side pressed lightly against Chernak's thigh.

There he stopped, sat, wrapped his tail neatly around his toes, and yawned.

Captain Waitley was heard to laugh.

"Grakow is not impressed," she said, possibly to Hevelin.

His vocalizations, however, only became louder, and Chernak found herself soothed somewhat. In that, the sound was like Grakow's purrs. Perhaps that was what interested the cat.

Hevelin again halved the gap. Grakow offered no complaint, nor any visible sign of welcome.

Again, the norbear came forward, and offered his paw—his hand.

Grakow bent his head and sniffed.

Rusty purring began. Grakow stretched out, belly to the floor, flank pressing into Chernak's thigh. This put his head within easy reach of the norbear, who rubbed the cat's head with soft, careful fingers.

For several minutes, the only sounds in the room were quiet breathing and the mingled pleasures of murble and purr.

Chernak allowed herself to relax minutely. Hevelin the norbear ambassador had specifically wanted to meet with Grakow. Now that this desire had been granted, might he forget about . . . communicating with Chernak? Possibly they could scrape through this without putting their mission in danger, or testing the efficacy of the mental shields that had been installed at such a cost.

Beside her, Grakow sighed and stretched, both longer and closer. The warmth and solidness of his body was comfortable, much the same as Stost's hand in hers. It was good to have a comrade nearby, to guard her back and to take the mission forward, should she need to stay behind.

The memory of a face stirred; she recognized the build type and the gear of an M grade soldier—then recognized the soldier himself, though she had never known his name. He had formed part of the guard that had ensured their departure from Rijal, for their papers, their mission, had been more important than the doomed citadel.

He looked up and she had a clear view of his face—high cheeks, strong nose, grim mouth. The eyes were black and showed humor, even anticipation. An M going into battle . . .

The memory faded into another—another M, this one in light-duty leathers, with a civilian at his shoulder. Neither was immediately familiar; she must have seen them in passing, during a station sweep or port ramble...

A sneeze, or a sound very close to a sneeze, brought her eyes open. Across from her, Captain Waitley was grinning.

"That is my father," she said. "Hevelin matches him with someone else. There's a similarity but they are not, I think, the same person." She paused, head to one side. "Who is the person you remember?"

Chernak looked to Stost, who returned her gaze without expression. Waiting, was Stost; she noted that he squatted, rather than sitting full camp-style. That was wise, he could be on his feet in an instant, at need.

"How do you know my memories?" she asked Captain Waitley, who raised a pale, slender hand.

"Hevelin communicates directly, by emotion and illusion. He heard you remember a person and attempted a match with another... record. Norbears collect networks; they try to connect people and objects and places with other people and objects and places. These two people resemble each other, as if they are from the same gene group—" she frowned, as if *gene group* did not completely describe her intention.

"If your friend is from the same gene group, I'd like to know who he is. There are others who would be interested."

Chernak tried to stir up a sense of outrage, or danger, but she felt as calm as if she were standing a dawn watch on a deserted world.

"Not a friend, but a comrade. An M soldier, part of a rear guard, which allowed Stost and I to make our ship and lift." She paused, the word *father* echoing curiously in her head, and added, "Ms are by design infertile."

Captain Waitley grinned.

"Obviously, then, not my father, but a chance resemblance. Sorry, Hevelin."

The captain then tipped her head and smiled slightly. "That's Coyster," she said, though not, Chernak thought, to either her or Stost. "You know that."

Chernak blinked—and blinked again as cats arose, seemingly from her memory. She knew better this time, for Grakow was the only cat she had known... and there was an image of Grakow, following a sense of warmth, and then a man's face, spare and ruddy, with thatched grey brows and grey hair cut tight to the skull; there was a faint clank, as if of tools shifting on a belt, comfort suffused her and—

She recalled him—recalled him as last seen, injured and bloody, applying pain patches to ease wounds even a soldier might find enervating, and the fingers of his good hand, dripping gore, groping among the med kit, looking for the dose that would release him to duty's reward.

She looked back as they rounded the kink in the hallway, saw the figure slumped and wracked—

A scream rent through her head, battle rage rose in her, and a berserker's need to tear and rend.

She shouted and threw herself sideways, thinking that here it was, at last, the protections Command had put in place, endangering the civilian, endangering the mission, and there was grace, cold against her palm. Quick, she must be quick, before the rage separated her self from her sense—

A hard hand closed around her wrist.

"Chernak!" Stost snapped, and she froze where she was, relying on his judgment, as the rage...subsided, unspent, leaving her panting and exhausted, one side of her face burning, as if she had abraded it against the rug.

"What is our situation, my Stost?" she managed.

"Stable. The ambassador norbear soothes Grakow's grief. Captain Waitley stands backup."

He released her and she rolled into a sitting position.

There was Grakow, lying on his side, panting. There was the norbear, both small hands on the cat, murbling and murmuring, softly, softly—and there was Captain Waitley, daring, as they watched her, to stroke Grakow's head.

The cat gave a long, shuddering sigh.

"I understood some of that," she said, looking at them over her shoulder. "The wounded man was Grakow's owner?"

"He who gave us the ship, what remained of it, and the keys to the repair bug, and called our duty upon Grakow, the only civilian survivor." said Stost.

Chernak wondered if he had seen, or dreamed...remembered, too. That question was for later. For the present—there was Captain Waitley, speaking again, this time to the norbear.

"Is he well?"

There was a pause.

"Are you satisfied?"

Another silence. Captain Waitley stroked Grakow once more and rose to her feet.

They also rose, Stost first, reaching down to offer his hand, assistance that she did not need, but which she accepted gladly.

"Hevelin is happy to have met Grakow and to have shared memories with Chernak," the captain said. "He hopes to continue these conversations soon."

She paused.

"On a related matter, your schedules will be synchronized with first watch. You will join crew in the galley for the start-shift/end-shift meal. Win Ton will guide you. After the meal, assuming Stost has no ill effects from his learning, Chernak will learn while Stost continues his studies.

"Am I clear?"

"Captain," said Stost, bringing his fist smartly to his shoulder. "You are clear."

"Good," she said. "Thank you for allowing Hevelin to visit Grakow. My apologies for any dismay that he caused to yourselves or to Grakow. Chernak, are you well?"

"Captain." She saluted. "I am uninjured, Captain, and able to serve."

"Good," the captain said again. She bent down to pick up the norbear, carrying him cradled in her arms, as if he were a child.

Stost sprang forward to open the door for her. When she had gone and the door closed again, Chernak looked to Joyita's screen, which showed only silver. They were to understand that they were alone.

She turned back. Stost was leaning against the door, worry plain on his face. She took a breath and he raised a hand, snapping off a terse sign.

We need to talk, it was.

"Yes," said Chernak.

CHAPTER SEVENTEEN

Arak ek zenorth
En route

PILOT ERTHAX HAD SURVIVED THE PROCESS OF REMOVING THE bombs, and returned to the safety of their ship having lost not so much as a finger. Were the universe Balanced, as Liadens insisted was true, he would at the least have left an arm behind.

Perhaps the disbalance in the universe was what broke his sleep. Or perhaps it was the lack of exercise. Or the lack of anyone to talk with.

Whatever the cause, Vepal thought, there would be no more sleep for him this off-shift. He ought to bring up his screen and research their next most likely port of call.

He did rise and dress, and sit down at his desk—but he stopped short of bringing the screen live.

Instead, he considered that last thought, that he had no one to talk with.

Erthax was an adequate pilot; before his so-called promotion to the mission, he had flown transport and supply. His off-duty interests tended toward beer and games of chance—though not, as Vepal understood it, such games as put his own skin at risk. Very likely, he also spied for Command, filing reports on the sly. Vepal had long thought so. That Erthax had not considered it his duty to bring suspicions of sabotage to his commander... that was only confirmation.

161

There was, in truth, little for him to discuss with Erthax beyond those ordinary matters of piloting and shift arrangements, which had for many cycles satisfied Vepal, who did not *like* his pilot.

Ochin was somewhat more to his liking, but Ochin was a simple creature: a Rifle, concerned mainly with his commander's honor and dignity. Should Vepal attempt conversation, he was certain that Ochin would *try*. But he knew so little. So very little.

There was, after all, a reason that Explorers kept aloof from the common Troop and preferred comrades from their own ranks.

Vepal, an Explorer born and trained... Vepal had become accustomed to his own company. Or so he'd thought. His recent interactions with Commander Sanchez, short as they had been, had wakened in him the desire for... comradeship, a meeting of minds, and exchanges of views.

Commander Sanchez was by no means an Explorer, but she had been intelligent and surprising, and he wished that they had met each other at least once more before he had quit Seebrit Station to pursue the mission once more.

The mission.

Well, and there it was—the mission. His most glorious accomplishment, a find that ought to have earned him another starburst. Information that would have—that *should have*—started the Troop on a bold new adventure, with glory assured and purpose renewed.

A mission the goal of which was nothing less than the survival of the Troop.

He still recalled his excitement; how he had shivered with something very near the euphoria, as he gazed upon the file he had discovered and understood what it was.

The orders.

The orders.

The very orders from Headquarters—Headquarters!—which covered what the surviving elements of the armed forces ought to do after...

... after they had mounted rear guard for those fleeing the Great Enemy, covering the retreat, buying the lives of the vulnerable with their own—which had been their duty.

Protect the civilians; resist the Enemy. *That* had been the two-pronged duty which they had been created to meet—a history taught to Explorers and commanders, but no longer given to the common Troop.

After—the war lost; the escape successful. Headquarters had assumed the survival of Troop, of *some* number of Troop—and Headquarters had cut orders.

He had assumed that present Command would be eager to embrace orders from legendary Headquarters. He had assumed...

Yes, he *had assumed.*

Worse, he had, in his capacity as Hero Explorer, researcher, and Troop historian, made a presentation to Command entire.

The summation of his presentation?

Why, that the Troop's present existence was an accident of history. The orders—the precious orders he had uncovered—had been lost in the confusion of the crossing. The surviving Troop had regrouped—which was well. They had formed a command structure among themselves—which was necessary.

And they had established Temp Headquarters, to await High Command, bearing the direction of their future—which had been an error.

A fatal error.

It had taken years—hundreds of years—but the wait for the arrival of authority had eroded the Troop. They lacked the resources to do more than rebuild and overbuild the ships in their possession. They lacked goals, they lacked skills, they lacked a culture that would have allowed them to evolve.

Pressed for resources, their only skill war, they had turned to conquest and that solution had extended the life of the Troop.

But it could not save them. They could attack until the last Rifle fell, but they had no core to hold.

There was worse, which had long been known to Explorers and to the overseers of the creches.

The design was failing. There were fewer viable births every cycle, even with the relaxed standards.

He had told the highest Command this—and lived, but not because they were given new hope by what he had discovered.

No, he had lived because he was a Hero, a Senior Explorer who had claimed several resource-rich worlds for the Troop. A certain dwindling segment of Command was composed of former Explorers, and among that group, he was well-liked.

He could not, therefore, be killed outright or attached to an underprovisioned strike squad and so find his way to glory.

Instead, he had been given a budget, a ship, crew and...a

mission. A glorious mission to realize the promise in his greatest find for the Troop.

He was to go out into the Unaffiliated Worlds, seeking a worthy power before which the Troop might lay their knives, and swear allegiance in the name of—peace.

The mission was in its nineteenth Standard Year and was no closer—was perhaps farther away—from being realized than it had been at the start.

The mission, so he had come to understand, would never be realized. He had several times, in recent years, considered abandoning the mission, putting in to some small port or another, and simply walking away from ship and from command.

Honor...

And was it not an odd thing, that *honor* which was not enforced by the design, nor mandated by biology...

Was it not an odd thing, that *honor* should be so difficult to ignore?

Walk away from the ship, and what of Erthax and Ochin?

Shot for being Yxtrang, if they dared step out onto any dock. Shot for having failed in their assigned duty, if they raised Temp Headquarters again.

Vepal might abandon the mission, but he could not abandon his command.

The only option then, was to be certain that they all attained glory together.

Or that he found some way—soon—to save his race.

· · · ✳ · · ·

The chimes sounded, the pathfinders rose and made themselves ready in their ship-given clothing. It was notable, thought Chernak, alert for anomaly, as she and Stost had agreed that they must be until their situation clarified...It was notable that Joyita's screen remained blank. She considered summoning him, then decided not. Better to let events flow.

Win Ton arrived punctually and gave them good shift in an accent that was somewhat improved. Chernak weighed this, recalling that it had been Win Ton who had recognized the language of the Troop and who had first spoken it with them. His accent had been terrible and his grammar beyond mention, but he had a grounding. Further, to their observation, he was quick-witted and he, with the rest of the crew and captain, would have been studying. His improvements, weighed thus, fell within the parameters of normal human learning.

Chernak acknowledged that she felt relief.

"Follow me to mess," Win Ton said now, and they stepped out into the hall, forming up behind him.

They walked not so far—*Bechimo* was not Troop transport, after all—merely to the cross-corridor, where they turned right and very shortly raised the galley.

Again, by the standards of Troop transport, it was not a large room, though certainly roomy enough to accommodate *Bechimo*'s normal crew levels. The addition of themselves did, Chernak thought, have the effect of making the room seem smaller, but that was often the case when Troop entered rooms made for and by civilians. Even Ms, with their smaller form factor, could overfill such a room through mere exuberance.

Win Ton paused just across the threshold.

"Pathfinders, here is Kara ven'Arith," he said, as a yellow-haired woman of very modest height moved to join them. "Kara, here are Pathfinders Chernak and Stost."

She looked up at them, her face impassive and her carriage erect. Chernak approved. It might well be that Kara ven'Arith was frightened, for she looked to be a sensible woman, but that was not for them to know.

"Kara," Stost said, making his voice soft, perhaps in respect of that militant calmness, and speaking his newly acquired Trade language, "Chernak and I thank you for your part in our recovery. Captain Waitley is fortunate in her engineer."

Most of the words slid by her ear, but Chernak knew her junior well enough to easily understand his intent. A compliment to skill was always in order. Accordingly, she smiled her civilian-soothing smile and added: "Kara, is fine."

There might have been the tiniest easing of the eye muscles, otherwise Kara maintained her expression and her stance.

"Chernak, Stost," she said, speaking the pidgin they had developed for, Chernak realized, *her* benefit. "Is fine." She glanced to Win Ton. "Translate, please?"

He bowed slightly, hand over his heart. A flicker of expression crossed Kara's face, but Chernak did not know her well enough to recognize either irritation or humor.

She faced them and spoke, Win Ton translating into the language of the Troop.

"In addition to my duties as engineer and third board, I am also the ship's medical technician. You were, of course, scanned when you came aboard. However, the scans look for large problems—contagion, broken bones—and often miss smaller concerns. If you have any wounds or worries, please bring them now to my attention."

"Chernak fine," Chernak assured her.

Stost pushed his sleeve up and offered the wounds Grakow had inflicted. Kara stepped forward, holding his arm steady with one fragile hand under his elbow, while she slipped an instrument from her pocket with the other.

It was perhaps a hand-scanner, though different in form from others Chernak had seen. Stost appeared to experience no discomfort as the beam moved down his arm. The device emitted a faint buzz; a telltale glowed green and Kara nodded, slipping it away and releasing Stost's arm.

"There is no infection; the wounds are healing normally." She paused and deliberately looked up to meet Stost's eyes.

"You were wise to bring those to my attention. Cat scratches are tricky. Is there anything else?"

"All fine," Stost assured her.

"That is well, then. I leave you to your meal."

She bowed slightly, as had Win Ton, though without placing the hand over the heart, and moved away into the room.

"We continue," Win Ton said, beckoning them forward.

They followed him to the left, past a screen—and there was Joyita, still in his tower. No, Chernak thought, surely it was *again* in his tower. He wore a different shirt—beige, when last shift it had been green. The sleeves were rolled up to reveal muscular brown forearms, and a broad bracelet clasped 'round one wrist, of the same silvery brown metal as his rings. He was turned half away from them, his attention on something to his left. The top of a desk was in view of the camera, and there, a carelessly flung book, the cover offering familiar, readable script: *Recompiled Troop to Trade Dictionary with Notes and Comments, Copy Two.*

"These devices will provide a hot beverage." Win Ton's voice drew her away from screen and book, but not before a hopeful thought occurred. Was it possible that Joyita was a savant?

There were such—some Ms achieved that level of function, able to absorb in a matter of hours maths and languages previously strange to them.

A comforting thought, yes, but there was still Hevelin to—

"These dispense hot beverages. Touch the green unit lightly on the white pad, and it will deliver tea; the brown unit dispenses coffee," Win Ton continued, interrupting the thought. "Stimulants. There is juice in the coldbox."

He moved a hand, showing them the next counter, which displayed foodstuffs familiar to them from their previous meals.

"Take what you will, eat your fill. We do not ration here." Win Ton turned to them.

"Unless you want my company, I will also leave you to your meal. The captain will arrive soon and will have questions." He smiled, very slightly. "It is the nature of the captain to have questions."

"We will eat and make ourselves ready for the captain's questions," Chernak told him, and Stost added, in the Trade tongue, "Thank you."

They gathered food and juice, not wishing to risk the effects of unknown *stimulants*. A bench, somewhat larger than the other seating options in the room, had been placed before a small table. This, they took for their own, Stost arguing that it had been placed deliberately for them.

As they ate, they watched. Stost watched the room, which held Kara and Win Ton and Clarence. Chernak watched the screen, Joyita apparently busy at various tasks. Was there comm traffic in this new location? There had been none, except that between the repair bug and *Bechimo*, in the previous location.

"I wonder . . ." she began, and stopped herself, looking over her shoulder at the sound of a nearby step.

Clarence raised his hands, palm out, an effect that was slightly spoiled by the fact that he was holding a mug in one hand and a half-eaten muffin in the other.

"Don't mean to disturb you," he said, pausing well within Stost's reach and pointing at Stost's plate.

"That," he said. "*Veggie roll.* Is fine?"

"Fine," Stost agreed, and Chernak added her own affirmation. "*Veggie roll*," she said. "Fine."

"We make," Clarence said. "Kara grows veggies, I make roll."

"Fine," Chernak said again.

Clarence grinned. "You learn today," he said to her, badly, in the language of the Troop. "Soon, we have better than *fine*." Another grin. "Fine, eh?"

Stost snorted lightly, so the comment had been meant as a joke. He tipped his head slightly to one side.

"Trade language for Chernak? Reading?"

"Captain orders. Both."

Stost showed the soft fist. "Fine," he said.

"Now?" asked Chernak.

"After captain," Clarence said. "Soon."

He moved in the direction of the drink dispensers, where Win Ton was drawing a mug from the green. They exchanged a greeting and Win Ton turned, moving rapidly toward the galley door.

It slid aside in the instant before he extended a hand to the plate and he stepped back, bowing with an air far different than that in which he had bowed to Kara.

The captain entered, giving him a nod of acknowledgment, looked around the room, and walked toward their table.

Win Ton continued out into the hallway; the door whisked shut behind him.

The captain arrived. They began to rise to her honor and were peremptorily waved back down.

"This is a civilian ship," she said. "We do not keep military protocols." She pulled a stool out from under another table and sat on it, facing them.

"Stost, are there any ill effects from yesterday's session in the learner?" she asked. She was *very* fluent today. Within another shift, Chernak thought with dismay, her accent would be indistinguishable from theirs.

"Captain, no ill effects."

"Good. Chernak, have you concerns about your session today?"

"No, Captain. Stost has explained the process. I will be glad to be able to converse in Trade, with all members of the crew, and to review the histories."

The captain nodded.

"Have you eaten enough?"

"Yes, Captain," said Stost, and Chernak allowed his answer to stand for both.

"Good. Before Clarence takes Chernak to the learner, there are a few things we must discuss.

"First, you may move about the ship freely. Certain areas, such as the bridge, are off limits, but you do not need to stay in your quarters. You are not prisoners, not overtly or specifically; you have access to the exercise room, to the galley, to hydroponics and other areas. Am I clear?"

"Captain," said Chernak respectfully, "you are clear."

"Good. Are you done here? I would like to show you something."

They were done. They quickly cleared their table and crossed the room with the captain, to Joyita's screen.

"When you were being brought in, did you notice the pod that we carry?"

"Yes, Captain," said Stost.

"It appeared to be a ship," added Chernak.

"It is a ship. What I need to know is what sort of ship it is. Joyita, may we have a visual, please?"

"Yes, Captain."

There was the ship-pod on the screen, very clear.

"Are you familiar with this class of ship?"

"Captain," said Chernak, "it is a small cargo ship, or possibly a packet boat. We are familiar with the class."

"Do you know what it ought to have, in the way of standard equipment? Would you be able to pick out nonstandard equipment—anomalies?"

Chernak looked at Stost, Stost looked at Chernak. They both looked back to the captain.

"We have been on such ships, Captain," Stost said carefully. "We know the standard equipment and most common add-ons."

"Good. I may have need of your expertise very soon. Tell me now, do you have any immediate needs?"

"No, Captain," said Chernak.

"Then Clarence will escort Chernak to the learner," said the captain, looking past them and lifting her hand.

"If that route passes our quarters," Stost said, "I will walk with them, and resume my studies. There is...a great deal of data to sort through."

Captain Waitley nodded.

"If you need any high-level data crunching done, apply to Joyita. He will run the numbers—through the ship's computers."

Stost saluted.

"Thank you, Captain."

"Ready?" Clarence asked, arriving at Chernak's shoulder.

She took a breath and met Stost's eye. He smiled.

"Yes," she said. "Ready."

CHAPTER EIGHTEEN

. . . .

Bechimo
Exercise Room

THEO WAS SPRINTING HARD, GRIMLY MAKING FOR THE TOP OF the incline.

Bechimo was talking.

"I have been comparing my results with the suggestions of the other pilots, Theo, and I am unsure, which is to say that I do not find their calculations superior to my own. Some suggested ports are completely unacceptable."

Her hair was sticking to her forehead; she was breathing deeply, but not struggling. There was a worrisome sensation of pushing harder off the left leg than the right. If that was so, the readouts ought to report it, but she saw nothing save the usual—blood pressure, oxygen use, how far she had run up the inclined repeating track, how far she had to go. No, she *felt* that slight unevenness in her stride, which meant *Bechimo* was feeding the information to her directly. She should be able to smooth—

"Landsdowne, for instance, is far too risky a port, in my estimation, and yet *several* of the projected travel sets take us there. In the meantime, I—"

"Let me concentrate on this," she said to the ceiling, there being no one else about. "A quarter shift without analysis won't hurt anything, will it?"

There was a pause. Theo sensed currents shifting and felt a

171

degree of . . . separation, though not a complete withdrawal. She could still feel the uneven pace.

"Yes, Theo," *Bechimo* said. "It won't."

Theo sputtered. Had it been Joyita she might have expected intentional wordplay, but from *Bechimo*, she wasn't sure. He had a sense of humor. She thought. If he was trying to expand his repertoire, then that was good.

She put that thought, with the suggested routes and ports of call, out of her mind, and concentrated on her pace and stride.

· · · ✳ · · ·

Theo pushed, hard and harder, sweating with the work she demanded of her body. *Bechimo* monitored her vital signs anxiously. He knew that work was necessary for strong muscles and a healthy biologic system. Exercise was key, also, for a balanced mind. It was only . . . she was so *fragile*. If she fell from the machine, she might break a bone; certainly, she would be bruised, which she would shrug away as an inconvenience, if even so much.

She increased the running rate still more, and though he also knew that she was . . . made irritable sometimes by such attentions to her comfort, he angled a fan and increased its airflow, so that it cooled her more efficiently. He adjusted the lighting, too, so that there was less strain on fragile optic nerves, and reversed the direction of a second fan, so that the flow from the first was softened into something he hoped resembled a "breeze."

She voiced no complaint of these adjustments; indeed, her concentration was such that she might not have noticed them. If he was wise, he would adjust nothing further, but relax into the bonding space and learn.

Learn, for instance, what it felt like to use muscles, to feel strain; to feel strength rise to match it. There was joy, fierce and bright; and a sense of well-being.

He had been bemused by her insistence on the sprint mode, thinking that she would exhaust herself and be unable to address the several important issues before captain, ship, and crew.

Now he knew—he felt!—how wrong he had been! Far from a wanton expenditure of energy, this was a renewal!

And, for him, a revelation.

· · · ✳ · · ·

It was good to be really working out, Theo thought; the dances, stretches and other exercises were fine, but there was nothing like a good hard run to sharpen up all systems.

The incline was gently falling back to zero, and the tread was slowing into the cool-down phase. She sighed, in mingled pleasure and regret.

She'd ask *Bechimo* to put a run on her schedule every third shift. Wouldn't be good to overdo, but she'd been underdoing—and that was *definitely* not good.

Sighing, she closed her eyes and raised both hands to run her fingers into her hair, and lift it off of the back of her neck.

"Chong chong," came a low voice, imitating a call tone. "Chong chong. The ... Captain. Chong chong."

The imitation was quite good—and that was yet another sign of recovery.

Theo opened her eyes, automatically adjusting her stride as the tread slowed again.

Win Ton bowed, a complex, subtle thing that she wanted held in *Bechimo*'s cache so she could study and decode it at leisure.

Right now, she saw that the bow was not entirely shipmate to shipmate, nor crew to captain; that it held a stronger stance, a flutter of hand and shoulder indicating ... something. He had managed to warm the movement with a touch of comrade and nothing at all of former lover and mentor. Also missing was the dip of the shoulder that indicated one was barely a pilot. Which was, Theo realized, completely accurate. When he had first emerged from *Bechimo*'s special healing unit, he had been prone to tangling himself in his own feet; he had been frail and, frankly, weak. Now, she saw a pilot when she looked at him, if not a completely recovered Scout pilot. In desperate times, he might even take them into Jump.

Dismounting, she pulled a fresh face wipe from the dispenser, sighing at the pleasure of the low humidity breeze from overhead. She smiled, too, at *Bechimo*'s subtle failure to mention Win Ton's arrival. Another step taken for AI personhood, there.

Win Ton might not have known the source of the smile but he received it blandly, and repeated his bow note for note.

"Thank you," she said in Terran, which was courtesy and far better than embarrassing them both with an inept bow in reply.

"I hope you haven't been trying to get my attention for very long."

"I only arrived as the incline began to fall," he said. "But you looked so focused, I thought a warning that you were not alone would be courteous."

"Appreciated," she said, "and well done. Have you been practicing on your off-hours?"

"I must confess it a natural talent. I can also imitate a tea kettle."

"That's going to come in handy," she said seriously. "I assume you wanted to see me alone for some specific reason?"

"Indeed. I have . . . information that the captain should also have available, if you will permit me to share it."

She tipped her head, considering him. He was in total Liaden bland-face, but she knew him well enough that she could read the expression he wasn't showing.

He was nervous, but not, she thought, of her. Was he about to break a confidence, and that was why he had made an effort to find her alone? Or—

"The captain needs the information, but not the complement?"

He nodded this time, his face brighter. "Exactly so. Precisely."

"But you need my permission to share—and to share only with me, the captain?"

She let that question have an extra doubtful note of query, a trick she'd learned from both Father and Kamele.

His face was set and serious now.

"That is correct, Captain."

She waited and saw the corner of his mouth twitch, though he wasn't so improper as to actually smile.

"Call it a *melant'i* issue, Captain. I consider it possible that you will find the information useful in your conduct of the next phase of our voyage. While it is not, precisely, confidential, it is . . . primarily held by certain persons with a need to know." He paused, and this time the smile was definitely there.

"Which you have become. Ordinarily, the group consists of portmasters, station masters, Scouts, and some levels of security personnel. It concerns a situation that some say is improbable, at best. Some deny it can be true at all. It came to me as part of my previous official duties."

Theo considered, recalling the last time Win Ton had involved her in something that had come his way in the course of his duty.

"Is it dangerous for me to know this?"

Win Ton went still, then bowed very slightly, acknowledging a hit, a bow Theo happened to know well. Padi had used it often, and it was amazing how much nuance, not to say irony, could be fit into so modest an inclination of the torso. Comparatively, Win Ton's offering was...stiff, as if he had been hit, in fact.

"The information is not dangerous to anyone. Technically, it is public knowledge; anyone *may* know it. Once it is in your possession, you are free to use it as necessary, if necessary. It can be confirmed at any port with proper facilities; indeed, *Bechimo* may be able to verify."

"If *Bechimo* has it, and it's so important for me to know, why hasn't he brought it to my attention? Or," she amended, "why do you assume he hasn't done so?"

"The nature of the information is that it is often believed to be nonsense. *Bechimo* may have it in a—an *interesting rumor* file. Such things are not necessarily useful to you in making decisions which involve...lives."

Theo shook her head, Terran style.

"No?" He interpreted, and she managed a small laugh.

"I don't think I've ever had someone try so hard to convince me that I need to know something, Win Ton. So what is it you want to tell me—the coords to Temp Headquarters?"

He took a step back, face tightening, then softening into mere polite blandness again. "Those are not for me to know."

Theo looked hard at him.

"Does anyone know them?" she asked interestedly.

"That, I cannot say."

She let the pause lengthen, but he added nothing. *Bechimo* was in the background, measuring her heart rate, and probably Win Ton's, too.

"All right," she said at last. "What is it, Pilot yo'Vala, that the captain should know?"

Some tension went out of him and he bowed, acknowledging receipt of her permission.

"There exists an Yxtrang ambassador, Theo. He often travels, but he has his own very small embassy. It is on the border of the Clanave Sector and the Carresens' holdings. He may hold a...more viable solution for the pathfinders than either allowing them to...strike out on their own, or placing them in the care of the Scouts."

"An Yxtrang ambassador? Why would anyone let him run free?" The thought and the exclamation arrived together.

Win Ton outright grinned. "Did I say that the information protected itself by seeming to be nonsense? To the question—would you arrest the Yxtrang ambassador, Captain?"

She shook her head. "What would I do with an arrested Yxtrang?"

Win Ton bowed, very precisely, and well beyond the measures Theo had for such things, even reinforced with *Bechimo*'s notes. She thought she caught an edge of one of Padi's more ironic notations of a hit . . . delivered at its core.

"Indeed, what *would* you do with an arrested Yxtrang? Or, perhaps, two? Consider this carefully, my captain and my friend, very carefully. Never consider the pathfinders as mere passengers."

With that he bowed, slowly enough that she would be certain to read it correctly—*Thank you for listening*—and left her.

Theo sighed and *fuffed* her hair out of her eyes.

"*Bechimo*, did you record that?"

"It seemed prudent. Shall I delete?"

"No, keep it."

She sighed again.

An Yxtrang ambassador. Really?

"Are you able to verify this information?"

"I will search my files, as Win Ton suggested. If I have nothing, then verification must wait upon our arrival at a port."

"Right."

"What will you do, Theo?"

"Do? Well, first, I'm going to take a shower. And then . . . I'm going to hold this information until we can verify. Does that seem prudent to you?"

"Yes, Theo. It seems very prudent, indeed."

She grinned suddenly.

"See? I can learn, too."

CHAPTER NINETEEN

Bechimo

THE PATHFINDERS HAD FALLEN QUICKLY INTO ROUTINE. IT WAS, after all, a known routine, even a soothing one. *Mission prep*, that was it. They were quick studies, and they studied to good effect. As much as Ms loved battle, so did pathfinders find joy and purpose in study. Immediately, they had shortened their sleep shift; one read or compiled their notes while the other took learning in the device, which they had decided must be an acceptable risk. It would have been better to reserve one, and not risk both and the mission itself, on a device of which they must, by policy, be wary.

In the end, they *must* trust the device provisionally, for both needed language and information, and above all else, *context*. And information was more quickly gathered—and understood—when two harvested together.

Language learned in the manner of the device required periods of active practice or the learning would fall out of memory. They therefore spoke the Trade tongue to each other and read the texts provided by Joyita, reinforcing their ability to communicate.

Willingly would they have added another—or all!—of the several tongues spoken shipboard, but that had not been allowed.

One language at a time learned from the device, to avoid confusions, that was Joyita's advice, which the captain accepted, so they learned Trade with a ferocity that might have given even an M pause.

In addition to language, the device was able to impart history.

The process was finicky, but they quickly developed a system whereby one would, with assistance from Joyita most often, though Win Ton and even Clarence sometimes had suggestions to make— one would learn a particular event, or period, in broad outline and, after, read in more detail, thus reinforcing history and their grasp of the written form.

In truth, it was exhilarating, even as they learned the shape of a universe that was at once strange and dismaying.

There seemed, indeed, to be no ascendant civilian authority at the feet of which they might place their knives. Nor yet did there seem to be Troop. There was what they must suppose to be a splinter group, which named itself Troop, and held a so-called Temporary Headquarters. Those not of the group referred to them as Yxtrang, which was not a Troop designation—but no matter the name, it was apparent from the histories that they were not *Troop*, but pirates and marauders.

The pathfinders' routine included walks about the ship and time in the galley with whomever they found there, or only themselves, if they were askance the shifts. Though in truth, they rarely found themselves alone for the whole of a walkabout. Most often, they were joined by Win Ton or Clarence, less by Kara, and least often, the captain.

They never met Joyita during these small outings, though he was their frequent partner at study, available at the speaking of his name to suggest a text, a word, or an approach to further research. They would from time to time invite him to meet them in the galley, or to join them in walking about *Bechimo*'s few corridors, but always he declined.

Duty, he said, and he seemed to have a surfeit of it.

It was Chernak who found their duty in the matter of Joyita. This was not unusual, as she was both the elder and, of the two of them, held the sternest sense of duty.

When she brought the question to him, Stost admitted that he had been worried for some time about the lack of presence in someone who seemed to be always present.

"I placed the mission first, Elder," he'd said in the patois they spoke between themselves. "If we engage this and do not survive this journey to a place where duty resumes, the mission ends with us."

"So you thought to lie low?" There was no anger in her

question, nor any suggestion that he had placed his priorities wrongly. By this he knew that she had been considering the case for some time and had not arrived at her conclusions lightly.

"Yes," Stost said, "I thought to lie low."

"At first, I thought so, too," Chernak said. "Then I thought further. If this is an instance of the Enemy, then the mission is in danger, because the Enemy has become aware of us. We must *know*, Stost. And when we know, we must act without hesitation."

He sighed, but she was right.

"Yes," he said.

And so the plan was formed.

They had discovered in their chance-met conversations that, while Under-Captain Clarence was the most recent acquaintance of Captain Theo, it was Kara who was the most recent addition to the ship's company. She had shared training with the captain, and had come from a socially unstable world which had lately tipped itself into turmoil.

Kara was Liaden, as was Win Ton, though he hailed from what was dignified as the *homeworld*, as distinct from Kara's *outworld*. There was a difference also in training. Kara had trained as pilot and mechanic, while Win Ton had previously stood as a mentor to the captain, his titles and experience making him perhaps the equal of a pathfinder pilot. Clarence—an open and even voluble source of information—was of the opinion that Captain Theo had an edge on Win Ton, the student having outpaced the mentor.

There were no doubts expressed by any of the crew, at any point of conversation—no doubts *at all* of the captain's competency, young as she was. Neither was there any doubt expressed by crew of the competence of any other crew member. And, yes, in addition to other specialties—Captain Theo, Clarence, Kara, and Win Ton, each and every, was a pilot.

It was not said, if Joyita was likewise a pilot.

Yet, four pilots in a crew of five on a small tradeship?

That alone was cause for astonishment, nor, according to Clarence, was it an accident. Captain Theo had high expectations of her crew and involved them in ship's business to a notable degree.

"Consensus-building," Clarence had said with a laugh, and a look over her shoulder at Kara. "Young-learning sticks all the way down your life."

Kara had shaken her head at him.

"In truth, Theo would make a very bad tyrant."

"Now, I think she'd be a fine tyrant, myself," Clarence had countered. "An' it's all to her credit, that she works so hard against her nature."

The ship itself, proud *Bechimo*, was revered, as her battle scars deserved. A worthy ship, a ship of distinction, which had brought her crew safe out of not one, but several risky ventures. A good ship, a ship of many parts—and who could find fault with such?

During one break, Chernak and Stost found Clarence and Win Ton together in the galley. The discussion went wide, as it might when Clarence was involved, and somehow—ah, it had been their description of Grakow's attacks upon a handmade toy of stuffed cloth which Captain Theo had personally provided—that a discussion of violence had come to the fore.

"Cats can be cruel," Clarence said, "but only to a point. They'll attack a vulnerable toy, forget it, then go back to it, playing predator, almost like they're laughing at it. But they won't do that to a port rat—with rats, cats're pure business. You know, you might even call them a nexus of violence!"

He had laughed then, and Win Ton, too. Win Ton allowed the smile to openly linger, while Clarence's grin was broad and his eyes danced.

Stost had shared a glance with Chernak before venturing, "We are not much familiar with companion creatures. Is it a language lack that I do not see the joke?"

Win Ton's fingers had moved quickly, with what might have been a warning, but Clarence shrugged it off, a chuckle still sounding.

"Here's the joke, then, if you got time to hear a story," he said, settling back in his chair, as like one of the Troop preparing to entertain the mess with a ribald poem or an epic.

"Now, Captain Theo was sent to a piloting academy in order to learn what could be taught her," Clarence began, his voice taking on the rhythm of a storyteller. "Understand, in the normal way of things, she'd've never left her homeworld, and likely would've followed her mother's path to being a teacher and a researcher. By unlikeliest chance, she *did* leave her homeworld and came to the attention of a Scout, who not only realized what Theo was—or could be—but was able to take action on her behalf.

"What this Scout did was send Theo off to the Anlingdin Piloting Academy on Eylot World, and what you have to know about Eylot is that it was as full of politics as it was possible for one planet to be and not flash out into civil war."

"What prevented it?" asked Chernak, this naturally being of interest.

"Time," Clarence said promptly, "and proper agitation. It all come to a boil while Theo was on-world." He shook his head, sadly it seemed, but perhaps not, because Stost noted that his eyes danced still.

Clarence continued. "Long story short, the agitators needed a sacrifice to the war effort, and they figured Theo for easy prey. Apparently, they didn't bother to research their subject first."

"An error," Chernak put in. "Insufficient information can be fatal."

Clarence bestowed one of his more delighted smiles on her.

"Right you are. Now, in this case, there weren't any fatalities, but that wasn't the fault of the agitators.

"Them—well. They set a mob on her, near enough. Theo will tell you it was half-a-dozen bullies and four of 'em already drunk. Kara, who was there, will tell you it was a cadet class of forty, some carrying edges and bats, looking for somebody to hurt."

"The captain was injured?" Stost recalled the smallness of her. Quick, yes, and fierce, as they had seen, but even a pathfinder might be hurt if a mob fell upon him.

It was Win Ton who answered that question, fingers tossing something unreadable, but intent, at Clarence.

"Theo fought them to a standstill. She was injured, but not badly, nor were any who came against her *badly* injured. Or killed. Kara will tell you that as well."

His tone made it seem, subtly, that Win Ton felt it had been too bad that the captain had chosen to stay her hand.

"Were they disciplined?" Chernak demanded.

"It was not the first incident," Win Ton said, "and the mob was acting under direction. As Clarence said, they thought to make her an example, to their own profit."

"Stupid idea, from boots to hat." Clarence took up the narrative again. "It was Theo who got disciplined. The board ruled she was a 'nexus of violence' and threw her outta school, just short of finishing with her first class license."

Clarence had taken a long swallow from his mug then. When he put it down, he looked at them, one by one, his face more serious now.

"She had contacts—not just Scouts and pilots, but contacts on-world. Pretty quick, she was hired on as second board on a solid ship, where first was a good pilot—and patient, too."

"Now to be fair," Clarence went on, "they might have had a point about that nexus of violence, because people have taken shots at us—you'll have seen the marks on the hull, coming in like you did. Can't say we did one damned thing to bring it on, but—hey, speaking of Eylot. It did finally hit the flash point like I said, and the politics wanted to take over the station, too. That put pilots and long-time stationers at risk. So this ship—*us* and Captain Theo in the chair—we went to that station and we took off pilots and crew before anybody got hurt—and more than one ship followed our lead."

He leaned back in his chair and nodded.

"Throw her out? Tell her never to come back? Didn't she just spit in their eyes and come away with the official gratitude of the Pilots Guild *and* an ambassador on board to boot."

He nodded at them, smiling again.

"So there, Laughing Cat on the hull was her own idea, and her own business. Plays hard, does Captain Theo; she's always practicing, always alert, and knows the difference between a toy threat and a real rat."

"But she never finished...this piloting academy?"

"Got her first class Jump ticket flying, the old-fashioned way. Master pilot gave her the tests, and her training pilot gave her the jacket. Got hired as a courier pilot for a...pretty demanding employer, that was before she come to *Bechimo*. Don't you doubt her piloting, now. Kara—same school, right, but kept her head down, graduated with a second class provisional, which she was better than, but that's what happens when you let politics in the door. All that got straightened out with the Pilots Guild, on-station."

Win Ton had risen then.

"My shift begins," he said and, with a small bow, left them.

Clarence glanced at the clock and raised a hand to stifle a yawn.

"And it's my rest shift," he said wryly. "Any other stories you'd like me to tell, you wait 'til next time we're together."

They'd left soon after Clarence, walking slow and thoughtful back to their suite and their studies. They had a possible course now. An entry point to the truth.

Kara.

The youngest, the lowest rated pilot, the last hire, the newest crew.

CHAPTER TWENTY

. . . .

Bechimo
Among the Sweet Growing Things

IT WAS HER HABIT TO LOCK OPEN THE DOOR TO HYDROPONICS while she tended to the plants and the equipment. Hevelin most usually accompanied her, sitting on her shoulder and commenting on this and that. This shift, he was uncommonly chatty, sharing news of Grakow, whom he had visited recently in the pathfinders' rooms, and putting forth the opinion that the cat ought to be allowed the run of the ship, as Hevelin was, himself.

"You must convince Theo of that necessity, my friend," Kara answered, speaking to him aloud, as was her habit. "And then, you must convince *Bechimo*. Best, perhaps, to allow Grakow the comforts of the pathfinders' suite, where his opportunities to find trouble are limited."

She was allowed to know, in Hevelin's peculiar dialect, that Grakow was a peace-loving and sensible creature and, besides, he would have Hevelin to guide him and Hevelin *never* got into trouble.

"Now that is very true," Kara said. "You are never in trouble. But that is because you are overindulged."

That gained her such a sense of self-important preening that she laughed as she opened the door to Forcing Room Three.

Warmth greeted her entrance. The tree did not grant her visions, as it did to Theo, but she never failed of feeling welcomed when she came to check on it. Hevelin grew quiet, though she retained a muted sense of his communication. It was very much like hearing a conversation through a wall—voices carried somewhat, but individual words were lost.

She checked the readouts first, finding that all was well. They appeared to have found a mixture of moisture, light, and temperature that was most beneficial to the tree's continued good health. In the short time it had been on board, it had grown two pods, which Hevelin had stolen. Theo had told her this, speaking of norbear overindulgence, and asked her to be especially attentive, in case the tree should show some harm from either the effort or the theft.

In fact, the tree had shown quite the opposite. It had started two new branches and had definitely leafed out. Those new leaves were a deeper, glossier shade of green than the dusty grey-green of the older leaves.

Kara turned from the instruments to do a visual inspection and walk-around. Hevelin, his voice still muted, extended a paw and touched a leaf very gently, as if he was touching the cheek of a child.

There were, she saw, several pods starting—eight by her count, but she might have missed any number hidden among the leaves.

"Do be prudent," she murmured. "We don't wish you to overexert yourself. You might also give some thought to your height. If you become much taller, we will not be able to extract you when it becomes time to do so."

There was a rustle, as of leaves moving in a sudden breeze, though the airflow in the forcing room was constant. She felt a cool tickle on the back of her neck, which may have equally been imagination or communication.

Kara shook her head in bemusement. If her life had gone as planned, she would even now be living in the clanhouse on Eylot, and a junior mechanic-pilot in the clan's business. Instead, politics had seen her exiled in fact, if not in name, from her homeworld, crew aboard a sentient ship, where a second machine sentience sat as comm officer, and crewmate.

That would be strange enough for any two lives, but Kara ven'Arith was more fortunate than most. In addition to the independent self-aware logics, she had daily interaction with a norbear, who was proving himself to be something rather more than a simple barometer for emotion, and a handy sort of pet for Pilots Guild guildmasters.

She had also lately added to her list of acquaintances a possibly talking but definitely sentient tree and two Yxtrang soldiers from a universe that had ceased to exist hundreds and hundreds of Standards in the past.

To round out, the self-aware ship had been designed as a long-looper, and traveled on contract under the Tree-and-Dragon. Routine business, which in these times included being stalked and fired upon.

"My life," Kara said, possibly to Hevelin, possibly to the tree or to *Bechimo*, who she was certain listened, even when he did not speak. "If my life were to become less interesting, I would not regret it."

There came another loud rustle of leaves—did trees, even sentient trees, laugh?

Hevelin murbled from his perch on her shoulder and patted her hair lightly.

"Thank you," Kara said. "I appreciate your sympathy."

She concluded her walkabout, made a note in the log, and turned to face the tree.

"You will be pleased to know that, by every measure I am competent to make, you are healthy. You may also be pleased to learn that the captain has authorized the construction of a wheeled conveyance, so that you may be moved about the ship and, particularly, to the bridge. Hevelin has been your staunch advocate; you may thank him as appropriate."

From Hevelin, then, she received a vivid picture of *Spiral Dance*'s bridge, and the tree grey-taped to the copilot's chair.

"Indeed, the tree *has* been a pilot," she murmured, glancing once more at the control board, to be certain of the settings.

"Good shift, Tree," she said. "We will be in the big room. Should you need us, only call out."

· · · ❄ · · ·

Stost paused outside the open door, listening. Kara was often accompanied by the norbear ambassador Hevelin. It appeared that this shift was no different than others in that regard. The norbear ambassador . . . was a concern. He and Chernak had read the histories, and the survey reports suggested by Joyita, regarding these creatures. The documentation would have them as native to this new universe, discovered some number of years in the past. Their inclination to form connections and to project those connections via a natural and, so stated the documentation, minor empathic ability was found to be useful to such persons as guild- and portmasters. Hevelin's personal history included long years as companion creature and reader of emotions to a master of the Pilots Guild.

Norbears were said to be sentient, but not intelligent; they made no tools, though some had been observed to use tools. They were not considered a risk of any kind. By anyone.

Hevelin had several times come to their suite in order to visit Grakow. There had been no repeat of the incident involving Chernak, though Hevelin made certain to greet them each with what, Chernak had speculated, might be the norbear equivalent of a comradely wrist grip.

"Yes," Kara said from inside the hydroponics room, "I'll be forming the pot as soon as I get back to the shop... Yes, it will have wheels! Indeed, I have no doubt that it will be so much nicer for everyone... No, I don't know any other traveling trees... Madoes, yes, we grow them so they travel with us... What is that? Madoes are boring and don't know anything? And yet you enjoy your madoes, do you not? In fact, you might enjoy them just a little... Excuse me? Madoes know they're thirsty and that's all?"

She laughed.

"I'll take your word for that, my friend. Now, if you please, I must have less society, so that I may perform my calibrations. Perhaps you might like to visit the long grasses? Thank you..."

Stost took a quiet breath and slipped silently into the room.

· · · ❋ · · ·

Make no mistake, Brulilt System was boring.

Win Ton had gone to get tea.

"*Strong* tea," he'd said, coming out of his chair into a long, interesting stretch. "We must, after all, set a good example for Joyita."

Joyita, head bent over some work on his desk, didn't even look up. If he'd been flesh and bone, Theo would have suspected that he was having a catnap for himself.

Theo sat up straighter and glared at her screens, which did not oblige her by showing anything more interesting than rocks and drab space.

You wanted boring, she reminded herself. At least, you didn't want any more flotsam.

"Theo." *Bechimo's* voice was soft inside her ear, and she was, abruptly and simultaneously, concerned, confused, and on high alert. Which were, she understood, *Bechimo's emotions*, which in turn triggered a state of high alert in her.

"I believe there is a situation developing in the hydroponics bay."

This was Kara's shift in 'ponics. But—a *situation*? Had one of the units—

"Kara and Hevelin went to hydroponics, as per schedule," *Bechimo* continued. "Stost arrived later, having gone by the most direct route from the pathfinders' suite. He then stood outside the door, making no attempt to announce himself, listening, I believe, to Kara talking with Hevelin.

"When Kara suggested that Hevelin leave her to work for a time, Stost entered the room, moving with extreme care."

Theo's heart was racing now. Stost was stalking Kara? That was—Kara had distrusted the pathfinders from the start. But surely he wasn't going to hurt—

"I am unsure of Stost's motivations and cannot discern his intentions. I am monitoring. I detect no overt signs of anger or hostility in Stost. His readings are completely calm."

Stost was an Yxtrang soldier, Theo thought. She'd lately been reading way too much about Yxtrang soldiers: the design, care, and keeping thereof—including the information that conflict was their natural emotional environment. Stost with violence on his mind might well be perfectly calm.

"I'm going up there," she snapped. She leapt from her chair— and froze, meeting Win Ton's eyes as he stepped into the bridge bearing two mugs.

"There's a situation in 'ponics," she told him. "I'm on it. Joyita!"

"Yes, Theo?"

"Where is Chernak?"

"At study, in the pathfinders' suite."

"Lock the door. I don't want her wandering the halls," Theo said. She looked back to Win Ton. His face was completely emotionless, like it had been when he stood witness to her bonding with *Bechimo*.

"Get Clarence to the bridge, quietly," she said. "We're on alert. *Bechimo*, brief them."

• • • ❖ • • •

Hydroponics was peaceful, especially now that her chatty companion was amusing himself elsewhere. Kara checked the instruments first, as she always did, and logged her readings. In theory, *Bechimo* could transmit the readings to her at any hour, or hourly, at her station, obviating the need for her to spend a half-shift every three in the 'ponics room.

In the case, theory was misleading, for plants were more subtle than mere instruments. The readings might all and each of them be good: humidity within tolerances, light levels steady, cycles in sync—and still the peas planted in row eight might fail.

Her aunt Feramayn had insisted that plants liked companionship just as much as anybody else and, without it, would wither and fail to thrive. There had been chairs set out in her garden, and the elders of the clan could often be found there of a sunny morning or afternoon, talking with each other or silently communing with the plants, while the gardener herself more often than not sang as she worked.

Aunt Feramayn's vegetables routinely won prizes at the agricultural shows, and her flower gardens were consistently rated among the best on Eylot. She was certainly an expert, and it was never wise to ignore an expert's advice.

Therefore, after logging her readings, Kara walked 'round the 'ponics room, stopping at each growing table to run her hands over the plants and murmur occasional pleased compliments. This system also allowed her to thin overgrown sections and cull any plants which seemed less than perfectly robust.

She hummed a little as she worked, soothed by the simple connection with growing things. So must Hevelin feel, when he was among his leaves. Certainly, he trilled and murbled over them.

In the back corner of the room, farthest from the open door, she was humming over a tray of madoes. She did not hear him, but she saw a shadow move where there ought to have been no shadows. Kara spun away from the table, as much as she could in this cramped space, dropping into the core *menfri'at* stance: centered, legs flexed, hands ready. Her heart was pounding in her ears. She ignored it.

Stost, for it was Stost whose shadow she had seen, stopped where he was, at the intersection of four rows, which handily boxed her in. He raised his hands to belt height, palms out.

"Kara," he said. "No threat, Kara. I need to ask. I need to *know.*"

She took a deep breath, keeping her eyes on his broad, stoic face.

"Ask what?" she demanded; it wasn't sensible, the fear constricting her stomach. Stost was civilized; he had not offered them any threat or harm. She knew that.

But some part of her, that knew other, darker things, was focused on the fact that here was an Yxtrang; that Yxtrang preyed, especially, on Liadens; and that she was alone here, with the enemy of her race.

She swallowed, holding her stance. She ought to calm herself, she thought, but she did not care to remove her attention from Stost for even the few seconds required to mentally review a relaxation...

He took one step forward, and bent, perhaps in an attempt to put himself more on her plane. Or perhaps, whispered that darker part of herself, to more easily deal a blow. She held firm with an effort, while her heartbeat spiked.

"Kara, we must know. We must understand this thing and know if our mission is in danger. Is it so that this Joyita—*is Joyita the ship?* Is the ship alive, with us in its belly?"

Kara moved, a feint to the right, though there was no place for her to go to the right or to the left. But if she could put him off-center for a moment, it would give *Bechimo* time, perhaps to act. *Bechimo* was watching this, wasn't he? Didn't—

Stost spread his arms, hands open, boxing her more tightly.

"I have to know, Kara. *We* have to know. We have a mission. Are we foredoomed to fight the Enemy here? Is this ship one of the Great Works?"

"I don't know what—" she began, but even as she spoke, she saw Stost's eyes widen. An orange and grey blur moved along the misting tube to her right, resolving into Hevelin as he came to rest on the tube between her and Stost. In that position, he was very nearly eye to eye with the Yxtrang.

Warily, Stost straightened, hands still turned palm out.

"No threat," he said again and raised one hand, forefinger extended, toward Hevelin, as he would greet Grakow.

Hevelin *hissed*.

CHAPTER TWENTY-ONE

· ·

Bechimo
Pathfinders' Temporary Base

CHERNAK PUSHED BACK FROM HER STUDY SCREEN AND SPOKE SO softly she scarcely heard her own voice.

"Joyita, are you there?"

The screen, which had been displaying the at-rest display—a calming swirl of blues and greens—flickered, and there he was, just as always.

Joyita had very good ears, of this they were certain.

He was in his chair. There was a mug near his hand that bore the four rings of brown-pink metal. Visible behind him were the usual screens.

She and Stost had excellent observational skills, and they knew ships. They had seen and concentrated on the shape of *Bechimo* during the initial encounter, and while they had each considered type and mass, they had also noted easy details such as the likely conning zone, apparent view ports and hatches, mount sites and mounted objects, the shape...

Clearly the engines were somewhere and the crew somewhere else.

And yet...where was Joyita's comm tower, from which he never emerged?

On those frequent occasions when they met others of the crew in the mess, they had sometimes shared food and often they drank together.

But the comm officer, for all his ubiquity as librarian and vocal go-between, the comm officer—did not eat. His several cups and mugs appeared on his desk or, occasionally, in his hand, but never in the common areas where Kara, Theo, Clarence, and Win Ton each had their favorite drinking vessels, nor in the wash-up unit.

But Joyita...He was never mentioned as at exercise, he was available instantaneously at any and all hours, and as Stost had pointed out to her, he had no history other than the histories he shared from the library.

On a ship such as *Bechimo*, where comrades shared experience, and knew much of each other's lives before the ship?

Did not Clarence mention the names of mates who dealt with dockside thieves and the shipping of cat food? Did not Win Ton mention this clan and that, and from time to time, this world and that? Had not Captain Theo been mentored and taught by several named persons, landing on this world and orbiting that? Some of Kara's instructors shared names with some of Captain Theo's, and her family...

Yet among such a talkative crew, where the comm officer knew the state of the ship at all moments, the whereabouts of all crew, the schedule and the time—there was no mention of a shared past with Joyita, nor did he himself mention comrades not present, or tales out of school; the names of favored mentors, nor worlds where temptations had been accepted, no regrets.

"I am here, Chernak," Joyita said, looking at her, and for a moment it was all bright foolishness, for how could those eyes, dark and bitter and knowing, belong to—

She cleared her throat. The Enemy's deceptions had been many and artful, and wore what seeming they would. Remember, she told herself, the children, so pretty and so small, with the death of a fortress and all who had manned it on the tips of their rosy fingers.

"I wonder," she said aloud in this time and place, "if I might visit you in your tower? I have a matter to discuss which is..."

Her voice faltered as she met his eyes.

He smiled, fierce and proud, and pushed back into his chair, his arms straight before him and his hands against the edge of his desk.

"I see that I have been maladroit," he said.

Chernak's mouth dried. If Joyita *was* the ship and a Great Work, then she was a dead soldier, and Stost, too, unless—

Joyita turned his head abruptly away from her, snapping forward in his chair as if he had seen an alert on one of the background screens. When he turned back, his face was grim.

"The door to your suite has been locked," he said, "captain's orders. Please remain calm."

Chernak took another breath and asked calmly, "Where is Stost?"

"Stost is in hydroponics."

She decided not to risk his temper by asking Stost's condition.

"Thank you," she said and composed herself to wait.

· · · ✳ · · ·

Bechimo updated her on Kara's situation as she turned the hall into 'ponics.

"Tell her I'm coming," Theo said—or meant to say—and slowed from a run to a rapid walk as she moved through the open door. Hydroponics was a crowded room; best not to run.

According to *Bechimo*, there wasn't any *reason* to run now.

"Theo?" Kara called. "I am in back, by the madoes!"

"Coming," she said, rounding the corner.

She stopped.

Stost was flat on his back on the deck. Kara was kneeling next to him, a wad of absorbent toweling in her hand. The toweling was red.

"Is he—"

"I think he hit his head on the corner of the tray when he fell. Really, as large as he is, it's a marvel he didn't do more damage—to the plants or to himself! Scan shows no harm, other than the cut. He seems to be...sleeping. Brain activity is consistent with a dream state."

Theo stepped forward and knelt on Stost's other side. Information...she knew Stost was sleeping; there was a finger-long cut on the right side of his head, which was bleeding, but which wasn't, she knew with a certainty that must have been *Bechimo*'s, life-threatening.

"What happened?"

Kara sat back on her heels and pushed the hair off her forehead with the back of one hand.

"He—surprised me. He said he *needed* to know, because of their mission..." She shook her head.

"I was . . . frightened, and Hevelin—Hevelin must have understood that because he came racing to my rescue along the mister rods, stopped about six centimeters from Stost's nose and—Theo, he *growled*! I've *never* heard Hevelin growl!"

"Me, neither. He must've been trying to make a point. Where is he now?"

Kara looked down.

"Well, Rogue? Here is the captain, come in all haste. How will you explain yourself to her?"

A rusty orange shadow moved by Kara's knee, as Hevelin used Stost's belt to haul himself to the downed man's abdomen. He bumbled over to Theo, and she helped him up onto her shoulder.

"What did you do?" she asked.

She received a flutter of hesitation and a strong sense of reluctance.

"You don't have to do it to me," she said. "But I need you to tell me what you did to Stost. Did you hurt him?"

Vehement denial.

"That's good to know," Theo said honestly. "Will he wake up?"

Yes, of course Stost would wake up. That was conveyed with a slightly wounded air.

"Also good to know," said Theo, pausing before she asked, "*When* will Stost wake up?"

Indeterminate. She was left with the impression that the waking-up part of the process was entirely up to Stost.

Theo sighed and looked to Kara, who was kneeling, head down and shoulders rounded in an entirely un-Kara-like attitude, the bloody toweling clutched against her knee.

"Kara?" she murmured, thinking, *She's not hurt. Surely Bechimo would have told me if Kara had been hurt!*

Kara raised her head. Her face was drawn and rather pale.

"*Are* you hurt?" Theo demanded, extending a hand across Stost.

Kara sighed, got one hand free of the toweling, and met Theo halfway. Her fingers were cold.

"I'm not hurt, Theo," she said. "Only frightened."

"Do you know what Stost was trying to do? He threatened you?"

"No . . ." Kara frowned and shook her head.

"He said *no threat* several times, but he was clearly trying to block me, to keep me at the end of the corridor, and I—panicked.

I tried to feint, and then Hevelin—bah! I am disordered! I ask your pardon."

"No, it's okay. I'd be disordered, too, if I'd heard Hevelin hiss."

From the norbear on her shoulder came a feeling of smug satisfaction. Kara snorted a laugh.

"It was . . . startling. As to what Stost wanted . . . he wanted to know if—if Joyita was the ship, and if the ship was a Great Work."

"A Great Work?"

"It is what he said. I was about to tell him that I didn't understand, when Hevelin leapt forward to defend my honor."

"By growling and doing—something . . ."

"Whereupon Stost stepped back, as if he had, indeed, been struck—and fell, senseless, to the deck." Kara looked wry. "As you see him, even now."

"Hevelin—" Theo began, and stopped as a picture began to form in her head.

She was suddenly facing a large, doglike creature. It had a long muzzle full of sharp teeth which were *much* too close to her face; so close, she could smell the stink of blood on its breath. There were others behind her, she knew it, and she knew they were hers to protect. She gathered her . . . brought all of her . . . to the front of her mind, leaned forward, hissed—and *pushed*.

The dog-thing squealed, once.

And collapsed.

Theo felt a thrill of horror.

"Is Stost damaged?" she demanded.

A strong negative from Hevelin. She caught a faint whisper in what might have been Clarence's voice, "That's one way to get an education."

Theo looked at Kara and shook her head.

"Stost isn't damaged and Hevelin might have taught him something. Or not. Apparently, the growl is reserved for predators, who fall over, stunned or dead, when it's unleashed."

Kara sighed.

"Then I am triply pleased that Hevelin has never had occasion to educate one of us," Kara said and looked down at Stost, still sleeping quietly.

"Shall I fetch a blanket? Certainly, we can't carry him to a more comfortable situation."

Inside her head, Theo felt a click, and a sense of engagement.

For a couple of seconds, she had three viewpoints, then the sensation faded, and she blinked at Kara.

"One of the remote sleds is on the way," she said. "We'll lower the bed, roll Stost onto it and take him back to Chernak."

"She will be pleased to see him in such a case," Kara said drily.

"Stost takes his orders from Chernak," Theo said. "She probably sent him to . . . get information from you. From *you*, specifically, here in the 'ponics room where Joyita doesn't have a screen, asking questions about a living ship . . ."

Kara's eyes had widened. She pressed her lips together and nodded.

Theo felt the sled slide comfortingly over her skin and stood up, offering a hand to Kara.

"Sled's here," Theo said.

· · · ※ · · ·

"Are you the ship?" Chernak asked.

Joyita shook his head.

"I am not the ship."

"But you are a Work, even if not a Great one."

"I believe that I don't understand your terminology," he said. He glanced aside, as if at a readout, and returned his dark gaze to her.

"Stost approaches, escorted by Captain Waitley, Pilot ven'Arith, and Ambassador Hevelin."

"An honor guard, indeed," Chernak said and pressed her lips together. With such an escort, Stost had taken no lasting harm, and that . . . relieved her.

"Please remain where you are," Joyita said. "Door opening in 3 . . . 2 . . ."

On his *one*, the hall door opened to admit Captain Waitley, with Kara visible in the hall behind. Of Stost, who ought to have been perfectly visible, Chernak saw nothing.

Once clear of the door, Captain Waitley stepped aside, to allow the utility sled to move deeper into the room: the sled bearing Stost—limp, lifeless, and bloodied—with the norbear sitting tall on his chest, a diminutive, furry hunter proudly displaying its trophy.

Someone cried out—a wordless thing that was half battle cry and half despair—and Chernak was on her knees at the side of the sled, which had stopped, and the creature was gone, leaving Stost—Stost . . .

"Stost!"

His eyes were closed, and it struck her, like a knife to the gut, that she would never again see herself reflected in them, nor hear his voice, nor feel his hand. She had no one to guard her offside now; no one to mount watch while she slept; no one to watch for; no one...

"Chernak!"

A shadow moved. On her knees, she spun to face it—her.

Captain Waitley's pale face showed... pity.

"Chernak, Stost is not dead."

She stared. The words made no sense for a moment. The little captain must have seen as much, for she bent over Stost and placed her fingers on the pulse point under his jaw.

"Alive," she said. "He's sleeping."

"*Sleeping?*" she repeated and placed her own fingers to the pulse, felt it beating calm, steady, and strong. Strangely, the knife in her gut twisted harder, and she gritted her teeth.

"When will he wake?" she managed to ask, around the pain.

"Soon. We hope. Will you put him to bed, and then tell us—what is a Great Work?"

· · · ✳ · · ·

"Stost has been received by Chernak," *Bechimo* said.

"How'd she take it?" Clarence asked.

"She reacted with strong dismay, having leapt to a theory unsupported by logic—that Stost was dead. Once Theo showed her the error in her reasoning, she became less dismayed."

Win Ton shifted in his chair, and Clarence threw him a grin.

"He'd've said, I think, if Chernak's dismay had led her to trying to hurt anybody."

"I did come to that conclusion, after a moment's thought," Win Ton said gravely.

"There was no reason for Chernak to harm anyone," *Bechimo* said, sounding slightly aggrieved.

"Now, you and me, we agree," Clarence said. "You'll have noticed that, with humans, sometimes dismay disconnects the logic circuits."

There was a small, palpably disapproving pause before *Bechimo* spoke again.

"Theo, Kara, Joyita, Hevelin, and Chernak are going to speak

together, regarding the pathfinders' necessities. Will the bridge observe?"

"The bridge will observe," Clarence agreed promptly. "Might as well everybody be on the same page."

"With the exception," Win Ton said, as a window opened in the bottom right corner of his secondary screen, "of Stost, who is sleeping."

CHAPTER TWENTY-TWO

Bechimo
Conference Circle

THEY SHARED JUICE OUT OF THE COLDBOX RATIONS AND SAT IN a circle on the floor. The circle included Hevelin and Joyita. Sitting circle for such things was common across their cultures—well, Chernak corrected herself. Work circles were known across the cultures represented by Captain Theo, Tech Kara, and herself. Perhaps Hevelin had familiarity, also, through his webwork of contacts. But, who could know what...a Work such as Joyita might think or know of circles? He had only nodded when the little captain proposed the formation.

Chernak paused and sipped juice before she continued.

"Formidable as they were, the Enemy did not limit itself to organic weapons. It also created...machines. Some were small, so that you could hold them in your hand or slip one in your pocket. It would then influence the fool who had taken it up and gradually enlist them to the Enemy's cause.

"Others were larger in scale—self-directed units of destruction. They were...machines, but self-aware. Some looked like armored vehicles, others looked like armored men. Some...were ships. Still others ate worlds, as you or I would eat a piece of cheese. A very few were space stations.

"The world-eaters and the stations, those were the Greatest Works. They were, as I said, self-directed, *alive*, and wholly in service to the Enemy."

She took more juice and found that she had not quite exhausted her topic.

"The Great Works... one appeared about Planet Tinsori, at the site of a station that had been destroyed in the First Phase. It was as if the Enemy was making reparations. The Troop would have seen it destroyed, but it was in civilian space; the natives claimed it for themselves, the convenience—the symmetry—blinding them to their danger.

"On that world, there was a religious order, the initiates of which had long studied the Works and had developed tools and techniques for neutralizing them. Tinsori set a group of such initiates upon the—Tinsori Light, they called it, after the other, which had been destroyed. They trusted that the initiates would influence the agent of the Enemy to forsake its duty."

She drained what was left in her cup.

"Did they?" asked Captain Theo. "Influence the Light to forsake its duty?"

Chernak turned her hands palm up.

"There was no news of massacre out of that sector before the Retreat, which the histories we have been reading style the Great Migration."

She sighed and said, formally, "I have finished."

Captain Theo nodded, but did not immediately speak. Chernak closed her eyes, concentrated on her breathing, and tried not to think of Stost, asleep and most ably guarded by Grakow.

"The Enemy," Captain Theo said at last, "remained in the Old Universe."

Chernak opened her eyes.

"So your histories state," she said politely.

"You do not believe the histories?" Kara asked.

Chernak looked at her and at Hevelin curled beside her.

"I have seen what I have seen," she said carefully. "And I have seen evidence that following the First Phase, the Enemy rewrote histories and records from afar, in order to sow chaos and to hide those points at which it was vulnerable. We—The Enemy did not win the First Phase, but neither did those who opposed the Enemy. The opposition had developed weapons, and they were sufficiently potent that the Enemy chose to withdraw, and for a time to work from afar. Where the weapons had been stockpiled, the records were altered, the stockpiles lost. The true outcome of the First Phase itself was miscast to teach that the Enemy had been routed, and so complaisance was sown..."

She looked up then, into Joyita's face. He smiled at her and shook his head.

"Right," said Captain Theo. "You don't trust the histories."

"If you trust none of our records, nor our own account of ourselves..." Kara began.

"It's not necessary that Chernak believe the records," Joyita said. "In fact, it's better if she continues to question—everything. After all, she's a pathfinder. I imagine that a pathfinder, like a Scout, will stop asking questions only when she has no breath left to ask them."

That was apt, and Chernak smiled.

"You give an accurate accounting of us," she admitted, and turned her head at the sound of a footstep as familiar to her as her own heartbeat.

Stost stepped into the room, accompanied by Grakow, tail held tall and proud.

He stopped to see them all in circle, and Joyita in his screen a part of it. Grakow continued into the formation and butted heads with Hevelin.

Chernak came to her feet to face him.

"Are you well, Pathfinder Stost?"

"Yes, Pathfinder Chernak. I am well."

"And your wound? Will your wound present a problem?"

He raised a hand to his temple, face wry.

"My wound will not present a problem. I have learned much, Pathfinder Chernak, to the good of the Troop."

She saw it in him and raised the soft fist in acknowledgment.

"We will debrief later. For now, will you join us at work?"

"Yes," he said and came forward to take his place at her side.

· · · ✳ · · ·

"Joyita's got something up his sleeve," Clarence commented.

"I wonder if Theo knows what it is," Win Ton murmured, his eyes on the larger screens.

Dust and rock, and more of the same. Occasionally, something would spark in the sullen prospect, or something would—

"Jump glare!" he said sharply—and immediately doubted himself, for the screens were muddy and the instruments showing calm...

"Nothing seen here," Clarence said.

"No, nor here, now," Win Ton admitted. "A reflection, then? *Bechimo*?"

"Break-in pattern acquired; match program running."

There was silence on the bridge, then, while the ship worked. Clarence worked his scans hard, while Win Ton reset his board. In the right bottom corner of the screen, Kara was pouring juice into cups 'round the circle and—

"I have a match," *Bechimo* stated, and Win Ton felt a thrill of relief.

"Don't keep us in suspense," Clarence said, glancing toward the ceiling.

"No. It is the ship I encountered once before at this location. I was not able to get an accurate reading, then or now. It may equally be a pirate ship, or one such as myself. Previously, they were as anxious not to be seen as I had been."

"Increase shielding," Win Ton said.

"Certainly, Pilot, if it will make you feel safer. I do not believe that the other ship will approach us."

"Best to make sure there's no misunderstandings," Clarence said. "Just in case they don't follow the same pattern as before."

"Agreed," Win Ton said.

"Shielding increased," *Bechimo* said.

· · · ✳ · · ·

"What you need to know," Theo said slowly, "is that you *can't know* everything about us. This ship, this crew—we're unique. We hold secrets, because everyone holds secrets. For instance..." She looked from Chernak to Stost.

"For instance," she said again, "you each brought a case aboard my ship. While you willingly relinquished your clothes and your weapons, you kept those cases and hid them."

She glanced to Joyita, who gave her a wry smile and a shrug.

"Because we asked you to relinquish your weapons, we assume that the contents of those cases is something...other...than weapons. We make that assumption because you are honorable people. We do not, even now, ask what is in those cases, because *we* are civilized people and know that everyone holds secrets. We trust that you have not endangered us with yours."

She paused for a sip of juice and looked at Kara, who was watching her closely, her face smooth and calm.

"Continuing on that same course, we don't intend to endanger you with our secrets. Luck—" she stopped herself, just, from wrinkling her nose and made a mental note to ask Anthora, the next time they met, if it was possible to *get rid* of Korval's so-called *luck*.

"Luck brought us together, and we intend, frankly, that you won't be long among us. You have your mission and we—I won't hide from you; I *can't* hide from you!—that we're an odd ship. We're also a dangerous ship to be associated with. You don't *want* our secrets. I would guess that your own are dangerous enough."

She paused and placed her right hand over her heart, looking from Kara to Chernak, to Stost, to Joyita.

"I certify, on my honor as captain, that the ship *Bechimo* is *not* a Great Work. The ship has provenance. We know who financed her construction; we know her birth yard and the date that she was put out to space."

She lowered her hand.

"Does this satisfy?"

Chernak saluted, and Stost did.

"Captain, your oath puts our concerns to rest."

That might or might not be true, Theo thought. But as long as they all remained civilized and pretended that no one was concerned or afraid, they ought to get through this next stage without anyone taking harm.

"As for the crew—" She shook her head and turned her hands palm up.

"You know some of our minor secrets. For instance, you surely know that I'm a so-called nexus of violence, because Clarence doesn't miss a chance to tell that story. But you don't know who Clarence was before he came to sit second on this ship.

"You know that Win Ton is, like you, an explorer of the starways. You do not know what brought him to this ship—and you don't *need* to know.

"Nor do you need to know how Kara landed on this deck, or all the ports Hevelin has seen in a long life of travel."

"Captain," Chernak said, saluting again.

"One secret that we *can* share," Joyita said, "is the secret of my nature. I am not the ship; I am, in fact, the comm officer. I am...an experiment. I also have provenance; I know who is responsible for my being present on this ship. The captain and crew share this information."

He paused and looked at Theo, who reminded herself that Joyita's judgment was sound—most of the time, even when she didn't know what he had in mind—and signed for him to continue.

"Thank you, Captain. I am, as I said, an experiment: Can a fully aware, unique logical system become, let us say, human? I have bent every effort to not only learning to be an individual, but to appear as a human to humans. I'd thought—" Here he looked wryly at Chernak.

"I thought that I was progressing well, but obviously, I made errors. Errors that endangered the crew, the ship, and the pathfinders. I would ask, with the captain's permission, that the pathfinders, who are, after all, trained observers, be allowed to assist me by pointing out my errors and by suggesting ways in which I might improve myself."

"I have no objection," the captain said, "if the pathfinders are able and willing to assist you."

Chernak and Stost exchanged a glance. It was Chernak who spoke.

"Captain, we would be pleased to assist you—and Joyita—in this experiment. We must point out, however, that illusion goes only so far. If there is no tower, nor comm officer inside it..."

"Agreed," Joyita said crisply. "I am working on solutions at those fronts."

Was he? Theo thought. That was...interesting.

"Are we agreed, then?" she asked the circle at large. "The pathfinders will study, and assist Joyita as they may. The ship and crew will do what the ship and crew does. We will enjoy the comradeship of the pathfinders and Grakow, while they are with us, but we all agree that we will be parting ways in a very short time."

"How short a time," Chernak asked, "Captain?"

"As soon as we can find you a safe harbor. We're compiling options and will present them to you within the next four shifts."

"Thank you, Captain," Chernak said and looked to Stost.

"We will increase our study shifts to battle prep status."

"Don't endanger yourselves," Captain Waitley warned.

"No, Captain," Chernak said. "This is a known protocol. We will take proper precautions so that we are fit and alert when it comes time to debark and forward our mission."

"Excellent. This work session is finished. The circle may open."

She stood, bent to offer Kara a hand, and helped her to her feet.

"Thank you," Kara said, bending down in turn to pick up Hevelin and bring him to her shoulder.

"We leave you now to your studies and the discussion of your duties," Theo said to the pathfinders. Both saluted.

· · · ✳ · · ·

"Joyita sets himself up as a shield for *Bechimo*," Win Ton murmured. "There is only one self-aware logic present . . . and he is not the ship."

"Joyita is in no danger," *Bechimo* stated.

"That's right," Clarence said comfortably. "Good piece of fancy dancing, on the part of the comm tech and the captain."

"Did it sound to you as if Theo will be moving very soon?" asked Win Ton.

"It did. But if we wait a couple minutes, we can ask her."

The door to the bridge opened with a snap and Theo strode in, Kara and Hevelin some paces behind her.

"Crew meeting," she said, sounding tired and snappish and nervy. She ran her hands through her hair.

"Wait," she said. "First, I felt something—almost like Jump flare—when I was in the meeting. Do we have visitors?"

Felt something? Clarence thought, but did not ask, given her current testy nature. Win Ton was already answering the captain's question, his face full Liaden and smooth.

"We entertained a visitor very briefly, Captain. *Bechimo* IDs as a vessel he has met in this space before, which is known to be of a retiring nature. Shielding has been increased, as a precaution only."

"Good," she said briefly. "*Bechimo*?"

"I believe that we are in no danger from that ship, Captain. The last time we sighted each other, it was quick to hide."

"Good," she said again.

"Want your chair back, Captain?" Clarence asked.

"No," she said, moving over to the observer's station and pulling out the stool. "You keep the chair and the watch. This shouldn't take long."

He nodded and ostentatiously gave his attention to the screens, while she closed her eyes and did some deep breathing and, probably, a quick calming dance inside her head.

Felt that ship come in-system, had she? That bonding had gone deeper than he'd hoped, and for a moment he imagined he was facing Daav yos'Phelium and trying to explain what it was that Clarence O'Berin had let his daughter run her head into. By his reckoning, he'd already cost Daav a wife—though Daav never did seem to reckon it that way. If he was going to cost the man a daughter, too . . .

"All right," Theo said, from her perch on the observer's stool. "We just had a situation that could've gone bad real fast, except for Kara's quick thinking and Hevelin's intervention. We've got an agreement based on mutual self-interest in force right now, but the reality is that we're going to have to part from the pathfinders sooner, rather than later. *Bechimo* has generated an annotated list of our four top ports. You should each have that information on your screens. We'll meet again here in six ship-hours to make a final decision for our first port of call, and following, we'll Jump out as soon as is practicable.

"Questions?"

"Captain, we have not done the final inspection of *Spiral Dance* with the pathfinders," Win Ton said.

Theo sighed.

"I don't think mutual self-interest extends that far. *Bechimo* and Joyita have been over it, and nothing scans dangerous. You and Kara have done a hands-on inspect and didn't find anything dangerous. Unless I hear an objection, we'll assume that Pilot yos'Phelium locked her ship down proper before she set it on its way. I'll entertain further discussion of that at our meeting in six hours. Other questions?"

There were none.

"Good, then. Kara, you're off-shift. Clarence—"

"All respect, Captain," Clarence said, "Clarence is on-shift and Win Ton is off."

"With all respect," Win Ton murmured, "I am perfectly able to continue the shift, after a brief tea break."

Theo opened her mouth, closed it and, after a long moment, actually produced a grin.

"That's mutiny," she said. "But I'll let it go this time. C'mon, Kara, we're both off-shift."

A ship in the Jump configuration preferred by most starfaring groups neither comes nor goes. If the Jump is not calculated properly, the ship stays where it is within the frame of previous motions. If the Jump is calculated exactly, the ship's energy and contents become one, contracting dimensionally, and the ship and its force packet vibrate their way into a crystalline state that adjusts space around it. The goal is to achieve an energy level meant to match that of a "place"—a star system, a nebula, a rendezvous point—where the matched energy levels permit the ship to reappear in normal space. Transferring from place to place in this way requires minimal energy once the Struven units stress the base ship-and-energy packet into a unit; space rearranges itself around the packet until the ship emerges—or occasionally fails to emerge—at the target location.

The energy of the underfields is not the same as in so-called "real space"—thus, a star a mere twenty light-years distant may take longer to get to subjectively and practically than a star two hundred light-years away. The difficulties of knowing the exact local conditions at a star before arriving are mediated somewhat by the necessity not to overlap the fields produced by the Struven units with the gravitic underfield of curved space-time; it takes extreme computing power and reaction time to arrive safely on a consistent basis. The revised ven'Tura Piloting Tables permit both longer and more complex voyages to be safely computed for most conditions.

—From Advanced Space Travel
for Dummies, *17th ed.*

CHAPTER TWENTY-THREE

··

Bechimo
Aubernet System

BECHIMO WASN'T THERE, AND THEN HE WAS.

He found a word for the transition among the fettered thoughts of others—he'd not realized it before—but there it was: *joy.* He was pleased to be away from his former hideaway and pleased to be doing something. He'd spent many decades without the pleasure and companionship of crew.

Despite this newfound joy—or, perhaps, because of it—he did not relax the standard security measures. He arrived with as small a Jump signature as possible, some energies baffled and dispersed across the transition barrier itself.

He pulled in external information: guide stars were found and measured instantaneously; the local solar cycle compared to records centuries old; the faint electronic and nucleonic scents of ships and power plants registered and recorded; the noise of purposeful transmissions converted into data streams; and the echoes past of Jumps into and out of near-space weighed for specifics of mass and time.

Internally, information was processed, also along planes and at levels which were less natural to him.

Theo at her station acted as both filter and junction point.

She simultaneously looked within and without, as he did. Within, all the crew continued respiration; the pathfinders,

Grakow, and Hevelin were comfortable within the confines of the family suite, and the Tree, still unsure of its name but full of travel excitement, was doing something that sucked extra nutrition from the hydroponic drip Kara had added to its room. Hevelin, through Stost of all people, had requested that he and the Tree be added to the control room for the in-Jump. Theo had disallowed it, but it appeared that the Tree did not need screens to know when it was in Jump, and when it was exiting Jump.

That was . . . interesting.

Bechimo tagged that observation as worthy of later reflection.

In one corner of his thoughts, as secret as might be, but not as secret as he would prefer, *Bechimo* worried over Theo, and in another corner of his thoughts, also not quite as secret as formerly, he shared information with Joyita, and marveled.

Joyita's ratiocination was different than his. Though Joyita's understanding of the universe was not as encompassing as was *Bechimo*'s, it was more definite where it came to humans. The comm officer, *Bechimo* decided, though he was in Clarence's apt phrase, *his own person*, also reflected the master on whom he was modeled; the mentor who had brought *Bechimo* to himself, long years ago. After he and Theo were more stable, *Bechimo* wished to follow that thought as well, and explore the myriad and fascinating possibilities with Joyita.

Joy faded into busy; he had data streams to ply and orders to carry out. They had been in-system for seven seconds. No one, except themselves, knew that they had arrived. They were hours away from being noticed by even the most careful of scans and could be away well before that, if required.

Within their bond space, *Bechimo* felt Theo sift and analyze what they were sensing. She used the filters well; his concern that she would be overwhelmed by his sense had proved without basis, as so many of his recent fears had. The habit of worry, however . . . was difficult to release. Caring for crew was . . . a difficult balance. Too much care and they would feel constrained; too little and they might damage themselves.

Theo, now. They were becoming a better team with every Jump. For now, she was content to observe and learn, leaving the play of plasma and ions to his discretion. If there were signs of dangers in the magnetic fields, he would be the first to see it and to react. She knew that. And trusted him.

Knowing that she trusted him...that was a different, more potent joy.

"Would you like to see the overscan, Theo? We are too far out for many of the local feeds and so Joyita is looking for whispers; we've yet to decide which of the three activity centers is best for the mission."

He felt her hunger before she answered.

"Show me."

· · · ✳ · · ·

There was always a little shock of dislocation when she came back to her board from a session with *Bechimo*. It felt a lot like putting aside a book, knowing that the experience left behind was no less real than the experience here and now, though it was far different.

She'd *lived* the micro Jump that had brought them closer in, had felt the rush of new information, *denser* information; sorted through it with *Bechimo*, until it seemed that she was *Bechimo*—but no. She was Theo, and her here-and-now priority was the board, the bridge, the crew, and the approach to system.

Bechimo's in-Jumps differed fundamentally from the in-Jumps of ordinary tradeships. To begin with, all weapons were a half-notch from live, and the screens set to target rather than scan. Rig Tranza would've politely inquired if she was going for pirate, if she'd had *Primadonna* on those settings, coming in.

Clarence had only nodded and said, "Smuggle-running, that's all. It'll tire you down if you do it every in, though, lass."

Which just showed the difference background made. Rig had been a straight-flying pilot with an honest trade line. Clarence... had, she thought, been honest, as much as he could be. But he hadn't always flown straight.

"Then, we'll have to practice more," she said. "If your captain has a reputation as a nexus of violence..."

She'd meant it to be a joke, but she felt a touch of extra tension, not inside her own self, but in the glances and gazes of her crew.

It was Joyita who broke the small gulf of silence.

"We're pulling in good feed," he said, and now the screens were showing potential targets as their signals were recognized and analyzed. Traders—at least a dozen signals—and two freighters. They were scattered around three small orbital stations, and several more were docked. The screens showed designee numbers, then ship name or owner and PIC.

"Anybody seen a warn-away?" Clarence asked. "Anyone know a ship?"

That was the advantage of having crew: more eyes meant more coverage. Theo therefore let the crew work, bent now on deciding which of the stations would be best for their particular brand of reconnaissance. Knowing a ship meant connections good or bad, and until they had a count and IDs...

"Fifteen..."

"Unknowns," said Kara, and Win Ton murmured, "ID *K'achoodie*, please, Joyita."

Theo scanned Minot Station's roster of docked ships, not really expecting to recognize the names. She didn't know that many ships, after all.

Clarence was looking right at her when she saw it; the thrill of recognition like an ice cube down her spine. She felt *Bechimo* snatch the information from her, a half-second before she managed to vocalize it.

"*Primadonna*! At Minot Station."

Now the stations could see *them*, and the other ships, too. Her hand was on a call button when the status lights showed an uneasy truth.

Primadonna listed no Pilot in Charge.

The roster said, "*Primadonna*, Hugglelans, Port Lien for Necessaries."

The system, like the star, was called Aubernet; like many systems the gas giants were still hugging the star. Eventually, of course, would come the disturbance that would launch one or more of the six of them into far more distant orbits and rearrange the orbits of the three stony worlds... but for now the center held and the shipping was all about the middle stony world's livable atmosphere and the easily accessible natural satellites.

"Prefer the Minot feed, Joyita, and find out what the hall there has available for trade. We've got some bundles we can move— send the small hold's basics and see if we get any requests. Also do the standard info search with Minot. Advise and update the bridge. News, social news, too. Whatever seems useful."

"Adjunct information search begun, Theo."

"Not landing on Frolich, then?" That was Clarence.

They'd considered Frolich because of their library. Nothing like Delgado, of course, but the guidebooks claimed they had a University-certified head librarian—

"And check the staff credentials for Minot's library or info service."

"Yes, Theo."

"Better stick with the orbitals, don't you think?"

"Did think so, if y'recall, but I understand, Captain."

Theo laughed gently. Of course he understood. It was hard to stop being a copilot, even if one had changed ships.

Joyita managed to make the incoming information sound interesting, and normally it would *be* interesting. Theo listened with one ear as she considered her necessities.

"There are no outstanding warrants for any of us under our license names. There are no liens or outstanding bills on *Bechimo*. Laughing Cat is not yet registered. Sorry, Laughing Cat is in the process of being registered, please advise before doing business. Minot does not require a customs check of items shipping through. Tourists unfamiliar with low-grav are advised to hire a guide. No visible high-energy hand weapons, please. This is strictly enforced. No open flame intoxicants permitted in public areas. This is strictly enforced. Language order for public dealing is Terran prime, then Trade. Liaden is not a commerce language at this outpost..."

To begin with, Theo thought, *Primadonna* was off ordinary routes—and that was information, right there. Well, Hugglelans was expanding, after all, trying to take advantage of Korval's recent reversals. Rig Tranza now—

"TerraTrade recognizes trades in Aubernet System," Joyita continued. "The Minot Pilots Guild circuit office is scheduled to open again in thirty-two days. The Frolich Pilots Guild office is scheduled to open again for sixteen days in twelve days. Minot's two trade bars are full service and always open. Liaden is not spoken in Coville Corner."

"Joyita, can we get a pilots-on-station update—just send it to my Screen Seven, Terran alphabet. Also," she added after a moment, "I'd like to see what the proceedings against the Hugglelans ship *Primadonna* are and anything on crew. Any recent civil disturbances we should be aware of on station?"

She could feel *Bechimo* working in the back of her mind. Kara and Clarence acknowledged or repeated, as necessary, particular bits of Joyita's information.

"Docks twelve and fourteen are dry, with airlock and comm interface only. Day rates only, no discounts. Dock sixteen is out of service. Dock twenty is available for midterm full-connectable lease only. Two refreshing docks are open, one owned and operated by Waysn Unlimited and one operated by Minot Port Authority."

"Dry, I'm thinking?"

Theo signed *Yes* to Clarence, but Kara called her on it.

"Records, Theo. We've got a lot of input right now."

So Theo signed *exactly so* and called out, "That's correct, Clarence, thank you. Run us in, if you please, as PIC. Kara's second."

"Yes," he said, and Kara said quickly, "I'm live," which was plain on Theo's screen, and also in that space in her head that she shared with *Bechimo*.

Several images re-formed around the ship as Theo got down to the hard parts.

"We have library and infofeed rates, Theo," Joyita said. "Net rates are high, but there's no scramble at all on open radio."

"Clarence is on PIC. All the way in. Clarence, dock us dry. If you can spot *Primadonna*, pick a spot for the best visuals going in. If they ask, just tell them we're recently commissioned out of Waymart and are on a route-building and shakedown run. We've got some small goods to trade and will consider odd-lot or pickup trade."

"Yes, Captain."

Theo closed her eyes, the better to access *Bechimo*'s feed. The space around glittered with ships and energy. There were no long-range single ships at dock, no obvious cutters, no major military presence. Minot Station had some defenses but it was no battle station. Frolich and its stations existed for trade, and there was a reason for that.

Minot Station in particular was well located with regard to multiple Carresens destinations and enough local trade to make it an entrepreneurial haven for those fond of living off of market vagaries. With Frolich and the gas giants' moons to work with, they also had decent raw materials for export as well as to feed their small ship repair and ship-building industries, industries growing now that the heavy gas-and-carbon nebularity had moved beyond the Carresens trade domains.

In light of the recent upset in the trade balance, old routes were being reopened, and new trade opportunities were being formulated.

In short, Minot was due for a boom. And here was a Hugglelans ship, likely on the same kind of mission she was on: search out the future for an expanding fleet of ships and traders.

Bechimo's presence became more definite to Theo as he again offered the power of the deep scanned images: energy levels, heat maps, projected orbits, ships with obvious maintenance issues and those without, ships with low level shields still in place, and still the local and regional magnetic field strength and plasma flow.

Bechimo was sensing data on so many levels that Theo fought to understand what was before her—around her. It reminded her of her first time in a sailplane, with a working airport's sky worth of information and no surety of which details were important.

She felt that she was just beginning to understand some kind of a whole when the glittering influx of information dimmed. She was, Theo realized, seeing Minot through an overlayment—the image of another station! And then another, and another...

"What are we doing?" she asked. Abruptly the overlays came clear to her—*there* was Ynsolt'i, then Cresthaller, Chustling and... Eylot, which overlay got stronger as Ynsolt'i's dropped entirely away.

"I compare and model," *Bechimo* said. "First, I search for coincident ships. I search for risk factors. In fact, I search for any coincident conditions besides our own presence. I consider information I have learned within the ship as well."

"And have you arrived at any conclusions?"

"I have observed," admitted *Bechimo*, "that we seem to frequent older and smaller ports of call. Also, ports with a Terran bias. This may be seen as unusual for a ship with ties to Tree-and-Dragon."

There was then, within the flows and energies of the system, Jump glare. The nonchaotic wave front would be several moments before giving over ship IDs, but again came the feeling of overlays matching matching matching...

"I believe that is a Liaden ship, Theo. I have alerted Joyita, who will alert Win Ton, as the pattern matches that of a Scout observer ship. There, yes, they call themselves a packet ship. I have no ID verification as yet. I will alert you when they broadcast. Now, your attention will be needed at docking."

CHAPTER TWENTY-FOUR

. . . .

Bechimo
Minot Station

DOCKING TOOK ATTENTION, INDEED.

Joyita was handling basic comm. Clarence, Kara backing him, was on ship dock, which included negotiating with the portmaster's office. Win Ton was on scan.

Which left Theo on for the decision trees for both trade opportunities and supplies.

A rush of queries came in once Laughing Cat was registered with the station. The news that they were a Tree-and-Dragon contractor brought another rush. In the meanwhile, supply catalogs starting filling a side queue.

Then, Theo had to take her own comm for the Minot Admin desk's query about their claim to consular status for Hevelin, which they needed before docking. Some ports specifically banned norbears; others had livestock regulations.

Minot didn't ban norbears, which was good. But it had numerous and—judging from the fact that Theo's contact in Admin had to twice check with an "expert" for clarity—confusing livestock regs. Finally, Hevelin's certifications were accepted, but there was additional delay while a particular set of high-ups was chased down or waked up, and final lockup to the station was put on hold until that had been accomplished. Apparently it wasn't every day that an ambassador deigned to visit Minot Station.

Clarence chatted with his contact in the portmaster's office while they waited for the high-ups to be found. It was banter mostly, and apparently pleasing, because the voice warmed up some—but, there, Clarence had an easy way with him, Theo thought. People liked Clarence, unless he wanted them not to. He chuckled and said something low which had the cadence of a word she'd heard from Clarence on comm back a docking or two. A code word? Connections from his former career as a Juntavas Boss? Or just old pilot code for comforts available and invited?

It might have been the latter, because the voice gave a low laugh in return, her tone warming appreciably this time.

"Well, Pilot, we're not Terra or Liad, but we find ways to amuse ourselves on the off-shifts, and you have my name. But you know, we do have a five-hour quiet shift—that's five out of twenty-five—that the galleries and bars are closed. Happens that the lights go dim right about the time you're set for latching on, so if you're making walkabout decisions you'll want to keep that in mind. Not that the dockside's closed, that's always up for ship stuff, and we staff all hours here. The public social though, that closes five hours…'Member that!"

Theo shook her head—likely no one noticed. It appeared that her copilot had a talent for connection. Well. Connecting with people, that's kind of what he'd done as a Boss and as a pilot, wasn't it? It was good to have that talent available to the ship.

She flicked her fingers—not quite a nonsense gesture—and returned to her lists and lineups. Clarence's luck or lack of it was information.

In five hours they could at least take a look at whatever came across the comm lines, and take a break, too. Ship and crew could sync with Minot time, and maybe find out what the station offered ambassadors once they received permission to dock.

Clearly they were going to need more or better documentation from the Pilots Guild. For that matter, they were going to be needing the Guild regarding the pathfinders. She had no wish to hang around the station for a ten-day or more for the official Guild office—surely *someone* must represent the Guild in emergencies, even when the office was closed.

"Theo," Joyita said, interrupting these thoughts, "I have begun passing two screens to the pathfinders in their stateroom. They are receiving the general Minot approach vids, without your commands or comments, and they are receiving our general system scan, again without voice commentary and without the targeting overlays."

"They're pilots," Theo allowed. "They ought to find this instructive. After all, it's their first port in a new universe. Are they still at studying, in between?"

"Yes, Theo, they are, with Grakow's aid and assistance. From their conversation I would say they regard the vids as a sort of relaxation. An entertainment."

"Excellent," Kara said, low, but still to the bridge entire. "The last time one of my approaches was amusement for other pilots we were still back at piloting academy. I had hoped to have outlived it!"

Theo grimaced at the undertones and the heat; that much anger could be a problem...

Unbidden, there rose in her mind three charts: one of Kara's vital signs sitting pilot alone; another, measured during the emergency at Ynsolt'i; the third, here and now.

Yes, a spike of heat and blood pressure now, but...

Theo concentrated and the images vanished. She didn't want to be monitoring Kara. It was—she didn't *want* to know Kara this way.

She felt a sense of chagrin—not hers—and took a deep breath.

Inner calm, she told herself, and looked again to her board.

"Theo." Within their bond space, *Bechimo* offered her an image: the incoming ship now both identified and targeted on a scan map not yet mirrored on the bridge screens.

"Joyita will share this information with the crew. You should know that I have seen this ship before, while I was at rest. Before our bonding, before the firefights, were I without a mission or captain, I believe I would flee before this ship. Now, Theo, I find it... an interesting development."

"Are you in danger from this ship?" Theo demanded.

"I believe not, though it would have been different were I not crewed."

"We'll be careful, then?"

"That should be sufficient, yes."

She blinked fully back to the bridge just as the scan image changed.

"This incoming ship has finally identified itself," Joyita was saying. "It reports as the *Chandra Marudas*, a Scout packet boat out of Drasto Yards. My guide to ships is not entirely up to date, I find, but a dozen years ago this ship was listed as a survey vessel out of Solcintra, Liad."

There was a sharp intake of breath from Win Ton's station, followed by a sigh. He moved his hands, as if in indecision, then turned his chair to face the bridge and made a seated bow of privileged communication.

"I share knowledge for the crew, here and now," he said, looking directly at Theo. "It is not to be taken elsewhere or bandied about on port. It is not...safe, we will say."

Theo nodded and motioned for him to continue.

"Yes." He sighed again.

"I know this ship. *Chandra Marudas* is an observation and surveillance ship, long involved in Scouts' mission of the sequestration of Old Tech."

"Is Minot a port known for Old Tech? I saw nothing in the..."

"Minot fits in a gap, Theo; it is located between several powers...and thus will be a place where the nearly reputable may trade with those above reproach. The system is one that requires checking for contraband from time to time."

"But the home port change," suggested Joyita almost eagerly. "Is it not true that the removal of Korval from Liad has altered many things within the Scouts—the organization of Scouts is what I mean. Might this ship have been repurposed now that it has a new home?"

"As a packet ship? Unless...well, but how could you know? Drasto Yards has long been a center of quiet work for the Scouts. I was there as part of my duties. In my judgment as a Scout—no. I think that a purpose-built ship like the *Chandra Marudas* is unlikely to find a new life as a simple packet ship. Surely it has holds and might be disguised, but I do not believe it has given up the thrill of the hunt."

Kara sat up straighter. "Is it looking for *Bechimo*?"

Joyita in his screen shrugged.

"As the captain explained to the pathfinders, *Bechimo* is not Old Tech," he said. "The ship has provenance. We know the names of the investors, the name and location of the yard that built—"

"Does a ship that just recently came through as flotsam from the Old Universe count as Old Tech?" Clarence wondered aloud.

Theo stared at the side of his face. He didn't turn his head. "It's cargo," she said.

"Illegal cargo's been confiscated by authority before now," Clarence answered.

Theo took a breath.

"It belongs to Clan Korval," she said.

"That might play better." Win Ton spoke before Clarence; the older pilot smiled, eyes on his screens.

"However, Captain—with all respect—it would be good to have clarity before we must declare *Spiral Dance* to authority."

Theo stared at the image in her head, the one that showed increasingly accurate targeting information for all that the Scout ship was nearly a day from dockside.

Not a solution, she said, and the image faded, leaving behind the whisper of her own voice.

Not a solution...yet.

She sighed and looked round the bridge at her crew.

"It would be good," she said, "if we could find a representative of the Pilots Guild to talk to."

· · · ※ · · ·

Crew was at liberty, now they were at dock. Win Ton had retired to his cabin, and finding himself neither tired enough to sleep nor yet awake enough to attend a vid or a book, had taken to dance.

"*Chandra Marudas* has not filed for Minot Station, Win Ton."

He'd been deep in the dance, his mind filled with the movements and perhaps a variant of a song he'd once meant to sing to Theo of a private morning. It therefore took a moment for the words and the meaning of the words to reach him.

Reluctantly, he allowed the song to fade, as his body found a natural end to the sequence he had been exploring and brought him to rest in the middle of his cabin. He bent and picked up the towel he had draped over the back of his chair and wiped his face.

The screen in his cabin was filled now, not with Joyita, whose voice he had belatedly recognized, but with what was likely a scrubbed version of the main system scan.

Towel between his hands, he considered the screen and—yes, there was *Chandra Marudas*, destination listed as Frolich, via a premium insertion orbit.

In addition to *Chandra Marudas*, and the other local ships, the station's bulk was a ghostly layer, seen through by the combination of direct sensors, stolen feeds, and *Bechimo*'s increasingly capable interpretive signal gathering.

He looked again at the legend for the Scout ship: *Chandra Marudas*, Frolich, premium.

Yes, precisely, he thought, doubting it, for the captain of *Chandra Marudas* was no fool, nor likely to lose the trail of valuable quarry.

Still, the ship, in either persona, was not prone to errors or to jokes, although Joyita was attempting puns of increasing sophistication. He did not, therefore, ask if they were certain of the ship's bearings, but asked a question, instead.

"Thank you for the news, Joyita. Will they have seen, or had news of, us?"

"Not yet, Win Ton. We won't appear on their scans for several hours, and then they may pass over us. We're locked to the station now, and they won't find our signals easily. We are very picky about frequencies and power levels, you know."

"Yes," he agreed, flashing the hand-sign of *maximum agreement* toward the screen. "We are very good at not being seen, for a ship that is so well-known in some quarters, are we not?"

"Perhaps we are," Joyita allowed, "but here it is easy to be underreported. Local ships are careless with their signals. They cover the spectrum with small talk and chatter, and love notes, and recipes. The ciphers we've seen have been simple and uncomplicated—some smuggling, some trade-advantage, some local intrigue having to do with a weather prediction . . . To find one ship, inside all of the noise of Minot Station, would take dedication."

"Scouts have on occasion displayed dedication to a task," Win Ton said dryly. "Especially to a task they believe to be vital."

"We will keep close watch," Joyita said, not quite as if he was soothing a child. "If conditions change, we will sound an alert."

Win Ton bowed, there being no more to say at the moment.

"*Chandra Marudas* is not all I have to speak with you about, Win Ton. Have you a moment?"

Win Ton bowed again.

"I have a moment; several, in fact. But I wish you will have a face before we proceed, friend Joyita."

"Certainly. Please forgive my lapse."

The screen divided: half continued to display the system scan; the other half showing Joyita in his tower, sleeves rolled, mugs to hand, and rings gleaming.

"Well met," Win Ton said. "How may I serve you, Joyita?"

"I have compiled a new iteration of the pathfinder dictionary, informed by their discussions between themselves of the material they are learning, and also by feedback from the learning unit. You may be interested in sleep-learning portions of it."

"Indeed, I am interested. However, our honored guests have, by the captain's order, what Clarence dignifies as *first dibs* on the sleep learner."

"Yes!" Joyita nodded and smiled. "You anticipate my subject. *Bechimo* has discovered several items under the Founders' Seal which may prove to be useful to us.

"The most important to our current case is a...not a list precisely, but a notation of items which have been stored—for crew—since Joyita himself was aboard."

The phrase "Joyita himself" had been spoken with such diffidence that Win Ton was reminded of a raw recruit in awe of speaking of a Scout commander. But, newly discovered items, which had been stored away for...centuries?

"I assume that there are learning units among these stored items," he said. "They will be...very old and not, I think, standard."

Uncharacteristically, Joyita laughed aloud. It was a good wholesome laugh, and Win Ton marveled at the strength of the programming that might produce a person from circuits.

"No, they're not at all standard. There are, so far as the notation would have us believe, three of them. They had been packed for the crew-that-never-came and were supplied by the Uncle himself."

Win Ton sat on the edge of his bunk.

"I have been discussing this possibility with Kara, who believes that the units may be made usable, and would like to see them unpacked so that they can be tested."

"I see. Kara would like these units tested? Am I to be the subject?"

It was just; he was fourth and the most expendable of the crew, though he was, he thought, much stronger and very nearly back to his previous speed. He had hopes, some days—hopes that he would fully regain what he had lost...

"Kara will test the units with Clarence standing by," Joyita said. "As the fourth pilot, she...is in line for such things."

Win Ton looked up into the screen and met Joyita's eyes.

"Kara is fourth? When did this develop?"

"It is a recent development. *Bechimo* has been monitoring your recuperation. I understand that you have made recent gains with regard to reaction times and in your general speed and balance. If you would like to see the entire analysis, please apply to *Bechimo*."

"Thank you, perhaps I shall. What, then, is to be my role in the...discovery of these learning units?"

"The units were, as I said, stored with other items, which were likewise procured and packed by the Uncle, into crew storage. Among the notes left for us are the instructions for opening the storage units. They are...rather complex and, again, security which was put into place by the Uncle.

"You, in short, are required in your *melant'i* as safety officer, to be certain that all instructions are followed exactly and to abort if it seems the operation has gone awry."

Win Ton sighed.

"Is there a problem with this? You *are* the ship's safety officer."

"Indeed and I do not dispute it. I only wonder if it might not be less perilous to subject my brain to the mysteries of an ancient sleep learner."

"No one will endanger themselves. That is the captain's order. If the units cannot be tested and certified safely, then another solution will be found."

"I hope that the solution set does not include buying a sleep learner from Minot or Frolich. I see from the incoming catalogs that their prices are only ruinous!"

Joyita smiled. "I think Theo is thriftier than Minot."

"So I should hope."

There was a pause, but not, to Win Ton's ear, an end to the conversation. He was about to ask when Joyita spoke again. "There is," he said slowly, "a third topic. This one is...personal. Have you a moment to speak as a pilot?"

A call to *melant'i*. Seated as he was, Win Ton bowed.

"I am pleased to speak as a pilot with a pilot."

Joyita shook his head slightly.

"That is the crux of the matter. I am no pilot and I wish to be—for myself and for the increased safety of the ship."

Win Ton frowned.

"Joyita, are you playing *melant'i* games with me?"

"How so?"

"When first you were ever seen on the bridge of *Bechimo*, you were wearing a pilot's jacket! I have it—"

He stopped, because Joyita had turned his face slightly away. If he had been Liaden, that gesture would have signified embarrassment.

"Tell me," Win Ton said. "There should not be confusion between friends."

"I made an error," Joyita said slowly. "Jermone Joyita was a pilot. When I first was seen, I was ... not wholly myself. I was modeled from *Bechimo*'s files and memories, and so I was given—I used—Joyita's jacket. For ... verisimilitude. But I—*I* did not earn that jacket. *I* am no pilot at all, according to the Pilots Guild, where B. Joyita has no file."

Win Ton blinked as understanding overtook him.

"You want to create a records trail. For ... verisimilitude."

"Yes! I think we can agree that I am *able* to pilot this ship. I would like it, Scout, if you would consider testing me. A first class provisional would, I think, stand me in good stead with most ports and pilots we're likely to meet."

Win Ton held up a hand—*wait*. His mind was racing. As a plan, it held together. A Scout pilot was the equivalent of a master. He was, indeed, qualified to test candidate pilots and assign rank. But such a test, for such a student ...

The challenge! He thrilled with it.

"There are," Joyita said diffidently, "complexities. For instance, the captain would prefer you to be taking an ordinary live watch, though of course without naming you as PIC. So, I thought that I could be a pilot of record at need."

"Comm officer is not sufficient?" Win Ton asked, because it was necessary that he ask the candidate such questions. For himself, the matter was already decided. All that remained was designing the test.

"In some cases, comm officer is not sufficient."

"How if the captain made you senior comm and added a stripe to your sleeve?"

Joyita heard the irony. He inclined his head with just the right angle to convey this.

"My intent is not to raise my rank, nor to substitute for you, but to be understudy. We shall have to have papers; my history needs to be . . . solid. This, I learn from the pathfinders. I need a past, not only a present."

Win Ton considered the hard brown face in the screen, with its lines and its scar and its beard.

"Are you truly not *Bechimo*, Joyita?"

"Truly, I am not *Bechimo*, but my own self, Joyita. And recall, Win Ton, that *Bechimo* lacks a pilot's certificate as well."

Win Ton laughed. "Now there is *melant'i* played with perfect touch! Surely *Bechimo* is among the finest pilots in this universe or the last!"

"Hold," said Joyita, his face abstracted. There was a moment in which he seemed to gaze into middle space before he turned his attention once again to Win Ton.

"*Bechimo* says, 'Now, now that I am bonded with Theo Waitley, *now* I am that pilot Win Ton names.'"

Win Ton drew a breath . . . and slowly exhaled.

"Ah," he said, "now."

"Forgive me if I am blunt," said Joyita. "The case is that we both—you, Win Ton yo'Vala, and I, Joyita comm officer—need the confidence to sit first chair in an emergency. I propose that we take advantage of our docking here at Minot Station to fly sim enough for a Scout to make a determination for a candidate pilot. We need to have confidence, in ourselves and in each other."

Win Ton stared at the screen, wondering how deep the ply of trust and confidence ran. Was this Theo's idea? Or Clarence's meddling? *Bechimo*'s?

"Consider it, please," said Joyita. "We can speak again tomorrow before suggesting it to the other pilots. Should we go forward, then elsewhere *Bechimo* can achieve his own certificate. The more we have records and paperwork, the harder it becomes for them to put us aside as mere AI."

Mere AI? thought Win Ton, though he did not say it. Instead, he inclined his head and asked the other question that he must ask of a candidate.

"And this is your own desire, friend Joyita? It is no order from the captain, nor compulsion from *Bechimo*, nor any other coercion which has led you to this and to me?"

"If I am to be a proper Joyita, and serve ship and crew, I must be a pilot. It would please me greatly if you were to sign my certificates."

CHAPTER TWENTY-FIVE

. . . .

Bechimo
Sync Shift

EVEN WITH *BECHIMO*'S INTERCESSION, IT TOOK THEO A FEW MIN-
utes to comprehend the request, made as it was on the open bridge
with Win Ton bowing a complex bow of request in front of his
shipmates before explaining that he and Joyita had conceived an
interlocking skills test which might require the captain to bend
a *minor* rule or two in order that they might see it to fruition.

Bechimo admitted privately in bond space that the idea, while
not his, was excellent. Yes, Win Ton's recovery was still ongoing;
in fact he had progressed rather further than *Bechimo* had thought
he might, there in the depths of the cellular repairs. And yes,
other than a test to destruction, which it was understood that
Theo might not sanction for a number of very good reasons—not
the least because it was good to have the resources of a Scout
available to them—then the best way to see how far he'd come
was to challenge him with multiple challenges at once, which
surely the inculcation of master-grade piloting would provide.

Under this dual assault, she'd managed to nod, and everyone
brightened.

Clarence, grinning, shook Win Ton's hand and saluted Joyita.
"I'm for it! Nothing wrong with a ship full of pilots that I can
see. Right?"

He shook Win Ton's hand one more time, with enough vigor
that the Scout winced. Clarence winked at him.

"We'll do this again when we get the test results in—and I'll bow as proper as you like it then. Deal?"

Win Ton smiled.

"Deal."

Hevelin bounced about between Theo and Kara, then to Win Ton, and then to Kara and Clarence, showing amazing agility for an old norbear. He showed them all a bridge—not *Bechimo*'s bridge, and maybe not even an actual bridge anywhere, but a composite, which Win Ton did not think of until later—with a break-out screen displaying a successful Jump completion, so he at least knew the basic topic of conversation was flying a ship or piloting one. And yes, there was another screen on *that* bridge, and Joyita's image was there.

Theo slowed the celebration of what had yet to happen with a wave of her hand.

"Apparently, Joyita and Win Ton will do this thing, and we're all agreed that it will be a good thing. But! . . . it will wait until we have clear time. Maybe we won't need to just have a sim flight. I'm thinking that real flight is more compelling, if we are interested in records, but that discussion will wait, too.

"For the moment we'll take our rest as we can. Joyita's on comm, and helping me with research lines and leads. Unless we discover something urgent—by that I mean life-threatening—we will not be taking on supplies here. Everybody double-check necessities and let Clarence know if there is something vital that needs replacing before we leave dock. Despite that we aren't doing any serious shopping, we're going to give evidence of interest in ordinary things while we discover what's happening with the ship I was copilot on."

Theo turned to Kara.

"Opening and doing a thorough inventory of the crew locker is a priority. *Bechimo* says that it hasn't been opened since it was filled. There is only a very hasty description of the contents, as if Uncle had not only been in a hurry, but packed it himself. It's unlikely that the teaching rigs were unreliable when they were packed, but the age of them argues for care. We'll do no-load testing and the like. We want to have as many functioning learning units available as we can, but not at the expense of one of us, am I clear?"

"Yes, Captain," said Kara.

"Good. I have the unlock instructions here—Win Ton, there's a copy for you—and the keys."

She looked around the bridge, seeing her crew alert, and Win Ton maybe a little uneasy, which was fair enough given his background and his training. She wasn't completely easy herself, though maybe not for the same reasons.

"All right, then. Let's get this done."

· · · ❋ · · ·

"Hevelin approaches, Pathfinders." Despite his eagerness to learn even more of their language, Joyita understood the need for them to practice their newly acquired language, and so spoke in Trade. "May I open the door to him?"

Stost looked up from his study screen and met Joyita's eyes. The comm officer looked fresh and alert, as befit a man coming on-shift after a good sleep and a filling meal.

"It would be a kindness," he said, "though Grakow is sleeping."

"That seems not to limit the ambassador's enjoyment of the visit," Chernak muttered, deep in her own screen.

Stost nodded—there was a useful gesture! It came from the Terran lexicon and was apparently readily adopted by all who met it. And it was true that Hevelin, finding Grakow at nap, would likely simply curl up with his friend and wholeheartedly join the venture.

Half of Stost's attention returned to his screen, he heard the door open and close again, but paid no mind until there was an insistent tug of the fabric at his knee. He looked down at the furry ambassador.

"Grakow," he began, but got no further before images of space, Jump space, Joyita and Win Ton arrived in his head, all a-jumble and infused with such joyous anticipation you might have thought the creature was going into battle.

Stost bent and brought Hevelin to his knee.

"*Mezta, mezata,*" he murmured in the language of the Troop, and then, in Trade, "Peace, little one, let me understand."

The flow of images slowed, leaving the sensation of anticipation and the fading sense of Jump.

"What does he say?" asked Chernak.

"It would seem that Joyita would take his piloting tests, administered by Win Ton," Stost said and looked to the screen.

"Congratulations, it is an honor to be allowed among the ranks of pilots."

"Very much so," Joyita said, inclining his head slightly. "I am particularly fortunate in my teacher."

That was properly said, but there remained a mystery.

"The ambassador is very happy for your good fortune," Stost commented.

"So I am informed. Perhaps he merely likes pilots and believes we ought to improve ourselves. He traveled with a master of the Pilots Guild for many years."

"So you had said. Well, we are informed of the joyous news, Hevelin. The Troop is enriched."

There arose in Stost a feeling of fulfillment, as if he had finished a particularly tricky bit of navigating, and Hevelin wriggled slightly under his hand. He bent and replaced the norbear on the floor and saw him off in the direction of the second bunk room, where Grakow was asleep on his pillow.

"Joyita," he said, his eyes lingering on the retreating ambassador. "Yes?"

"Does the captain plan a long stay at this Minot Station? Is there—" He glanced at Chernak, who was watching him with interest, though not alarm. "Is there anything for *us* here? The captain spoke of someone who might take ourselves and our mission in hand."

"I believe that one of the reasons we are at this dock is to search for recent news of this person," Joyita said. "There has been a complication, but you are not forgotten."

"Recall us to the captain," Chernak said, "should this complication be eased by the presence of trained soldiers."

"I will remind her," Joyita said. "I leave you now to study, unless there is else?"

"None else," said Chernak. "Thank you, Joyita."

"You're welcome," he returned, and the screen faded into swirling patterns of blue.

· · · ✳ · · ·

The locker slid all but silently from the bottom of the storage wall, four more like it stacked over it, each as tall as Kara. Win Ton stood ready as safety officer, and also to assist with the unpacking and inventory once the locks were opened by the captain.

"This is something we couldn't do before the bonding," Theo said, trying hard not to be too pointed.

She frowned at the green line on the floor and waved Win Ton back a few steps. The locker slid out until its leading edge hid the line.

"Did you ask?" Kara said, carefully neutral in her turn.

Theo kept her face as noncommittal as she could and shook her head in a good Terran *no.*

"I couldn't ask what was here because this storage wall didn't show as a storage wall. The manual pull rings double as tie-downs, so when I inspected this area I couldn't see that we had anything *in* storage; all I knew was that the area was marked 'crew storage' on the ship plans."

"This means that *Bechimo* kept information from you before you bonded."

Win Ton pushed at this point; it was one of the few things he shared with Kara, this distrust of the fact that *Bechimo* had hidden things from them, from the captain, until he'd gotten his way and bonded Theo to him.

"It wasn't *Bechimo*'s rule," Theo pointed out. "It was the Founders' decision. *Bechimo* knew there were things he couldn't tell me or *us,* but he didn't know what those things were. The Founders blocked certain knowledge from his conscious mind." She sighed and *fuffed* her hair off her forehead.

"If you ask me, the Founders have a lot to answer for. They might have had enemies and been afraid for the ship's safety, but hiding information is a sure way to make sure mistakes are made."

"Indeed," said Kara.

"The Uncle, however—" Win Ton began, but Theo cut off whatever he'd been about to say with a quick pilot's chopping motion: *stop.*

"According to our records, the *Founders* made the decision. The records—the records that we couldn't have access to, *either,* until *Bechimo* had a bonded captain—also show that Uncle recused himself from a lot of the board's decisions. I know it's the fashion to mistrust him—and I don't say we should trust him entirely. But it seems to me that Uncle has been more careful in certain areas than his reputation would indicate."

"*Our* records?" murmured Kara, but her question was over-ridden by Win Ton's more forceful tone.

"You believe that the Uncle has a fine understanding of *melant'i*?"

Theo sighed again.

Kara stood close enough in the cool storeroom that Theo could feel her warmth; Kara carried the mechanical keys for the locker's cables, straight from the captain's safe, while Theo had the codes.

"I think," Theo said stepping up to the locker, "that the Uncle is a very careful person. His understanding of *melant'i* probably *is* fine. In my dealings with him, he maintained a...a *careful advantage*."

She tapped the first string of code into the keypad. There was a tiny exhalation of air, as the bar the first mechanical lock was attached to turned, exposing the lock's true face. The front side had been a fraud.

"That's odd, isn't it?" Kara said, stepping forward, key in hand. "I wonder what would have happened if we hadn't had the instructions and tried the key in the first lock?"

"But we have the instructions," Theo said. "I'd prefer not to know what defenses might be built in, given Uncle's involvement."

"This is 'careful advantage,' is it?" Win Ton said from his observation point. It was his job to point out anomalies before they became problems.

Theo decided that his question was rhetorical and consulted her clipboard.

"Kara, insert key one. First to the right, a single complete turn, then to left, one complete turn past the original insert point."

Kara did as bidden—

"It turns as new," she said, sounding surprised. "And—there!"

The lock silently fell into her hands. She gave the gleaming mechanism a long thoughtful stare before slipping it into her work pouch.

Theo nodded.

"Good. Now lock number two. You're to insert the key straight in, gently, blue edge to blue dot, with no torsion. When it feels seated, push hard."

Kara did these things and that lock, too, fell away, this time with an audible click that surprised with its power. It joined the first in Kara's pouch.

Theo looked to Win Ton.

"Safety Officer? Is all well?"

"Indeed. My reading of the instructions matches yours. We now proceed to the next step: captain enters codes."

Theo again leaned to the keypad. The code was on her clipboard, but she didn't need it. The code rose in her mind, her fingers moved, and the bar slid a hand's width under power, revealing cables securing the unit to an undercarriage of sorts. She stepped back.

"Kara, key three is to slide into each cable, in order, from left to right. After that, we see what we have."

Carefully, Kara inserted the key into each cable; the uncoupling took only seconds. Three common stasis seals remained between them and the contents of the locker.

"I think," Theo said, "that this is another example of the Uncle's work. He has given the crew of *Bechimo* something. He maintained his careful advantage, and he addressed the Founders' concerns for security. Once security needs are met, the rest ought to be easy. Uncle's careful advantage, Win Ton, isn't a simple thing—I think it's meant to be a safety margin for those participating in his arrangements."

Theo backed away, permitting Win Ton access to the seals.

Theo continued, "When I was one of Uncle's courier pilots, he made sure I wasn't at a *disadvantage*. I was sometimes *at risk*, but I always had the means *to do* something about that risk. He didn't risk me or the ship needlessly. He doesn't do things carelessly, as someone with his reputation might be expected to. Balance? *Melant'i*? Surely, he understands those concepts. And he understands and acts on them for other people, not just for himself."

The seals parted with a breathy exhaust. Win Ton pulled the lid up, revealing numerous boxes and cases. The items in sight were marked with large bright blue Terran numerals, none lower than fifty-two. The exception was a stasis box with Liaden script on the outside, which Theo made out to say, *tea for the captain*.

It was Kara who saw the flimsy between the tea and box fifty-seven—

"It's a packing list, Theo! With a signature."

Theo glanced at the familiar hand and nodded.

"Himself," she said. "I see it."

She paused, sighed, and stood away from them.

"You know what to do and I'll leave you to it. I'll be on the bridge, if you need me."

Joyita was in his tower when Theo entered the bridge, and Clarence was in his chair, intent on the station feeds, if she had to guess. Neither looked up at her arrival.

She took her seat, looked at the incoming, sighed, and glanced again at Joyita intent on . . . something, his uniform a little more wrinkled than it had been earlier, when they'd been celebrating his soon-to-be rise to pilot. Good attention to detail there.

Closing her eyes, she accessed a quick relaxation exercise and sat, eyes closed, a little longer. There'd been a story—she thought it had been a story and not a history—about ancient logics built to look like humans. She wondered if there was a way to do that, really; if there'd be enough computing power in something as small as a human-shaped head—that would let Joyita move among his crew mates.

She remembered then, that he'd told the pathfinders he was working on there being a comm officer in a tower for the idle to see—and made a note to ask him what he'd meant by that.

She opened her eyes and he was still in his screen, glancing up as if he had felt her eyes on him.

"Captain," he said, "it is good that you're here. I have some reports to send you . . ."

So that was official business, something Clarence wasn't getting along with everything else.

"Send it on," she said, and to Clarence, "Available for backup, Pilot."

Clarence glanced over and nodded. "Welcome back, Pilot. *Bechimo*, sign over to Theo."

"Yes, Pilot. Thank you, Pilot."

Clarence returned to his task. There was synchrony going on, with each flip or click and sound pulse on Clarence's board being echoed, or maybe twinned, in Joyita's comm tower lighting and sounds.

Theo opened her screens.

It was just as well that *Bechimo* didn't have his own image now, wasn't it? As it was, she suddenly found that he knew small details: things of little note, but of some interest. She knew, for instance, that *Rofflager* was on cable clamp only, which meant an imminent departure. The station was adjusting internal pressures in waves instead of modules today, it being a good routine check of systems.

Primadonna was cable-locked, clamped, *and* tagged; crew status listed as zero.

"Tab Two on the note board," said Joyita and she repeated "Tab Two" in acknowledgment as she opened it on her screen.

Tab Two made her catch her breath, it being a stationary four-way image of *Primadonna* with a sidebar of information. She knew *Primadonna*; she'd been copilot on *Primadonna*; earned her jacket and her first class card on *Primadonna*. She knew the Hugglelans logos and where *Primadonna*'s markings varied from the routine of the marque—there on the ventral she didn't have the usual orange blotch of tech number or a variety, she having been first of that exact line, and there under the Hugglelans logo *Primadonna*'s nameplate was almost twice the size of most of the line's ships. Lost in new data and old memories, it took her a moment to figure out what was wrong.

"Joyita, have we purchased a security camera feed contract with Minot Station?"

She flipped through port, starboard, north and south on the images, finding nothing amiss other than each entrance being tagged with a bright yellow lock symbol, likely affixed with some kind of ugly adhesive that would take a real scorcher of an atmospheric landing to be rid of. Rig would be furious.

"A moment, Captain."

A moment, Captain?

That thought she shared with *Bechimo*—and received no response. *Bechimo* felt ... distant; in fact, it was the feeling that she got when he was concentrating on a problem.

In his screen, Joyita moved in wonderful imitation of someone hard at work.

"Actually, Captain, as far as I can tell from a careful inspection, one cannot purchase an internal security scan feed from the station. It is not available on the main menus nor on any sub-menu I can locate for station services."

"I'm relieved. That's not something you usually *can* purchase openly. So tell me, please, what is the source of—*this*?" She waved her hand at Tab Two.

"Yes, Captain. We're taking the feed as available across the cable, which flows continuously both to Station Security and to Port Command, and across separate channels. Since we're monitoring all cross traffic we effectively have our own feed. The side feed is the post of the orders in force at the moment.

"Here," he continued, "are the upper passage cameras. There are several walking guards or police on patrol. They appear to take no particular interest in ship locks, though we have only a very short history to date and don't know what open-shift might—"

"Stop."

She looked at the information, the images, the list of orders in force. Distantly, she was aware that the sound of diligent triage was no longer audible from Clarence's station.

She looked to Joyita.

"The cables are so poorly shielded that we can simply…"

"You did ask for all routine searches, Captain."

Theo sighed, careful of nuance.

"And so routine now includes invading the surveillance systems of the ports where we dock? When was this protocol put into force?"

"We began, belatedly, at Jemiatha Station, Captain. *Bechimo* feels strongly that, had he been more diligent when we first took dock, he would not have failed so signally to protect his crew. Here at Minot, we've been monitoring all available communication lines in as much depth as possible. We have tapped the usual video and voice feeds, decrypting where useful. We continue to monitor for mentions of our ship or crew IDs on all accessible channels. We also take available open-radio trade, supply, emergency, maintenance, and entertainment channels. Since we are stationside, we also make use of whatever telemetry nearby ships are relaying."

"I see."

Theo looked at Clarence. Clarence returned her gaze with something very near to Father's blandest, most polite expression. No help from that quarter.

Theo tabled the matter in favor of more pressing matters. There would be plenty of time in Jump to instruct her two erring AIs regarding data theft.

Right now, since they already *had* the data, they might as well use it.

"Is there any word on Rig Tranza? Is he here on the station? And the rest of his crew?"

Joyita paused to glance down, as if he was checking a note on his desk.

"There appears to be no 'rest of his crew,' Captain. Rig Tranza is currently being housed in short-term pilot housing *here*."

Here showed up on her screen as a live-action video image of a closed door bearing the legend, *Transient Crew Cabins, shift-to-shift rates*.

"Do we know anything more?"

"He is not free to travel beyond the area, Theo."

"Under restraint?"

"He is allowed the lounge, a cubby, access to food. According to the hearing records, he awaits information, counsel, money, and support from Hugglelans Galactica. The station is billing him for his stay."

House arrest, Theo thought, in cramped short-term housing meant to be base for a two- or three-day turnaround at best. For a pilot used to the comforts of his own ship, food, and music, it would be torture. She shook her head, considering his music and his idiosyncrasies. But surely, the station would have let him gather up his kit and his necessaries before they sealed the ship. That was only civilized.

"How long has he been in there?" she asked Joyita.

"Thirty-nine port days."

She grimaced, scanned the sidebar. Thirty-nine days? Someone should have been able to do, well, *something* in that time. The Pilots Guild should have been called in, until . . .

"Hugglelans. Have they sent somebody?"

There was another pause from Joyita. A very long pause, even for a flesh-and-blood person. The answer, when it did come, was not what she expected.

"That section of the station's hearing files is still being decrypted, Captain. *Bechimo* reports that he expects a breakthrough shortly."

CHAPTER TWENTY-SIX

. . . .

Bechimo
Crew Lockers

THE PACKING LIST WAS REMARKABLY HELPFUL IN THE TASK OF sorting the unopened boxes and bags according to potential usefulness, and Kara was a pattern card of efficiency.

She put the tea aside to go to the galley; the still-functioning stasis box was reserved for possible later use.

Among the contents of the locker were boxes that had held sweets and other edibles that would likely end up in general recycling—they went into a pile. There were garments, some that might still be wearable though they were museum items now, fashions hundreds of years out of date, as well as a collection of static toys—high quality unpowered stuffed toys meant to be hugged or held, throwing balls, including a six-pack box of bowli balls and...all left sealed in the search for the additional learning units.

They largely worked in silence, exchanging such information as had to do with the sorting. Kara's choice of language at the moment was Trade, which was, Win Ton admitted, reasonable given the nature of the task. He had assayed a small pleasantry between comrades, in Liaden, which met with a noncommittal reply. After, he limited himself, also, to Trade and to sorting.

However, though Kara continued to sort efficiently, consulting the packing list as necessary, he began to feel as if she were...

dismayed. Even distressed. Given her earlier rebuff, he wondered if he should speak, offer a comrade's care, or if he should merely work on, pretending to be oblivious.

At that moment, she took the decision out of his hands, rounding on him so quickly that he barely controlled the urge to step back.

"Do you know what we have here, Win Ton? Do you see?" Her voice was tight, as if the words had been forced out of her by the strength of her feelings.

He opened his hands, gently encompassing the piles and the goods yet to be sorted.

"What I see is miscellany. Some minor tech goods, some..."

Kara snatched a box from the pile at her knee and shook it at him.

"This claims to be honey-sweet flat biscuit. There," she pointed, "*there* is a bundled box of four mixed syrups. *There*, travelers' filters for backworld water safety. Next to it, a small personal first aid kit."

"Miscellany," he offered again, keeping his voice soft and unthreatening. He considered the results of her sorting: five divisions, but by what rule they were divided, he did not know.

She took a breath and bowed as between comrades, and it was in comrade mode that she spoke next.

"Win Ton, this is not trade stuff. These are household items gathered by someone who was not of the household, for people being rushed into a ship called for service suddenly. *Bechimo* did not know his crew, being only newly aware himself; the Uncle was called upon to stock what might be needed."

She moved a hand, showing him not the piles divided, but the content of each pile.

"Child items, you see? Soft toys and amusements. Several sets of generic socks across multiple sizes, the same of ship's mocs. The captain's own tea. Socks and comforts! Sleep training units? Yes, of course, for people flung into a course they'd not finished readying for."

She handed him a small box that he had passed to her only moments before.

It was labeled *Box 13* in a very neat hand and under that was written *Meefa*. Beneath the slightly cloudy outer seal was packaging easily read, in Terran.

"Child's Encyclopedic Library of Games, Jokes, and JeeJaws?"

"Yes. Look on the other side." She spoke in safe, unnuanced Terran.

"Ideal for children eight to eleven, with family games included."

Win Ton felt the tension, felt her eyes on his face as if she was willing him to hear what she hadn't quite said.

"Meefa," he said now, changing his intonation toward the Terran, realizing that there had been small inscriptions on some of the other boxes, which he had simply ignored, deeming them not important. Hardly the sort of attention one expected from a Scout, he thought, cheeks heating. Apparently, he had more to recover than mere reflexes and muscle tone.

He handed the box back to Kara with a bow thanking her for her instruction, and pulled another box at random from the bin, this one small and dense. *Box 17.*

He repeated the number in Terran, out of respect for the list, and read through the transparent seal, "Jigat's personal set of ten gaming dice?" He paused, considered, permitted his sigh to escape. "I see that we have not thought this through."

She bowed in agreement, very lightly, with neither irony nor superiority inflected.

He was senior, here and now; it was for him to speak, to acknowledge what was here, and how it came to be here.

"The crew of *Bechimo* inherits from the crew of *Bechimo*. All honor to them, to the Uncle for equipping them as kin, and to *Bechimo* for guarding their estate. It is as if we have received their debt books."

They bowed together, in the direction of the bin and the boxes.

"We will record the names, so that we may properly explain to Theo," he began, but Kara had already pulled out her note taker.

· · · ✳ · · ·

"Theo?"

"Clarence?"

The bridge had been quiet for the last quarter hour. No new input from *Bechimo*, no news from Kara and Win Ton down at the locker; no answer to her request that someone from the Pilots Guild get in touch with her.

They *had* been getting running summaries—some of them quite pithy, as if Joyita had found the sarcasm-and-irony generator deep inside his programming—of the offers, catalogs, and off-topic messages streaming to them from Minot Station.

Joyita shared out the incoming for them to double-check and generally delete.

"Have you considered how you're going to visit Pilot Tranza?" Clarence asked.

"*How?*" Theo glanced at him and saw the question was serious. She hadn't actually *said* she was going, but—

"*How.*" He was talking Terran and let his emphatic native accent climb into it for extra measure.

"I take it for granted you've decided to go. Never was anybody in your line could leave a friend in trouble. I reckon that's hard-wired into the DNA. But we're under backup mode, if I'm remembering right, so you'll need somebody else to go with you. There has to be official contact made with Minot, letting them know you got a vested interest in the man. And you need to officially find out what got his ship arrested."

Joyita harrumphed, and not over a catalog.

"Clarence, pardon, we have a file. We have been diligent."

Clarence glared up at the screen and snapped his fingers.

"We can have all the files you can snabble off the wire, comm tech, but we gotta have that info *officially* else they'll know we're reading their mail."

Silence. Theo, who was watching the screen, saw Joyita frown.

"I see," he said, and glanced at the work screen on his left. There was some fiddling going on, as if he was entering something into a keypad and—

"I have located the port workers' social message board. I believe that as docked pilots, you have full access to this board. There have been several threads asking about *Primadonna*'s situation as well as discussions of Pilot Tever, now absent. I will send the contents and suggest you join at your earliest convenience."

Clarence half-looked at the ceiling, half at Theo, and laughed.

"Port gossip's about as official as you can get, I guess. 'Course everyone wants the inside news...geez. So it's all fine now that we're reading their mail, right?"

Theo watched Tab Two grow an edge that eventually designated itself Tab Three. She accessed it and blinked at the webwork of threaded conversations, until she saw a thread labeled *Primadonna*, and toggled it.

A couple of postings in, and she to admit that the Minot Station workers had the news all right, inside layers and layers of supposition, confusion, and truth. She read on, until she sort of felt Clarence *waiting* for her to answer him.

Without looking away from the screen, she said, "I'm going to visit as a former copilot of record. You'll stay here, in case of customs or a welcome committee for the ambassador.

"I'll take..." She paused, as she read past the gossip to the information.

Minot Station was a rougher port than she liked, though she'd been on rougher, and Pilot Tever, lately copilot on *Primadonna*, had gained himself a minor reputation as a quick-tempered, brawling conman, and a bigger one as a thief. The casual acceptance among the posters of back-hall fights made her wary. Absolutely, she should take someone with her. Crew should go in pairs on this port. She reminded herself to make that clear.

Almost she said, "Stost," into Clarence's waiting silence but, no. Stost's ID was from the Old Universe. He was more invisible than Joyita, so far as a record trail went. And she really didn't want to start a panic, if somebody decided there was an Yxtrang on-station.

So, if neither Stost, nor Chernak, nor Clarence, then who, Theo? she asked herself kindly and *fuffed* her bangs off of her forehead.

"You're right, I do *have* to go," she said at last. "This doesn't seem a friendly port for Liadens, but Win Ton will have to come with me. He's taller than Kara, and me, if it comes to that."

She heard a sort of strangled noise from her copilot, like he'd laughed and sneezed at the same time, but when she looked over, his attention was apparently on his screen.

"I'm taller than Win Ton and Kara together, in case that's escaped you. Captain, I volunteer to go as your emissary."

He paused, pushed a button low on his board, and nodded.

"I'm getting the rest of the feed now and the gossip sheet. *Up to the Minot*, is it? Somebody's sharp enough to cut."

That was a Liaden phrase. Brought into Terran, it had all the subtlety of a star hammer against hull plate.

Theo managed not to laugh, but she did grin—and there on her screen was the legal feed, and the gossip sheet, too.

She found the threads she'd been reading again, saw that they were even more complicated than those Joyita had provided. She copied and shared with Clarence one commentary:

Pilot Tranza's not going to have happy bosses. Don't say much for him or his security if he can't keep the copilot out of the treasury.

Another was more animated: *Tever ever shows his face where I can see it, he'll find out a McKathy can hit a man from behind, too. I swear my head's still ringing. Me, I'll use a wrench or a hammer on the gasper!*

Theo stopped reading, hand to forehead in exasperation and worry.

"They used double-truth on Rig, this one thinks. Do we have any records on this Tever anywhere? That's Aiji Tever, lists Walston Harrow as a home port."

From Clarence, a long, low whistle.

"Tell you what, Theo. I'm thinking this isn't just somebody jumping ship with the cashables. Port's arrested the ship all right, says here in the gossip that second board ordered all kinds of special and expensives on ship's credit, and walked away with them. So's not just whatever cash happened to be in the boot, but he drained the ship's account, too. Just happened to be a ship from Walston Harrow on-station at the time. Bet is there's more than one hand in the batter here. Your Rig's probably famous for his honesty, and that's the easiest target there is. In the meantime, the bad actor and his accomplice get away with the goods and the cash, and the ship can't pay her docking fees."

Theo sighed.

"I'm wondering where Rig got him. He had to have come from Hugglelans; Rig wouldn't take an indie on, not on *Primadonna*. And Hugglelans screens applicants *hard*."

Clarence shrugged.

"I'll ask him the question for you, Pilot, once I get to see him."

He said it like it was settled, but she let it go for the moment in favor of curiosity.

"Joyita, assemble what's available on Tever, rumor and facts, and for that matter on Walston Harrow's piloting schools and trade associations. I'll look at the report at shift end. Nobody's leaving the ship before then, anyway."

· · · ✳ · · ·

Win Ton and Kara had finished clearing the locker, placing those things that they knew to be spoiled into recycling. Each of the other four piles went into its own crate, clearly labeled as to contents, and placed, pending captain's orders, into an empty, unsealed locker.

The learning units, they carried to the engineering workroom and left them on the bench.

Then they went to the bridge, Kara with note taker in hand, to find Theo.

She was in discussion with Clarence, but broke off when they entered, and spun her chair to face them. Win Ton stood slightly behind Kara and to her right, so that she might speak first.

"How's the work going?" Theo asked.

"We have finished a preinventory sort," Kara said. "Our priority was locating the learning units, which we have done."

Theo smiled. "Excellent! How many?"

"Three portable units, Captain. We've taken them to engineering for testing."

"Do we have the ability to test them fully?" Theo asked. "Did you find instructions?"

Joyita answered before Kara could speak.

"We have the test equipment—the engineering workroom has the equipment to verify circuit integrity. Assuming all or any of the units pass integrity testing, we can run mock learning sessions before we embark on short-term volunteer testing. I have all of the instructions, as does *Bechimo*. The units should be serial numbered. We can test serially, or in parallel, as Kara sees best."

"Good," said Theo. "Thank you."

She nodded to Kara and glanced to Win Ton, meaning, so he thought, to dismiss them to their meal. He believed he had himself under control—certainly Kara had recovered her composure—but Theo apparently saw . . . something, as her next question proved.

"There's something other than the learning units?"

"Yes," said Kara, "there is. There is this."

She handed Theo the note taker.

"I see a list of names," Theo said, after a glance at the little device.

She looked up, again to Kara, and then Win Ton.

"Who are these people?"

"They . . ." Kara looked to him, and he stepped forward to her side, so that they might speak to Theo equally.

"We believe that these are the names of those who comprised *Bechimo*'s intended first crew," he said, and hesitated.

Kara caught up the narrative. "There were games and stuffed toys in the locker, with clothing and other items of a more personal nature, such as tea marked for the captain."

"There were children among the first crew?"

"*Bechimo* had been built as a long-looper," Win Ton reminded her. "A family ship."

"The first crew never arrived aboard," Clarence said quietly from his post, as if he were simply reminding them—or perhaps he was reminding Theo. "*Bechimo* got an emergency warn-away, and he went."

"A warn-away and a confirmation," Theo said, her eyes downturned, perhaps reading the names again or perhaps not.

"*Bechimo*," she said very calmly.

"Yes, Theo?"

"Do you remember the last time we talked about your first crew?"

"Yes, Theo."

"Do these names mean anything to you?"

She raised the note taker.

"Yes, Theo. Those names were on the crew roster I had from the Founders."

"All right."

She lowered the note taker and offered it to Kara, who took it and slipped it away into a pocket, with a worried glance at Theo's face. Win Ton didn't blame her; he was feeling slightly alarmed himself. A quick look aside found Clarence watching with interest, but no apparent concern.

"The last time we spoke about your first crew," Theo continued, "you said that the identity of the person who gave you the emergency order to withdraw was available only to the bonded captain. I ask the question now, as your bonded captain: Who gave you the order to withdraw?"

She did not say, Win Ton noted, "...and abandon your crew," a wise omission in his opinion.

"The order to utilize emergency programming came from Jermone Joyita, who had been my mentor and brought me to full consciousness."

"Joyita wasn't a Founder." That was Clarence, reminding one again that a man who had been the Juntavas Boss of Solcintra Port for more than twenty Standards could not be an idiot. "I'm

guessing there were codes involved to initiate emergency opera-
tions."

"Joyita was not a Founder," *Bechimo* agreed. "The nature of
his work with me made it necessary for him to have the codes."
He paused. "I believe that the captain-elect was to have changed
them upon arrival on deck."

"But she hadn't got on deck before the emergency," Theo
finished. "Who gave the confirmation, *Bechimo*?"

"Founder Yuri Tomas. It was Founder Tomas who told me
that my crew were no longer available to me and who advised
me to *await developments*."

"Yuri Tomas?" Theo repeated.

"Joyita addressed him as Uncle," said *Bechimo*, "though they
were not related biologically."

"I thought Uncle was banned from your decks," Theo said.

"That was after. He was a Founder. He had the codes and
the authority."

"Both of them ordering you to go into full emergency mode
says to me—understand, I've got some experience here—It says to
me that your crew had already been lost. If that hadn't been the
case, they'd've given you return orders or a rendezvous point."

There was a long pause before *Bechimo* spoke, and when he
did so, his voice was somber.

"Thank you, Clarence. I believe that you must be correct."

Theo sighed.

"Thank you, *Bechimo*—and Clarence. I'm glad to know the
full history. Now."

She looked at Kara. When she moved her gaze to him, Win
Ton dared a small bow. She ignored it.

"What needs to be done—with these names?"

"We need to...honor them," Kara said slowly, clearly struggling to fit the concepts that came so naturally in Liaden thought
and Liaden social structure, into the crude framework of Terran.
"We—it is as if we have been given their debt book. It is...
too late to Balance for them. But we can *remember* them, and
remember that what we have—ship, captain, and crew—comes
to us from their hands."

It was, thought Win Ton, a good effort. Whether it was sufficient to make the matter plain to Theo or would require...

"All right," Theo said, and stood up.

"*Bechimo*. Joyita."

"Yes, Theo," *Bechimo* said.

"Captain."

"I want the two of you to collaborate on finding the histories of these names—these . . . honored members of *Bechimo*'s crew. Also, find out what happened to them and why it happened. When you think you have enough biographical data, let me know. We'll arrange a whole-crew fancy dinner, to hear it all out and— celebrate them. In the meantime, please let the log show that we acknowledge ourselves as *Bechimo*'s second crew, inheriting from the first crew—and list the names. *All* the names."

"Yes, Theo," said *Bechimo* and Joyita together.

"Is this sufficient?" Theo asked, looking from him to Kara. "Is there anything else that should—that needs—to be done?"

Kara bowed, honor to the captain, though so deeply and held so long that it came perilously close to honor to the delm.

"Their honor is made whole. It is what we may do. Thank you, Captain."

It was Win Ton's turn to bow, and he abruptly found himself of Kara's mind, and thus bowed too deeply to the captain's honor, and counted the heartbeats—not the full six, but five—before he straightened and smiled at her.

"It is done well, Captain. Thank you."

"Thank you for bringing this to my attention," Theo said, inclining her head, as if she were delm, indeed, and took their bows as her due. Which was well enough, Win Ton thought. Theo was . . . not entirely well versed in the matter of bows. She would have seen *honor to the captain* and been satisfied there.

Well, no matter, he thought. If Theo could not read it, at least he—and Kara—knew what they had given.

He turned toward the galley and the meal break, and in so doing met Clarence's speculative eye.

Ah, yes, of course.

Clarence O'Berin, once Boss of Solcintra Port and very well versed in the language of bows, also knew what they had given.

CHAPTER TWENTY-SEVEN

. . . .

Bechimo
Bridge

KARA HAD EATEN QUICKLY AND TAKEN HERSELF OFF TO ENGI-
neering to begin the circuit checks on the three learning units,
leaving Win Ton the sole occupant of the galley. He ate a quiet,
leisurely meal, thinking about *melant'i*, about his clan, and about
the fact that, despite a Liaden father, Theo was Terran.

In the midst of these ruminations, he was joined by Hevelin,
who sat in his lap and murbled gently, seeming to have nothing
to share save the considerable comfort of his presence.

At the quarter hour, Win Ton reluctantly relocated his lunch-
mate to the next chair, rose, put his bowl and cup into the washer,
and went out to the bridge to relieve Clarence.

Absorbed still in his own thoughts, he did not notice Hevelin
until the door slid aside and the norbear excitedly rushed past him—

—straight into Clarence, who scooped him up with the admo-
nition, "This isn't your shift, you old PIC-grabber!" and bore him
off to the galley, sparing Win Ton a nod as he passed.

Theo ran the ship clean and tight—and it was *Theo* in this,
Win Ton knew, not *Bechimo*. Left without guidance, *Bechimo*
would do too much for his crew. A benefit of the bonding, perhaps, was that they were *not* coddled.

In any wise, a clean, tight ship, which was how the captain
had been taught to pilot, so he'd been told, first by Master Pilot

251

Orn Ald yos'Senchul, who had taken an especial interest in Theo at her ill-gotten piloting academy, and reinforced by Pilot Rig Tranza, who had held his copilot to a high standard indeed.

Taking the vacant chair, Win Ton found the board properly set: Clarence had made sure everything that was off was off, that anything that could be armed was safed except if in use, and for that matter, that his seat was properly adjusted... for him.

Win Ton sighed. It was a problem: a seat tuned for the last copilot was detuned for the next, and the second seat lacked the automatic controls that adjusted Theo's chair to her as she sat down.

"I'm in," he said, as soon as the chair was properly adjusted. "Board live. Comm live."

Theo nodded, turned a glare he was pleased was not directed at him at her screen, and sighed before leaning deliberately back in her seat.

"Let the incoming fuzz-mail talk to itself, Joyita. Hold anything that doesn't look urgent." She looked at Win Ton. "I'd like the three of us to discuss Joyita's testing protocol, in private."

"Certainly," Win Ton said and looked to his prospective student, attentive in his screen.

"At least, Joyita, you'll not have to delay a piloting session while you manually adjust the high-back support tension lock!"

Joyita smiled.

"Yes, that's so, but I do have to recall that I must not be PIC via video for any port expecting to meet me *in situ.* Sleep-learning is not so available to me as it is to you, or even to *Bechimo.* The pathfinders have been teaching me much in this regard; I thank them for the information with each lesson!"

"So," Theo said drily, "since you don't have to teach him how to adjust his chair, what are your plans for testing Joyita as a pilot?"

Win Ton closed his eyes and reached out, ticking off sections of the board, pleased to find his hand sure and his touch firm.

He opened his eyes and met Theo's.

"My plan is to treat Joyita as any other pilot candidate. I will prepare a short verbal quiz to administer before the first level of hands-on testing begins. I will, if necessary, require the candidate to assure me that all work we see will be his, aside from the delivery of information through systems which all or any pilots on board access through the grace of *Bechimo*. I understand that if required I may trust *Bechimo* to verify."

Win Ton signed *verify* as well, looking to Theo and then to Joyita in his comm control room. Joyita's gaze was elsewhere: anyone not familiar with him would assume he was in the process of adjusting his seat to sit properly at board.

"Yes, of course you can," Theo agreed out loud, while Joyita raised his hands and produced something that might have been *witness crew agrees test boss*.

Win Ton shared a smile with Theo.

"Hand-sign too? How many languages do you have? I will also mention—as one who is your teacher and wishes you to do well—that was ... somewhat awkward."

"I speak Terran, Trade, Liaden, and a pre-diaspora language specifically developed to make communication quick and accurate for those of the soldier caste."

He paused, frowning as if at a screen, then raised his head.

"I see that the sign was not only awkward, but unclear."

He stood and bowed a very credible student accepting correction from the master.

"The dialects of hand-talk are not yet firmly in place, due to variations in body language, and what I will call, lacking a better word, accent."

"Accent's as good a word as any," Theo said. "Everybody has their own style. As long as you're clear in an emergency, developing your own accent isn't a bad thing."

"I will take that under advisement," Joyita said gravely.

He turned as if to sit down, paused—and flung himself into his chair in full emergency haste. Win Ton came half out of his seat in response, then sank back as Joyita spun and smiled gently upon the bridge.

"My seat here has been a hand's width too far away from my board since I added my new screens—long before we acquired the pathfinders' company. I'm pleased to have made the adjustment before my tests.

"Also, you should know that the pathfinders have been teaching me by secret example several dialects they have yet to share. *Bechimo*'s crew might take advantage of these forms to provide ourselves an extra range of communication, since not all of the crew is yet bonded."

"Indeed, indeed! As time permits, a ship dialect is a good plan, and in fact it is a tradition among certain branches of the Scouts..." Win Ton's hand-sign to the bridge was simply *good plan*. "However, we wander from the point. The captain wished to talk about the testing protocol."

"*And*," said Theo briskly, "how long will it take you to devise an appropriate test, Pilot? If we have a free day, *will* that be sufficient?"

His hands shaped an automatic *we take this slow* in the Terran mode.

"A full and complete testing will include real-time transitions, a docking or two, full check-outs, and at least one Jump. A continuous test of local work, then a Jump with both ends handled by the candidate, that would be appropriate, I think. I believe that it is *most* appropriate to do this by the book, as nearly as practicable. I—we—are going to be setting a precedent which others may need to follow. It must be above reproach and hold up to the closest scrutiny."

Theo looked startled.

"Do you think...that there will be others?"

"I must assume that there will be. Joyita suggested that *Bechimo* ought to be licensed as well, and, on consideration, I agree. *Admiral Bunter*, if he has survived, ought also to be tested and certified.

"Licenses, paperwork, test results—these are the things that pilots, that *people*—accrue. If there are others—there must be others, Theo! Korval has the services of one such, certified sentient by the Scouts."

Theo blinked. Jeeves, of course. She hadn't thought to wonder...

"How did that happen, do you know?"

"It happened because Er Thom yos'Galan, so far as I heard the tale, was a clever, ruthless man who was not afraid to call Balance due."

"He threatened a Scout?"

"Balance," Win Ton corrected. "He was owed; both parties agreed. And his Balance was that the tests be made, and what certifications there might be, awarded, *as if the Complex Logic Laws did not exist*."

Unexpectedly, delightfully—Theo laughed. Win Ton grinned to hear it and nodded.

"Yes, precisely. But to return to our topic—we must assume that there are others, and so we must not err."

He took a deep breath and looked up to find Joyita watching him, rapt.

"I must do this correctly," he said, to Joyita as much as to Theo. "If I fail, if I make an error, all my training and all my deliberate variations from my training will have been worthless, and all yours as well. And if that happens...we'll all likely be dead for having dared."

Theo opened her mouth to speak, but Joyita broke in: "Theo, I'm declaring an urgent situation within the parameters you set at the start of our meeting. There's a new day posting of *Up to the Minot*. There will be a hearing on the *Primadonna* situation within six shifts, as an officer arrives in response to a message Rig Tranza sent via courier. I'm sending the posting to your screen tabs now. Also, *Bechimo* believes the key is within his grasp."

Theo pulled the screen up immediately, as Joyita continued in Liaden: "Win Ton, I never meant to be a danger or a burden to the crew. If my existence destroys you, I will—"

"Stop!" Win Ton was on his feet without quite knowing how he'd gotten there. Theo and Joyita were regarding him with some wonder—as well, he thought wryly, they might.

He took a breath to calm his tumbling thoughts, and bowed, suggesting quiet and harmony. He bowed, first to Joyita—his student—and, second, to Theo—his captain.

"Of all of the people on this ship, the most blameless, aside from Grakow and Hevelin, is yourself, Joyita. You must never assume or accept blame for being alive.

"The rest of us, *all* of us, put ourselves here at this time and place by our own willful decisions. For the most part, we could have been elsewhere. I could have remained on Liad, a dutiful son of my clan. Theo could have been a teacher on Delgado. Kara might have decided to debark with the others on Codrescu Station, instead of accepting an offer to crew on this ship. Surely, Clarence had options before him, and yet—we are here because we will it. It is as if we are a gathering edge of change that must happen to cure generations worth of errors, if we survive.

"You, Joyita, *are not* one of those errors. Neither is Hevelin, nor Grakow. You are carried along on this edge of ours."

Win Ton bowed to Theo, a bow of contrition.

"If we seek to place blame, the most of it must be given me, in any case. I had not meant to do this to you. I had only meant—but we have discussed this. And you, too, have been gathered unwilling into this edge of change. I hope you will, one day, forgive me, Theo."

She held up a hand, the Terran signal to stop. She stood, stretched, looked between Joyita and Win Ton. She bowed, a stark thing, yet perfectly intelligible: *necessity is.*

"Win Ton, you were right. We, all of us, chose to be here, on this deck, on this ship. I had choices. I could have sent the key back to you. I could have decided that the ghost ship I kept seeing was just what everybody else said it was—a blip in the sensors. I didn't make those choices. I'm here because I opted in. So did you. So we *are* in this together; all of us with *Bechimo* are this edge. Do you understand?"

Win Ton inclined his head.

"Yes. I understand. We are crew and comrades, no matter the reasons we are here."

Theo gave him a smile.

"Now, let's get back to—"

"Captain," said Joyita. "Two inquiries have just come in from Minot Station Control.

"The first is a query into the status of the ship we have docked to us, which we have not referenced in any way in communication with the station. Apparently, they have visually identified the ship as a ship, rather than a pod. Possibly, they have been monitoring it for shiplike activity, and are confused by their readings."

There was a pause.

"I discover no indication of active probes, so I assume visual and passive monitoring only. I have not replied to this inquiry as yet.

"The second inquiry is perhaps first in priority. There is a question from the Port Administration offices as to our intended route and availability of a mount for a mini-pod. This is in response to our docking statement that we will have minor items to trade and will consider pickup trade and goods. Port Admin explains that they have been authorized to act in the case of time-sensitive cargo which has been unduly delayed. They offer a split upfront and on-delivery payment."

Theo sat in her chair, as did Win Ton.

"We can take a mini-pod," she said slowly. "I'm curious though, Joyita. How many mini-pods are there among the ships currently on-station?"

Win Ton's Screen Three came live; he supposed the image was being shared between them. There was a quick camera scan along the docks, which settled on a single such pod...

...attached to *Primadonna*.

The image grew and ancillary information appeared along the bottom of the screen: dimensional information, pod make, mounting style...

Theo sighed.

"Joyita, please let Port Admin know that we're interested in their proposition, and ask them what the next step is."

CHAPTER TWENTY-EIGHT

. . . .

Bechimo
Bridge

"NECESSITY EXISTS!"

Deliberately, Theo said the phrase in Liaden, with a glance to Kara and to Win Ton, who both bowed acknowledgment of a point well made. Clarence inclined his head with a fluid hand motion, which meant he'd heard her, and nothing else. His face was properly bland, and he seemed, in that moment, to be completely Liaden.

Which was, Theo admitted to herself, annoying.

She shook her head and *fuffed* at the hair straggling over her forehead. Clarence was pushing hard on his point and...and *Bechimo* was concentrating on something else.

"Look, First." Clarence had shifted to backworld, low port Terran, but he was still somehow drawing on Liaden body language, so that he was speaking from the strength of considerable experience, edged with a brawling, port-tough tension she'd never seen from him before.

"*Look* at the case," he continued. "We got station debating between themselfs if they gotta send somebody down here to take a close, personal look at our pod mounts. We don't need that; we don't need the questions that happen, after." He took a breath and continued in an accent that might, Theo thought, have been the dialect of his youth.

"Well, now, the luck of ya! Just happened t'find a ship laying around loose, is it? Well, well, ain't that fine. But what we have

259

to be wonderin', in an official sort of way, if ya get m'drift—we're wonderin' where the crew's gone to. And, comin' to think on it a wee bit more, we're wonderin' who the owner might be. And, with all that said, why! It ain't too much to wonder if the lot of ya ain't just pirates, after all.'"

Theo glared at him.

"The ship belongs to Clan Korval," she said grimly.

"Which might, as Win Ton had it, play well—but only if the cards come from *your hand* as captain of this ship who signed a contract with Clan Korval, and from your own personal call, whether you care to let 'em know who your brother is—on a port where they don't talk Liaden."

Theo drew a breath, but Clarence wasn't done yet.

"And that means, *Captain* Waitley—" he said "Captain" with so much vehemence that it almost cut—"*that* means *you* need to stick to the ship in case they send a boarding party. The ship is your duty."

He paced; she stood with arms folded, not exactly pleased with being lectured, and especially in such a mode. Modes. He came 'round again on his orbit and stopped, facing her.

"I can see we want to take a look at trade, and I can see it'd be fine if we could get your mentor out of his troubles. But... you're the very captain named me executive officer of this ship. And I'm saying that *my* call as exec is that I go see these details in *my* person. If I got a question, I can call in. I've written a few contracts myself, and I can spot a bad pod from the other side of a yard. Still, if you need it, page sets can get couriered right to this ship, for the captain's review. But... *you* stay on board until they decide they don't need to do a tour. Do we have an accord?"

Theo closed her eyes.

Things had gotten complicated, that was true. It appeared the port fiscal admins wanted a way out of what was becoming a black hole for them in the form of a ship locked to dock with a cargo they'd preagreed to handle with haste. It also appeared that the dockside of port wanted to be sure of security. Also, they might, yes, be suffering from a surfeit of curiosity, given a very old ship carrying a ship of a design that no one in this universe had seen flying, well—ever.

"Faster is better, I'm thinking," Clarence continued, just speaking plain Terran now and sounding a little tired.

"The money folks get paid more, so if we can get them moving we make it so the docksiders have got to go along. The bet is to look at documents and pull on some beards to make things go fast."

Theo opened her eyes to frown at him, not recognizing the idiom. From the looks on their faces, Win Ton and Kara were even more adrift than she was.

"I believe that beards are a commonplace among elders of Clarence's homeworld," Joyita offered. "The longer a beard, the more important the person."

"That's it, and a long time since I've thought at all about either," Clarence said and sighed lightly.

"C'mon, now, lass; your Rig'll keep fine for another couple hours. And station admin won't think anything out of true with the exec coming in the captain's stead. Captains're understood to be busy by nature."

Theo sighed, too. He was right. She *was* the captain; she could delegate. And if anybody came asking official questions, she could explain *Spiral Dance*. Well. Sort of explain *Spiral Dance*.

So she nodded, first to Clarence, then to Kara and Win Ton.

"Joyita, please let Minot Station Admin know that yes, we are a tradeship, and yes, we would like to hear more about their situation and how we might help them. On the other front . . . we've made our assumptions about what they want. Ignore that query for the moment."

She paused, one hand up, signaling *wait*.

"Joyita, have you sent yet?"

"I have not. You appear to be in the process of consideration."

She nodded.

"Right. Let's cancel that first message and try this instead.

"Apologize for the delay on a reply. Tell them we're still syncing our shifts with the port shifts. So far they've only asked if we're interested and capable of handling a mini-pod. Reasonable question—it's not likely we're on anyone's ship capacities lists yet.

"So tell them—yes, we are interested in principle, and that we have an open pod mount. Let them know we're prepared to send our executive officer and our chief engineer to Station Admin, to discuss how we might help them. If they ask about performance bonds and the like, tell them those details will be part of the discussion they'll be having with the exec."

She paused, nodded once.

"The other query appears to be informal, not official. It might just be some docksiders being curious. We'll just leave that unanswered. If we get a formal inquiry, start it with the juniormost available crew member. Stall, without seeming to, while the rest of this works out."

She finished and Clarence nodded.

"I hold myself ready, Captain. We'll also have to consider Win Ton's—space! All of us ought to have consistent name badges for ports like this. Carrydocs all need to be in Terran, and any showing sigs in Terran, too."

Win Ton sat up as if he were going to object, then sank back into his chair, nodding.

"I can have those documents ready immediately," Joyita said.

"Captain's gotta agree," Clarence suggested, but Theo shook him off.

"Executive officer's got to do something, I guess, since we have one. It does sound like they're a little touchy here. I'd really like to finish our business and roll out without any...unpleasantness. Now, what about for Liaden ports, should we all have a Liaden port kit ready as well?"

"Table that 'til we're at one," said Clarence. "That would be my say. But we'll want to be set if they call me down to the office, so I'll go over what we've got on your friend's situation."

Clarence looked at Joyita.

"Can you send me that info in two? One coded to show what's in the public view and the other for what we've picked up on the side? Don't want to start off knowing too much when I'm talking to the top Johnnies, do I?"

There was a slight pause as Joyita reached out to a toggle. There was an audible *click* from his screen and he turned back with a single nod.

"Your tabs and Theo's are now color-coded. Blue is for public documents and local news reports; green is information garnered from the port newsletter and from general port directives. The white tab covers information taken from private correspondence and internal directives."

"Thank you, Joyita," Theo said and looked around at them, her gaze touching each face in turn.

"So, it's settled," she said. "Clarence will represent the ship to nder Stost?" came the now-familiar voice.

espects to the captain, and a reminder that we are

ards. It would be an honor to serve."

convey your message to the captain," Joyita said.

anks." Stost said and turned to meet Chernak's eye.

my Stost?"

it, Senior; the prospect of walking unfamiliar halls

ing new air, though it be station air, beguiles you."

now me too well," Chernak said and went back to the

tain's reply came more speedily than Stost had expected,

of course Joyita who brought it to them.

ptain thanks the pathfinders for their willingness to

ates that she has already considered you in the capacity

ort. She asks your patience while circumstances clarify

ks that you hold yourselves ready should need arise."

rned to Chernak, seeing the surprise he felt reflected

you, Joyita," she said. "We are ready on the captain's

said Stost.

Chernak agreed and stood. "I will shower and dress,

do not shame the ship should the captain call."

ep was her privilege as senior and she hurried to

lf ready. It would be best, she thought, if they were

should the captain call.

Minot Station in this if they nee

will go with Kara, our chief engi

this isn't a comfortable port. W

want all intelligence gathering

high priority, information that

"Questions? Remarks?"

There were none.

The moment of silence was

"Bridge, we have complete a

engine, as well as several Stan

We have access to station stay

"Excellent!" Theo said aloud

in the field of sense and info

to her. An image of Rig Tranz

memory she'd never had, a ma

ted himself to become, more..

face. Rig Tranza had been a ha

an effort to see good news in

Bechimo spoke again, this ti

a line from one of those Liaden

"I believe, Theo, that *Prima*

accident of theft. I am accumul

has been treachery—and I beli

. . .

Stost and Chernak considere

granted them, perusing both th

broadcasts with equal interest.

from study, while proving the

were the equal of *Up to the M*

not. The news broadcasts might

they were captioned in Trade.

spoken Terran while gaining b

to exercise those skills in whic

"An unruly station," Cherr

Up to the Minot. "One hopes

tions. She can ill afford to lose

"True," said Stost, who ha

on his screen, Grakow asleep

said, not loudly, "Friend Joyita

"Pathfi

"Our

capable gu

"I will

"My th

"Bored

"Admit

and breath

"You k

news sheet

The ca

and it was

"The c

serve and s

of crew esc

and also a

Stost tu

on her fac

"Thank

word."

"Well,"

"Well,"

so that we

First p

make herse

both ready

CHAPTER TWENTY-NINE

. . . .

Minot Station

"BUMP COMING!"

Clarence's pace was steady and comfortable, slow enough that his caution came in good time to warn Kara, if she'd needed it. He led them according to a printout they'd both memorized rather than wearing the in-ear and letting *Bechimo* or Joyita guide them, as *Bechimo* had clearly preferred.

Theo, though, had been adamant. "We don't want to look like we think there's anything strange—nothing like we suspect treachery. Most leaves, crew has comm and personal arms. So that's what we'll have, too, unless Clarence or Kara won't feel safe..."

"I'll feel safe enough, Captain," Clarence assured her, with such a degree of earnestness that Kara had regarded him thoughtfully before making her own answer.

"I will feel perfectly safe, Theo. After all, we will have a stationer escort."

That was only for part of the way, but Theo had nodded, and they were away across the docks.

The bump Clarence had warned of at the transition point was stronger than Kara expected, but then Minot Station's docks were built for spacers and not for casual cruise ship passengers. The decking was clean, if worn, and there was a spot right *there* that would have had her out with a meter and test probe if it had been *hers* to deal with. The gravity was suspiciously variable, and Kara sniffed disdainfully. Fluctuating gravity might have something to do with the restraints on *Primadonna,* which were likely on the same grid. That thought made her feel somewhat better. A station that arrested ships on a routine basis would surely have a grid dedicated to restraints.

Traffic was light, foot and cart, and when Clarence brought them around the next bend in their path and past two sets of auto-seal emergency doors, the lighting changed to a hue more comfortable to civilians.

"Lift ahead, then right and three doors, and we'll be arrived."

Kara aimed a walking bow at Clarence's back. Being Terran-sized, he took Terran-sized steps; if they'd walked in cadence she'd have fallen behind or had to strain her own stride.

She caught up to him when he paused at the lift. He signed *comms still live* to her before the door opened and they entered.

Kara looked around. The lift was an old grid design or retrofit locally rebuilt. It offered no clues as to its original builder, and the dated inspection certificates that should have been prominently displayed—were not. Kara sniffed again at that lack.

She could see no obvious surveillance, but for all she knew the floor did that work. If there was an active video monitor aboard, it was cleverly concealed. There were scarred grab bars on the lift's back wall. Someone lashed cargo there, Kara thought, else there were autocarts that locked themselves in against the bars.

The controls were actual touchpad. She sniffed at that, too, when Clarence's hand wave was insufficient to start them on their way. Well...at least *she* wasn't going to have to troubleshoot it.

Clarence was probably as busy as she was watching the equipment. If he noticed the notched insets as anything special, he didn't mention it—but to Kara it looked like at some stops there were side feeds for 'botcarts. The pattern of wear on the decking gave some credence to that theory.

Five levels down and four changes of gravity later, the lift opened its doors upon their destination and they debarked.

Once they locked on Avenue A and the pressure equalized enough to permit them to enter the hallway, their path was left, right, and straight ahead. The hall was moderately crowded, shipfolk and stationers intermingled and vastly incurious. They passed some dayside shops. Flowing arrows on the overheads promised trade bars, all-nighters, and something called a curio.

They turned their final corner and there paused. Kara frowned in irritation, for the promised guide was not—Ah, but no!

A blandly uniformed youth easily three hands taller than her stood with drink in one hand near the door. He was studying a device held in his free hand, which must have informed him of their arrival, for he suddenly looked up and at them.

He pocketed the device and moved toward them, surreptitiously dumping his beverage container into a convenient trash chute.

Clarence pivoted toward him, and she stepped up to his side.

"*Bechimo* staff?" inquired the youth.

Clarence tapped the ship's badge pinned neatly on his left breast and nodded for both of them.

"Right here. I'm executive officer." Clarence was speaking in one of his...less couth dialects of Terran, retapping the badge in emphasis.

The young man nodded and turned to Kara. He hesitated, plainly startled.

"And...engineering officer?" he said tentatively.

Kara produced a cool nod, which was an ironically proper greeting to a person of...substandard manners.

"Myself," she said, in a Terran less colorful than Clarence's choice. She tapped her badge: *K.v.Arith Engineering*.

"Oh," said their supposed guide. "I thought from the image that...that you were older."

"I am as you see me."

He reached into his pocket and brought out the device, holding it toward her.

It was, Kara admitted, a good likeness, and one she ought to share with her mother eventually. Though why it had been taken from the work deck where she was full deep in hydroponics equipment and concentrating on a—well, it *did* make her look older and disguised her height as well.

"You know who we are," Clarence said. "Care to return the favor?"

The youth's pale face flushed pink.

"I am Admin Intern Eidalec," he said, slipping the device back into its pocket. "If you will follow me, I will guide you through the inner halls. This way, please."

✳   ✳   ✳

The intern wore his permissions on his hands. At least the doors to the inner halls were of a higher order of elegance than the lift; nothing so crass as a touchpad.

Intern Eidalec was also a quiet guide, and his uniform fit him well, as Kara saw from time to time, as she glimpsed him on the far side of Clarence. He flashed his hands left or right, waking muted sounds in reply. Pneumatic slide doors with pressure seals slid aside for him. There was rhythm to his gestures, almost a dance. Kara nearly smiled; she could appreciate someone who took joy in his work.

As well as he moved, Intern Eidalec had not yet mastered the art of patience. He swung energetically out, without even a glance to be certain that his charges remained with him. Indeed, his headlong course made her realize that she needed to increase her routine workouts. It would not be good to become incapable of working in other environments, forever shipbound for lack of strength or stamina. Watching him made her consider bowli ball for the first time in . . . a long time, though where one might play on *Bechimo* . . .

Ahead, the intern stopped, so quickly that Clarence nearly overran him. He waved his left hand, but failed to rouse the door, though it had produced a small chime in recognition. Or, perhaps, in apology.

His sigh was loud in the quiet corridor. He lowered his hands and turned, looked beyond them toward the busier hall they had just quit.

Reflexively, Kara also looked that way and saw two men coming toward them, one in uniform and one in a more formal business attire.

Their guide muttered, "Of course," very quietly, and then, more loudly, to them, "Please, these officials will have the key. Let's step aside to let them through."

The officials were Dock Supervisor Franksten, in the rather well-used uniform of one personally doing day-to-day physical work, and Corp Veep Semimodo, wearing a bright, multistriped civilian suit that reminded Kara of the clothes her clan's elders had worn when she was a child. She'd seen texts at Anlingdin about the ebb and flow of fashion, even did the Econ section on the power of fashion to change cultural necessity. Now she wondered if that meant Eylot was in that culture funnel that went from Liad, bounced to Terra, bounced back to the Liaden subcenters, then spread to...

Kara realized that the man in the suit was speaking again, as if all was agreed on.

"And the case is that we'll need to use a tug or even two and cross-pull the pod, since *Primadonna*'s apparently not going anywhere soon. Or ever."

Veep Semimodo was expansive and—soft. His motions were not those of a dancer or a worker. His hands moved constantly as he pointed to this and that on the display screen that none but he could see clearly. He spoke rapidly, his voice high and as soft as his hands.

It might have been easier if they had been in a conference area but the seating in the inner office was cramped. Intern Eidalec had been relegated to a stool near the door, while she and Clarence sat on bare metal chairs, facing Semimodo across his desk, while Supervisor Franksten stood beside it.

The big display screen was angled in such a way that it favored Clarence and Semimodo, which meant that Kara and Franksten had to crane and peer. The intern had no view of the screen at all, and Kara noticed that his eyes were on her far too often.

Clarence had told them to address technical questions to her. Thus did Supervisor Franksten ask about *Bechimo*'s necessities regarding the state of the pod upon receipt.

"*Bechimo* can receive the pod docked or undocked," she said. "If it is the standard mini-pod, we will attach it to a free podpoint. We will, of course, need to establish that the pod self-checks. I assume it contains a standard power reserve and automatics."

Franksten nodded. "Standard mini-pod, so far as she checks out to us," he said.

"Excellent. Have you the values to hand?"

He looked to Veep Semimodo, as if for direction, but the administrator was studying the display.

Finally, Franksten lifted his hands, fingers fluttering *don't know*.

"We don't have the current values," he said, sounding both apologetic and irritated. "We ought to, mind you, and in the normal way, we would have 'em. Fact is, the ship's not forwarding to our comms on this."

Kara blinked and sent a quick glance to Clarence. He gave

vent to a dramatic trader's sigh before he took up the conversation, with Semimodo as his target.

"I'm able to sign for the ship if we've got a good cargo. It ain't always you see a cargo coming off a ship under arrest, but self-contained cargo is cargo if we got a destination. Cargo has to be in good order. Carrying order's gotta be good, too. Cargo history's gotta be clean."

Semimodo nodded at Clarence's points, visibly agreeing, then holding up his hand for a pause.

"The point you raise is correct. The cargo . . ." He cleared his throat, his voice going even softer. "A moment, just a moment." He looked to the intern perched on a stool. "Caffeine or beverage for those who do. You, also. This may take a bit. Use this! You know mine!"

The intern took the proffered object with a nod and turned to them.

Clarence nodded to the admin, "Thanks."

"Standard hot caff for me, no 'toot," he told Intern Eidalec. "If what you got is 'toot, I'll take water, cool or cold."

Clarence nodded at her, and Kara caught herself before recalling where she was. Not a tea, then. Well, she'd lived on Eylot; she could stomach coffee, if she had to. "The same for me, if you please."

The intern made a dancer's turn and slipped out the door with an elegant flick of the wrist.

Veep Semimodo waited until the door had closed fully before he leaned forward, his eyes on Clarence's face.

"Now here's the thing," he said, almost whispering. "The cargo's got a clean history, just longer than you might think. We've been looking at the trade situations out there toward the center of things and we offered, a while back, to be forwarding agents ourselves if it would help. We also do some of our own financing, when we can find cargoes and ships that ought to be compatible but don't have the business. Was going to put together a full proposal for you, but then we got in the middle of this muddle and it's had my attention a bit."

He sat back, waving his hands meaninglessly at the screen.

"So here, the cargo's going through to Lefavre. We don't have anyone on a regular route from here to there. Since you're route-building and haven't got a firm schedule, this felt like a fit." He smiled, uneasily to Kara's eye.

"We solve each other's problems, see? And a nice piece of profit in it for your ship."

Clarence didn't return the smile, and after a moment, the man continued.

"What's happening is that we'd been working with the Hugglelans folks on a project, on account of the situation there on Eylot. We offered them a spot if they'd want to bring some of their equipment out this way. See, you might want to consider us, route-building like you are. We give easy access to Carresens space, and through them you got a chance to do some backdoor Liaden trade and Terran trade, too—depending on how you want to go. The Hugglelans aren't so bound...well, anyway, we've done some work on this and found a few cargoes, including this one, off *Primadonna*. The Hugglelans gal now, she has a plan, and she's paid a hold fee, going to be leasing a few dock spots, all good. But this came through and we figured the timing out. She said she'd get a good reliable ship to it, and all things considered, we agreed to be forwarding agents for the cargo—goodwill, you understand. Guaranteed delivery.

"So *Primadonna* picked it up and brought it this far, stopped in for refresh and was to take it beyond, on to Lefavre. That history's clear."

Veep Semimodo paused, perhaps expecting a question or agreement. Clarence said nothing. Taking him as her model, Kara also said nothing.

Semimodo cleared his throat.

"Well, there. The ship arrived, docked, and was on kind of a counterschedule. The pilot says they were doing back-to-back shifts to make the route. What we knew was that we had orders for stuff coming in, and the ship paying fees from her own account. We knew Hugglelans—like I say, we got an arrangement with them. Still in force, far as I know. Another ship popped in—we'll forward all details to you soon's the meeting here is over—and next thing is the copilot's gone. So's a lot of expensive supplies and equipment. *Primadonna*'s got no money, account gone empty inside of a three-day layover. Pilot claims all stolen...but not our problem; bills still have to be paid. Can't release the ship until we're even—and we're not.

"On the other side, we got good evidence that the pilot got took and maybe even Hugglelans got took, which is too bad all around, but don't make a difference to our bottom line. We have to hold the ship until we get paid. But we're stuck, too, with late fees if the transship doesn't go through. Minot Station guaranteed that if the cargo started, it'd go through."

There was a sheen of sweat on his smooth brow, and he paused for breath, which Kara, at least, begrudged him not at all.

"So there it all is. Station would be obliged if you—if *Bechimo*—will take up the cargo and see it through."

There was a still moment before Clarence nodded and raised a hand to touch his chest.

"Now, I'm a pilot, so I gotta ask. *What about* the pilot? The one got took? Under arrest for theft?"

"Well, not theft. Not arrest, really. He's detained. Was, that is. Actually, now, he's on what Hugglelans calls *on furlough*, because of that situation on Eylot as much as the situation here. Had a hearing, heard from the bosses too. *He's* in the clear; no fault on him. But, see, he's stuck, too. On furlough, he can't take the ship out of here, even if either him or the ship had the money to settle those fees. Which they don't. Supposed to be somebody from Hugglelans coming to get it all straight. It's their ship, isn't it? And theirs to rebank. Guild regs say a ship can't leave where it is if it can't pay for intake at the next port. In fact, the pilot's drawing basic budget up in transient, piling up quite a bill. The pod—see, *the pod's* not arrested. Minot Station is transshipper of record. The pod *needs* to move on."

Kara took a careful breath to settle her stomach. She had never met Rig Tranza; she only knew of him from Theo's stories of her time as his copilot. Still, a pilot abandoned struck far too close to her own history for comfort.

"The pilot," she said, looking from Veep Semimodo to Supervisor Franksten. "Can he not simply . . . retreat to his ship, live on its resources, and so cease to be a burden on the resources of the station?"

Franksten nodded.

"Seems logical, at first looksee," he said. "But, see, Engineer, we're about talking a ship locked to station, an' taking station feeds. Empty, she don't use so much, but with a pilot aboard—well, it'd cost more'n it does to feed him and give 'im place to sleep stationside. Not only that, you got this problem of having a pilot on his own ship—well, the company's ship—which is the crux right there. Pilot's been furloughed by the company 'til such time as a rep comes to straighten us all out. An' see, there's this other thing. The pilot—no fault on him *here*—but he's...what do they say? Noncompliant, according to Eylot, which is Hugglelans' home port." He shrugged.

"Anyhoot, he let us pick 'im up and gave us a key. But the ship won't talk to us—we had him about a day for the hearing, then kept 'im on-station, like I said. Two days ago, though, the ship stopped confirming connections. Now the pilot's upset and doesn't have anything much to say to us.

"Legally, he says—an' the Pilots Guild would have to weigh in—legally, while the ship's under arrest and he's on furlough, he's not the pilot. While it's under arrest, he's not responsible. If somebody'd been on board, they'd've got the request and could have done what was needed to keep it unlocked. He says that's automatics, and the only one can stop 'em is somebody with the backup codes. Somebody like the owner, and maybe the code and key that went off with the copilot who's gone, they could do it. But Pilot Tranza, he's real clear that he's not *Primadonna*'s pilot right now. We tried to talk to him while he was under for the truthing, but the way in to that ship? That didn't come out."

Kara stared at her hands, thinking that...there was some-thing...not quite correct about the situation as explained, some-thing that had been left out.

She glanced to Clarence, hoping he might read her concern, but at that point the intern returned, bearing drinks and disruption.

The intern came close, handing Kara her drink. She nodded politely, seeing with relief that it was cool water and not coffee.

"And that mini-pod?" Clarence asked, receiving his own bev-erage. "If the ship ain't talking to you, how's that coming loose to transfer over to us?"

Franksten nodded at him.

"We're working on that part. I got some ideas. Oughta be soon we can do something, there. And that's what we need to talk to you about, particular."

"But, you have a shipyard here," Kara said. "Can they not extract the pod? Surely..."

Semimodo put his hand up, shaking his head.

Kara ignored him. "A yard capable of building and updating ships certainly has the tools required for an extraction!"

Veep Semimodo sighed, nodded, and looked from Franksten to the intern. As soft as he already was, still, it seemed that he deflated.

"Things aren't always as straightforward as they appear to a . . . trade-runner," he began, and then simply seemed to run out of energy.

He looked to Franksten, hands waving senselessly. The supervisor nodded. The intern, back on his stool, did not nod; his face grew grim.

"Engineers," said Franksten, "an' maybe young engineers particularly, think solutions are all in a row. Change this, fix that, done. It isn't always that way—sometimes you have to take things out of order, or wait for orders, or maybe even . . . fabricate something."

He said the last with reluctance, dragging the Terran into a quiet slur.

Semimodo spoke up then, his tone annoyed.

"There is a problem dealing with the shipyard right now. Shipping's up and sometimes the yard's working close to limit. Yard boss wants to take over my dockside and consolidate so *everything* to do with ships goes through the yard. They want in on long-range decisions and station business. That's not the way here, *never* been that way here. Station does the refuels, delivers the consumables, we—dockside and Minot Station Admin—that's our responsibility."

He stopped suddenly and produced a wan grin.

"Sorry, Pilots. Politics is all it is; nothing to bore you with."

Clarence took a sip of his water and shook his head.

"Well, now. I don't believe I've ever seen a mess as fine as this one. My suggestion is that we just take a little time with our drinks here. Then, we'll put all these points and contentions in order, an' see if there's any agreement to be made that benefits us all. Let's just all think for a space."

CHAPTER THIRTY

. . . .

Minot Station
Administrative Offices

THEY THOUGHT FOR A WHILE, WITH CLARENCE AN AGREEABLE guest, and agreeable still when it came time to listing all those points and contentions, with Semimodo taking notes toward producing a contract.

In this phase, Kara was silent, Clarence being the elder in matters of contract and advantage. Indeed, there was much that she might have learned had she given the discussion more than half her attention. The neat disarming of Veep Semimodo's discourse on financial necessities, as well as the acquisition of a guarantee that, even if the pod were not released in a reasonable time, *Bechimo* would receive a "kill fee" to, so Clarence said, compensate them for *lost opportunity*.

No, even given the rare chance to watch a master at his work, Kara found herself thinking not of the business at hand, but of Eylot.

Eylot was her homeworld; her clan and many friends were still on-world. The few words that had been spoken regarding the "situation" there filled her with foreboding.

Staring into what remained of her drink, she struggled with herself and her need to know...

There! They were talking about lift systems, a topic in which she normally had a great deal of interest. Now, she merely waited until there was a break in the conversation and addressed Veep Semimodo in her best approximation of the High Tongue's imperative mode, were the High Tongue rendered in Terran.

"Forgive me, sir. We have been in transit, all of our attention upon the possibilities of this port and that. In reference to the furloughed pilot, you mentioned a *situation* on Eylot."

She glanced aside at Clarence, who inclined his head and raised his cup for another sip.

Feeling more certain of her course, she continued.

"Our ship was recently through Eylot's system. When I was a student pilot, I was employed by Hugglelans as a part-time tech. I hired onto *Bechimo* from the station there, when it was...absorbed by the government. I wonder—have matters on-world worsened?"

She had almost said "pirated," which would not have been... diplomatic. Of course it would have been wrong to say; that she had even thought the word was a testament to the depth and degree of her unease.

Semimodo, in the meantime, had been caught by a point of trivia.

"Pilot, you say?" He leaned forward, as if to get a better view of her.

"Pilot *and* engineer? Worked on a station, too? As young as you look? I can't imagine how a pretty..."

Clarence broke in, with a smile Kara could not, herself, have mustered.

"*Bechimo*, ship and crew, we pride ourselves on keeping young-looking, Corp Veep. But, young or not, the engineer's concern is legit. Don't mind sharing the fact that we had ourselves a tense situation there. All worked itself out, and we been away awhile. What's that news?"

The admin awarded the "keeping young" quip a chuckle before shaking his head.

"I don't keep up with all of it; seems to change every time we hear, and I got the station to run, of course. Intern Eidalec here, he's your man for up-to-date news. He pays attention on account of his studies—that's sector history, public service, politics, policy, and I don't know what all else, when he's not working with us."

Intern Eidalec beamed, mostly at Kara.

"Yes. I'm very interested in the history of conflicts and also about world and station security issues.

"As for Eylot, I can't say things have *worsened*," he said. "More accurately, they are *clarifying*. I have files and files of the government news releases, and I've read through the basic proposals that Mayko Ikari and the planetary advisory team have been working on."

He shot a glance at Veep Semimodo, who nodded and waved an indulgent hand.

"Yes. What's happening is that the Eylot government is consolidating, after a troubled period and some internal problems. It appears that the unrest caused by the nonnative populations has been subdued and good order is being restored. Unfortunately for Hugglelans, this more robust government is absorbing—they call it professionalizing!—some of the functions that their business has historically handled, for private profit. In order to better function . . ."

It was good, Kara thought, that she had begun this from a formal mode. She preserved her countenance and controlled her breathing, though the intern was clearly approving of this more robust government and the steps taken against the nonnative populations.

Nonnative? she thought, in momentary outrage. She had been born on Eylot, and three generations before her! And what did good order restored portend? Had there been—a war. Her clan . . .

But, here, the intern spoke on.

"Many of the Eylot government's actions are actions we would take on this station, in the case of security issues. I can't imagine that a planet ought to be under less control than a space station. I mean, there are so many more people to protect. And here—on this station, the policy has always been to ensure that there's no confusion of language or culture. Station Admin in the past has discussed making the official station language Terran, but there are so many Terran dialects, allowing Trade to be spoken is absolutely the better solution, in the service of less confusion. Why—"

Veep Semimodo made a rolling motion with his hand. The intern flushed and fell silent.

"Getting back to the case before us, Hugglelans gives us to understand that they have considerable . . . assets. Yes, considerable assets, which have never been on Eylot or even in that system, and they feel—and I think rightly—that they should take this opportunity to reorganize elsewhere. At the same time, see, the government's been assisting in the negotiations and the redistribution of assets.

"Now, of course, Minot Admin finds much to admire in Eylot's stronger security. In turn the Eylot government finds Minot Station more acceptable to them than—well, no sense naming names. We'll just say, *other stations!*"

He smiled. Kara gritted her teeth.

"In the case of Pilot Tranza—he's not a strong supporter of the new government or its work, plus he wasn't born on Eylot. And he holds a Terran Guild license. Not that a Terran pilot *needs* to have an Eylot license, but see, Minot Station will be able to help Eylot be sure that only Eylot certified pilots leave for their system from here. Like Eidalec said, it does appear that Eylot is getting itself in order. If you like, I can have some of the press release files and news sent to you."

Kara managed to nod politely. "Thank you, that would be a kindness. Also, if you have cites and references to other news services, that would interest me as well."

"Ah, of course, a scholar as well as a very pretty pilot *and* engineer. I'll be happy to provide—"

"And I believe," Kara interrupted, deliberately rude as she turned to Supervisor Franksten, "if you can provide the model number and serial information for the mini-pod, I may have a solution in mind. I will need time to look at it and run a few sims from my own desk, of course, but if you can certify that the pod is yours, engineering may be able to solve the problem of moving it."

"Right!" Veep Semimodo said and abruptly stood.

Clarence came to his feet and Kara followed his lead.

"So, thank you both for being so generous with your time and consideration of our little problem. I'll get this contract into order and send it over the wire to *Bechimo*. Proposed contract only, see? Something for you and your captain to look over and to talk about."

"Sounds fine," Clarence assured them, and with a few handshakes and shapeless bows, they escaped into the corridor.

· · · ✴ · · ·

Given their journey and the manner of it, news reached them oddly, often long after notable events had transpired.

So it had been with the attack upon Liad, a Troop's highest dream of conquest. Sadly or, Vepal thought, happily, the attack had not been delivered by the Troop. Yxtrang had never yet penetrated the defenses guarding *that* rich prize. In fact, if one had a taste for irony, which Vepal had acquired over the cycles, one might find it exquisite, that the blow had been struck by a Liaden clan, of a name even Yxtrang knew.

Clan Korval, so the reports had it, had either delivered Balance to their homeworld, else they had acted with a hero's decisiveness to rid that same homeworld of a hidden enemy.

Their motive scarcely mattered to Vepal; he had never looked for allies on Liad, being fonder of his life than was perhaps seemly in one of the Troop. Still, a fact that remained remarkably consistent across all of his sources was this: Clan Korval included within itself...

Three Yxtrang soldiers.

Vepal felt a thrill, as if he were about to engage, and took a moment to calm himself and think.

There were several possibilities, after all, and this news was nearly a cycle old.

The first, and most likely, possibility was that the reporters had gotten their facts wrong. This happened often, though he could not recall a previous occasion when *all* the news sources had reported the same error as fact.

The second possibility, which was only second because Liadens were remarkably lax in discipline, was that Clan Korval, and all those subordinate to them, had been executed.

The third possibility—but this game was unworthy of him. The news packet was old, but it was possible that it was recent enough to report what had become of Clan Korval, and its three Yxtrang soldiers.

The search returned multiple answers.

Once again, all sources were in agreement: Clan Korval had been banished from Liad and had removed themselves, all personnel and such property as they could manage, though where they had gone *to* remained unreported.

The trade papers provided that answer.

Surebleak, in the Daiellen Sector.

· · · ❖ · · ·

Their time away from the ship was not officially leave, but Semimodo's parting hope that they would avail themselves of the station's amenities, coupled with Clarence's known tendency to wander toward anything resembling a shopping opportunity, meant that Kara was unsurprised when his hand-sign suggested they turn right rather than taking the lift directly to the docks.

If it was a direction chosen at random, it was stereotypical for crew just in. Just around the corner they found quiet bars and carts with prepacked snacks and finger foods, boards advertising crashpads by the quarter shift—and not two hundred paces in, Kara caught a glimpse.

"We are being followed." She spoke low, in Liaden.

Clarence remained visibly absorbed by the sights, watching, as he usually was, for specialty baked items, breads, spices.

"Yes? Is it *we* or is it *you*?"

Kara sighed. "I don't know."

She pointed at a displayed specialty dish that she doubted she would ever be hungry enough to eat.

"How can something made of spun sugar be a rarity?" she asked in overbright Terran.

Clarence leaned close, apparently to get a better view of this item, and she continued in quiet Liaden.

"He is very clumsy for someone who moves so well."

Clarence nodded and pointed to another item in the same display.

"One should know the play before one acts it," he said, also in Liaden, and despite her irritation, Kara very nearly laughed. Instead, she bent her head slightly.

"Indeed," she said solemnly. "Guruki's deathbed scene is full of sense and nuance, do you agree? Do I find a devotee of her work?"

Clarence did laugh, but quietly.

"I am caught out," he murmured. "In my former position, I was often given tickets to the plays. Entertainment cries out for exploitation!"

She seized this opportunity to scan behind them. Yes, there.

"Certainly," she said to Clarence, "one cannot help but admire act three of *A Clan of Mysterious Melant'i.* It is a classic." She sighed. "I suppose the *nubiantil* doesn't realize that I find his height conspicuous."

"Young sweet thing?" Clarence did a translation on the fly and chuckled, cocking his head to the right.

Kara followed him, and he slowed his pace to match hers. There was sufficient traffic in the hall that Liaden might be over-heard and call unwanted attention to them.

"He's got some cute if you like the style, I guess," Clarence continued, in dubious Terran. "Low on sense, though. Don't think anybody on board would appreciate him much, not even Grakow."

Again, Kara did not laugh, but it was a near thing. She glanced at the shop they were passing and held up her hand. Clarence obligingly stopped.

"Let us go in here and I will buy us a loaf of that round bread, with the ingredients listed. It reminds me of something I miss from home—from Eylot. Once the pathfinders are set on their way, I will add a tray of chekin seed to the 'ponics mix. It will go well, I think, with some of your loaves, and you may not know it." She glanced over Clarence's shoulder.

"There he goes—beyond us. Ah! He thinks we may have gone into that bar. I wonder how long he will watch it."

"Long enough for us to buy your loaf and walk soft back to the ship," Clarence said, waving her toward the shop's door.

She paused a moment more, thinking about Intern Eidalec, then looked up at Clarence.

"My clan no longer keeps a book of Balances, but he tempts me to begin one."

CHAPTER THIRTY-ONE

Bechimo
Bridge

"WELL, SURE IT *CAN* BE DONE. BUT THAT DON'T MEAN IT *OUGHT* to be done!"

Kara sighed. Upon their return to *Bechimo*, they had reported to Theo; then, as the promised draft contract had not yet arrived from Veep Semimodo, Kara sat down in third seat and opened her files.

As she had recalled, there was a protocol for releasing pods for which there were no codes in hand—but Clarence, who ought to have been delighted to hear it, was arguing again.

And pacing again, too.

"Well, why *shouldn't* it be done?" Theo asked reasonably, from second chair. Win Ton, in first, had his head down and his eyes on his screens, where he was, so he had said, devising a piloting test for Joyita.

Clarence turned to face Theo.

"Do you—do *we*—want it to get about that *Bechimo* has a touch with breaking a pod?"

Theo blinked. "If the contract—"

Clarence held up his hand.

"No, no, lassie. You're too innocent to be a captain, no offense intended. I'm speaking from experience here. I know we can break the pod loose. Used to be a fair hand at it myself, though

283

it got to be I hired an expert when the work had to be done. *Melant'i*, that was. And breaking a pod loose from its rightful ship is close enough to piracy. Even if there's ways—which I'm not arguing—good ships and well-behaved captains pretend they've got no idea."

Kara sighed. Hevelin was sharing her seat, demanding to know . . . something, which was distracting her from the matter at hand.

"Hush," she said to the norbear. "I need to speak with Clarence."

Surprisingly, Hevelin hushed, though he did not leave her side. Clarence spun on his heel to face her.

"Listening," he said.

"At school we—Theo and I—had a cargo master teaching one course. He'd retired after fifty years in space, he said. Therny Chirs, his name was, and he was Terran. A very blunt, unsubtle man, so you would think from his lectures. Then, come the tests you would understand just how subtle he was.

"As much as he spoke to the importance of properly filled-out paperwork, and the necessity of obeying rules and regulations, he also spoke to those times when the rules must be . . . circumvented.

"He taught that we needed to know the difference between law and rule, rule and custom. And he said that it was vital to know the difference between possible, useful, practical, and fatal."

She pointed at her screen.

"Here I have the practical procedure for loosing *Primadonna*'s pod. Certainly, then, such an action is possible. It would be useful to accomplish this as soon as possible."

"And fatal to the ship's reputation, if we're the ones who do the deed," Clarence finished grimly.

Kara frowned at him.

"Professor Chirs also warned us that the closer we got to a cargo's destination, the more important it was that the most recent waypoint's credentials and tracking be clear. If I go into this pod's externals and open it, those are going to show—it's not a pod we own and it isn't a pod that Hugglelans owns—"

"My point!" Clarence interrupted. "There's already enough talk about this ship without the scuttle getting around that the engineer's able and willing to hotshot a pod. You heard them at the meeting. Excuses all around, and politics, too. They *want us* to remove that pod, and they were pushing it at us as fast as they could dance. There's something under the deal they think might burn them and they'd rather it was us instead."

"So," said Theo. "If the local yard won't remove the pod, and we—" she wrinkled her nose, "*ought not* remove it—and you make a good point, Clarence. We don't need any more rumors around this ship! If the pod can't come loose from *Primadonna*, then there's nothing to transship and no deal. We might as well call Veep Semimodo and tell him not to bother sending over the contract."

"Now, now, not so fast, Captain," Clarence said. "There's no harm at looking the offer over, and it might be we can make them so desperate they *will* get a tech over from their yard to do the needful. Then Kara can watch it done in real time, to back up what she has from theory. There's your possible, useful, and practical test right there. Let somebody else do it and we'll avoid the fatal."

Kara looked to Theo, who was frowning at the pirated screen feed of *Primadonna*. Motion on that image caught her eye—

"Theo!"

"It's back again," Theo said, turning her chair around with a shrug. "Just a drone. *Bechimo*'s been tracking it. So far, it's just been looking at us."

She rose suddenly and danced a step or two of a relaxation sequence.

"All right. We haven't signed anything yet. We haven't even seen the draft contract. We'll wait for that and see what they're offering. If Clarence thinks he can manipulate them into removing the pod themselves—they guaranteed delivery, didn't they? There must be penalties if they *don't* deliver, so they might be getting worried about that..."

Hevelin murbled, loudly, with an overtone of complaint.

Theo frowned.

"What's he saying?"

Kara moved her shoulders.

"I am not certain I have it all. No, perhaps I do. I think Hevelin is excited because he thinks he's met—or maybe someone he knows has met—Professor Chirs. I see him from Hevelin, but younger—much younger—than when we knew him, Theo. The location...I'm not certain, but there is another norbear present.

I think not Podesta, but...they could have met. Hevelin thinks there's something *important* about this."

Theo nodded.

"Remind me about that. For the moment, the pod—we'll wait for the contract, but it might just be that Rig Tranza would be willing to give us a release code. Which is another reason for me to see him—"

She held a hand up, palm out, toward Clarence.

"But, there's good reasons why I shouldn't leave the ship. So, Clarence will go see Rig. From what I hear about that intern, I think it's best if Kara *doesn't* go."

Kara glanced up sharply—and withheld her comment. It was prudent to avoid trouble, even the possibility of trouble.

"Clarence will go," Theo continued. "In fact, Clarence and Win Ton will go. Kara, please explain to Win Ton what you understand about the technique for unlocking the pod from *Primadonna* and the best way for us to relock it securely. Then, if he'll talk about it at all, we'll find out what Rig Tranza thinks."

"Yes, Captain," she said.

"Yes, Captain," said Clarence.

Win Ton looked up from his screen, and inclined his head. "Yes, Captain."

CHAPTER THIRTY-TWO

. . . .

Minot Station
Transient Crew Cabins

THE SHORT-TERM ACCOMMODATIONS AND READY ROOMS WERE close by. Not quite so near as *Primadonna* herself, which was scarcely a hundred steps from their own berth, but only that hundred steps on dock level, down a single level, and fifty paces back toward *Bechimo*. Not by any means an arduous journey.

Nor did they encounter any trouble as they walked. Win Ton had not himself *expected* any trouble dockside. In his experience, dockside trouble was found in restless crowds running between strange shifts.

There *had* been trouble of sorts at the ship, with arguments presented by both *Bechimo* and Joyita once Theo heard out what they'd learned regarding Rig Tranza's situation—and were still learning. Unprecedented: Theo called for a private conference between herself and the ship's AIs.

In the wake of that conference, Clarence and he were required to check arms and to each accept a personal locator. They were also each given a Terran kilobit coin. Win Ton had been dubious, but Clarence had raised no objection to carrying one, though they were large and showed easily on metal detectors.

Theo had seen his frown and nodded.

"I'd give you a cantra for just in case, but there's no proof this place accepts cantra as money."

Then came the dangerous items.

"You're sure on this, Theo?" Clarence asked.

Theo was serious. In fact, she was adamant.

"I am. They'll go to dust if you overtwist them. If Rig's not interested, that's what you'll do. If you get stopped by ... *anybody*, that's what you'll do."

"And elsewise, we're carrying info that we don't know so we can't repeat it?" Clarence was not a happy man, Win Ton saw. Well, and neither was he.

Theo frowned.

"Do you want me to do this? It would be much easier, and I was set to go, but my exec wouldn't hear of it. So, call it an order."

Clarence bowed his head, caught, as the saying went, on his own hook.

"Yes, Captain," he said, and Win Ton said likewise.

The itinerant pilots' short-stay quarters were at the end of a shadeless antiseptic swipe-clean passage of indeterminate color. The door opened when Clarence touched the plate, and they entered, going left into what proved to be a small, largely empty automated cafeteria.

The sole occupant of this cheerless room was a large Terran, who looked up when Clarence said they were looking for Rig Tranza.

"That'll be me," he said with a nod. "Pardon the crush, Pilots, right? You got here at a good time, though. One of the outgoing pilots did me good; took my letter and sprang for a 'fresher run for me and my clothes. C'mon, sit down and be comfortable! Welcome."

He spoke loudly, did the large star pilot, and shrugged his way into a corner of the room as if he had a dozen visitors, rather than two.

He wore a clean khaki shirt, with TRANZA in Terran script over the Hugglelans logo and, as if he'd seen Win Ton's glance, he said, "You know who I am, right? Come lookin' for me by name. There's only one abandoned pilot here on this station and that's Rig Tranza. You can ignore the 'lans part of this"—he tapped his chest—"'cause right now I'm on station ration."

He pointed at a small table and benches.

"Sit, sit. I been doing a lot of that, so let me lean just here, if you don't mind."

His hands went from massive, meaningless movement to tightly controlled hand-sign: *survey system sound plus video behind me,* his fingers said, while aloud he continued, loud and affable, "I do thank you for taking time out from a busy day."

Win Ton bowed and sat at the table indicated. Clarence, however, stepped up to Tranza, offered and shook his hand, even patted him on his arm as if they were kin or intimate friends. Something transpired there that Win Ton didn't fully see, some signal passed...

"Any port in a storm, that's a saying, isn't it?" Tranza said, patting Clarence's arm in turn and releasing his hand. "But I'm not quite into storm yet. This is more like sunspots 'round the rim."

"Understood, Pilot, understood."

The two large pilots parted, measuring each other. Tranza was younger by more than a dozen years, but no youth; alert, yet showing a profound weariness in the lines of his face.

Clarence took a seat at the table, and Tranza went on.

"I get borrowed and side information here—get to see the arrivals. There it was, large as you like it—*Bechimo*, Laughing Cat. Theo Waitley, Owner and Pilot! And not a courier, neither, but a capable, decent-size ship, and a couple of pilots to run backup, too. Knew she had it in her!"

He held up a hand, reaching to his back pocket with the other.

"Just a second, right?"

From the pocket came a small, flat device Win Ton recognized as a local receiver. Tranza tapped it on and music flowed; not loud, but noticeable. The pilot leaned carefully against the wall and sighed. A fluctuating beat with a persistent undertone—perhaps bells or voices—settled over the constant whisper from the air vent like a blanket.

"Hope you all don't mind a little music...helps take the hiss out of the air. Sorry it isn't anything civilized or got any choice at all; all my music's on the ship and this is the only feed I can get that's not all advertisements for stuff I can't afford to buy even if I wanted it."

Win Ton doubted the music could cover their entire conversation, but he hand-signed *is perfect, do.*

"By all means, by all means," Clarence said heartily. "Theo told us you was one for music!"

Tranza sketched a salute, his grin wan.

"So tell me," he said, "how you like running an old ship? Looks in good shape—must have some quirks though, right?"

Clarence laughed.

"Show me a ship and I'll find you some quirks. Gotta tell you, though—one of the best close-in handling ships I ever handled. Else, has some comm and view stuff newer ships could use, but pilots got out of the habit of. Beside that, I got Theo in first seat, and she makes everything look smooth."

Tranza nodded and spread his hands in question.

"So, right. *Did* Theo send you?"

"Did. Sends regrets she can't come herself."

As he spoke, Clarence leaned in, quick hands sliding through *affirmative* with hints of *special research info* that Win Ton couldn't be certain that the other pilot picked up.

Clarence was continuing, still in that cheerful, hearty voice, "Unnerstan, I'd've prolly stopped by on mine ownself's interest, if you know what I mean. I been on a lot of docks, and I'm always looking to find out what's really happened when there's been a hoorah. Half cat, *máthair* swore it. Other hand, Theo wanted to get your side to this. Is it contract issues? Flight time?"

Tranza sighed.

"No, nothing like that. Was just like this, see, Pilots..."

The tale he produced was as near to what they had seen in the port news as made no difference. He spoke clearly and to the point—which Win Ton admired—adding details, as well as some unlikely ancestors into his account of the rogue copilot, before he began to account his own errors.

"Tell you what, Pilots—*always* let your instincts into your decisions, always! A boss brought me that one, with better credentials than Theo came with. Well, I felt something was a tad off, but—really prefer not to run entirely solo. And I'd had a bit of a tiff with that boss not long ago, so I thought maybe I should go with. Clear I was right, and a damn fool not to refuse him!"

Win Ton bowed, acknowledging the correctness of a statement tempered with experience in proving it.

"Got that," Clarence said with a nod. "That's how I ended up as exec on *Bechimo*. Got an offer from the captain on short notice; she'd got advice from a source she trusted. All of it instinct, I guess. Took a look at the ship and the flight deck and I was in—but there, the choice was plain, right there in front of me. Been some interesting times since, but I wouldn't have skipped them."

Win Ton felt two gazes on him. Clarence's was backed by a quirky grin, Tranza's with ordinary interest.

Win Ton bowed again gently, seeing that this was a bonding, a winning of trust for themselves and not only on Theo's behalf. "I also fly with *Bechimo* on instinct, Pilots. I cannot tell you all of it—the captain may relate her own history, if she wishes—but this I will tell you: she is my captain now because when I first met her I was...captivated. So young, so strong—so capable! She was a student, an excellent student and so much promise! Then she...was gone from my orbit and we lost contact. Then, the universe threw the dice in my favor, placing me on the deck of the ship she commands now, quite unexpectedly. Nor would I have it otherwise."

Tranza nodded vigorously, his grin becoming a laugh.

"Don't have to tell me," he said, "Seen her grow myself. Little leery at first of assuming too much command..."

Clarence laughed out loud, and Win Ton permitted his smile to widen, so that Rig Tranza might read it.

"I think," Win Ton said, "that...our Theo has the instinct for commanding loyalty, the instinct of command itself. Thus, we are all at her command." He inclined his head.

"And you—your status? Your ship is arrested—this is the first time I have encountered such and would not have known it was possible, save for a law course I've long ago let go."

Tranza resettled against the wall and touched the little device. The volume of the music increased somewhat.

"Yeah, I'm stuck, is what I am. And I made enough mistakes I'm not likely to get that ship back, even if I get my job back. First mistake though, was not trusting my instincts. Tever...I *never* should've took him on. One of the bosses—"

Clarence held up a hand, cutting off the repeated recitation of error.

"News is that a pilot's got to do what a pilot's got to do," he said. "Pilot's choice."

Tranza nodded.

"Always the way, right? Always."

He said nothing else and seemed about to sink again into his own thoughts. Win Ton dared to put a question of his own.

"Do you know the other reason we've come?"

Tranza sighed, his expression dour.

"I'm guessing, right, that they want you to take the cargo, right? More stupid shoved down—" He shook his head, cutting off his own commentary, and flung out a brusque sign that fell somewhere between *tell more* and *out with it.*

"Yes. The mini-pod has been offered to us—to *Bechimo*—as a cargo. Costs prepaid."

Tranza whistled and shook his head.

"Politics," he spat out. "More of the damn politics! What I need to do is find me a quiet place to fly back and forth and forth and back where they don't suffocate me in politics!"

Head slightly to one side, Clarence waited. Finally, Tranza waved an annoyed hand.

"Might as well do it. I'm not telling no pilot I trained to turn down an honest offer." He flipped his hand—palm up, palm down. "Sure, do it. Not my skin at this point. Not my ship neither, more's the pity."

"Ah," Win Ton said softly. "About that. There is the matter of releasing the pod. It would be better for all, if we could find a noninvasive way of releasing the pod."

Tranza looked into Win Ton's face, his own grim.

"Would, wouldn't it? Trouble there is that they—Minot Station Admin, that is—they have my keys. Wouldn't hear me when I asked to get my music and my gear so I could live off-ship like a pilot instead of a prisoner. Wouldn't hear me when I told 'em the lockout would happen if Mayko triggered furlough—which she did, fast enough you'd think she'd been sitting there waiting to hear there was trouble. My keys—the ones they got—they might as well be playing cards, for all the use they'll be, unlocking *'donna*. I can't even reclaim what I own 'til somebody from Hugglelans shows up."

He closed his eyes briefly, opened them, and shrugged.

"Not my ship, gentlemen. Can't help, hate to disappoint. Now, thank you both for dropping by—and give Theo my best salute."

This was a clear attempt at dismissal. Win Ton hesitated, looking to Clarence, who had leaned forward somewhat, elbows on the table, one hand slightly extended and cupped, as if he held something beneath.

"I wonder, Pilot, if you have time to look at a couple things? One's something that Theo wrote to you—haven't seen it it myself, unnerstan—just something she said she saw in a contract and wanted to remind you about. Other one—haven't seen that one, either—she said it was commentary on the topic at hand. Win

Ton's got that. No need to feed 'em through the station's reader—you can borrow mine."

Tranza's tight mouth showed he wasn't amused.

"I got no lift scheduled," he said stiffly, coming out of his lean and stepping toward the table. "Might as well read what she's got to say."

Clarence lifted his hand to reveal the chip, simultaneously bringing the reader from his right pocket. Win Ton offered his chip left-handed, leaning far in over the table and close enough to shield Clarence's hand-signs, *special comm system interception*.

Tranza looked between them cautiously and gave the chips a knowing glance as he sat down across from them.

"Well, right. If I recall things, Theo had a special interest in contracts... lemme take a look."

"Let me spring for some snacks," Clarence suggested, pushing his chair back. "Got no place else to be for a bit, and maybe we can answer questions, if you got 'em."

Clarence brought a loaded tray back, handed out drinks and left the snacks on the tray at table center, where they were in easy reach of all. He leaned back in his chair and considered each of the snacks in turn, as if considering how to make it.

Win Ton watched Tranza with Scout eyes, a more interesting prospect than giving his attention to the music interspersed with poorly produced recountings of the goods available in the station shops.

Tranza's face softened as he began reading Theo's letter, then slowly hardened, tension lines growing around his eyes. There came an involuntary motion of his right wrist and a hastening of the reading.

Head down, the pilot ejected the first chip and inserted the second, but instead of immediately returning to reading, he looked up, meeting Win Ton's eyes, then Clarence's.

"Right. Well, Theo's smart; always been. I'm done with this, Pilot, if you want to take care of it."

That meaning was clear, and the first chip's powdery residue joined a less-than-palatable edge of overcooked pastry on the corner of Win Ton's plate.

Tranza took a deep swallow from his cup and bent once more to the reader.

The information on this chip was denser, thought Win Ton, watching Tranza's face. Denser and more disturbing. The lines about Tranza's mouth deepened; there came minute tremors of the jaw, as if the pilot were holding back choice commentary. His eyes grew hard.

Occasionally, he would pause in his reading and look up to reach for his cup, drinking as if he wished it were something more potent than flavored fizz water.

At one point, he stopped reading altogether and stared down at his fingers as he flexed them, apparently deep in thought.

At last, he reached an end. He handed the reader back to Clarence after ejecting the chip and personally spreading the dust over the snack remains on his plate.

"'Preciate the loan, Pilot." He sighed, and picked up his cup for a more moderate sip. "Might be something, right? I get my messages twice a day; got nothing answering the first letter I sent. 'S'posed to be hearing something official soon, any whiles. At least I *thought* I was."

Tranza pulled one last sip, tossed the empty onto the same plate the chip's powder decorated. "So tell Theo this: Mayko brought me Tever, face to face. And I took him as a special favor." He nodded firmly. "Yeah, tell her that.

"Tell her, too, if I got no news come next mail call, the song's on the last stanza."

He stared at Clarence when he said the phrase, then moved his gaze to Win Ton.

"Tell her that particular, right? *Song's on the last stanza*. It'd be good if you got your contracts all set and signed before then."

CHAPTER THIRTY-THREE

. . . .

Bechimo
Minot Station

"CLARENCE AND WIN TON HAVE RETURNED, CAPTAIN," JOYITA said quietly, as if Theo hadn't felt the lock cycle and their footsteps down the long corridor.

And, she thought, looking up from her study of Minot Admin's contract to transship a mini-pod, *does Joyita know I know that? Joyita isn't part of the bonding, and I don't know what Joyita feels—if anything—when the main hatch opens.*

So.

"Thank you, Joyita," she said courteously. "Please ask them to come to the bridge, if they're not already on course. I'll meet them there."

"Yes, Captain."

Theo sat first seat. Kara was at third, still searching for a protocol to unlock the mini-pod from *Primadonna,* Hevelin sitting on the arm of her chair.

Theo felt weight in the hall outside. Maybe Hevelin felt the same thing or was informed by another sense; he scrambled down from his perch and rushed across the room, just as the door slid aside.

Win Ton entered first, walking Scout-silent, which he usually remembered not to do on board, his face stringently bland.

Theo felt her stomach tighten. The meeting with Tranza had been bad, then...

Three steps into the room, he stopped and bowed, managing Hevelin's leap into his arms as if he had planned it.

Clarence came onto the bridge, walking not so silently, but more slowly than was usual. He crossed the bridge and sat, carefully, in the second chair.

"Captain," he said neutrally, giving her a nod.

"Second," she said, trying to match his tone and missing.

Win Ton was still standing, Hevelin on his shoulder. Theo looked at him and he took a breath, possibly to center himself.

"Captain," he said, "we bring a message from Pilot Tranza. Also, Clarence has a report."

Formality, Theo thought, implied import. Her stomach hurt. The meeting with Rig had gone *really* bad, then, though she couldn't imagine...

Well, she didn't *have* to imagine, did she?

"Report first," she said. "Win Ton, sit down, please. I don't want to put a crick in my neck, looking up at you." That, she told herself, was better. If she wasn't grumpy on her own behalf, he would take the request that he sit as a comment on his strength. Or lack of it.

"Yes, Captain." He sought the observer's chair, Hevelin effortlessly riding his shoulder.

Clarence cleared his throat.

"Your man's on his last tank of air, Theo," he said, less neutral now. "He's decided his ship's lost to him—declared himself abandoned, and that's not something a pilot wants to ever say. Claims he has expectations from the Hugglelans, still...wants 'til the next mail, thinking there's a message."

She shook her head.

"He's that way, Clarence. He wants to be exact. To be careful. To be sure. He likes to be sure. The info we sent him...makes it clear that there's no rush for anybody from Hugglelans to come get him. He'd written direct to the home office, to the head of the company—Rig and him were youngers together, he told me. It was how he got *Primadonna*, fresh and new, to call his so long as he ran goods for Hugglelans.

"So, he sent to the top, but the boss never saw the letter. Tever screened it—and sent it on to Mayko, since she's coordinating the

expansion in this sector. Mayko answered that they were busy right now and they'd get to him eventually."

Clarence sighed.

"He said that Mayko brought him Pilot Tever."

"That's in one of the sends, too," Theo admitted.

Clarence nodded to Win Ton.

"She'd better hear that message, then, boyo."

Win Ton looked like he'd eaten one of the sour cherries from one of Father's "bird trees," but he inclined his head.

"The message was thus, Captain." He took a deep breath and delivered it word for word, as she must suppose, his inflection perfectly Tranza's own.

She shivered, nodded, and repeated it: "...song's on the last stanza."

She closed her eyes, trying to think. Nearby, she could feel *Bechimo*, a patient presence, watching her think—that was the notion she had, anyway. All the pieces, they ought to come together—contract, pod, Tranza, the pathfinders...yes. She felt a jolt of something that may have been surprise—*Bechimo*'s surprise—and opened her eyes.

"Clarence, I need an amendment to this contract from Veep Semimodo, quick as you can manage. Get me a contract that authorizes us—in fact, *pays* us—to remove the mini-pod from *Primadonna*, as an item separate from the transshipping agreement. The language has got to include..." she paused, remembering the classroom and Therny Chirs at the front, reciting a list of Ten Essential Contractual Clauses.

"It's got to include this phrase: 'Hold harmless crew, staff, contractors, and administration of the spacecraft *Bechimo* and of Laughing Cat Limited for incidental alterations or entry to *Primadonna* in the course of this work'—or whatever. The important phrases are 'hold harmless' and the list of our personnel."

Clarence nodded, a decided gleam in his eye. Theo thought maybe he hadn't cared much for Veep Semimodo.

"Also, given that they've got a pilot abandoned—Hugglelans should have been here for him days ago!—tell them that we'll be prepared to add a passenger and expect to depart immediately after that pod is transferred and locked."

"But I'm not *certain* that I can make the pod dismount and remount—" Kara began, but Theo shook her head.

"Your job will be to make sure the remount's done correctly. *Bechimo* will back you up. I'll do the dismount."

She paused, reviewing her plan. Right.

"Joyita will be PIC. Chernak will hold herself ready to assist in any way required—"

"Chernak!" Kara stared.

"I'm not done yet," Theo told her. "Joyita, the pathfinders need carrydocs acceptable to Minot Station and nametags that indicate they're security—wait."

The entire bridge waited, staring at her in flavors from amused to amazed.

"Make that *ambassador's security*, if there's a guild class for that, please, Joyita."

"Yes, Captain. I have appropriate papers for the pathfinders ready. Searching... There is a symbol for security attached to an ambassador's team. I will produce appropriate badges."

"If Chernak is holding herself ready," Kara said carefully, "where is Stost going to be?"

"Stost is going to be helping Clarence and Win Ton escort Tranza back here. Just in case there's trouble."

"Which there's bound to be," Clarence commented. "I been seeing an underthread in the station chatter, saying that, being as Tranza brought the blight that was Pilot Tever on-station, it's Tranza oughta pay stationer damages. If word gets around he's free on dock, things could get... inneresting."

"So Stost goes," Theo said.

"Be pleased to have 'im," Clarence assured her solemnly.

"That's it, then," Theo said briskly. "Joyita, please give the pathfinders my compliments and relay their assignments to them."

"Yes, Captain."

"Clarence, the faster we get those amendments to the contract, the faster we can leave this port."

"And won't that be a fine thing," he returned, with a grin. "On it, Captain." He spun his chair to face his screens. "Joyita, Veep Semimodo's good news to my Screen Three, if you will."

"Minot Station contract to your Screen Three, Clarence," Joyita replied. "Captain, the pathfinders hold themselves in readiness; they have chosen the working surname *Strongline*. Ship's list identifies them as security personnel attached to Ambassador Hevelin's office. Papers and tags have been delivered."

There was a pause before he added.

"The pathfinders beg the captain's indulgence and ask that their personal weapons be returned to them."

• • • ☼ • • •

Theo danced, and she danced hard, seeking inner calm.

Bechimo adjusted airflow, temperature, lighting. He monitored her heart rate, breathing, and endorphin levels; he did not intrude upon her thoughts or upon the silence in which she wrapped herself.

Elsewhere, the crew was in a state of preparation, according to the captain's orders.

Clarence was on comm with Veep Semimodo, fighting for the wording Theo had indicated to be of importance. The extra money had been agreed to with scarcely a hesitation, but the words—the words were being resisted...

"Well, then, I'm guessing we'll just let the deal go, Veep," Clarence said, eyes closed and leaning back in his chair, letting it take most of his weight. "Good day to you and thanks for taking time with us."

His hand moved toward the comm switch...

"No, now, Clarence, let's not be hasty!" *Bechimo*'s analysis of Semimodo's voice indicated that the man was near panic. "I'll... that is, where did you want that clause inserted?"

Eyes still closed, Clarence smiled.

Kara was taking a tea break in the galley. She sat with eyes closed, hands wrapped loosely around the teacup, possibly reviewing the pod transfer procedures.

Win Ton was researching ready room rates and food costs, in an attempt to predict how much money would be needed to pay Pilot Tranza's debt to the station.

The pathfinders were also doing research—Joyita had provided them with a map of the station, with the route to the ready rooms outlined and every entrance, stairway, and lift marked.

In the meanwhile, in the solitude of the exercise room, eyes closed and face set, Theo danced.

• • • ☼ • • •

"Theo, you have achieved your euphoria and will be at peak for the next five shifts. Dance longer and you will exhaust yourself."

It was something like talking to herself as she moved in the dimness. His presence meant she might have danced in the absolute dark and would have an absolute sense of location . . . so she knew whose voice she heard, even if *Bechimo* didn't always reach conversational mode now: sometimes information just became apparent; data manifested, images arrived and were mentally absorbed. That he reached this time for words meant that he was concerned. And he was right to be concerned. If she were at less than peak, she would endanger them all.

She shifted her stance and entered a series of forms that would lead, soon, to a satisfying conclusion to the dance.

"Do you think I've been foolish to commit us? Expose us?" she asked.

Bechimo's pause was no longer than a polite conversational break.

"You have reached a decision and established a course of action. I cannot measure the future interactions of the humans you are dealing with. I have no evidence that either the decision or the course is a foolish.

"Clarence has achieved your desired changes to the contract; it is awaiting your signature.

"Win Ton has achieved an estimate of the total of Pilot Tranza's financial obligations to the station.

"Kara is practicing the pod transfer on sim, based on my assurance that the approach will be at an appropriate angle.

"I am monitoring external communications. Rig Tranza has not received a reply to any of his transmissions. The various shipyard committees continue to speak to each other on the need for an intervention in response to Minot Station's search for an outside fixed-base operator to assist the station. I have acquired copies of the contents of portions of the shipyard files and portions of the libraries and data of other local ships. There's also some sentiment blaming Rig Tranza for the actions of the missing pilot. I monitor as many lines of . . ."

"We shouldn't . . ."

"You have not determined that I should not; you have not requested the data searches be limited. Information is useful. The more information we have, the better we may protect ourselves."

Theo couldn't argue that, and she didn't. Instead, she brought her attention wholly again to the dance, its conclusion a mere two forms distant. As she defined space with her movements, she concentrated on a different space, which she used to know well. *Primadonna,* the bridge and passages; the location of the cabins. If Tranza had taken her out of the computer; if the cues had been changed . . . This next throw depended—over-depended—on the hope that nothing had changed, that Mayko's furlough order hadn't triggered changes more dire than the ship simply wrapping itself in silence. It was possible. Mayko had been Tranza's student before her; Mayko had known the ship well . . .

Theo brought her hands together, sweeping them to the right as she extended her left leg back, and transferred her weight. She finished the sweep, pushed off of her back leg. Her forward hand became a battering ram, her trailing hand right behind it pushed palm top to palm bottom, her weight centered over poised feet. She was a wall withstanding an attack and remained so for the count of three deep breaths, whereupon she brought her hands before her in a quiet ball as she went completely to center, gathering energy with one last sweep, and absorbing it as her arms came down with a sigh.

And there. She was now fit to ask the questions, *Bechimo* being present and the questions still needing to be asked.

"Are you satisfied with the state of the bonding, *Bechimo*? I had feared the bond originally. I was . . . concerned . . . that I would be overwhelmed, that I would be absorbed and . . . controlled. I never liked to be controlled and I've always fought to be myself, sometimes in stupid and silly ways."

She stepped into her cooldown, allowing *Bechimo*'s subtle ministrations in the way of air currents and temperatures and humidity to caress her.

"And now I . . . I'm worried. About you. About . . . us, I guess. Win Ton, the night I first sat second on a spaceship—he told me that I'd *entranced* him, made him drunk with me. We were . . . pretty tangled up at the time and sweaty and not done yet, and I thought it was, ummm, love play. But here he is now. Is he in a trance? Did I cloud his judgment? He gave me a set of wings and helped make me a star pilot."

She stood entirely still and looked into the dimness at his walls.

"And you, my friend. Are you in a trance now? You've made me captain of you and all you are and all of your future. Do I cloud your judgment? Do I make us all unsafe because you're drunk with me, because you admire my, my...*mystery* and let me do what I will, even if I'm making a mistake that will kill most of the people I care about?"

There was no answer at first, and the pause lengthened. Light came up unbidden, the cool breeze became more pronounced.

"Theo, I have considered this myself. I have considered that I am less confined to absolute safety. And I have considered what Win Ton has said to me and to Joyita in preparing for his piloting test. I think—and this is considered thought—that Win Ton may have the right of it. We have come to be bonded very nearly by chance; accident after accident falling together. I consider my source and I consider yours. I believe that we are part of this gathering edge of change—and that *we must be*. Unbonding... I will not consider.

"My goal is that we survive. When I see danger I will report it. If I see an erroneous decision, I will report it. You are my captain and I will have your commands. I have no greater joy than this, Theo."

CHAPTER THIRTY-FOUR

. . . .

Minot Station

THE IMAGE ON THE SCREEN WAS FROM A STOLEN FEED; *BECHIMO*'S zoom from the wider image showed Theo appearing nearly waiflike in the oversized and battered jacket she wore. She was approaching *Primadonna*'s docking vestibule, walking away from the camera source.

Despite the image, Kara wished for a word from that calm, strolling figure. It was quite ridiculous, and the decision not to use comm on dock a sensible one. They did not, after all, wish to rouse the surveillance mics, nor to share their business with Minot Station security. Still, it was a chancy thing Theo undertook—

Kara shook her head, cutting off the thought.

This was Theo. *Of course* the thing was chancy.

Kara frowned at the video. Theo was very nearly arrived at her destination; the camera had zoomed, building the image to better detail. In fact, to suspiciously good detail.

"Are you interpolating and interpreting the video now?" she asked Joyita. "If they have that good a camera on her..."

She had seen Theo this closely herself, knew the small scar at her hairline, had brushed it gently. It ought not to be quite so clear on a security feed!

Bechimo answered her, sounding, if such a thing were to be believed, sheepish. "You are correct Kara. I *am* correcting the images, both for lighting and detail. I am monitoring and watching closely for preliminary signs of concern, or danger."

303

The screen now displayed another shot of Theo, much more distant, tracking.

In his tower, Joyita waved a hand at a console and it mirrored the image Kara studied now.

"This is the live camera feed from dockside that Station Admin sees. The slow zoom is the one they are tracking manually. *They are expecting activity.*"

The activity they might be expecting was not exactly what they were seeing. Admin had been told that a tech was going down to *Primadonna* to look at the remote panels sometimes used for planetside work. Admin, of course, knew that Kara was a pilot; perhaps they thought that they were seeing Kara or yet another *Bechimo* crew member moving to the task, at least as long as they hadn't studied a dossier on Theo.

Kara sighed lightly. Hevelin was sitting on her lap, to all appearances entranced by the images. He had been quite excited earlier, when the feed had shown them Clarence and his back-ups on the way to their appointment. Each had worn a weapon openly, for Clarence carried... quite a lot of cash for Pilot Tranza's buyout. Theo had insisted on cash, and Clarence, for a wonder, had agreed wholeheartedly.

"I gotta have room to maneuver when it comes to bribes and hints. 'Sides, Admin'll think they're smart for getting some of what they paid us back on the spot."

The image on the screen changed again, briefly meditating upon the drone tug station-keeping *Primadonna* as promised. The operators claimed that they needed less than a Standard Minute to pluck the thing away, once it was unlocked.

Kara sighed as the screen again showed Theo's face. The security image displayed Theo in shadow, captured through a dust-fogged lens. *Bechimo*'s enhanced image showed Theo, calm and steady, clear and bright, as if she every day made a not-quite-illegal, but not-exactly-legal entry into a ship on a port far from home. It also showed strain lines in Theo's face that Kara had not previously noticed. And—Kara's eyes were sharp—the outline of the hefty weapon sometimes carried as her public gun.

Mentally, Kara danced three forms in order, centering herself. Events occur, let them... her breath evened. She touched the internal comm button.

"Chernak, are you well?" she asked the pathfinder, who was on call in the galley.

"I am well, Kara. I see the captain has almost reached her goal."

Kara looked to the screen, saw Theo steps away from *Primadonna*'s hatch.

"So she is. The next minute will tell us—everything."

"I watch," Chernak said, and Kara nodded, releasing the button.

Her concentration was firm, the transfer script memorized, but still ready on her screen. She had done pod-connects before, though most frequently from pod racks rather than the tug style they'd be doing today...

...Hopefully be doing today.

"Kara, I'm getting a communication from Admin. Something about a delivery from that intern you spoke of?" Joyita was getting good at Terran inflections.

"Now?"

She only half-swallowed the rest of her reaction, using a recheck of boom-lock positions to cover her language.

"Advise them the PIC suggests the ship is busy at their necessity, if you please," she said. "Crew will not be receiving until after the transfer is complete."

"Yes," Joyita said.

Kara looked again to her screen, as Theo's hands touched *Primadonna*'s exposed control pads. The security shrouds deployed, enveloping and hiding her even from *Bechimo*'s augmented surveillance.

Kara sighed with relief at that: the shrouds would have failed to deploy if the ship had failed to recognize Theo. One potential obstacle was overcome.

Now, all she—they—had to do...was wait.

· · · ❖ · · ·

Dockside controls were always cold on the hands in Terran space, where the docks weren't heated above bare necessity.

The shrouds not only shielded her from the eyes of the curious, but also deadened external sound.

Distantly, Theo heard the vague clang and stubbed walk of a pedestrian unused to the dock grid, but that was no concern of hers.

She uncovered the twin scanners looking into the deep-welled camera that checked her face and features. The lights above the panel failed to respond, which was as it should be. An absolute stranger would have needed to display an optical-scan card to go further. *Primadonna* remembered her—or maybe it remembered the jacket. Rig Tranza's mind was not an easy one to know, and it was possible that the scratches and wear patterns were not all accident. Deep breath now. At least she wouldn't have to sing, though Tranza would have preferred it.

Theo's gloves were still pocketed; bare hands flawlessly pressed the freezing-cold flat plates in the proper order, at the proper angle. The door plate glowed, and a three-note query sounded, high and clear, as if struck from fine crystal.

Theo relaxed, elated. Almost in! One more security test to pass.

She took a breath and recited the arcane words without difficulty.

"Sing a song of sex pants, pockets full of dry, four and plenty blackburrs, staked in a pie!"

Three breaths now, four, five... She wondered if Clarence had ever cooked a blackburr pie, or if he would.

Her triumph faded. The hatch remained closed and locked, no entry—and this was a single-use code, which was wiped on successful completion.

The three notes sounded again.

SECOND VERSE flashed dull red in the security screen.

Theo's stomach tightened.

Pharst, she hadn't studied the thing! He just always sang it when he was in that mood where he might sing songs for days, or he might have a brew and stare at the stuff he called art...

Well, she hadn't come here to fail. She had a good memory after all. She just needed to visualize Tranza, in his favorite corner of the galley, eyes half closed and the beer to hand...

"When the pie was opened," she began slowly, "the burrs began to sing. And... wasn't that a dainty fish, to catch... before the ring?"

Eyes squinted, she watched the screen.

THANK YOU flashed the message, and there was a distinct *clunk* as the hatch mechanisms began to work.

The inside of the ship smelled the same, but it felt cramped and alien, with too many Hugglelans logos everywhere. She'd not recalled them feeling so overbearing when she'd been copilot—and hadn't really realized how roomy and even luxurious *Bechimo* really was.

The hall ahead of her was shadowed. *Primadonna* was on standby dims until she announced herself. Theo stepped beyond the vestibule, feeling the hatch close behind her.

The three notes sounded.

"Who am I?" she asked the air, knowing there was no real intelligence behind the routine she was going through, just programming aimed at security.

"Theo Waitley," said her own voice, of several years gone by, sounding young and naive.

"Correct," she affirmed.

Lighting came up and fans began to hum. Her seat—what *had been* her seat—hummed as settings she'd assumed had been long ago logged off reasserted themselves. A double *thunk* came from the direction of crew quarters, the sound of inner airlocks opened to ship normal and inner doors unlocking.

She crossed the bridge and took her chair. Second board.

Screens came up, displaying information meant for a pilot, information meant for—

"Oh, Tranza," she sighed, between frustration and dismay. He'd never taken her out of the ship's command line, and now here she was, setting up to take the ship's cargo, close enough to pirate—but no. Rig had cleared the removal, and his was the only permission she cared about. Hugglelans ship it might be, but she'd always thought of *Primadonna* as belonging to Rig Tranza.

The small screen set into the top of her board was asking her to set a new code. A new *captain's* code.

She looked around, feeling an extra presence and an awareness— if she wanted to use it, she had the authority, right now, to reset herself as captain of *this ship* and become a pirate in truth. She could do it; there were ways to automate things...

It was tempting. It was astonishingly tempting. And it would be so very easy.

Theo took a hard breath and—thought of Kara. Kara, who would *never* be tempted to steal a ship simply because she could. Kara, who knew right from wrong, even if Theo didn't.

She was concentrating so hard that she could very nearly see Kara—no.

She was *actually* seeing Kara, hunkered over her boards on

Bechimo's bridge, her face serious, as it would be. Not only that, but she could hear—she *was hearing*—a voice demanding to know if *that ship* had been boarded, if the pod overrides were internal after all...and that was bad. She had to hurry.

Bechimo's bridge faded, the demanding voice cut off in mid-demand, and she was seeing *Primadonna* and the boards, live.

Three slaps at the controls and piloting comp gave way to cargo; two more and the logs were up and the pod controls to hand. Cargo controls self-checked, three-noted, and waited.

She nearly requested contact out loud—but this ship didn't take voice commands, as prepped; Tranza having said on more than one occasion that he might sing to himself, but he was damned if he was going to talk to himself. Theo fingered the switch for the low-power, ship-to-ship comm used in port, and selected the freq.

"*Bechimo* Engineering, *Primadonna* Cargo here. We have control lights. Power's up. Pod hears and obeys."

She released the fields that tied the pod to the Struven units, making the pod alien to inertial ship movements and ready for reposition and plucking.

"We have time issues. Confirm."

Kara's voice answered, without Joyita's intercession.

"Confirm, *Primadonna*, time issues. I've told the pickup team we're live. Please make sure the beacon is *on*."

And there, so simple a thing, forgotten, like she was a novice... of course the beacon had to be *on*; they were doing a spaceside live double transfer, not a crane pull.

"Confirm!" she said and before the word was finished her hands had completed that task.

Her awareness was all around her—the pod felt ready to go, beacon on, only the lightest of physical break-away latches now kept the pod still and in place.

"Ready," she said to Kara. "Inform the tug."

"Informing tug," said Kara as Theo leaned back in her chair. All she had to do now was wait.

· · · ✳ · · ·

They waited for word: the deal had been that once the pod was successfully mounted on *Bechimo*, *Primadonna*'s role in the transfer would be seen as over—and the burden of all the other legal travails would fall to the arrested ship and not to the pilot.

Rig Tranza could walk out then, so long as his up-to-the-second charges for room and board were covered to the bit.

Tranza was, improbably, recording a local audio-only feed supplying music archived from one or another of the station's private holidays and made by amateurs.

"You'll watch that for me, right?" he said to Clarence. "I want to get what I can of this—I've got cuts from the last three of these and want to grab... just let me know when we're ready to go, right?"

Clarence nodded, Win Ton bowed, Stost... surveyed the cramped and dingy area, eyes bright.

They were all three armed, of course, with the burden of most of *Bechimo*'s cash treasury shared between Clarence and Win Ton.

Clarence felt better about Win Ton's state of mind now; the lad had properly blanched when he realized how much cash Theo was apportioning to this little task. For all his Liaden inscrutability, Win Ton's face and posture were both edged with tension, his pose favoring, just slightly, a left-handed gun draw, and a right-handed blade.

Stost, good laddie that he was, stood solid as a wall behind them, his back to the screens. He'd gotten a good look at the cafeteria itself and was now giving most of his attention to the door they'd come through. Anybody who wanted to use the lounge would have to pass him, if they dared, though of their party of three, he alone showed no weapon. He wore the shirt, vest, trousers and boots from his once-and-former uniform, with a Laughing Cat logo conspicuous on the right shoulder.

On the left breast, there was the *Bechimo* crew badge bearing his name, and a small triple star along the right bottom edge, which was on all their badges now. According to Joyita, the stars were the proper symbol for crew serving an ambassador's ship—in theory giving a wee bit of extra privilege to such crew. Stost's badge also bore a red triangle, which declared him security personnel.

Clarence glanced at Win Ton, who was sharing Stost's interest in the door and the screen over the door, which showed the state of the hall beyond. Which left Clarence to watch the feeds for news of Theo's progress.

He stepped over to the screens, which were all displaying the public visual feed. It took a bit of squinting to find the screen that interested him, but he managed. The view alternated between a long-range topside-scan camera with a five-rotation-per-minute rate and four blink-cameras aimed out from the spinning core, two north and two south. Topside, of course, was the active docks while the south blink covered storage. It wasn't the optimum way to cover current events, but he'd had plenty of experience. Since the station wasn't all that busy, he had a good notion of which motion was important and which wasn't.

During a lull in the action, Clarence glanced over to Tranza's mock-patient form leaning over the table. He was abruptly and sincerely glad that Theo hadn't had the paying and walk-back to do. Tranza moved his left hand like he was striking some percussion instrument, and his right foot was on beat. His eyes were closed and lips compressed in a curious unstraight line suggesting his tongue was swinging with a third line of music.

Tranza was as close to breaking as might be, that was Clarence's measure. Lost his job, lost his ship, abandoned to a backwater after a decent and honest career... nobody deserved that. No blame to him for not watching the action. Following the feed took patience and the man was just about full out.

Clarence shook away that line of thought. A part of his job as a Juntavas Boss had been to put people in situations like this one; maneuvering them until they didn't have a choice, except to cooperate or be stranded on Liad.

He was well out of *that* now and pleased to help an honest man stay honest.

As for the buyout, Theo'd been clear: pay what was asked and argue later.

He was carrying a fair amount of Theo's personal cash, along with most of *Bechimo*'s treasury, that was his feeling.

Well, and if it came up short, he'd toss in a few bits himself.

· · · ❈ · · ·

The tremor was light and familiar. Theo had ridden out many a pod transfer when she was *Primadonna*'s copilot. She looked to the screens and gave a nod of approval; whoever was piloting the drone tug had obviously done this before.

Lights changed: the blue light, which meant the pod system was cycling, clicked into green, meaning available. The latches read empty. The tug had the pod; her part was done.

Right hand touching keypads, Theo closed her eyes to recall; pod docking and undocking systems went from active to neutral, flashed from neutral to locked. She powered those systems down, hands working while eyes and thoughts scanned the flight deck.

The ship was still pleading from the small screen, begging her to confirm as captain.

Ship's chronometer gave her six more minutes before that option was no longer available. Good enough, she'd be out in under five. The screen blinked again, insisting, and she began to feel guilty. A ship *should* have a captain, after all...

No, she told herself, *Theo, it's not a plea. The ship isn't begging; it doesn't* know *it lacks a captain; it doesn't feel the need of a captain.* Now, *Bechimo* had *wanted* a captain; had known that he was incomplete until a captain came to him.

But this...was a programmed insistence, words thrown at the screen. There was no intelligence behind it.

Theo turned away, letting the words blink.

· · · ❋ · · ·

There, on the screen—motion! Lucky for him the scan caught the change in attitude, showing momentary jets of reaction fuel.

The drone's careful approach was smooth and accurate. Could have been a textbook show, that, with the double catch locking clean as could be and, a few seconds later, the extension locking.

The view scanned away but he could see the blink-camera view from the north now. Didn't seem to be any issues there... he counted mentally, figuring on—yes, straight ordinary pickup and a rotation toward *Bechimo.*

He felt a presence at his elbow and turned his head to meet Rig Tranza's eye.

The other pilot nodded at the screen.

"Good, right? Good pilot on that thing."

With sudden spirit, he pulled a card from his pocket, crossed the distance to the order wall and, slipping it into the query slot, laughed.

Eyes showing a teary relief, Tranza laughed again, pulled the card from the slot, and snatched the printout pages as they came from the slot.

"Got my bill, Pilot. They've registered me as out and owing."

Smoothly, he handed the printout and the card over.

Clarence received them in one hand, signing *good work* with his free hand, and turned away from the screens.

"Ought to be somebody from Admin down here for us any second. We'll settle right up and get moving. Kara'll have that pod locked in no time." He switched to Trade.

"Stost, boyo—might be a good thing if you come over here and stand behind Pilot Tranza. Win Ton'll take point and I'll do the talking."

CHAPTER THIRTY-FIVE

· ·

Minot Station
Transient Crew Cabins

CORP VEEP SEMIMODO HIMSELF LED THE WAY, SMILING WIDELY; behind him were two others, in uniform, both looking far harder used than the veep. They carried highly visible sidearms and showed grim faces. Even if Clarence hadn't once employed a brace or two himself, he'd've recognized them as bullyboys from the swagger.

"That's done, Pilots, that's done very well." Veep Semimodo was positively beaming. "The exchange is made, and now we can add up expenses and—"

Tranza pointed at the printouts Clarence held.

"The exec officer here, he's taking my part, you know—they told you. Clarence, he'll be paying off anything due."

"Well, it's always a pleasure to see Clarence," the veep said heartily. "Now, Pilot Tranza, we'll get you on your way as soon as we add up the totals. The number you have there, Clarence— that's the residential total. There are some additional expenses that need to be dealt with as well."

Of course there were, Clarence thought; he'd've been disappointed in the veep if there hadn't been additional expenses.

Semimodo bustled over to the serving counter, pulling a mathstick out of one commodious pocket as he did. He immediately fell to shuffling papers and inputting numbers.

The bullyboys, in the meantime, were doing sums of a different sort, trying to sort the four of them in order of threat level.

Himself and Win Ton, they took at face value, maybe deducting a couple points from Win Ton, for him being small in all directions.

Tranza, they dismissed as a prisoner, though that was over now—and . . .

Clarence managed not to laugh. *Just* managed not to laugh.

Stost . . . wasn't anything like they'd expected to have to deal with. They counted, then counted again, 'til Clarence was almost sorry for them. It was a hard call, on account of Stost having a lot of what you'd call *presence*, plus with him standing behind Tranza like he was, it was hard to see if he was carrying anything besides his badge and his lunch. About then, it occurred to the pair of them to badge-check, and bully eyes widened when they saw that red corner on Stost's badge.

They exchanged a look and took a step forward, by way of testing their group's mettle.

Win Ton failed to fall back despite being a head and more shorter than the bullyboys. They leaned in and over. Win Ton stayed put.

"The space is small," he pointed out in perfectly polite Trade. "Please, give Veep Semimodo and Exec O'Berin space to work."

Clarence took his cue, turning to the side. Win Ton waved him past with a languid hand, his half-turn leaving him sidewise and an even smaller target for the bullies.

"Sure, and there's always details," Clarence said, as Tranza left Stost's shadow to approach the counter. One-handed, he formed a surreptitious sign, *not agreed*.

Understood, Clarence sent back, stepping up close to the front of the counter, while Tranza continued around to the back.

"I understand, Veep," Clarence said. "Always something, isn't it now?"

Semimodo continued to rustle hard copy and play with his math-stick, Tranza, behind him, craning and trying to see the numbers.

Clarence glanced back, but the bullyboys remained in place. Stost had stepped up to Win Ton's side, standing there quiet and calm, hair within a handspan of the ceiling.

"Yes, here we are," Semimodo murmured. He shuffled his papers one more time noisily, then, apparently satisfied, he gave a nod and put them down.

He withdrew from his other pocket a walletlike leather folder and opened it to withdraw even more hard copy.

"There is, you see, the matter of the medical care that was provided for Pilot Tranza. Medical services are not covered by the standard housing fee, as I'm sure you'll—"

Clarence felt a lick of pure anger, and he knew right then how he was going to handle this. Theo'd told him to smile and pay. Well, and he knew how to smile, now didn't he?

· · · ✳ · · ·

Theo stood up from second chair and took the full step to first board. An inner pocket in Rig's old jacket yielded a gauzy slick bag.

She sighed, relieved. On the flight deck itself, Tranza's habits held. The right-side bin on his seat held sealed snacks. She grabbed a few, but it was the left side that held the treasure she'd come for.

"Backups, right?" She mimicked him without mocking his routine, scooping the chips up quickly.

The bin held the usual three-course backups, and those she left temporarily on the seat while she searched for the color-coded records. She had no desire to take Hugglelans' information and no need to know the ship's history.

But the other chips and slips—backups, indeed.

Whenever he bought new treasures, he copied them to his private directory in the ship's computer. But he made mobile chips and kept them ready close, ready to go at a moment's notice. The chips in his chair bin were largely greens and reds, with a few blues and a purple . . .

Her breath caught. Purples were his favorites—he'd often dragged out a dozen or two at a time while she was PIC, sometimes going back and forth among them searching for some mysterious *that*, as in, "Now *that* was worth hearing again. . . ."

He'd tried hard, to share his *thats* with her, but she'd been undereducated in some few of the musics he offered and entirely ignorant of many of the others.

The chips clicked into the bag along with a couple more of his favorite pack snacks, then . . .

"No, Theo," she said aloud, stopping herself from reaching to the dashboard.

The dash only ever held current mission stuff for Tranza,

and there was no longer a current mission for him. Then, she second-guessed herself, opening the hard copy bin, scanning—there! There were a couple of music notes among the hard copy, and those she took. The rest she left for the Hugglelans rep or whoever took charge of *Primadonna* next.

She left the bridge, three rapid steps to the short hall, a right turn—and face-about. Her former cabin, she passed by; whatever was in there now wasn't hers, and Tranza wouldn't have stored anything in his copilot's quarters.

She put her hand briefly against the pad on Tranza's door. It slid aside, the room lights coming up to full bright.

Theo'd never been in Rig Tranza's cabin. He'd never invited her in. Now, mindful of time slipping past, she opened the top drawer, pulling music first, half filling the bag—how could he have listened to all of that? Worlds and worlds worth of music...

She finished with the drawers and pulled open a door. Recognizing one of the rare civilian shirt-and-shorts suits he'd allowed himself, she flung that into the bag, and opened a second door, hating the necessity of going through Tranza's stuff—his private things—like a thief.

"It's in a good cause, Theo," she told herself, and pulled open the last door.

There was his leave bag. She hefted it; it felt ready to go. Grabbing the handles, she yanked the bag out, only to find another cache of bagged coded memchips. Purples and plains and—

Time.

She stuffed what she could into her bag, opened a nearly empty unlocked side pocket on Tranza's bag and stowed the rest there.

She felt a very slight vibration through the floor, and suddenly she was looking at *Bechimo*'s cargo boards, screens confirming that the mini-pod was attached. There was a timer live, too, counting backward.

Yes, she needed to be out—and soon.

She closed the closets and the drawers, stepped out and waved the door shut, Tranza's bag over her shoulder, her bag in hand. The door to her quarters was on her right. Before she thought, she put her hand against the plate.

The door opened, but she didn't step in, shock holding her where she was. Disarray and vandalism met her eye: drawers wide open, doors loose, the 'fresher all untidy. Mayko had a lot to answer for, else Tranza'd been enraged...a hard thought, that, but now she was angry. Angry for Tranza and for the ship, which he'd kept so tidy and clean.

Enough, she told herself, and waved the door closed, half-running to the bridge, Tranza's bag knocking painfully against her hip.

· · · ❋ · · ·

Clarence smiled.

Smiling, he shook Tranza's printout at the veep's chest, just hard enough to make the paper rattle.

"Now, this medical cost which isn't included in...what's that for exactly?"

Semimodo didn't even bother to look abashed.

"The pilot was given several injections of Truth. He had an... unusual reaction to the drug and required a doctor's care, and several days of close monitoring in sick bay."

Clarence smiled.

"So, not only did you arrest this man for no reason having to do with him, but you decided to try to drag info outta 'im while you had 'im in hand. He had a bad reaction to the drug, which isn't unusual with your double-dosing, and needed a doctor. Am I getting this right?"

Semimodo beamed.

"Exactly right, yes."

"So, you're not only charging the pilot for the truth drug you decided to administer, but you're charging him for both the drug and his care when he got sick from it."

Still smiling, Clarence shook his head.

"Seems to me, if the Pilots Guild heard whispers o'this—and there's nothing surer than that they will—well, Veep, if the Pilots Guild was to be called on to adjudicate this invoice, I'm thinking they wouldn't be too happy with Minot Station. Might even demand restitution on behalf of the pilot here." He paused before inclining his head very slightly.

"So, that course, you'd not only be losing your additional costs, but needing to pay more to the pilot, as an apology."

Semimodo glared at him.

"This station is not a charity. We must recover our expenses."

Clarence raised his hands soothingly.

"Nobody said elsewise. But I'm betting, Veep, that you can just hold that medical bill and pass it right on to the Hugglelans as a usual and normal charge for your tender care of their pilot—and they won't bat a lash before taking out their wallets."

The veep stood taller, his round face showing heavy lines, as he spoke: "Pilot Tranza is the one who received medical care, therefore the expense is his to pay. We could have just turned him out onto the docks, sick and with no place to sleep. Some other stations would have done just that. Minot Station elected, without being coerced, to give the pilot medical care and also to provide a place to sleep, and food. We will not be cheated of our reasonable charges."

Clarence waved the printout with more energy.

"You'll want to think hard on that, Veep Semimodo. We—that is, *Bechimo*—we've done you one favor already, and we haven't been on your dock three whole rotations. Yeah, it's business, but it's a favor still. We'd like to know that we can trade here, without prejudice and with no danger to our ship or crew."

Clarence looked aside to Win Ton, seeking a nod affirming the point. The Scout gave him that with great promptness and a visible touch of a smile.

He turned back to Semimodo.

"Now, here's the thing about favors. They can evaporate just like they never was. So, since the Pilots Guild appointed our ship to carry one of their ambassadors—it would likely trouble Ambassador Hevelin to find that a pilot was...mistreated here—well, knowing him like I do, I'm thinking he'd be having us report the situation to the commissioners, and you know how that's likely to go."

He paused. Smiled.

"What I'm suggesting is that it would be worthwhile for you to find that you made an honest mistake and that bill got into the wrong pile. Now that you discovered it, you can just set it aside for the Hugglelans to settle.

"In the meanwhile, we'll pay this bill, here"—he rattled the printout again—"with a little left over, since I don't have small change. We'll have done with the brangle, and we can all leave before that mob that's been growing on the middle decks gets down here and starts breaking up the furniture."

He smiled. Semimodo paled, his eyes seeking the screens.

He looked back to Clarence and, credit where it was due, made a credible effort to get the glare back in place.

Clarence tempered his smile with sympathy.

"That really is your best deal," he said.

. . . ❊ . . .

Veep Semimodo's bluster evaporated completely as the sound of many voices and feet approaching their position grew louder. He took the lesser payment, and an in-hand bribe, and even marked the printout "paid" and signed it with his official chop.

Then, he folded his math-stick, his wallet and his papers, and moved hastily around the counter.

"Let me through!" he snapped at Win Ton's back.

Win Ton, a thing of grace and beauty, swung lightly out of his way; Stost pivoted on one heel.

One bullyboy had already hit the door out to the hallway, the other brought up the rear, Veep Semimodo bracketed between them.

Clarence grabbed Tranza by the elbow.

"Time to go, laddie," he said and set off after Semimodo. Stost and Win Ton fell in behind.

Ahead, the veep and his men had reached the intersection with the main hall and ducked to the left, opposite to all the noise, scuttling down a hand-railed side hall.

Short of the side hall, Clarence turned, one hand still holding Tranza, and signed with his free hand, a simple point at the deck coupled with *here hold short*, and flicked his fingers from palm to full hand four times.

Behind them, Win Ton heard the door to the transient lounge close.

He nodded, turned about, not surprised, but pleased, to find Stost with him still, as the elder pilots disappeared down the side hall, in the wake of Veep Semimodo.

"We hold," Win Ton said in Trade, and the big man looked down at him with a smile, eyes bright.

"No problem," he said in Terran.

Win Ton recognized Clarence in the phrase, but did not laugh. *No problem* indeed; Stost's business, far more than his own, was force.

The crowd was approaching quickly. Win Ton sighed and centered himself.

"Tever owes me, owes all of us!"

"Money's gotta get paid afore that ship leaves!"

"Cut m'brother, stole his watch!"

Echoes and anger herded splinters of conversation ahead of the approaching stationers.

"Five," Stost said conversationally in Trade. Win Ton frowned— then realized that his companion was counting seconds.

And here they came, rounding the corner in disordered haste—a compressed mob of docksiders, some in uniform, riding the gravity shifts along the hallway without trouble, without notice. Several were armed with pipes; some others with hammers. Win Ton fervently hoped that no one would try to deploy their weapon; their ranks were so tight that they would surely harm each other before ever they touched Stost or him.

Finding the hall blocked, the crowd slowed, casting puzzled glances at each other.

Win Ton stood, centered and calm, hands crossed on his belt, waiting.

"It's another star-froze Liaden! What're we? Invaded?"

Then they saw Stost, standing calmly, his pose mirroring, Win Ton realized, his own. It was a moment before the crowd comprehended him, a head taller than any present, nearly too large to be seen.

"Don't block us, we're going in there!"

"Ten," said Stost, *sotto voce.*

One of the leading edge of docksiders pointed past Stost to the closed door.

"We got cause, and we got the right. We're gonna—"

Win Ton raised one hand, palm out, in the age-old sign for *stop.* The other hand, he extended, fingers flashing a sign well-known to space workers and stationers: *cut jets!*

That brought their eyes to his face.

He kept his palm extended, lowering the other hand. He met the eyes of a square-built individual in mechanic overalls who stood a little ahead of the rest, the head of a mallet resting against one broad shoulder.

"You have arrived too late, if I understand your intent. Veep Semimodo and others of his party have returned to his office. Likely you will find him there, if you wish to speak with him."

There were nine of them; far too many to reason with, but

perhaps bored indifference would turn the trick. Briefly, Win Ton wished that he had Theo's skill in dealing with crowds.

"You're blocking the door," said the woman with the mallet. "We know who's in there, an' he ain't flying outta here 'til we get—"

In the distance Win Ton heard the sound of the mistuned lift rising to dockside. Under it was another sound, rapid steps descending the stair system. They slowed, then after an exchange of hushed and undecipherable murmurs, regained pace.

"Fifteen," Stost said, very nearly cheerful.

The leader had stepped forward, her mallet held cross-body now, one hand gripping the stock just below the head. She stopped a short arm's reach in front of Stost, which was not well judged, for she had to crane dangerously, sacrificing her balance in order to see his face.

"Outta the way, Long Drink. Make room!"

Looking down at her, Stost extended one hand, palm out. The leader frowned, words stopped for a moment—and a moment was all that Win Ton required.

"I repeat—you will find no one beyond that door. If you wish to speak to Veep Semimodo, seek him in his office."

"Let us through!" shouted someone from the back of the crowd. The front of the crowd moved uneasily forward.

Stost said, "Twenty."

Win Ton dropped his warning hand, though he did not take his eyes off of the knot of angry people before them.

"Troop, stand aside," he said in Old Yxtrang. "We two shall move on to duty elsewhere."

Stost took one large step back, and another to the left.

Win Ton likewise stepped to the left—and the crowd surged past them, rushing toward the lounge door.

Win Ton caught Stost's eye and pointed to the side hall whence Semimodo, Clarence, and Tranza had vanished.

Stost waved him ahead, and the two of them began to hurry.

CHAPTER THIRTY-SIX

Bechimo
Bridge

"WE'RE NOW IN PROCESS, *BECHIMO*. CONFIRM TRIPLE BLUE STROBES are our pod target!"

"Confirmed, dockside. Triple blue."

Kara's concentration on her boards was very nearly trancelike. This sort of maneuver—when an ill-timed delivery could hole a hull—*this* was when engineers and cargo masters earned their pay.

Minot Station was operating the transfer drone, with Kara standing by; the push of a single button would take the operation to manual should anything go awry.

So far, everything was proceeding smoothly. Theo's work had been done well: the pod announced itself live, set itself to release-ready, and finally releasing to the transport lock. No hesitation, no glitches.

Dockside also did well, for all that the transfer was across no more than three of *Bechimo*'s lengths. Working close-in like this was nerve-wracking, as she knew from her own experience. Minot Station displayed nothing but calm competence.

Once released from *Primadonna*, the mini-pod happily chatted with the drone's systems, and with *Bechimo*'s; the temp link registered properly on Kara's board and that of the drone pilot, the low-speed rotations syncing easily in the shared orbit.

"We have an approach and are ready to commit when you say the word," Minot Station said.

"Everything looks good here," Kara answered. "We use a shorter commit range for the mini-pods. Can you tighten it up a tenth?"

The closing drone responded immediately.

"Oh, aye," the drone's pilot said, possibly to herself or to her second. "That's a Waymart ship. We'll bring it in."

Kara frowned as irritation briefly disturbed her concentration. As if there was something *wrong*—something suspect—about ships registered at Waymart!

She took a breath, focusing on the task in hand.

"Please do bring it in, Pilot; we will be fine."

And there! The pod was in position, just shy of physically touching *Bechimo*'s mount points. Kara's lead docking screen was in 3D mode in case she needed to take over, but everything, including the close-ups of the regular and the Jump clamps, was orderly.

"All good," she told the drone pilot. "Commit when ready. Automatics will accept."

She saw the pod slide gently onto the mount points; half a dozen status lights lit on her board, verifying the connection—yet she never felt the linkup.

"Mass and dimensions analyzed and adjusted," Joyita said.

"Sharp job, gang," Kara said to the drone pilot, pulling from Clarence's dockside vocabulary. "Everything here is right and tight. You may clear the area. We'll test the pod's shield integrity."

As soon as the drone cleared the bounce zone, she did just that, to the limit possible while still attached to the station. All by the book and everything *binjali*.

She leaned back in her chair, letting the work trance go. Theo should be back aboard soon now; as well as Clarence, Win Ton, Stost, and their passenger. Then, they would leave this dreadful place for—

"Kara," Joyita's voice cut through this pleasant train of thought, "there are multiple security issues of which you must be made aware, as the ranking crew member aboard."

Kara sat up, dread replacing the warm glow of accomplishment and anticipation. She met Joyita's eyes.

"I'm listening," she told him.

· · · ※ · · ·

They had been forced to vary, not once but twice, by the ~ent of angry stationers. It was then that Win Ton learned that Stost had studied the station maps as closely, or perhaps even more closely than he had.

The corridor they were presently traversing showed signs of being a less-favored route. However, the station map had it ending at a gate in not many more steps, and the words AUTHORIZED PERSONNEL ONLY had been writ large and red. They had met no one since they had ducked out of the sight of three persons running noisily toward the lift on the level above, and they passed down this corridor as silently as a brace of ghosts, the pathfinder walking as silently as the Scout.

"We go down a level there," Stost said, pointing ahead. "There is a utility corridor and a stair at the south end."

Win Ton remembered the utility corridor hazily. He had not, truth told, been thinking in terms of descending into the belly of the station when he had made his study. Stost was apparently possessed of a more suspicious nature.

"A good plan," Win Ton approved. "If we cannot go through them, we will go under them."

The stairway Stost had indicated was steps away, and Win Ton swung into it, finding the way...rather thin.

Stost's shoulders would be rubbing the walls, he thought, but heard nothing behind him. A glance back showed the pathfinder descending sideways, speed and balance unimpaired. Win Ton nodded and increased his own pace downward.

· · · ※ · · ·

Chernak had been watching the man outside the main hatch for some while now. Joyita had asked her to lend her eyes to the task and she was pleased to do so, though the man and his actions puzzled her.

Ambassador Hevelin had joined her in the galley, climbing companionably onto her knee. He, too, watched the security feed, and with an intensity that suggested not only understanding, but concern.

"I think that, himself, he is not a danger," she murmured in Trade, as he offered no commentary of his own. "As you see, he is a civilian, neither pilot nor soldier. Young, but soft. There is a weight in each jacket pocket, but not the same weight. Weapons? We assume so, and we remember that this is what the captain styles a *rough port*. It may be prudent here to go armed. He has not placed anything against the hull. He has not announced himself. Yet he occupies our dock. He waits, but for what event? Can he know that the captain is off-ship? Does he have business with the abandoned pilot, soon to arrive? That is likeliest, I think."

She stirred.

"Friend Joyita."

"Chernak?" came the reply.

"The returning pilots have Stost as escort and need fear nothing from this one at our door. The captain, I think, has no escort. I do not say that she is vulnerable, but it might be wise for her to acquire a guard before she returns."

She paused.

"I might go out now, and roust him before any returns. I can be very firm."

There was a small sound and Chernak looked to Joyita in wonder. He was chuckling.

"You learn, and learn again," she commented, trading him one of her true smiles.

"I am taught by masters," Joyita said gravely. "As for your offer, I believe that you can be very firm. In this instance, Kara must make the decision, as ranking crew aboard."

That was the correct chain. Chernak bowed her head.

"Tell Kara, please, that I stand ready to receive her orders."

· · · ✳ · · ·

"Call Station Security and have him removed," Kara said, staring at the image of their dock and their loiterer. She was *angry.* How dare he remain there, before their hatch, after she had denied him? Obstinate fool.

"I called Minot Station Security when it became obvious that he wasn't going to leave, despite your firm refusal to see him." Joyita sounded nearly abashed. "I was informed that all Security personnel are involved in containing and dispersing a riot that started near, or in, the transient crew cabins."

Kara stared at him, suddenly cold.

"Clarence and Win Ton, Stost and Pilot Tranza—they *are* on their way back to the ship?"

"We have received word from Clarence. He and Pilot Tranza are en route and should arrive soon. However, the party became

separated. Win Ton and Stost are using another route, and their return may be delayed."

Kara glared at the image of Intern Eidalec, shivering with anger.

"Also," Joyita said.

She transferred the glare to him. "There's more?"

"A potential security issue," Joyita said apologetically. "*Bechimo* reports that *Chandra Marudas* has docked at Minot South, and six of her crew are on-station."

It took her a moment to recall the ship name.

"The Old Tech hunters. Do they hunt us—*Bechimo* and... you?"

"Insufficient data," Joyita said, his voice flat and machinelike. "We are monitoring."

"And in the meantime, that fool of an intern sits outside our lock," Kara said, welcoming the warmth of her increased anger.

"Chernak wishes you to know that she stands by to receive your orders to remove him. She states that she can be very firm."

Kara hiccuped a half-laugh against her anger.

"I don't doubt that. But, no. He wishes to see me, and apparently he is prepared to remain until he does. I will go, with Chernak as backup. Please ask her to meet me in the hall."

"Yes, Kara," Joyita said.

. . . ❈ . . .

Their progress had for the last quarter hour been down corridors and up a series of ever-more-disreputable ladders however, they had achieved the second level, and the ba would no longer serve them. Accordingly, they had clir last ladder, this ending in a hatch above their heads ar by a simple mechanical lock.

Win Ton sighed, caught between frustration at shackle arrangement and relief that the matter y complicated. Had he been wearing a full Scout bel have managed any number of complex locking n he no longer seemed to have a belt-kit. Perha with the rest of his effects at headquarters.

Less than a minute later, he quietly raisec so that he could peer out into the hallway ?

"I see no one," he murmured.

"I hear nothing," said Stost, who, so he had learned, posse.
a pair of very fine ears.

"Then let us seize the moment."

He pushed the hatch fully open and pulled himself up into
the corridor, Stost following.

· · · ✳ · · ·

Kara set a brisk pace to the hatch, fists clenching and
unclenching.

She was angry, then, Chernak deduced, following. The soft
youth before the door offended her. To allow him to remain
when the captain was soon to return—it reflected poorly on her
ability to keep the ship, no matter the possibility of danger to
the captain herself.

Chernak moved carefully, not only because she did not wish to
overrun Kara, but because Hevelin had climbed to her shoulder,
insisting that he be made a part of the upcoming action. He was
making soft sounds, not the usual cheerful murbles and purrs,
but something closer to a growl, as Grakow might growl when
stalking the Great Enemy in his sleep.

He was also sharing images, quietly, overlain with a sense of
concern. Chernak saw people hurrying purposefully down a hall,
and perhaps a room being barricaded for defense.

They had reached the vestibule, and here Kara paused to open
a locker. Inside, hung in neat array, like with like, were hammers,
pry-bars, wrench-kits, cutters and other useful dockside tools.

"I do not think this matter will require force—he is stupid,
not violent," Kara said. "There are regulations concerning the use
of firearms on-station and fines for ignoring the rules. However,
there are no rules against using a star hammer or a pry-bar to
calm someone who has become agitated, or so far forgets himself
as to threaten violence against the ship or the captain. Do you
understand me?"

Hevelin murbled.

Chernak smiled, showing just a hint of tooth, as one might
th a comrade before battle.

"Kara, I do."

The answering smile was every bit as fierce, then Kara nod-
at the open locker.

Best you stand before this; watch and hold yourself ready.

If he is stupid enough to try, you will not allow this person into our ship. I don't think that he's *that* stupid.

"I will go out and dismiss him."

She triggered the hatch.

· · · ✻ · · ·

There was a sound behind them.

No, Win Ton corrected himself, nothing so unsubtle as a sound. Merely a small disturbance of the air.

"Two come," Stost said softly, "behind us."

Wonderful hearing, Win Ton thought, and nodded.

"Yes. Perhaps they are stationers who have no taste for riot."

Stost snorted lightly. "Stationers walk like cows; the floor rings with each step."

Well, that was true. Win Ton sighed and recalled that the captain of *Chandra Marudas* was by no means an idiot.

Carefully, he reached to his collar, fingered the chain, and had it over his head. His ship key. *Bechimo*'s key.

"Take this," he said to Stost, so lightly that he scarcely heard himself. "If I should be taken, return it to the captain's own hand, none other."

"The captain will certainly shoot me if I fail in my duty to her crew," Stost breathed in protest.

"She will not." He paused. "I think she will not, though she would certainly shoot *me* if I surrender that key, either willingly or through force. You will guard the ship and the captain best by keeping that safe."

The chain and key vanished somewhere on Stost's person.

"These who follow—do not fight them, but do not go with them. Allow them to take me, if the dice fall that way. Return to the ship and tell Theo—the captain—what occurred."

Stost said nothing.

The pair behind them increased their pace.

Win Ton increased his, walking briskly, with Stost keeping pace. Ahead, the hall curved to the left; he could see the pale light that signaled a public stair reflected on the decking.

He could also hear voices, as of a group of friends talking energetically among themselves.

Talking *Liaden* among themselves.

He sighed, looked to Stost…and signed, *we go on.*

CHAPTER THIRTY-SEVEN

· ·

Bechimo
Dockside

HE JUMPED WHEN SHE STEPPED OUT ONTO THE DOCK, LIKE HE hadn't expected to see her, even after all of this...unseemly display. Then, he smiled.

"Engineer! I'm so glad—"

"I am busy," Kara interrupted, speaking Terran slowly and distinctly, as if to an idiot, which certainly he was. "You were informed of this."

"Yes, I was! I understand that I came at an—an awkward time, with the pod transfer just starting. I didn't realize, that is...I'm sorry for interrupting you were busy.

"I listened to the transfer on my comm. You were very good; everybody—the drone pilots and everybody, I mean—they're all impressed with your work!"

"I am flattered," she said dryly. "However, I am no less on duty now than I was earlier. We will be undocking and departing very soon. I have no time to talk. You may go."

She crossed her arms over her chest, not trusting that he would leave if she simply turned and went back into the ship.

His smile faded and he drew back slightly, staring—then he forced the smile back into place. It looked very uncomfortable.

"Your ship can't leave until your exec is back from his meeting with the veep," he said. "Maybe I didn't explain—well, I didn't explain, and I'm sorry about that, too. But I brought those files you were interested in, Kara—Engineer! If you have just a half hour, I'd like to show them to you and explain them. I reserved a lounge for us, just right down the hall, so we could concentrate." He hesitated, then plunged on headlong.

"This is fresh information, just in from Eylot; it will only take a few minutes to show it to you."

Was the man demented? Surely even a fool could understand that she was not able nor interested in going anywhere with him.

She felt, through the anger, a tiny flicker of alarm and was suddenly very glad that she had brought Chernak as backup.

Well, one could only try again. If he did not leave this time, then she would go inside and call his superior to come and fetch him home.

Decision made, she spoke again, clearly and distinctly.

"I am on duty, Intern. I will be pleased to receive the files but I have no time to talk, and certainly no time to visit the wonders of Minot Station."

She moved her hand as if she were brushing an annoying insect away, deliberately insulting, and said again, "You may go."

She turned toward the hatch.

· · · ✳ · · ·

Hevelin was becoming fidgety, transferring weight even as he sat, giving the impression of Grakow preparing to pounce, showing patience and impatience at once. His shared thought was of a crowd of norbears rushing toward an unseen threat, preparing for battle.

Such ferocity! thought Chernak. Who would have expected so much? But there, this was a ship of the unexpected. Captain Waitley had spoken true.

The youth at their door was being difficult to dislodge. Too difficult. He brought to Chernak's mind a soldier sent ahead, to delay and disarm an enemy force, until his comrades could surround them.

Kara turned toward the hatch, clearly done with this nonsense. Chernak approved and shifted slightly.

"No, wait!" the ridiculous youth cried. "Please. At least let me give you the files!"

Kara turned back—a mistake. Chernak took one step forward.

The youth extended his bundle and Kara extended a hand to receive it.

Hevelin growled, low and menacing.

The intern thrust the package at Kara's face, lunged, and with the free hand grabbed her wrist.

Chernak leapt forward, Hevelin roaring inside her head.

Outside, the package flew up—and away. The youth retained his hold on her wrist, yanking her close while he pulled a small gun from his pocket.

Chernak cleared the door as Kara seemed to collapse toward the deck, her hand slapping at her leg.

The youth screamed. Chernak hit the deck in time to see the gun fly high out of his hand. Hevelin left her shoulder in a leap, skidding on blunt claws as he landed. Chernak let him go, her focus on Kara...

...Who seemed not to need her protection.

The intern hit the deck on his back, hard.

Kara kicked him once in the ribs, to ensure he stayed down, which was only sensible, and fell to her knees beside him, pressing polished metal against his throat. "Yield or die!"

There was blood on the deck. The downed man was panting, his face bleeding from a long cut. Kara's hand was heavy across his throat and he struggled to speak.

Chernak stood near, ready to assist, but not expecting that she would be needed.

"Yi-yield—"

That was well, but now came the pounding of feet against decking. Chernak looked up. From the hall nearest their position came Clarence and a second man at a dead run. The stranger was not as quick as Clarence, but he was quick enough.

They would reach the safety of the ship before the pursuing crowd caught them.

· · · ❊ · · ·

Arrayed on the stairs before them were four pilots in leather jackets. Comrades all. Technically.

"Well met, Win Ton yo'Vala!" The voice was pleasant, the language was Liaden, the mode was comrade, though comrade with a subtle edge to it, as if the speaker held a stick-knife, still folded but ready to deploy.

Ing Vie yos'Thadi was a subtle man and a ruthless one. Win Ton had last seen the good captain on Volmer, specifically upon the deck of *Vivulonj Prosperu*, the Uncle's own ship. Win Ton had been ill unto dying, the Uncle's questionable technology deemed the last long throw for his life.

And before bringing him to that last, doubtful chance, yos'Thadi had elicited a promise, an oath that, should the dice fall in Win Ton's favor, he would give yos'Thadi—yos'Thadi's team—the *Old Tech ship*.

"What, no kind word for a comrade? Was it not myself who brought you to your healing? Was it not myself who stood most faithfully by your door, and who allowed Theo Waitley entry, so that she might gaze upon your face, for all she could know, for one last time?"

"I see you, Ing Vie yos'Thadi," Win Ton said, as modeless as if he spoke Terran. Comrade—no. This man, at least, was no comrade.

"So brief! Would you deny us? But, there, you are in haste and have no time for pleasantries. So be it, we shall do business."

He bowed slightly, the knife's edge briefly shown, and straightened.

"It is time to pay your debt. Our side of the bargain is proved fair, as you stand before us, hale, strong, and in your own mind."

The pair of Scouts who had been following behind them arrived. Stost pivoted to face them, his back against Win Ton's. And what did it say about the path he had traveled thus far, that Stost at his back comforted him more than the presence of Scouts?

"I am alive, yos'Thadi; I agree. As to the debt—do you know that much of the universe believes a contract made by coercion is no contract at all?"

"Come, we had agreed to do business; amuse me at some other time. At *this* time, you will turn that ship over to the Scouts, for proper disposal."

He moved down one step, so that he stood before the rest, and extended a hand.

"Give over the key and return immediately to active duty. We shall include you in our company."

Of course they would. Make no doubt he would be among those who manned *Bechimo* on the last journey to the Scout's warehouse...where he would be destroyed.

"I regret," Win Ton said, in a tone that conveyed no regret at all. "I do not presently carry a key to *Bechimo*."

yos'Thadi considered him, eyes glinting, face bland.

"He tells the truth," said the woman at his right and one step higher. She met Win Ton's eyes and bowed gently, as between colleagues. "Menolly vas'Anamac, healer and first mate."

Win Ton gave her bow back to her. "Menolly vas'Anamac, I am pleased to meet you."

"So, you do not have the key," said yos'Thadi. "We shall contrive. You will not, I know, object to the escort of comrades. The ship itself will let us in."

He stepped aside; the Scouts ranged behind him did likewise, clearing a path up the stairs, to the dockside.

"Pathfinder, we go with these," Win Ton said in Old Yxtrang. "This is a matter for the captain."

Stost blew out a breath; perhaps it was a laugh or merely irritation that they did not merely knock over these upstarts and go on their way.

"The captain will solve this with knives," Stost predicted.

"That is the captain's choice," Win Ton said and walked forward to the stairs.

· · · ※ · · ·

She had walked out of *Primadonna* reluctantly once, full of necessity and hurt, Tranza urging her on to her future. This exit was instead full of sadness, hurry—even relief. Doing what she could, saving what she could.

Keeping her personal world in balance.

Theo shook herself and went through the hatch, out onto the dock, where the shrouds hung close until she stepped onto the dock, and all the noise and bustle of Minot Station opened before her.

The first thing she heard, close by, was voices, then echoes of multiple people hurrying, talking. Relieved to be away, Theo sighed and paused, shifting the bags to a more comfortable position.

The deck was . . . vibrating; nearby, she heard the sound of many feet, moving fast, and a tremendous metallic *clang*, closely followed by Kara's voice, yelling.

What was Kara doing on the dock? And she was in danger! Theo took one step—and stopped, as the images filled her head, blocking out the dockside.

Bechimo was . . . overwhelmed. He was not directly under attack, but rather beset by multiple threads of information, by too many decisions, and too many decision points, every one of them scrambled by the random actions of humans.

She saw Kara on the dock; Clarence and Tranza; Chernak guarding *Bechimo*'s entrance, star hammer in hand. A mob ranged too close to that entrance; she saw hammers, bars, pieces of pipe in angry hands . . . and *Bechimo*, near as she had ever felt him to panic, weapons not live, but a whisker from disaster.

Calm, she thought, standing in the bonding space, feeling him all around her. *I will handle this. Monitor the action. If anyone approaches or seems to threaten—no weapons! A loud noise: have Joyita make an official announcement—a warn-away and a reminder to respect our perimeter. Call Station Security, if you haven't already. I'm on my way . . .*

Theo blinked the dock back into existence around her, heard a yell—a scream—saw people running past her, toward *Bechimo*. Her ship was in danger, her people—

She ran, impeded by the bags, but she couldn't—she wouldn't—just drop Tranza's life and treasures.

And so she ran.

She would get there in time, before anything bad . . . *worse* . . . happened.

She would.

. . . ✳ . . .

"Seven lawns of Ligorra, woman! Who are you killing now?"

Clarence was looking down on the wounded intern, possibly amused. His companion stood in the shadow of the ship, recovering his breath, his attention fixed on the pursuing mob.

Chernak did not fault him for that. It was an unruly affair, this mob, and not a true weapon showing among them. However, pipes, hammers, and pry-bars could do damage enough—and would, unless they were dispersed quickly.

"See to this idiot!" Kara snapped at Clarence, which was proper in the command chain which had left Kara as field captain.

She came to her feet and ran for the open hatch.

"Come with me," she cried as she rushed past.

Chernak followed, to the tool locker, and received two hammers, one to a hand. They were ... surprisingly heavy, but Kara hefted hers as if it had no weight at all.

"Back me," she said, looking up into Chernak's face. "We have to stop them now."

"Yes," said Chernak, pleased to find her thus astute. Again, she followed at a jog.

Kara stopped at the orange line on the decking, which marked out *Bechimo*'s private dock.

"Leave!" She shouted to be heard over the low roar of the mob. "There is nothing for you here. The men you were pursuing are members of this ship's crew."

"The redhead, maybe so," one yelled from safe inside the ranks. "But t'other one, he owes and he don't leave until he's paid."

"That's it," said another, and stepped forward, deliberately challenging Kara's authority.

"I said—*leave!*" Kara shouted.

And she threw the hammer.

The challenger jumped backward, lost his balance, and fell to the deck; the hammer also struck the deck, with an enormous clanging that silenced all gathered.

The fallen man scrambled to his feet, leaving his pipe on the deck. Chernak hefted her own hammers, ready to rearm Kara or throw one herself.

The crowd, however—there came laughter from the crowd, and whistles.

"Never mess with a mechanic carrying a star hammer!" one called out.

"Space, no!" another called. "Mechanics always win, Thurlow. C'mon back here afore she gets mad!"

The former challenger took the wise advice of his comrades and disappeared into the mob. Kara remained where she stood, feet planted wide, and arms crossed over her breast; Chernak owned herself proud to stand honor guard to such a warrior.

The crowd shuffled its many feet, not quite decided on a course—and then separated hastily, giving way before a group of six strangers, Stost and Win Ton marching at their head.

CHAPTER THIRTY-EIGHT

. . . .

Bechimo
Dockside

THERE WERE TOO MANY PEOPLE AROUND HER SHIP.

Theo slowed to a walk, trying to make headway, pushing past people oblivious to somebody shorter than they were. Neither of the bags had sharp edges. Unfortunately. And her elbows were demonstrably not enough.

She pushed harder. The man blocking her way grunted and stepped aside without looking around, and she advanced another three steps.

Maybe if she started kicking kneecaps?

"Make way for Captain Waitley!" a large voice boomed over the crowd, and another, just as large, repeated, "Make way for Captain Waitley!" A clang punctuated that call, as if somebody had dropped a star hammer to the deck.

Not that she could fault the method; the crowd parted before her and she walked, finally unimpeded, to her dock.

She let the bags fall as she crossed the orange line and straightened up to survey the situation.

Kara was standing inside their perimeter, staring out over a mob scene, arms crossed over her chest like she was daring them to try *any*thing that would give her an excuse to have Chernak let fly with one of the two star hammers she held.

Beyond the perimeter, apart from the general crowd of

339

stationers, stood a cluster of leather-clad pilots, with Win Ton and Stost apparently in attendance. Stost also held a star hammer.

Clarence was over by the hatch, first aid kit to hand, and Tranza right with him. Together they seemed to be advising a down and bloodied person. Or maybe they were keeping him down.

So much she saw before Chernak brought one large boot down hard on the decking, waking a ring that was only somewhat less authoritative than the previous racket, and loudly announced, "Captain Waitley returns!"

Clarence looked up and gave her a nod. Tranza looked up and kept looking, eyes wide.

Kara turned away from glaring at the crowd and came to Theo, leaving Chernak to keep order.

"Captain." She saluted a formal change of command, just like they'd learned in Command Protocols, way back at Anlingdin.

Theo dragged the answering form out of memory and accepted her authority back.

"Welcome home, Captain," Kara said, sounding perfectly calm, despite her hair coming undone from its usual careful braid and the streak of dried blood on her face.

"Thank you," said Theo and spun slowly, surveying the situation and letting everyone there see her take charge.

They were looking at her, too, she saw. Eyes everywhere, set in faces ranging from surprised to worried to demanding. Terrans, Liadens, pathfinders, crew—and a norbear, walking on his back legs, a small gun cradled in his hands.

Theo took a breath.

First order of business, she told herself, *disarm the norbear.*

Certain of his attention, she bowed formally, to the honor of Ambassador Hevelin.

The assembled humans variously stood silent or murmured to each other, wondering. She ignored them, all of her attention, all of her thought, centered on this one very small person.

Mindful of her etiquette lessons, she shaped her bow to include their relative roles. She: captain, pilot, protector. He: ambassador and most honored guest; majestic representative of an ancient race.

She could feel Hevelin's regard as she bowed; indeed, *Bechimo* showed her his *actual* regard, eyes intent, posture upright and interested.

Theo blinked the vision away and finished her bow with

hands held wide, her right a little lower and more forward, in invitation for embrace or, in his case, for a boost to her shoulder.

Hevelin reacted well to the offer of majesty; he allowed the moment to stretch as he gazed benevolently upon her. Then, just when she began to think he was going to keep her in this new and interesting pose for the rest of the day, he uttered a surprising deep growling *chirup-chirup-chirup*. He adjusted his grip on the weapon he cradled—to all appearances deliberately—and quite carefully aiming it downward, marched solemnly across the deck to her.

The watchers all around stirred, whispering and quieting in response to repeats of *hush*! There was also a hurried exchange in Liaden, which she deliberately didn't try to translate.

Hevelin's eyes were on hers. *He* knew the theater of high office, having lived among it for decades. Theo briefly wondered if he had counted that pause, in order to increase his importance and the drama of the moment. Just then, he arrived, pausing a step away, at which point he dipped a shoulder, clearly indicating, to her if not to all present, that she should receive the ugly little gun.

"Many thanks, Ambassador," she said in Trade, and far louder than was required to reach his excellent ears. Hevelin permitted her to get a proper hand on the pistolene grip and remove it from his tender care.

Straightening, she checked the safety. It was off; she felt a chill breeze down her spine as she rectified that and shoved the thing into a pocket.

Stost was now within their perimeter, leaving Win Ton with the small group of Scouts.

Kara had rejoined Chernak at the line, each of them holding a hammer.

"Security Officer, attend me, if you please."

Chernak placed her hammer down on the decking, on the flat of its head. That put the stock within Kara's reach should she need to offer another demonstration of might.

"Captain." Chernak saluted.

"Please, carry the ambassador into the ship with all due pomp," Theo said quietly. "Put him with Grakow and tell him to stay with Grakow."

Chernak dropped lightly to one knee, offering her hand, palm up, to the norbear. Hevelin wasted no time in taking advantage of the offered lift. Chernak rose effortlessly and paused to allow

Hevelin to gain her shoulder, where he stood on back legs, mur-bling softly and gazing out upon the assembled crowd.

"Captain," Chernak said again, delivering a snappy salute, and spinning sharply on her heel. She marched like she was her own parade to the hatch and through it.

A sigh passed through the crowd.

All right, Theo thought, that was taken care of, and every-thing else seemed to be well in hand, as long as she didn't stop to think about *Bechimo*'s hatch standing wide open and all of his crew dotted about the dock, in view of potential adversaries.

Movement near the hatch drew her eye: Clarence and Tranza were helping the wounded man to his feet. They were not—*absolutely* not!—taking care of him, whoever he was. There must be someone in this whole crowd of gawkers who could—

Kara had apparently been thinking along the same lines, only faster, because she suddenly pointed into the crowd.

"You! Take this man to Station Security and tell them to review the vids. Hurry!"

Tranza it was who guided the wounded to the perimeter, even as a woman in a bright green vest with VOL stenciled on it approached from the other side.

Tranza was being real cautious about the line, and maybe the woman, too. He passed his charge on to Kara, who grabbed him by the arm and practically shoved him into the woman's arms. Tranza walked carefully back to Clarence.

Another problem solved, Theo thought, the knot in her stomach loosening somewhat. It only remained to get her crew to stations.

"Security Officer," she snapped.

Stost marched smartly to her, and saluted with vigor. "Captain!"

"You will carry my orders. To Kara: she's to immediately return to the ship, take second chair and keep the updates for our stated destination current.

"Clarence has two minutes to get to first seat. Two minutes by your mark, when you reach him.

"Please tell Pilot Tranza that these bags and contents are his. I would appreciate it if he would move them into the ship. Escort him, please. Joyita will assign him a cabin.

"Also, tell Joyita to stay hot as PIC. When you are done, take the other side of the hatch, with Chernak."

She nodded. "Go."

"Captain!" Stost said again, apparently delighted to receive these orders. He spun, not one bit less smart than Chernak, and marched toward Kara.

Theo turned her attention to their unwanted audience.

"Clear out now, people; there's nothing for you to do here and we're out in five minutes!"

"How're we gonna get what we're owed?" demanded a man holding a pry-bar over his shoulder.

Theo stared at him, trying to arrange her face like Father did—what Kamele called his *shocked and horrified* expression.

"If you got grief about Tever and what *he* owes, that's not on this ship, my crew, or my passenger. Tever was employed by Hugglelans; it's up to them to settle up. Mayko is the name you want, all right?" She spelled it out.

"Got that? Now *move*, people. We're out in five and we're not stopping for anybody!"

Amazingly, they began to move, to disperse, drifting back and away, where to, she didn't care, so long as they cleared her departure zone.

Behind her, she heard Kara say—"My wrench! Thank you!" and Clarence's laconic answer, "Better clean the blood off it before it sets and ruins the edge."

Theo turned. Kara had disappeared into the ship, and Stost was approaching Clarence and Tranza, carrying Tranza's bags in one large hand.

"Clarence, the captain's orders: you have two minutes to get to first seat. Pilot Tranza, the captain's compliments. These bags are yours. I will escort you onto the ship."

Clarence turned his head, caught her eye, and gave her a jaunty salute before leaping into the ship. Tranza followed more slowly, Stost at his back.

Theo sighed. Everybody accounted for and safe where they belonged.

Almost.

She raised a hand and beckoned Win Ton to her.

He came, moving lightly among the dispersing stationers. The other Scouts trailed after him, which she supposed she should've expected.

Surprisingly, they stopped at the perimeter line, allowing Win Ton to reach her first.

He stepped well within her personal space, his face blander than she'd ever seen it, all expression locked away. He met her eyes without flinching.

"Are you going with them?" she asked. "Back to the Scouts?"

"They offer that, yes," he said. "In exchange for *Bechimo*."

She stared at him, shock vibrating through her.

"You *can't* give them *Bechimo*," she said flatly, feeling the truth of it echo between them—captain and ship.

Win Ton's face softened a little, enough so that she saw amusement at the corners of his eyes.

"Indeed, I cannot, and so they come to you."

She gave him another hard look, seeing amusement, fading; hope, faint; and...purpose.

"They forced a bargain on a dying man," Win Ton said again, speaking quick and low. "If I should survive through their efforts, I would deliver the ship into their hands."

"I remember," she said, recalling their meeting at Volmer, Win Ton pale and weak—dying, yes, that. She remembered the team of Scouts escorting him, who wanted to catch and kill the ship. *Her* ship.

She looked beyond him, at the six waiting patiently at the perimeter.

"I only recognize one," she said. "The man with the short yellow hair..."

She caught a motion from the edge of her eye, turned her head to see two pathfinders standing guard at *Bechimo*'s open hatch, each holding a star hammer at ready.

She looked back to Win Ton.

"They come to me," she repeated. "Do they think *I'm* going to give them *Bechimo*?"

"They suspected that you might be weak or persuadable," Win Ton said. "Though they have been given pause, as they believe you have your brother's Yxtrang on security."

"My brother's Yxtrang?"

Win Ton outright smiled. "Why should they think there are any others?"

She nodded and raised a hand, signing *clarity*.

"You stand with *Bechimo*?"

He bowed, a serious bow of request and allegiance and some other things she couldn't read.

"If you will have me on your ship as crew, I ask that you speak with them, that they not interfere with our departure."

Theo sighed.

"We have a departure filed," she said.

Win Ton looked at her steadily, until she threw up one hand in defeat.

"All right, I'll speak with them," she said and raised her voice slightly.

"Stost, attend us, please."

"This man you have seen but not met, he is Captain yos'Thadi. He knows you and your credentials." Win Ton bowed—first to Theo, then to the Scout captain—and stepped back.

No other introductions were made. Stost stood at her back, star hammer in hand.

Captain yos'Thadi inclined his head so slightly that even Theo knew he was dancing on the edge of insult.

"Forgive me if I am blunt; we are informed that time is an issue."

He waved a hand toward *Bechimo*.

"This ship; it does not belong to you. It is an aberration, controlled by a machine intelligence, and dangerous to all who are elsewise. The Liaden Scouts have placed it under warrant. You and your crew will vacate immediately. We are authorized to provide transportation to a port of your choice in this sector."

Theo shook her head.

"The ship is mine, and I am his rightful captain. We have, as you say, business and an upcoming breakaway deadline. I doubt your authorizations, and consider you to be no more than underlings."

Captain yos'Thadi stood up to his height, which equaled Win Ton's, but fell very short of Stost's.

"Underlings?"

Theo shrugged. "You are a Scout captain. You follow orders. I am captain of an independent tradeship. I *issue* orders. *Furthermore,* Liad has no claim on me. The Scouts have no call on me."

"So. If you wish, we will play the game. Every port you raise, we will be waiting. Eventually, you must come to a Liaden port, or a port where a ship might be confiscated and a captain arrested, on the evidence of Scouts."

He paused, then snapped: "I command you to give over that ship!"

Theo felt buffeted, heard the notes of power there. Like the witches who'd tried to control her, like the bullies at the academy!

She closed her eyes, found *Bechimo* in bond space offering Balance, offering a glimpse of her bridge, where crew—*her* crew, her *people*—worked quickly and efficiently, prepping for their departure.

She opened her eyes and met yos'Thadi's expectant gaze.

"I do not surrender this ship and I will not be hounded, *Scout Captain*—" a touch of Clarence there, she thought, still keeping her gaze steady.

"The Scouts have declared this ship a danger and have placed it under warrant. If you wish to appeal that warrant, you must appeal to a Scout of higher rank."

Theo blinked.

Beside her, Win Ton spoke quietly, "Challenger calls the question; challenged chooses weapons."

yos'Thadi turned his head.

"You would make it a duel, would you? Another amusing trifle, yo'Vala. I believe you have missed your calling. You ought to have been a fool."

"Ah, no," Win Ton said gently. "I have merely combined careers."

Challenged—that was her, Theo realized. Challenged chooses the weapons.

She smiled and inclined her head—not far—to Captain yos'Thadi.

"Very well. We will bring this discussion to Scout Commander Val Con yos'Phelium, on Surebleak, in twelve days' time. I will stand by his word. As I know you will."

"Val Con yos'Phelium is an outlaw," yos'Thadi stated.

"And yet, he retains his rank," Win Ton said. "Weapons have been chosen and the time of meeting set. Surebleak, in twelve days, yos'Thadi."

He glared.

"Twelve days to Surebleak? You would have needed to Jump there directly, beginning yesterday, to achieve it inside of twelve days!"

Theo looked at him.

"Can't your ship make the timing? We can set another date, if you'll give me an idea of your capabilities."

"Of course *we* can be there in twelve days!" he snapped.

"Then there is no problem," a woman stated, coming forward to her captain's side. She bowed to Theo as between equals.

"I am Menolly vas'Anamac, Captain Waitley, first mate on *Chandra Marudas*. We accept your terms and will meet you on Surebleak, in twelve Standard days."

"Menolly—" yos'Thadi turned to her . . . and stopped, apparently silenced by what he saw in her face.

"Do not bait a dragon in its own den, Ing Vie. Continue and you will be burned. Captain Waitley is at an end of her patience with us."

A long pause.

"Minot Station gives us an amended breakaway time of six minutes from my mark," *Bechimo* said into her ear. "Mark."

Captain yos'Thadi bowed—*not* as between equals.

"Captain Waitley. In twelve days."

He turned and stalked away, his crew following.

Theo blew out a hard breath and turned to Win Ton.

"Six minutes to breakaway," she said. "Let's go!"

CHAPTER THIRTY-NINE

· ·

Lefavre, Clanave Sector, a Carresens Port

RIG TRANZA NODDED TO HER, ALL FORMAL, THEN TO CLARENCE, then Win Ton, Kara, and Joyita. Hevelin stood near him petting Grakow, a slow murble shared between them. Stost and Chernak stood doorside, official.

"Pilot Waitley, you done me a good turn. Understand, I'm not sure exactly how much of it happened, because there's a lot I don't know and haven't seen, right? Prolly a good number of things I won't see and couldn't remember if I did.

"What I want to say, right, is you've got a good ship and a good crew to match. You make me proud. Proud you were my student; proud of how you've come into your own self. I'm grateful, too, and that'll have to do, because there's no way I can repay what you and this ship done on my behalf.

"And for all the rest of it—well, I don't think you're running beyond *your* design limits, but by a swarm of ghost ships, you're running well past mine. I'll take that taxi on over to the *Challenger*, thanks—and I mean that, right? Thanks."

Rig's taxi was hours gone. Theo sat her station and looked at the beautiful world below them: a world she wouldn't set foot on, nor see a dawn on.

She was daydreaming, yes she was. And at that, it was better than going over Tranza's decision, which was logical by his needs,

349

to be away from *Bechimo* as soon as possible. She'd offered him a chance to come with them to Surebleak, to speak with Korval's master trader—she figured she could pull *that* out of the teapot at least!—and he might have met with Val Con, who might provide a recommendation once the other matter had cleared...

Anyway, the mini-pod had been collected by a station tug, and Tranza had caught his taxi, direct to *Gran Fuesco Challenger*, the largest tradeship in-system.

So, rather than think too hard on this or that, she watched a storm. They were, after all, at Lefavre.

Lefavre—the spaceport—sprawled synchronously above Lefavre, the planet, where a pinwheeling storm covering half the visible disk drew the eye mercilessly as a string of small satellites dotted the brilliant storm top in shadow. Every planetary year the storm sat just *there* for three hundred and fifty days out of a seven-hundred-day year. Just off one edge of the storm was the mountain chain that made its existence possible, as the winds roared away from the ice-capped south.

Bechimo's view of the planet was unimpeded now that they'd moved beyond Senior Captain Avra Carresens-Denobli's ship.

They'd barely been in-system when the senior captain called Theo, direct and in person, like she was family or at least a close friend of the family. She called to offer Theo a meal and an overnight on the *Gran Fuesco Challenger* and was saddened, she said, that Theo made such a short stay, but understood that if Theo and *Bechimo* had time-sensitive connections to make, that was how the universe flowed...

"The universe flows so. Time-sensitive connections—it is too bad. I am sorry we will not meet this time and look forward to that meeting in future. I have the highest recommendation from my daughter—that would be First Class Pilot Asha Carresens-Denobli—that I meet you. Asha was at Codrescu when you took away the ambassador, who I would also be very glad to meet. Also my cousin Janifer speaks kindly of you. But these pleasures are in the future. In present, tell me, is there anything I can do for you?"

It had taken not much more of a mention that she had a pilot as a passenger, Theo's own teacher actually, who was in need of a deck to fly since Eylot—

"Huh! Eylot! The fools. A teaching pilot, you say? Send me his records—better, send them and also let him come to me. We will see him properly situated! If it is possible, let him speak with me now."

Tranza had spoken with the senior captain—an interview, as it turned out to be—and come out of his cabin, eyes full of a new hope.

"You know these people, Theo. You know them, right, and they say things—I didn't know it was you at Codrescu, don't pay attention to places I don't go, right? And Carresens is top flight here. That one, she's a boss of bosses, right!"

It made her feel . . . odd to have Tranza defer to her. To have him amazed at her, when he'd taught her so much.

Eyes on the world below, Theo sighed, briefly considering how nice it might be to return one year and fly a sailplane from one of the three famous slopes on Cantankerous Citadel. Twelve hours, they said, was a short flight.

Bechimo gently altered the airflow of fans number seven and eight, brushing her ought-to-be-cut bangs down into her face. He'd been reading some of Tranza's epic love songs from Bothelair, where hardly a stanza was done until the beloved's hair was mussed.

"*Pfffwaow*, I know! Can't sight-see much longer. Who's checking Joyita?"

This was rhetorical, at best. Win Ton was checking Joyita, as were Stost and Chernak. The pathfinders were under Kara's direction in this—both of them wishing to learn their new universe—and Kara having found unexpected admirers for what Clarence called, much to her embarrassment, the Battle of Minot Docks. So that meant that everybody but Clarence and Theo was checking Joyita.

Joyita raised a hand and waved.

"I am checking myself to the second, Theo, and will go to the nanosecond when we determine exactly when we begin Jump and not before."

"Are we slowing you down?" she asked, half serious. "We could leave right now, except we're waiting for that on-delivery payment to transfer."

"I am content to wait, Captain," Joyita said, with dignity.

Theo grinned, her eyes drawn back to her screen.

Why, look at that tendril of storm; in the time since she'd been watching, it had changed from grey to hard white, bright and—

"Theo, we have the transfer," Joyita said, interrupting this reverie. "We also have a number of electronic mail packets for you."

"Joyita, you're PIC. That comes first. As you have time, you can fill in details."

"Yes, Theo. There are several notes from Master Trader yos'Galan. There is an official communication from Eylot, demanding that you return for trial. Another official communication from Eylot, demanding that you return Kara for trial. Eylot..."

"Skip Eylot," Theo said.

"There is also a communication from Minot. Minot Station Pilots Guild representative requests a full explanation of why the norbear ambassador was seen armed, in public."

Theo raised her eyebrows.

From second chair, Clarence laughed.

"Quicker'n a cat can lick 'er paw!"

"But that was my fault," Kara protested, looking up from the screen she shared with Chernak and Stost.

Theo watched that changeable wisp of storm and shook her head. "A full explanation?" she said pensively. "That's going to take some time and consideration!"

Clarence had the good grace not to laugh, this time.

"Well," Theo said, wiping the seductive view of Lefavre's storms from her screen.

"Let's go to Surebleak, Pilot Joyita. On your mark!"